The Glimpse

Claire wrote her first paranormal screenplay at the age of thirteen and named it after a road sign. *Danger Alive* never made it to the big screen, but she continued to write and daydream her way through school and university. Claire graduated with a first BA (Hons) in Film Studies, and spent the next few years working in the BFI. She worked as a runner and camera assistant, and fantasised about creating her own films. In 2000, she wrote and directed the short film, *Colours*, which sold to Canal Plus. Today, Claire is concentrating on writing YA fiction. She spends her time between Paris and London, along with her French husband and two young sons.

Find out more about Claire's books or contact her at www.clairemerle.com.

The Glimpse

Claire Merle

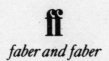

faber and faber

First published in this edition in 2012
by Faber and Faber Limited
Bloomsbury House,
74-77 Great Russell Street,
London WC1B 3DA

Typeset by Faber and Faber Ltd

Printed in the UK by CPI Group (UK) Ltd, Croydon CR0 4YY

A CIP record for this book
is available from the British Library

ISBN 978-0-571-28053-7

FSC
www.fsc.org
MIX
Paper from
responsible sources
FSC® C101712

2 4 6 8 10 9 7 5 3 1

For my husband, Claude, who always knew.

Prologue

Sometimes, when Ana hovered on the edge of sleep, she heard the patter of feet along the school corridor; she felt her best friend Tamsin close by – a near, warm presence like the imprint on a bed recently slept in; she saw the Board's saloon car pulling up outside the front of school, a white envelope glowing through one of their leather cases, whispering her name, her disease.

Of course that wasn't really how it happened. A little under three years ago, as Ana stood in home economics, large science goggles propped on the end of her nose to be ironic, she hadn't known they were coming for her. But sometimes, in the twilight between wakefulness and dreams she saw it all. As though part of her were trapped in the past, conscious of the threads that were weaving together, tightening their hold around her to create one shattering moment that would change everything.

I

Sleeper

Mrs Beale checked the temperature of the water in Ana's plastic baby bath. Behind them, Tamsin hunched over her own tub and mimicked their teacher, peering cross-eyed at the thermometer.

'Thirty-seven degrees Celsius,' Mrs Beale muttered. 'Very good.'

Tamsin's lips moved in sync with the teacher's words. Her eyelids fluttered, gazing high over Ana's head, just like Mrs Beale. Ana bit the insides of her cheeks, holding back laughter.

Beneath the sweet scent of warmed milk and baby cream lingered the tang of burnt cake. In another life, the lab had been used for identifying carbon dioxide gas with litmus paper and heating sodium-dipped flame-test wires over Bunsen burners. Now it was employed for warming baby bath water to precisely thirty-seven degrees Celsius, for measuring out bottle formulas, for learning to cook large family meals.

Mrs Beale strode past Ana's bench towards Tamsin. Tamsin dropped her impersonation and gazed up at their home economics teacher with wide eyes. Her dark fringe cut a straight line halfway across her forehead. She was pushing it more than she normally did. Recently, it seemed to Ana, her best friend wanted to get into trouble.

'Now, girls,' Mrs Beale said. Her high-pitched voice strained to be heard over the general class chatter. 'In an emergency, if you find yourself without a thermometer, you may test the water with your wrist. It should be warm, but not hot. Never put a baby in a hot bath.'

Tamsin's hand shot up.

'What if you've been in an accident,' she said, 'and lost your hands, or been burnt in a fire and have skin grafts? Could you test with your elbow, if you still had one?'

Ana squeezed her lips together and snorted. Her shoulders shook. Tamsin blink-blink-blinked her lashes.

'Your elbow would be fine,' Mrs Beale replied, 'should the situation require it.'

Several other girls on the benches nearby giggled. But not even a hint of a smile reached Tamsin's eyes. She wanted to be an actress. At times like this, Ana knew her best friend was practising, proving to herself she was good enough. But Pure girls didn't act; they didn't become concert pianists, like Ana dreamed of being, either. They were too important for that.

A knock sounded on the classroom door.

'Come in,' Mrs Beale trilled.

A small girl from a couple of years below entered.

'Yes?' the teacher said.

The girl blushed. 'The headmistress is waiting for Ariana Barber.' She curtsied then turned on her heel and darted out.

Ana stared at the life-sized newborn-baby doll lying on

the workbench, waiting for its bath. Head wanted to see her? Head never saw anyone. It was the deputy headmistress who took care of trouble, who handed out detentions and tasks.

'You'd better go,' Mrs Beale said. 'Leave all that.'

Sixteen pairs of eyes followed Ana out of the classroom.

*

Head's office lay off the front entrance to the school. Ana's patent leather shoes tapped the parquet floor and echoed down the empty corridor as she approached. The usual projected message shone on the closed door: Do Not Disturb. But beneath it lay a personalised instruction: Enter, Ms Barber. Ana's heart flipped into her throat as she reached out, twisted the handle, and went inside.

Five grown-ups sat around a large meeting table. Three, including Ana's headmistress faced the door; her father sat at one end; the last man had his back to her. Everyone but her father looked up as she entered.

Ana's breath caught in her throat. She rubbed her hands on her blue uniform skirt.

'Please sit down, Ariana,' Head said, gesturing to a chair.

She shuffled towards the table. Her mind fell blank. She flexed her legs to sit, but they gave way. Her bum hit the wooden seat with a slap. The jarring force travelled up her spine and rattled her brains.

'The Board,' Head said, introducing the man and woman beside her.

Ana's eyes flicked up to the ugly pair. Now she

3

understood her father's stillness. He was scared. The Board didn't visit normal people.

The female in the grey suit stroked the corner of a stiff envelope bearing the Board's gold stripe. Head's eye twitched. The man beside Ana, the Chief Warden from their Community, who was in charge of security, kept glancing at her father. The male Board representative cleared his throat.

'The Board of Psychiatric Testing and Evaluation,' he said, 'was established ten years ago, just after the Pure tests, to help contain our country's Mental Health Crisis and prevent it from spiralling out of control.'

His monotone sent a shiver down Ana's back. He obviously wasn't here to give her a history lesson.

'Science has classified the genetic mutations,' he went on, 'for three hundred and four Mental Illnesses.' His head bobbed, too large for his skinny neck. 'Each mutation is dominant.'

Ana gazed at her fingers in her lap. They didn't just tremble, they convulsed. Like there were tiny animals inside pushing to get out. She glanced at her father. His six-foot-two figure was all angles. His jaw clenched. He finally looked up, blue eyes locking on the male Board representative like he was preparing to take out a target.

'Human traits,' the man continued, 'are determined by variations in the genes. The Big3 – schizophrenia, depression, anxiety – are a complex mutation of these differences that depend on the state of several interacting genes.' The Board representative paused. He met her father's glare, a small smile on his lips. 'What perhaps you may not realise,

4

Ariana, is that if one parent is affected by the Big3, every child will automatically become a Carrier, at best. More likely than not, however, they will develop some variation of the inherited illness, starting off as a Sleeper and one day becoming Active.'

Ana stifled a gasp. The room seemed to shrink and fold in on itself like an inflatable castle at the end of a children's party. *Please, no, no. This couldn't be happening.*

'So,' the man said. He prodded a piece of paper on the table in front of him. 'Three months ago, you contacted the Guildford Register's Office for a copy of your mother's death certificate.'

A throbbing pulse began in Ana's neck and wrists. She and her father had moved to the Highgate Community when she was eleven, a month after her father had taken her to see a dying woman with yellow skin and no hair, who he claimed was Isabelle Barber. Ana had always been sure he was lying. The patient with the boiled-egg head and dark craters instead of cheeks didn't share Ana and her mum's grey eyes, nor did she have a mole beneath her lip like Ana's mum. Besides, Ana had seen her mum dead nine months earlier. Did her father think she'd forgotten?

Now, as she sat facing the Board, all she wanted was to take back ordering a copy of her mother's death certificate. She never thought proving she was right about her mum's death would feel so wrong. Because finally she understood. Her father's lies had been protecting her. She should have been raised in the City with all the other Crazies.

I'm not Pure.

Ana's bottom lip began to quiver. Tears blurred her

vision. Life in Crazy-land was a terror-filled battle for survival. You could get stabbed walking down the street, attacked in a supermarket, robbed for your hair, or thrown, possibly by yourself, off a bridge.

The male Board member turned over the paper before him with a flick of his wrist. He pretended to read the autopsy conclusion, but he obviously knew it by heart.

'Death by car-exhaust asphyxiation.' He looked up at Ana. 'Once a popular method of suicide, if that was what you were wondering.' He slid the certificate across the desk towards her.

The blood in Ana's body dived towards her feet, as though attempting to abandon ship. She bent forward, put her spinning head between her legs.

'The Board delivers death certificates now?' she heard her father say, his voice so hollow she barely recognised it.

'This is a rather special case,' the man replied. 'You, Dr Barber, are something of a household name in more educated circles.'

Nobody seemed to notice Ana half under the table, or if they did, they'd decided not to interrupt.

'The secretary at the Guildford Register's Office had read about your wife's battle with cancer,' the male Board member continued. 'As you might imagine, this certificate created something of a conundrum. Worth a little investigation. Once the secretary had verified that the Isabelle Barber of this certificate was indeed the same Isabelle Barber as your wife, she discovered that your daughter is registered as a Pure and alerted us. The big question, of course, is how could the daughter of a depressive possibly be Pure? It's impossible. Except . . . except that you, Dr Barber, are in the unusual position of having developed the DNA tests for the Big3.'

And therefore are capable of altering the results, Ana thought. Everyone else was thinking it too. The Board's insinuation left no space for anything else. Her father had covered up her mother's suicide and then faked Ana's Pure test.

A moan escaped her, low and whimpering like a trapped animal's swan song.

Oh God, what about Jasper? She and Jasper were due to be bound next month, the first steps two Pures took to becoming joined. Ana struggled to inhale, but she couldn't get any air.

'You can't possibly think that these accusations will stick,' her father said.

'We have already redone your daughter's test, Dr Barber.' A wooden chair creaked as the man leaned back. Beneath the table, Ana saw him press his fingers together in the shape of a steeple.

'The interface virus?' she croaked. Last week, several students had been sent to the school nurse after the deputy head announced that an interface virus had wiped a few student medical records. Tamsin had joked that the deputy was running a small business on the side selling Pure DNA for cloning.

The Board rose from their chairs with synchronised movements. A large white envelope lay on the desk before them, its gold stripe glinting in the morning sunlight. Ana's redone test results lay inside it.

She couldn't move, not even to straighten up.

Instead of living happily ever after with Jasper, she would be battling to survive the giant loony bin of the City, waiting for the day she would wake up and decide to kill herself.

The Chief Warden coughed. 'Sorry, Ashby, a couple of the boys are waiting for us outside. I'm going to have to take you in.'

Through spread fingers, Ana watched her father push to his feet. The Chief Warden locked metal cuffs around his wrists.

Ashby looked livid. 'I hardly think this is necessary,' he said. He crossed in front of the window towards Ana. A large, shackled hand pressed into her back. 'I'll be out on bail in a couple of hours,' he said.

The tears rolling down Ana's cheeks dried. Numbness spread through her. She had no idea how bad things would get from here on. But she did know that she would never let her father touch her again.

2

Binding

Two years, ten months, and nine days later.

The chauffeur-driven saloon cruised along Hampstead Lane, a mile-and-a-half-long road which stretched the border of the Highgate Community from the south-eastern checkpoint to the south-western one. Ana pressed her nose against the window, watching the ten-foot-tall wall crowned with metal spikes flash past. It was one of the walls that kept the Crazies out.

Lake, Ana's joining planner, sat beside her in the back seat of the car fiddling with a lighter. In her mid-twenties, Lake wore the oatmeal trousers and cream blouse Ana's father had paid for. She stank of cigarettes. Her frizzy curls were scraped up in a ponytail and she'd stripped her face of its usual heavy make-up, revealing eyes as light as summer. Joining planners organised the joining ceremonies and were on hand at the bindings to supervise dress, make-up and hair. Ordinarily, they came from the Community, not the City. But none of the joining planners from Ana's Community had been 'available'.

Open lighter, let lid drop; open, flick, close, click. The saloon's electric engine buzzed. Both sounds chafed Ana's nerves. Her stomach churned. All day she'd been too nervous to eat. She kept wondering if Jasper would show up for their ceremony. In half an hour, they were supposed to meet at the Hampstead Community Hall, and finally (two years, nine months and three days after they were supposed to) take their first steps to becoming joined. Following the binding ceremony, they would be allowed to spend time together alone. Over the next four weeks they would see each other every day, and at the end of the month they would each declare whether they wished to go ahead with the joining or desist.

This was Ana's last chance. In one month she would turn eighteen. If she and Jasper weren't bound today and joined before her birthday, she would be turned out into the City with the Crazies.

Ana squeezed her fingers together until the tops lost feeling. Jasper had postponed several times, but they'd never got this far before. She considered what she might say to reassure him when they saw each other. If he showed. She couldn't think of anything. Jasper wasn't the same boy she'd met at the Taurell Christmas party the year she and her father had moved to the Community. She would have known what to say to the bright-eyed, smiling Jasper who hadn't yet lost the big brother he idolised.

Ana closed her eyes, remembering how overwhelmed she'd been – an eleven-year-old country girl entering the Taurell's festively decorated mansion. The coloured lights and holly, the beautiful women in black and red evening dresses, and the chaos of the children's quarters.

She had slipped away through empty corridors to an

unoccupied wing, found a library overflowing with paper books and an adjoining chamber with a desk and a dusty upright piano. Without thinking, she'd sat down on the piano stool and begun to play. She'd played a melody her mother had taught her. She'd played barely conscious of the silent tears streaming down her cheeks. Off-key notes resonated from the untuned piano, but she didn't care, she poured her yearning into it, pretended the music could traverse time and space to reach her mother's ears. When she stopped, she became aware that she was no longer alone. Two boys stood in the doorway. One closer to a man than a boy – seventeen or eighteen. The other perhaps fourteen. They looked alike – blond, wavy hair, hazel eyes, strong, slim faces. She quickly wiped away the traces of her tears and tried not to stare at the handsome younger brother.

'Who are you?' the older one said.

'Ariana Barber.' Her voice sounded small and tight from crying.

The older one's eyes narrowed. 'The geneticist's daughter?'

She nodded.

'Why aren't you with everyone else?' he asked.

'There are too many of them.'

The younger one laughed. His face radiated warmth. 'She's right,' he said. 'There are far too many of them.'

They escorted her back to the party, the older one teasing the younger about a girl. 'She'll be joined long before you're old enough to express an interest,' he said. 'Anyway, what's the rush? Just because you can be joined at fifteen, doesn't mean you have to be. You could be eighteen, nineteen, twenty or twenty-five. A ten-year gap is nothing.'

The younger boy glanced at Ana, embarrassed and sheepish, and she stared back at him, hoping he'd take his brother's advice and wait until her fifteenth birthday when she became eligible.

The following two years, Ana anticipated the Taurell's Christmas party with love-sick longing, but she only caught glimpses of Jasper through the crowds. The third year, several months before she came of binding age, she decided she wouldn't leave the party until she'd talked to him.

She found Jasper sitting on the servant stairs at the back of the house with Juliet Mango, a pretty girl from the year above her at school. They were laughing and flirting and their hands were fastened together with a scarf. Devastated, she'd bolted out a back door, crossed several gardens, scrambled over two fences, and sprinted home in the bitter cold without her coat.

So on April 21st, Ana's fifteenth birthday, when Jasper personally delivered his binding invitation, she was beside herself with shock and joy. Like everyone else, she'd known the Taurell–Mango joining hadn't gone ahead because Juliet had returned to school after the Christmas holidays. But she hadn't imagined Jasper might ask someone else, least of all her, so soon after. Obviously last year, when Jasper had praised her piano playing at the school variety show, she hadn't made such an idiot of herself, nodding and blushing and being too stunned to speak, as she'd feared.

For three blissful weeks after the invitation, Ana dreamed she would have the future she'd fantasised about.

But then the Board came to school with her redone Pure test. And a fortnight after that, Jasper's brother Tom died.

By the summer, Ana's father was vindicated of all charges, the Board admitted a possible mistake on their part and Ana was given a reprieve: She could stay in the Community until her eighteenth birthday as long as her illness had not begun to manifest. If she and Jasper were joined during that time, her reprieve would be extended indefinitely until the day she became sick. But Jasper put off setting a binding date again and again. As the weeks turned into months and then years, Ana's hope shrank and her heart hardened, expecting disappointment.

And now it was really happening. She felt like the time when she was eight and her mum stopped getting out of bed. For days she'd prayed her mother would do something, *anything*. But the morning her mum shook her awake, threw clothes and books into the old car her father had left them in case of an emergency, and driven them away from the farm at high speed across bumpy lanes until the petrol ran out, Ana's happiness was crushed with notions of getting lost, becoming stranded in the middle of nowhere, crashing. She'd got what she'd wished for. And all she could think about was disaster.

The saloon slowed as they approached the south-western checkpoint. Two square cabins stood on either side of the road harbouring guards who let the traffic through. Ana sat up, alert. Nick, the chauffeur, handed over their IDs. Crazies could not enter any of the Communities without going through the Wardens' approval process, and even then the date and hours had to be specified. Pure men came and went as they pleased. Pure women, for their own safety, were always accompanied into the City.

The guard checked their ID sticks, handed them back, and raised the barrier. They advanced towards Whitestone pond, a man-made basin surrounded by roads. Once a watering spot for horses, the pond was now a mecca for Crazies. Hundreds of them waded in the water, pushing and jostling for space as they dunked and scrubbed dirty washing.

Only several hundred metres lay between the Highgate and Hampstead checkpoints. But to Ana such forays into the City filled her mind so that six hundred metres felt like six thousand.

The car inched into Heath Street. Nick maintained a steady fifteen miles per hour. On the whole, the crowds parted around the vehicle, but even at this speed people tumbled against the doors. None of the Crazies by the pond had bikes or e-trikes or rickshaws. Ana had once asked Nick why. 'Too crowded,' he'd told her. 'Nowhere to lock them up.'

As they passed the pond, a thump sounded on the car bonnet. Ana tensed. A bearded, scruffy man pushed against the front bumper. They edged forward and he pounded the windscreen, a blade glinting in his scabby hand.

Ana sucked in her breath. 'He's got a knife,' she said.

Lake gazed ahead, indifferent. Nick continued his steady advance down Heath Street. There came shouting. A scream. Ana peered through the back window searching for the bearded man who'd now disappeared into the throng. Her eyes locked on a girl of twelve or thirteen. Pain gripped the girl's round face. She was swooning and pressing a blood-drenched hand against her shoulder.

'Someone's injured. We have to stop.' Ana knew she was supposed to pretend she hadn't seen anything, the way her father and Jasper and all the other Pures did. But she couldn't. Perhaps because one day that girl might be her.

'We can't stop,' Lake said. 'We'll be late.'

Ana began to unwrap the silver scarf prettily twisted around the top of her dress.

'Don't do that,' Lake said. 'It'll take hours to fix.'

Ignoring her joining planner, Ana ripped away the scarf and pressed the button to descend the electric window. Lake reached over and fought to remove her finger. Ana stretched her legs, leaning her neck and shoulders out of the car.

'Pull her in!' Nick shouted. Lake's arms wrapped around Ana's waist and tugged.

Ana flourished the scarf at a woman. 'It's for the bleeding girl,' she called. The woman's hand snapped at the stream of fine material. Lake yanked Ana's hips and Ana fell backwards into her seat. The electric window zipped closed.

Nick frowned at them in the rear-view mirror. Like all those who worked for the Pures, he was a Carrier – he could pass on mutated genes to his children, but he wouldn't develop the illnesses he carried. Everyone who wasn't Pure either carried one or more of the genomes that caused the hundreds of mental ills, the 'Carriers'; were already sick, the 'Actives'; or would become sick at some point in their lives, the 'Sleepers', like Ana.

15

'Sorry,' Ana mouthed at him. She knew he'd have stopped if he considered it safe enough.

'She won't use it for the girl,' Lake said.

'She might.'

'She won't.' Lake's eyes roamed across what remained of Ana's binding outfit. Without the diaphanous scarf twisting around Ana's waist and across her chest to knot at the back of her neck, the pale, ankle-length dress looked ordinary. Lake pinched her nose, let out a huff of air, then sank back in her seat.

*

The saloon pulled up outside an eighteenth-century Queen Anne house, which served as the Hampstead Community Hall. Six girls in pastel dresses clumped outside the entrance like tame varieties of roadside flowers. Ana felt a pang of regret for the scarf. Without it, her forget-me-not blue dress looked the same as all the others – strappy shoulders and a long straight-down skirt. All of the girls wore their hair up in chignons and French twists.

'Do you want me to wait with you?' Lake asked. She was slumped back in the leather car seat, with clearly no intention of moving.

Ana glanced at the mothers and joining planners standing on the sidelines. Then back at the girls. They all seemed to know each other, which wasn't surprising. Most eligible Pures chose to attend the binding ceremony in their own Community Hall.

'I'll be fine,' she said.

Nick rounded the car and popped open the back passenger door. He offered Ana a hand. She took it, at the same time pulling free the centre pin holding up her French roll with her other hand. Soft, straight hair splashed across her shoulders.

'Or you could wear it down,' Lake muttered.

'Sorry,' Ana said, picking out the remaining hairpins. Lake had spent an hour brushing and rolling, but still, Ana felt instantly better. Just because people paid attention to her for the wrong reasons, didn't mean she wanted to blend in. Wrapping her shawl around her shoulders, she stepped on to the pavement. Sun seeped through a gauze of cloud but it was freezing. She wondered about the bleeding girl. The Hampstead Whittington, only ten minutes from the pond, would be the closest hospital. But the girl wouldn't be allowed through the Hampstead Community checkpoint. She'd have to walk around. A forty- or fifty-minute detour.

'Nick,' she said, as her father's chauffeur ducked into the driver's seat. 'Could you go back and have a look for that girl?'

'Only if you promise not to pull another stunt like that.'

'I promise.'

Nick cocked his eyebrow, pretending to decide whether he could trust her. For the last year he'd driven Ana to her piano lessons at the Royal Academy of Music in the heart of London. Seven months ago, just after Ana's best friend Tamsin mysteriously vanished, Ana had gone through a stage of appropriating funds from her father's illegal wads of cash and handing them out to teenage girls who looked

17

like they hadn't eaten for weeks. Nick had grown accustomed to her odd requests.

He smiled at her before getting back into the car. 'Good luck,' he said. 'I'll see you tonight. Your father's asked me to pick you up from the concert hall, after the celebrations.'

Ana waved goodbye. Behind her the huddle of chattering girls grew tense and silent. A lady in a brown suit opened the wrought-iron gates and beckoned them forwards. Mothers kissed their daughters goodbye. Joining planners made last-minute tucks of hair and sweeps of lip gloss. Ana was the first up the paving stone path to the listed Queen Anne house. She imagined the superintendent registrar would have said something if they were missing a male binding participant. But then the woman had barely looked at the girls, so maybe she wouldn't know if the count was off. They paused at the black front door, allowing the others to catch up. Ana focused on inhaling and exhaling but she felt as though she'd forgotten how to breathe.

'We will now proceed to the music room,' the registrar said as the last two girls tottered up. *Breathe, bend leg at knee, lift foot, bend other leg.* Thank goodness her heart continued to beat on its own, even if it was way too fast.

Ana followed the registrar into the hallway and first left. The music room lay at the front of the house. Wood-panelled walls glowed honey-brown in the afternoon light. The young men stood twelve feet away with their backs facing the door. Two rows of three. Six sets of dark-suited shoulders. Seven girls.

Ana lost her footing. Pastel colours rippled around her as the other girls swept across the wooden floor to join their respective partners. *Chest pain, dizziness and shortness of breath are all symptoms of a panic attack*, she warned herself. *You cannot have a panic attack.* She pressed her toes against the soles of her low-heeled shoes.

A plump girl reached the centre of the room and pivoted in confusion. At the same time the remaining young man glanced back. Oval face, dimpled chin, wavy hair. Jasper's hazel eyes met Ana's and the tension inside her burst. She wobbled towards him feeling light-headed.

Behind her a middle-aged woman shuffled into the music room. The plump girl gasped. The woman wrapped an arm around the girl's waist and led her away. On any other occasion, Ana might have found herself empathising with the girl and hoping the girl's partner was simply sick, but she was too relieved it wasn't her. Today she was on her own emotional roller coaster. She was going to have to hold on tight just to make it through.

The registrar rounded a desk at the back of the room to address them.

'Please take your binding partner's hand,' she said.

Ana peeked at Jasper. His eyebrows slanted towards the bridge of his nose. He looked psyched up for a fight and though it had been concealed, a faint bruise coloured the skin above his right eye. She wondered how he'd got it. At the same time, shame smothered her. She shouldn't be letting him go through with this.

He glanced down at her hand before gliding his bony fingers between hers. His skin felt soft and slippery. Nine days ago, the last time she'd seen him, he'd appeared troubled but not angry. He'd fiddled incessantly with a star-shaped pendant, and told her she should continue to play the piano 'whatever happens'. 'No guarantees, remember?' he'd said, and she'd attempted to brush off an impending sense of doom.

The registrar approached the boy and girl in front of Ana and Jasper. She bound their clasped hands with a long piece of fabric, then repeated the procedure for each couple. At school, Ana had been taught that the act of binding came from an ancient tradition of betrothal (also known as 'handfastening'). Hundreds of years ago, a betrothal was a serious commitment that could not be easily broken. It almost always ended in the giving-away of the wife to the husband. The Pure ceremonies reflected the serious undertaking of becoming first bound, then joined in marriage with vows which could never be undone. It was a reminder that there were no divorces for a joined couple, and that the couple's duty first and foremost was the preservation and strengthening of Pure numbers, through procreation and the raising of Pure children.

Ana and Jasper were the last to have their hands bound. Jasper raised their entwined fingers. Ana's hand trembled as the registrar looped the cotton ribbon around and around. Jasper tightened his hold to steady her. She squinted across at him. His eyes met hers, tenderly. She dropped her gaze. A dull pain bloomed in her chest.

The registrar knotted the ribbon and returned to stand behind the oak and leather desk.

'You are now bound,' she announced to the group. 'In exactly four weeks you will each be asked to declare whether you wish to become joined. Use this time to become acquainted. A joining is a lifetime commitment and may not be undone.'

As the woman's final words fell from her lips, Jasper leant in to Ana and whispered, 'I need to talk to you urgently.' She looked into his eyes and saw anxiety. Nodding once, she returned his firm grip, lifted her skirt with her unbound hand and hurried with him from the music room. They surprised the confetti throwers at the front door. Arms jerked into the air, releasing tiny paper hearts in their wake. Jasper didn't relent. He pulled her down the stone path towards the gate and jostled them through the gossiping mothers and joining planners.

Ana saw her father before Jasper did. Ashby Barber was leaning against a wall on the other side of the narrow street, arms folded across his suit, waiting for them. His blue eyes shone wolf-like in the dwindling afternoon light. The hint of silver in his blond hair made him appear distinguished rather than middle-aged. He resembled a movie star from the previous century, not a Nobel Prize-winning scientist.

Ana stopped abruptly, tugging on Jasper's arm. She felt a stab of guilt as well as surprise. Surprise because fathers didn't usually attend the bindings and though under the circumstances he might have stepped in to fulfil her mother's role, Ashby wasn't the type. The guilt was to do with Jasper's furtive escape, though they had every right to run off together. And the bleeding girl.

Jasper's eyes followed Ana's gaze to her father. He swore under his breath.

Ashby crossed the road. 'Congratulations,' he said, picking up their bound hands, which looked like some strange disfigurement wrapped in a tourniquet. Then he kissed Ana's cheek and shook Jasper's right hand. 'Sorry I couldn't get here earlier.'

'I didn't realise you were coming at all,' Ana said.

Her father smiled showing gleaming white teeth. Ana glanced at Jasper. He'd turned so pale he looked sick.

'Where's Nick?' Ashby asked.

'Jasper's chauffeur is driving us to the concert.' Ana didn't tell her father she'd sent *his* chauffeur off to take an injured girl to hospital in the City; he wouldn't appreciate blood all over the car seat. 'I told Nick I didn't need him until later.'

'Well,' her father said, addressing Jasper, 'your parents are waiting for us to have a celebratory drink before the concert, and you two probably want to take advantage of your first trip on your own. Fortunately, I held on to the extra driver. I'll follow you to the Barbican.'

'OK, Dad.' Ana pulled her lips into a tight smile, aware of how quiet Jasper was beside her. Almost rude. At least they'd be alone for the ride to the concert hall. Then finally he'd tell her what was going on.

3

The Concert

Jasper slouched in the back seat of the saloon car behind his driver. Ana sat beside him. Their shoulders touched, their bound hands were sunk in the gap between their legs. The vehicle crawled down Hampstead High Street towards the southern checkpoint near Belsize Park. Jasper hadn't uttered a word since cursing at the sight of her father. If during most of the ceremony he'd looked like he was preparing for battle, now it seemed he'd surrendered the fight.

'Jasper?' she said. 'What's wrong?'

His eyes flicked across to her, but they appeared focused on something in his mind, as though she were imaginary, not whatever it was he saw.

'Not now,' he said.

'Five minutes ago you said you had to talk to me urgently.'

'Well, now I don't.'

A chilling hardness seeped through her. If Jasper couldn't make himself accessible on the day of their binding, she wasn't sure enduring the Community and everything that staying in it meant – the Board's tests, the constant scrutiny and ostracism – was worth the trouble. But that was her anger and her pride talking. She could hardly give up on herself. She straightened the blue ripples of silk across her legs.

'Please, Jasper, we're going to be spending a lot of time together over the next few weeks. I was hoping we could be open with each other.'

His eyes came back into focus. 'Are you sure you want honesty?' he asked. His flat voice carried an air of such menace, she flinched.

Jasper's hand felt limp and hot against the skin of her palm. She considered untying the white fabric so that she could sit further from him, or jump out of the car when they stopped at the Hampstead checkpoint. But of course, she didn't.

'Yes,' she answered, 'I want us to be honest with each other. You can't go through with the joining because you feel sorry for me, or because you sent me a binding invitation on a whim before you knew I was a Big3, and now, out of some misplaced sense of duty, you feel responsible for my future safety.'

'I see,' Jasper said. A hint of amusement touched his ashen face. 'So this is how you behave the first time we're officially allowed to be alone together?'

'And this is how *you* behave,' she said. She would not be manoeuvred into avoiding a serious conversation. She knew what it was like to live with someone you didn't communicate with. She and her father had never connected. Whatever compromises she was prepared to make, a superficial relationship with Jasper wasn't one of them; not even to escape the City. She glanced at him and the sight of hopelessness in his expression softened her.

'I'm not sure I can ask this of you,' she said.

'Ask what?'

'Come on. You know what.'

Instead of answering, he scowled.

Ana rubbed the soft silk of her dress between her right-hand finger and thumb.

'So, how are your studies going?'

'Fine.'

'I could help you prepare for the bar exam if you like.'

Jasper looked up and stared at her. Perhaps he thought she was being ridiculous.

'When my dad was arrested I got interested in law,' she explained. 'And then you started your law degree. I kind of followed the syllabus.' She shrugged. It was probably better not to tell him how fascinated and obsessed by the subject she'd become. How a non-existent social life and boring school studies meant she'd read every paper from the three-year Oxford syllabus she could get her hands on. Law appealed to her natural ability to memorise and her enjoyment of rational and creative argument. Her school studies never required such mental gymnastics. If anything, they'd grown simpler and stupider the closer she'd come to finishing.

Jasper remained mute.

Ana glanced out the window, then tried again. 'I er . . . I was remembering on the way to the binding the first time we met,' she said, 'at your parents' Christmas party.'

'You were much shorter then,' he responded.

'I was eleven.'

'Well, that could be why.' The hint of a smile shone through his expression.

She raised her eyes and grew warm under his gaze. Perhaps pulling the old Jasper out of the new required skill and delicacy, like extracting the soft flesh of a prickly pear.

'I was sure you'd be joined by the time I was eligible,' she said.

'Well, there was one near-miss.'

'Who desisted?'

'It was pretty mutual.'

She nodded, but she didn't believe him. She couldn't imagine any impressionable teenage girl turning down the rich, handsome Jasper Taurell.

'You were playing the piano,' he said. 'The first time we met,' he added, by way of explanation. 'You'd hidden away in the old annexe near the library and you were playing the piano and crying.'

Ana looked away, embarrassed and amazed he remembered. 'Yes, and you and Tom found me and insisted I return to the party.'

Jasper smiled, but the smile quickly faded and his gaze grew distant.

'Do you prefer not talking about him?'

'It's fine,' he said. But a sadness crept over him – a heaviness she knew too well from losing her mother. Before she quite realised what she was doing, she reached out and brushed a fingertip across the bruise above his eye. He wrapped his right hand over hers and brought it up to his lips. He gently kissed the bottom of her thumb. She held her breath. In her mind she saw her disease oozing out of her skin where his mouth touched her and staining his lips blue; she saw it sink into his veins and mix with the blood coursing through his body. It was like a curse. He was her antidote. She was his poison.

*

The opening bars of the evening's final concerto resounded through the auditorium. Hunched in his balcony seat, Jasper tried to swallow the lump in his throat. The melody they listened to pained him almost as much as the confusion in Ana's ocean-grey gaze. Without thinking, his fingers searched beneath his shirt for the pendant he'd altered to conceal his brother Tom's research evidence. He'd wanted to tell Ana what was really going on for months, but he'd been afraid she wouldn't believe him, just as he hadn't believed his brother the week before Tom's death, when Tom claimed he'd uncovered the story of the century – there was something wrong with the Pure tests.

Rachmaninov's C Minor Concerto grew wistful. A hush descended on the stalls below. Jasper almost didn't notice the muttering and murmuring until moments like that – when it stopped. He gazed over the balcony at the Crazies standing shoulder-to-shoulder inside the wire mesh pen below. The Benzidox addicts were easy to spot. They twitched and jerked; they were missing large clumps of hair or wore badly made wigs. The majority of the ragged crowd had their interfaces switched on. The wearable, miniature computers projected spinning symbols and catchwords on the T-shirts and sweaters of those in front. Blurred images and letters throbbed in a sea of colour. One or two of the Crazies manipulated the digital information in time with the music, using hand gestures to alter the colours and forms superimposed on the world around them.

When the violins began to crescendo and the music swelled through the vast hall, the mumbling and fidgeting resumed.

The lump in Jasper's throat swelled to the size of a golf ball. He had to say something to Ana now. It might be his last chance. He leaned towards her. The scent of lemon and the glow of her silvery blonde hair momentarily distracted him. Sensing his closeness, she turned. Serious eyes settled on his face. Beneath the fabric of their bound hands, he tightened his grip and leaned forwards towards the balcony, drawing her with him. He began to speak, gaze trained on the concert pianist centre stage.

'There are things I haven't been able to tell you,' he murmured. 'I'm in trouble.' Her eyes widened. 'Don't look at me,' he said. 'Don't draw attention.' She nodded. Her face relaxed. She turned from him and rested the side of her head against his cheek, as though they were simply sharing an intimate moment; a gesture that concealed his mouth.

Jasper felt a surge of admiration for her quiet intelligence. And regret. He should have trusted her. Now it was too late.

'This morning I met an acquaintance in the City,' Jasper began. 'One minute we were talking, the next he was flipping out, going mental. The Psych Watch arrived within seconds. They sedated him, dragged him away. It was . . . because of me.'

On Ana's left, her father rose. She leaned back, allowing

him to squeeze down the row, forcing Jasper to do the same. As Ashby excused himself, Jasper's mother, sitting to Jasper's right, placed her hand over his. He glanced around and saw his own father, mother and sister all watching him.

His face began to burn. He removed his hand and shook out one arm from his dinner jacket. A piece of paper flitted to the ground. Instinctively, he let his programme drop and bent to retrieve both items, jerking Ana down with him.

'Sorry,' he muttered. He rested the programme on his lap and strained to read the scrap beneath. A telephone number. 'Ana,' he whispered, 'I'm sorry, I've got to . . .' He untied the binding knot and started to unwind the material folded over their hands. She paled. Though a couple didn't stay bound for the four-week courtship, removal of the ribbon was usually a significant, intimate moment full of unspoken hope. Often a couple would hold off doing it for as long as possible, believing it auspicious to stay fastened together until the very last moment when they parted for the night.

'Sorry,' Jasper repeated. He rose and passed his family to the end of the row. His heart pounded as he strode up the aisle, loosening his bow tie, which now strangled him. At the exit, he pushed open the auditorium door and stumbled into the corridor. The door sucked shut behind him, muffling the orchestra. Dim coloured lights in the floor lit the passage towards the bar.

It was only after Tom's 'accident' and the Wardens' 'investigation', which included ransacking Tom's room and confiscating all his possessions, that Jasper had started to believe his brother had been on to something. And then it had taken him weeks to pluck up the nerve to search Tom's locker at the golf club. He'd found the tiny disc wedged into the metal latch, exactly as Tom had described. He'd found it and hidden it again in the next locker along. It had taken him over two years of deliberation before he decided to finish what his brother had started. Then he'd begun slowly building up his contacts and determining the safest way to get the evidence out of the Community.

But all his planning had come to nothing this morning. The moment Jasper had handed over the only other copy of the research material to the transporter, the guy had gone nuts. A minute earlier there'd been nothing wrong with him. He'd obviously been spiked, and the Psych Watch had been waiting. Which meant there was a leak. The Wardens had known exactly what was going on and had taken out the transporter. It was only a matter of time before they caught up with Jasper.

He should have disappeared in the earlier confusion, glided through the cracks of London's chaotic city streets and buried himself. But he hadn't been ready to walk away from his life; hadn't known where to go. And though he couldn't explain what was going on to his mother, he'd hoped for the chance to tell Ana the truth.

Reaching the bar, Jasper turned to make sure he wasn't being followed. The overhead surround-sound vibrated as the concerto climaxed, trumpets blaring. The piano's refrain started over, staccato and swirling. He was familiar with the final piece of the evening, but the shift felt different this time, as if it had lost control. He skirted round the bar and with a last backwards glance, exited through a fire door.

In the stairwell, he waved his hand in front of him to activate his interface – a gold triangle enclosing a circle of ruby glass, which hung from his neck chain. The ruby lit up. As the device projected digital information from the internal computer, the red stone blazed against his shirt like burning coal. Quickly, he attached the magnetic scrambler on to the metal housing so the Wardens couldn't use his transmission to track him. He mimed making a phone call. The camera inside his interface picked up the hand gesture and the computer switched to phone mode, casting numbers into the air. He held his palm parallel to his chest and the virtual telephone pad focused up on it. Using his other hand, he keyed in the number that he'd found slipped into his jacket pocket.

The line clicked into voicemail straight away.

'This is Enkidu,' a male voice said. 'I'm busy so try again later. BEEP. Sorry no messages! I ain't no answering machine.' Jasper hung up and rechecked the paper. Scribbled beside the number was the word *Camden*. As he scrunched the scrap into a ball and shoved it in his trouser pocket, his interface beeped that he'd received mail.

Enkidu, *Camden*, he thought. If he could get there without being followed, he might stand a chance of eluding the Wardens. Employing the stairwell door as a screen for his interface, he opened the new message and saw an image of a guy in a strait-jacket, blood down his cracked nose. Mouth twisted into a scream. Forehead mashed up. Unre-

31

cognisable. But the eyes – the eyes were his contact's. The transporter.

Sweat seeped through Jasper's shirt and trickled down the sides of his face. He yanked off his bow tie and bent over, palms pressed into his thighs. His breathing was all over the place. The music, though barely audible now, whirled in his head.

Someone anonymous had sent the image to warn or frighten him. Either way, it confirmed what he knew – his contact going demented right after Jasper had entrusted him with the disc was no coincidence.

Jasper glanced at the overhead security camera, then turned and flew down the stairs. His hard shoes clattered on the concrete steps. At Level Two his interface flickered off and back on again as the wireless network booster kicked in. At Level Three he yanked open the stairwell door, panting.

Notes of a single oboe floated through the darkness. The plaintive reed instrument reached through the old car-park speakers, spilt around the wall dividing the level, and wrenched Jasper's insides. He faltered.

His mother deserved better than the mysterious vanishing of another son. Ana deserved better than this. He'd messed up.

The oboe glided and the piano motif started to climb, violins echoing the ascent.

Quickly pulling up a 3D map of the arts centre, he searched for a way out. Built in the 1970s, the Barbican was a sprawling maze of concrete stairwells, grey towers, and interlinking walkways. Jasper found what he was after and adjusted his interface projection so that it glowed dimly. He crept away from the stairwell, the only place where the fluorescent strip lights still worked, towards a tunnel. The tunnel led to a shaft of steps that emerged by a walkway linked to Moorgate station. His best chance of diving under the radar was going underground. The Wardens didn't have the surveillance power to cover the sprawling London Tube lines.

Jasper passed a row of derelict cars, which had been stripped beyond recognition. Twenty-three years ago, when petrol sources began to dry up and the Petrol Wars started, cars in their millions had been abandoned all across the country – in front of houses, in garages, in car parks just like this one. Limited electric train resources had been unable to support the hundreds of thousands who'd commuted daily by car and people had flocked to the cities, leaving the rural towns to slowly die.

Beneath the haunting melody, a battery engine hummed to life. Jasper blocked the light from his interface and crouched down next to a wide pillar to listen. The vibration seemed to be coming from somewhere behind. His heart began to thump. Hardly anyone used this lower level car park – there was no need; there was plenty of room for all the Pure chauffeurs to park on Level One.

Jasper narrowed the field of illumination from his interface into a sharp ray of light. Rather than groping his way along the exposed wall that led up to Level Two, he would use the beam to find the tunnel door first, then make a beeline for it in the dark.

He scanned the brick wall until he saw a metal door.

He mentally marked his route: eight paces forward at a quarter to two, side-step around a wide pillar, then four paces at three o'clock. He cut the projection and listened. Blood rushed in his ears. He could no longer hear the smooth hybrid engine. He breathed in sharply, stood up, and stepped out into the open.

Headlights snapped on, catching him in their beams. The vehicle accelerated forwards. Jasper burst into a run, crossing the twelve-foot gap in seconds. The saloon halted beside the pillar. Blinded by the headlights, Jasper pushed against the exit door.

It didn't budge.

With everything he had, he thrust his shoulder into the cold metal. Pain exploded in his arm. The door held. For a moment, the shock of what this meant paralysed him.

The headlights dimmed. In a spurt of defiance, Jasper bolted left towards the ramp that led up to the next level. A pinprick of light danced ahead of him in the darkness – the approaching projection of someone's interface. Jasper swung back the way he'd come. The saloon jerked forward to cut him off, trapping him between it and the spinning shaft of interface colour.

The slap-slap of shoes echoed down the tunnel.

'Leaving early, Jasper?' a voice asked. Jasper's stomach plummeted. His panicky thoughts took a moment to place the smooth baritone. But then it came to him. He'd been such an idiot! So naïve!

'You've put me in a very awkward situation,' the man said. 'I'd been hoping we might avoid this.'

Jasper squinted through the darkness. The figure carried

a metal rod in one of his hands. A tingling sensation zinged up Jasper's spine, intensifying as it entered his head and burst inside the back of his skull. He tried to lift his hand to the pain, but his arm hung by his side. He grappled to think; his thoughts were flying threads he couldn't catch hold of.

All that reached him was the music, reminding him of Ana, as it played out the concerto's final bars.

4

Abduction

An overcast dawn bled through the high basement windows. Ana sat cross-legged at the bottom of the swimming pool holding her breath, a brick weight between her knees. Eyes closed, she concentrated on the slow, steady beat of her heart. Her lungs burnt. She relaxed her arm muscles, her facial muscles, her chest. She counted. As the burn faded, thoughts of last night crowded in on her. She pushed them away, determined not to remember how Jasper had pulled off the binding ribbon as though it was meaningless, how she'd searched for him until the concert hall and the bar were empty, then been forced to admit that he'd left without saying goodnight.

A line of bubbles drifted from her. She tried counting as a distraction, but it was no good. She couldn't shut Jasper out. Even asleep he'd haunted her. She'd woken from a nightmare in the early hours of the morning. In her dream, she'd found herself standing over their matrimonial bed holding a knife. Blood had dripped from the serrated edge. Confused, she'd looked down and seen the covers folded over Jasper's form slick with liquid crimson. She'd woken trembling and sweaty and hadn't slept since.

Beneath the water, the air expired from Ana's lungs. She

swam to the surface and hauled herself up the side of the pool. She dried off. Then, gripping the towel around her shoulders, she climbed the basement steps. The cold stone sent shivers through her feet. She headed for the main block of the house, halting at the end of the corridor. Voices vibrated behind the thin kitchen wall. Male voices. A mixture of curiosity and anxiety ran through her. Her father never woke before seven-thirty, and he never had guests to stay, not even female ones. Something important was going on.

A kettle whistled. Ana peered into the sunken living room. The flatscreen above the low sideboard flickered, which meant her father had switched on his interface and would be coming back to watch. Seizing her chance, she hurried over the wooden floor and Turkish carpets, past the glass coffee table and her father's photographs of strung-out rock stars. She reached the raised platform where her baby grand stood and stopped. Someone had opened the key cover. No one touched her piano, not even the cleaner.

Suddenly, she heard her father's voice.

'I don't see,' he said, growing louder and closer, 'why they can't ban reporters from the Communities altogether.'

Ana bounded up the open wood-slatted staircase. She didn't want her father's guest to see her in a bathing costume and towel. And she was far more likely to find out what was going on if they didn't know she was there. Halfway up the stairs and out of sight, she paused to listen.

'We're going to have to put a couple of extra security guys out there,' her father went on. 'I don't want them climbing ladders to see over the garden fence.'

Pressing her hand to her chest, Ana tried to steady the rapid rise and fall of her breathing.

'Perhaps if you authorised a couple of 'em to wait out the front . . .'

'Out of the question,' Ashby said.

'Well, maybe you should give 'em somethin',' the other man suggested. His lilting accent sounded familiar. 'A photo,' he continued, 'or a quote to capture her shock when she finds out what happened. Then the reporters might let up.'

Her shock. The words rebounded in Ana's head. She felt her knees weaken.

'Here, it's on,' her father said.

The flatscreen volume went up. Both men stopped speaking.

'. . . Jasper Taurell,' the newsreader announced, 'son of David Taurell, CEO of the giant pharmaceutics company, Novastra, was abducted last night . . .'

The words jumbled, and then Ana couldn't hear them at all. She shuddered. Somewhere far away, much further it seemed than the living room surround-speak, the reporter continued. '. . . There is growing concern that his abduction is politically motivated. Novastra, patent-holders of the miracle drug Benzidox, are currently negotiating a billion-pound deal with the government's Mental Health Services – negotiations that have been the centre of great controversy over the last few weeks.'

Water dripped down Ana's back and thighs, pooling on the step. Her swimming cap pressed against her temples.

Her legs were barely holding. Any moment now she would collapse on the stairs in her swimsuit.

One hand grasping her towel, she scrambled up. Her free palm slapped the smooth grey wall, steadying herself as she climbed.

'Ariana?' her father called.

At the top of the stairs she barrelled down the corridor. The black and white photos of her playing the piano lit up as she ran into her bedroom. She locked herself inside the bathroom and huddled in the shower. The water came on automatically, spraying her from all directions.

Thick steam choked the air. She began to sob, anger and fear twisting inside her. How could the Wardens have let this happen? They were supposed to protect the Pures from the Crazies. And why did Jasper walk out of the concert early if he knew Crazies were trying to kidnap him? He'd said he was in trouble. Why hadn't he told his father or the Wardens?

Furious, she struck her foot against the shower wall. The thick glass shuddered in its frame. She should have forced Jasper to tell her what was going on in the car after the binding ceremony. She should have got up and followed him out of the concert, instead of hesitating for a minute and losing him.

'Ariana?' The sharp timbre of her father's voice carried through the bathroom door. She growled in frustration. Her father was worse than the Board. He constantly analysed her for signs of instability.

'Ariana, open the door.' Warning laced his clipped tone.

She pressed her sobbing gasps down inside her, sniffed

and clambered to her feet, yanking off her swimming cap. Her swimsuit squelched as she peeled it away and kicked it into a corner.

'I'm coming,' she said. She stepped out of the shower and put on her dressing gown. Her face itched with salty tears and chlorine. She washed it with cold water, then patted her skin dry. Besides her uneven breathing, the only sounds came from beyond the high bathroom window, birdsong and the wind whistling over the golf course at the back of the house. Finally, once she'd regained some self-control, she unlocked the door.

Her father was perched on her beauty table by the windowsill. His square shoulders and shadowed face cut a dark silhouette against the fuzzy light. She forced herself to meet his gaze.

'This is a setback,' he said slowly, as though she might be hard of hearing. 'Not a calamity.'

She snorted in disbelief.

'The Wardens,' he went on, 'will find Jasper. This will all be fixed in time for the joining.'

Ana's hands trembled with indignation. She wrung them together behind her back. His self-assurance when he had no control over the situation was unbearable.

'You think all that concerns me is the joining? Jasper could be injured or dead.'

'He's been abducted, probably for money, or to put pressure on his father about this Benzidox deal with the government. I'm not worried about Jasper and you shouldn't be either. The only thing that concerns me about this,' he said, his voice growing softer, 'the only thing that could turn it from a setback into a calamity . . .' He paused. 'Is *you*.'

His look felt like an arrow of ice hitting her between the eyes. Ana shivered and hugged her dressing gown tighter around her body. Trust her father to make this all about her fallibility.

'I'm fine.'

'It didn't sound like it.'

'Really? What did it sound like?' Her hand slipped around the iron sculpture on the table next to the bathroom door, tightly encircling the miniature partridge's neck. 'Like I might be a tiny bit upset?'

Her father straightened.

'The Board will be here in less than an hour. I suggest you aim for "deeply concerned, but staying positive for Jasper's sake".'

'And how do I think staying positive will help him?' she asked.

Her father shot her a dangerous look. 'Hold it together, Ariana. With something this big, the Board will be keeping a close eye on you.'

Inwardly, she shuddered. But she didn't allow the fear to register on her face. Ever since the Board declared her a Big3 Sleeper, they'd rigorously and unrelentingly examined her. She hated them. She hated how they'd managed to get inside her, residing in the part of herself that coolly observed everything she did and felt.

Her father stepped towards her.

'Ariana,' he said with uncharacteristic gentleness. 'I didn't say this would be easy. But you're prepared. And you've been through worse. The last thing Jasper would want is to come home and find the Board has declared you Active.'

Ana stared ahead, not giving him the satisfaction of meeting his look.

'Well,' he said, pushing his hands into his blue dressing-gown pockets. 'When you're ready you can come down. We need to go over what you are going to say to the Board.'

'Great.'

Ashby retreated around the bed to the door. 'Why don't you wear your white blouse with the grey skirt?'

'Fine.'

He paused on the threshold of her room and scrutinised her for a moment. Looking for cracks no doubt.

'Good girl,' he said finally. Then he closed the bedroom door behind him.

Ana stood there glowering as his footsteps receded down the hall, furious with both of them. Slowly the anger dissolved and she sank to the floor. Sprawled out across the wooden boards, she felt as though her heart was splitting. Not only for the Jasper that had been taken last night, but also for the boy that had vanished nearly three years ago when his brother died, whom she'd glimpsed last night on the way to the concert and who would probably be lost to her forever now. He'd changed overnight after Tom's accident. What would become of him after hours or days in the hands of cruel, Crazy kidnappers?

In her mind's eye she saw Jasper at Tom's funeral. Pasty, unshaved, his scowling eyes were sunk in grey half-moons. At the end of the proceedings, after all the guests had gone, he'd cornered Ana, as though he'd seen her sneak in and hide in the shadows at the back.

'Hello, Ariana,' he'd said. She'd frozen beneath his icy regard, afraid he would call security and have her escorted out. She didn't think she could stand any more humiliation than she'd been through in the last couple of weeks. 'So, how are you?' His voice sounded strange, metallic, like it could cut. She opened her mouth to say 'fine', then closed it again. Her immediate reaction was to answer as she would if the Board were asking. To make herself appear balanced, stable, shocked and upset in just the right proportions. But the sparks of hurt behind his stare incited her to respond with the truth.

'I'm finding it hard to sleep,' she said. 'When I close my eyes I can't stop spinning.'

'Not so good then,' he said. His mouth twisted upward. She gazed at him. Close up, she noticed his eyes were set slightly far apart and his forehead was bigger than she remembered. She blushed. An un-joined Pure girl shouldn't be alone with a Pure male, even if they were in a public place. And then her cheeks burnt even brighter. The rules didn't apply to her. She wasn't Pure. Maybe that's why he was talking to her like this.

'You came to the funeral,' he said quietly. She tried not to look puzzled. Was he feverish? Of course she'd come. Or perhaps he was saying she *shouldn't* have come. After all, she and her father had not been sent notification of the ceremony.

'I'm sorry.' She swallowed hard. 'I just wanted to see if you're OK.'

'And what's the verdict?'

'Not so good,' she said, echoing his words.

He almost smiled. 'I'm sorry I didn't come after, you know . . .' She knew at once he was referring to the radio silence after she'd received her redone Pure test from the Board.

'It was to be expected.'

He looked at her as though he felt sorry for her. She frowned. She didn't want his sympathy.

'How is your father's hearing going?' he asked.

'Fine. His lawyers are confident the case will be dismissed.'

So far, the prosecution had been unable to provide any explanation for how her father was supposed to have accessed the security codes to get on to the Board's system and alter her test. Apparently, inputting data was easy, but only three executives on the Board were privy to the codes that allowed someone to alter files. It seemed they wouldn't be able to prove what he'd done, but Ana knew he was guilty.

Jasper shoved his hands in his dark trouser pockets. He began to jiggle his left leg.

'I was thinking.' His words came with a puff of air like they were travelling at high velocity. 'Once your father's case is wrapped up, the Board will be making their decision about what to do with you.'

Ana grimaced. She was well aware of this fact and the way Jasper said it made her feel like a stray dog.

'I'm going to tell them I want to go ahead with the binding.'

A wave of heat swept down through her head, her arms, her chest, her legs. 'Why?'

'Because I still want to get to know you.'

'But we couldn't be joined. What would be the point?'

'It's not illegal for a Pure to marry a Big3.' Hearing him say 'Big3' made tears spring to Ana's eyes. She forced them back.

'You would have to leave the Community,' she said. 'I couldn't . . .'

It must have been a trick of the light – a cloud passing over the sun outside – because his eyes grew overcast.

'You're not Active,' he said. 'You've lived in the Community for years without incident. Why shouldn't you be allowed to stay?'

She stared at him as though he were mad. 'Because my illness could kick in at any moment. I might not even know it's happening.' Her hands trembled now at her sides. She couldn't be sure if it was the hope or insanity of his suggestion that made her body shake.

'You could be sixty, seventy, eighty years old. Who's to say it'll ever happen?'

'The Pure test says so,' she whispered. Their eyes met. Something strange flashed across his gaze. If she didn't know better she would say he was suffering the onset of an illness – bipolar or one of the many mood disorders her father was making her learn about.

'The Community is your home,' he said. 'You accepted my binding invitation. If the case is dismissed against your father, I don't think you should be forced from your home and made to give up your future. Why should you pay for the Board's mistake?'

'You're upset,' she said, suddenly desperate to get away from him. She couldn't think like this, couldn't allow herself to hope there might be something else for her other than banishment to the City. Holding up the long hem of her skirt, she croaked, 'I'm sorry about Tom.' Then she ran down the hall and out into the mild June sun.

5

The Board

Ana picked herself up from the floor. She got dressed, went downstairs and her father grilled her about Jasper's abduction until the Board showed up. He reworded her responses, directing her performance like she was an actress in a play. She knew he was tough on her so that it would be easier to cope with the Board's inquisition, but she couldn't forgive him for transforming her emotions into something so calculated and remote.

When the doorbell rang, her father left her with instructions to play something pretty on the piano, while he let the Board in. She bashed out *Chopsticks*, reminding herself that according to Jasper and some of the legal papers she'd read, the Board's existence was precarious. Dozens of religious and activist groups constantly petitioned the government to get rid of it or pass new bills to reduce the Board's overbearing domination in the field of Mental Health.

A stick figure stooped in the entrance. Ana stopped playing and looked up. At the same moment, a woman appeared beside the man, seeming lumpish next to his beanpole frame. The man's nose, lips and chin lay squashed against his face. The woman's mole-eyes stared at Ana through thick glasses, giving the impression of distance and altitude, as though she was looking down through a microscope.

Ana's heart began to gallop. She rose from her seat, descended the steps into the living room, and invited them to join her on the leather sofas around the coffee table. They entered stiffly. In unison, they clicked open their briefcases and set up their screens on the glass table. Ana fetched the prepared tea tray and biscuits from the kitchen. She wondered what her health and beauty teacher would say about the inner workings of this ugly couple, or why, for that matter, members of the Board were always so unattractive.

The front door rattled shut. Leaning over the kitchen sink, Ana peered out of the window at the driveway. Her father strode across the tarmac to his chauffeur-driven saloon. The Board never allowed him to stay for her interviews.

She returned to the living room with the tray and found a third figure by the hallway entrance perusing her father's rock-star photographs. The stocky man didn't wear the grey suit with gold stripes, emblematic of the Board.

The tea tray wobbled in her hands. The china clinked. The man turned to her and smiled.

'Jack Dombrant,' he said, moving to assist her with the tray. She returned his smile uncertainly. He was the man her father had been talking to earlier, when she'd heard the news about Jasper.

'You have an Irish accent,' she said.

'Ah, most young people wouldn't recognise it these days,'

he replied. 'You've got a good ear with your piano playing, eh? My ma was from Dublin.'

Ana remembered the open key cover of her baby grand and at the same time realised Mr Dombrant had to be a Warden.

'We moved to London when I was eight,' he continued. 'But I never quite managed to lose the twang.'

She nodded. He must have immigrated before the 2018 Collapse, when England closed her borders, and Scotland, Wales and Northern Ireland became independent. Which meant he was at least thirty-one.

Ana sat down on the sofa beneath the flatscreen, opposite the Board. The woman signalled for her to roll up her sleeve and attached a plastic strap around her wrist. Then she linked the monitor to Ana's interface. Both Board representatives leant over the coffee table to check their display screens. Ana tried to slow her racing pulse.

'Can you describe your feelings last night at the concert?' the man asked, without looking up.

Members of the Board did not introduce themselves or talk of themselves individually. Ana had learnt over the last three years that they wished her to address them in a likewise, indirect fashion. The men and women who came to question her were always different, but they managed to create an unnervingly unified presence, like they were the close-up parts of a larger animal, whose singular striations and skin texture were always recognisable as part of a distinct whole.

'I was happy and a bit nervous,' she replied.

The Warden helped himself to a Bourbon biscuit and

perched on the edge of an armchair. The crunch-crunch of his chewing grated on her nerves.

The male Board representative blinked at Ana. The female took notes.

'Have you been feeling guilty about Jasper?' the man asked.

Ana swallowed and shook her head.

'Do you feel any guilt,' he pursued, 'about the fact that if and when you join with Jasper Taurell, you may not give him children?'

'And if you accidentally fall pregnant,' the woman added, 'not only will you and the children be relocated, but Jasper will be forced to live in the disorder and squalor of the City, instead of working for his father as a respected defence lawyer?'

Ana straightened her grey skirt, watching her hands as they brushed the cotton fabric. She didn't see why living in the City meant Jasper couldn't work for his father.

Concentrate, she thought, mentally kicking herself. *They're trying to catch you out.*

Guilt was a symptom of Depression, Post-traumatic Stress Disorder, Bipolar Disorder and a dozen other MIs – Mental Illnesses. Her father had repeated it often enough over the years: No matter what, never, never admit guilt.

'No,' she said, 'I do not feel guilty.' From the corner of her eye, she noticed the Warden amble towards the platform by the French windows where her piano stood. 'Jasper is aware of the consequences of his choice,' she added.

The Board members gave curt, synchronised nods and

resumed filling in the Chart of Attitudes, which Ana knew they would now have pulled up on their screens.

Discordant notes resounded from the piano. Ana's eyes shot to the platform. She tried to keep the shock off her face. She couldn't believe Warden Dombrant would touch her piano without asking first or would behave so disrespectfully in front of the Board.

The Warden dropped crumbs on to the keys as he bit into a second Bourbon and tinkled with his biscuit-free hand.

'I have a couple of questions about last night,' he said. Ana suppressed her annoyance. She became aware of her ramrod posture, her interlocked fingers tightening on her lap. 'I saw Jasper in the foyer before the concert.'

She smiled tightly. 'That's not a question.'

'He appeared to be rather agitated.' Dombrant's eyes seemed to be laughing at her.

Ana shrugged, but the hairs on her neck and arms started to tingle. She thought of Jasper beside her at the concert, leaning forward on the balcony, whispering to her he was in trouble, asking her not to draw attention. He hadn't trusted the Wardens.

'I don't think he was feeling well,' she said.

'Did he do anything odd?'

Her heart began to thump again. The Board leant over their screens. Though neither of them spoke, they gave the impression they were somehow conferring – no doubt evaluating her skyrocketing pulse.

'Why would he do anything odd?' she asked. 'Do you think he knew he was a target for kidnappers?'

The Warden stuffed the last of his biscuit into his mouth and brushed crumbs from his suit.

'We're looking at all possibilities right now,' he said. He pushed his hands deep in his trouser pockets and skipped down the platform steps, surprisingly agile for someone so bulky. 'Jasper might have felt somethin' was amiss, or seen somethin' that bothered him but not wanted to worry anyone, or spoil your evenin'.'

But that's what the Wardens are for, Ana thought. She caught herself before she said it. Focused on regaining her composure. Jasper may not have trusted the Wardens, but why if he'd suspected he was in danger, had he made himself vulnerable by leaving the concert early?

'Now this morning,' the male Board representative said, claiming back the interview. 'Please tell the Board how you found out about the abduction, what you did afterwards, and how you felt.'

On safer ground, Ana began the rehearsed monologue of how her father had knocked on her door, awoken her, and broken the bad news. She was mid describing the shock, which after several minutes faded into worry for Jasper's safety, when she felt the Warden's eyes boring into her. Her attention darted to him for a second. A slight smile crept across his lips.

Inwardly, she cursed. *So stupid!* He'd been there with her father this morning. He knew she was lying. She dropped her gaze.

'Did it remind you of other shocks?' the male Board member asked.

'No,' she answered, starting to panic. She braced herself

for the Warden's interruption, struggling to think of excuses that would explain the lie. But the Warden said nothing. So she forced herself to continue.

'The shock of discovering that I'm not Pure,' she said, 'is something I saw a therapist about and have now thoroughly dealt with.'

'What about your mother's death? Shortly before your fifteenth birthday you contacted the Guildford Register's Office for your mother's death certificate. Why?'

Ana took a deep breath. She'd gone through this story so many times with the Board, she sometimes found herself believing it. The true memory she had of living on the farm and waking early one morning to find her mother missing and a car engine running in the locked barn, felt like information from an interface projection – images superimposed on real life.

'When I was ten, my father told me my mother was ill and had been hospitalised with cancer. I think he wished to soften the blow of my mother's sudden death. Nine months later, he took me to see a dying woman. He said it was time for me to say goodbye to my mother.'

'Yes?' the male Board representative said, wishing Ana to go on.

'The woman resembled my mother, but I doubted it was really her. After many years of wondering about it, I decided to contact the Guildford Register's Office for my mother's death certificate. When the Board informed me my mother had died by car-exhaust asphyxiation, I was surprised and upset, but not shocked. I had already accepted that she was gone.'

The male Board member adjusted his glasses and leaned towards his screen.

'Why do you think your father lied about the woman?'

'He thought he was helping me. His psychiatric training taught him I would need closure.' She spoke flatly, but she couldn't totally restrain her disgust for this particular part of her story; her nostrils flared. Her father hadn't taken her to see the dying woman to help her. He'd done it to shut her up; to stop her from asking him questions about her mum all the time.

'Say the first thing that enters your head,' the male Board member instructed.

Nodding, Ana focused on the task at hand. Free association was one of her strengths. She almost enjoyed the mental gymnastics. Answers were strictly limited to food, nature, or science – her father's Golden Rule. Replies had to come without the slightest hesitation, or else they'd know she was censoring herself.

'Rain,' he prompted.

'Drops,' she answered.

'Red.'

'Rose.'

They continued back and forth for over a minute: *Black – Bird; Open – Flower; Light – Sun; Defective – Genetic; White – Milk; River – Stream; Silence – Vacuum; Darkness – Dawn.*

When the bombardment of words ended, the Board members both leant over their screens again. They had a program that automatically analysed her answers and gave a percentile estimate of mental disturbance. Anything over forty meant a whole day of intensive testing. Ana steeled herself for the results. She hadn't got over thirty yet.

'Twenty-two,' the man announced, as if that settled it – Jasper's abduction had not sparked the onset of depression or psychosis.

Ana sighed gently with relief. The woman unfastened a leather case and took out a packet of papers.

'Behaviour test,' she said, placing a few stapled sheets square with the edges of the coffee table. 'Creative test . . .' She laid another block of pages beside the first.

'Every morning,' the man added, vigorously tapping the creative test with his forefinger, 'as soon as you wake up, write at least one page. The Board will return in three days. Questions?'

Ana shook her head. Her entwined fingers itched and her cheeks felt hot, but she knew better than to fiddle. It was almost over.

'I have a question for Ariana,' the Warden said.

Ana's shoulders tensed. She turned to look at him.

'I feel,' he continued, 'that I need to understand Jasper a little better. Could you help me with that?'

She nodded, her dislike for the Warden growing. His lilting accent was starting to annoy her as much as his bad manners.

Dombrant circled Ana's armchair and plumped down in a seat between her and the Board.

'The Big3 – schizophrenia, depression, anxiety disorders. Over forty per cent of the population are Big3 Sleepers or Actives.'

'Forty-two point eight per cent,' Ana said.

'Exactly. If one parent is affected by the Big3 the likelihood of a child developing some variation of the inherited illness is very high.'

'And your point is?'

'Well, it's not like you've got Readin' Disorder or Mathematics Disorder. Don't you find it odd that Jasper isn't bothered by the fact you're a Big3?'

'At first I was surprised, yes. But I think after Tom's accident, Jasper felt there were no guarantees, even for the Pures.'

'So, has Jasper shown any unusual attitudes towards folk in the City?'

'What would you consider unusual, Warden?'

'Friends outside the Communities for example.'

'Oxford accepts Carriers, Sleepers and even Actives. Jasper might have made friends with some of them, I wouldn't know.'

'Yes,' he said, 'Oxford accepts Carriers, Sleepers and Actives. I believe there are currently three of them at the university. None in Jasper's year.'

'If you know already, I don't see why you're asking me.' The Board representatives huddled over their screens, no doubt conferring about the hostility slipping through her comportment.

'Jasper had a friend called Enkidu. We want to get in touch with him.'

Ana shrugged. 'I've never heard of him.'

'Ah,' the Warden replied. 'He's turning out to be something of a mystery.'

'Do you think he has information about the abduction?'

'I'm not at liberty to discuss the investigation at this time.'

Ana's face stung as if he'd really slapped her. 'Isn't that what we're doing?' she said. She stood and moved over to the sideboard below the flatscreen. With her back to the room, she began rearranging the tall vase of sunflowers. 'What can you tell me? Has his father heard from the abductors? What do they want?'

'Well, it depends who they are. Could be a mercenary group doing it for a ransom. Could be paranoids, thinkin' Jasper's involved in a plan for Novastra to take over the world. Could be religious fanatics taking a stand against the use of Benzidox. Could be the Enlightenment Project.'

'So they haven't made contact yet?'

The Warden yawned, stretching his arms, irritatingly noncommittal. She extracted a floppy sunflower from the vase by the head of its stem and turned to him.

'Well,' she said, 'with the little information you have managed to scrape together, what would you say are his chances?'

'We're hopeful it's just some mad City folk after a bit of attention, knowin' it would make a stir because of who his father is.'

Ana's throat ached. She pressed the stem of the sunflower she held between her finger and thumb, crushing the stalk flat.

The male Board representative coughed. 'The Board has decided we will come back to see you tomorrow morning, Ariana.'

Ana snapped the broken flower at the top of its stem. The severed head dropped to the floor.

'Of course,' she answered, coolly regarding the Warden.

'Warden,' the male Board representative said, 'do you have any other questions for Ariana today?'

'That's it,' he replied. 'For now.' He leaned forward, nabbed two more biscuits from the tea tray and stood up. The Board members both shut off their screens and tucked them back into their cases. Their insignia, a golden triangle in a dazzling white circle, now shone from their interfaces.

Ana held up her wrist. 'May I?' she asked.

The woman nodded. Ana unstrapped the pulse monitor and handed it back.

'The Board will show themselves out,' the man said.

'And so will the Warden,' Dombrant said. Winking at Ana, he crammed both biscuits into his mouth.

6

Surfing

Ana watched from the kitchen window as her visitors strode across the courtyard and down the drive. The movement sensor on the metal gates picked up their approach. The gates swung open. As the Board marched through, the Warden turned and looked at the house. His eyes found her in the window. She glared at him, knuckles turning white around the tea tray. An expression of curiosity crossed his face. He smiled, doffed an imaginary hat and followed the Board on to the street.

Ana flipped the tray. The china cups, milk jug and remaining biscuits crashed into the sink.

'The Board would like to come back and see you tomorrow, Ariana,' she mimicked. 'Any more questions, Warden? Yes,' she answered in the Warden's Irish accent, 'I'd just like to know why I'm such an arsehole.'

She stomped into the living room and waved a hand across her chest to power up her interface. It came on, automatically synching to the flatscreen. She considered calling her father and telling him it was a fiasco and it was all his fault for not warning her about Warden Dombrant. But he would try to calm her down. He'd tell her she was over-reacting, that she needed to get a grip. Ana was sick to death of controlling herself. She wanted to scream, swear, smash things up. There was no way she could endure another session with the Board tomorrow without losing it. She'd end up telling them where they could shove their stupid association tests and creative writing.

For three years she'd kept her head down and done as she was told. Was she going to sit back and keep quiet now? Was she going to put her trust in the Wardens when Jasper hadn't? Warden Dombrant was spending time questioning Jasper's behaviour and who Jasper was friends with, when he should be tracking down the kidnappers.

Ana navigated to the BBC News website and stroked her index finger through the air, scrolling down the front page. On the left side of the flatscreen appeared all the day's breaking stories. She tapped her finger in the air over the article titled: Novastra CEO's Son Abducted. A page opened up featuring an old photo of Jasper and his father playing golf.

She scanned the article for information. It covered little more than the seven o'clock news. As yet, no demands had been made and no contact established. An information hotline number flashed at the bottom of the page.

Her gaze rested on the image of Jasper. Pressure filled her chest as she imagined him stuck in some underground hole, blindfolded, thirsty, beaten up or worse, much worse. She had to try and help him.

Ana initiated the interface virtual keyboard by pretending to touch-type. The keyboard appeared on the dark coffee table in front of her. She tapped in the words 'abduction', 'Novastra', 'Benzidox'. The projected words hovered distortedly in front of her chest. She pinched their virtual forms with her fingers and dragged them up to the search engine box on the flatscreen. Within seconds, dozens of pages from all over the net appeared on the screen.

TOMORROW'S UNITED CHRISTIANS claim NOVASTRA'S BENZIDOX DESTROYS FREE WILL.

HUSBAND OF NOVASTRA EMPLOYEE SAYS DANGEROUS ENLIGHTENMENT PROJECT SECT ABDUCTED HIS WIFE.

ANOTHER NOVASTRA EMPLOYEE DISAPPEARS, ESCALATING FEARS OF A BRUTAL ABDUCTION.

Ana scrutinised the results. She'd known controversy surrounded Novastra, but counting Jasper, that made three abductions for the pharmaceutical monopoly in the last twelve months. Her fingers hovered in the air in front of her.

She thought back to the concert. When Jasper had said he was in trouble, he'd spoken of an acquaintance he'd met yesterday morning. The acquaintance had gone mental in the street and been picked up by the Psych Watch. It seemed probable Jasper's abduction was somehow connected. The situation wasn't as simple as Warden Dombrant wanted her to believe. The Warden had been concealing something, waiting, watching, calculating. Which is why he hadn't pulled her up on the lie. With a shiver of anticipation Ana typed 'Enkidu' and 'Psych Watch'.

The top search result referred to an ancient Mesopotamian poem about a king who befriended a wild man called Enkidu. All the other results referred either to the poem or to the establishment nine years ago of the Psych Watch, the Board's right hand, enforcing their dictates and keeping the streets free of dangerous Actives.

What she needed was a list of all the Psych Watch arrests in London yesterday morning. She navigated to a missing persons website, one she'd become familiar with last September when she'd been searching for information about Tamsin. The website published the names of those seized from the streets so families with missing relatives could trace a loved one that had been taken by the Psych Watch to a Mental Rehab Home.

There were thirty-six entries for yesterday morning between nine and eleven-thirty. Ana scanned through the names but there was no one called Enkidu. She started over again at the top of the list, clicking on the provided links for more information. Some included eye-witness accounts of the seizures, some of the more violent episodes had small articles written about them. Ana was about a quarter of the way through the list when she came across a short piece which had featured on several local news sites: Yesterday morning, an ex-member of the Enlightenment Project experienced a sudden psychotic break and pounced on an unsuspecting young Pure man. The Psych Watch arrived in record time to halt the attack.

This morning I met an acquaintance in the City, Jasper had said. *One minute we were talking, the next he was flipping out, going mental. The Psych Watch arrived within seconds.*

Perched on the end of the sofa, Ana stared at the flatscreen. The circumstances fitted exactly. She would check the other remaining names listed, but what were the chances of another Pure being involved in an incident where the Psych Watch showed up so promptly? Which meant Jasper's acquaintance was an ex-member of the Enlightenment Project. And Jasper had got himself mixed up with a dangerous sect. The sect members lived in seclusion, hidden within the wall surrounding Hampstead Heath; the same wall that demarcated the southern border of the Highgate Community; the same wall that Nick drove alongside every time they went to the checkpoint. The Enlightenment Project leaders brainwashed their followers, starving them and locking them up until they yielded their minds to the sect's teachings; teachings that included a prophecy of a future where the Project would save the country from the evils of modern society.

After checking the remaining links to the other Psych Watch seizures and finding nothing, Ana sat quietly and considered what might possibly have led Jasper to take up such an acquaintance. Could he have been helping the ex-member that flipped out escape the sect? Someone called Enkidu? It would explain why he hadn't sought help from the Wardens. The Wardens and the Enlightenment Project had some sort of understanding. The Wardens steered clear of Project business, and the Project followers never breached the wall into the Highgate Community.

If the Enlightenment Project had Jasper, the Wardens wouldn't attempt to get him back. Jasper would be tortured and brainwashed. They would twist his mind until he wouldn't even want to leave. Ana couldn't let that happen.

What she needed was someone with insider information or someone who could get it. She would need to confirm whether Jasper was a prisoner behind the wall and if so, where. The Wardens wouldn't rescue him, but Jasper's influential father would. Just under three years ago, David Taurell lost his oldest son in a freak accident; surely he wouldn't let his only other son go without doing everything he could to prevent it. But first Ana would have to prove Jasper was in the Enlightenment Project because there was no way David Taurell, the CEO of pharmaceutical giant Novastra, would make a stand against the Wardens and risk alienating the Board or the government, on hearsay.

Ana tapped in 'Enlightenment Project', 'abduction', and 'ex-member' on the virtual keyboard. She dragged the suspended words up to the screen's search-engine and a moment later, scanned the results. Her eyes settled on one in particular.

NOVASTRA EMPLOYEE DISAPPEARS, ESCALATING FEARS OF BRUTAL ABDUCTION.
    An ex-member of the Enlightenment Project, COLE WINTER, was taken from his Camden residence for questioning, after another Novastra employee was reported missing.

Camden. A word Ana had seen scribbled on a piece of paper Jasper read moments before leaving the concert. It seemed like a fortuitous coincidence. There might even be some sort of connection between the two. At any rate, an ex-member, still harassed for abductions linked to the Project seemed like a good place to start. He might be willing to talk.

After running a search on Cole Winter, Ana disabled the

link synching her interface computer to all the flatscreens in the house. A flatscreen couldn't store web information, but she didn't know if her father could use the established link to recover her search history. This way she eliminated the possiblity. Because she definitely didn't want him to find out what she was up to. She was going to sneak into the City and enlist Cole Winter's help.

7

Wind Chimes

Ana spent the morning preparing to put her plan into action. After lunch, she checked the news again for any developments concerning Jasper's abduction – nothing. She dug out her old bike from the garage and sat for two hours plucking up the courage to go. Eventually, she wheeled her bike across the brick courtyard and down the drive. The security gates swung back, revealing the wide avenue and a neoclassical mansion across the way. She peered into the street. No sign of reporters. Well, she deserved some compensation for having Ashby Barber as a father. Requests for media permits to camp outside their house had to go through a special government-approval process. It had been like that ever since the national tabloids attacked her father – the trustworthy face of the government's Separation Survival Campaign – for falsifying his daughter's Pure test.

It was warmer today. A reminder that they'd already passed the first official day of spring. Sparrows and finches rustled in the sycamore trees lining the avenue. Ana propped herself on the angular bike seat. She hadn't ridden for a couple of years, and she felt awkward and silly in the old jeans she'd found. They inched up her ankles, chafed her inner thighs and made it hard to bend her knees. She wobbled off the pavement, fumbling to get her feet on the pedals. But then she was off. Her sense of balance, the sensation of the pressing wind, the feeling of freedom, were all at once un-forgotten.

Ana sailed to the end of the road. Without stopping, she careened left on to Hampstead Lane. The ten-foot-high wall running the perimeter of the heath loomed on her right. The wind whipped up around her. Beyond the wall, it soughed through the heath trees. She shuddered and pedalled harder.

The south-eastern checkpoint was just like the south-western checkpoint. It consisted of two square cabins on either side of the road, harbouring two guards. The pavements behind the cabins were sealed off, making it impossible to get in or out of the Community without getting your ID checked and logged.

The road to the checkpoint inclined steeply. Ana concentrated on getting her out-of-practice thigh muscles to complete the uphill task. She still hadn't found a feasible reason that would induce the security guard to break the usual run of things and let her through on her own.

A young guard – the one who was always beaming at Ana – was sitting in the cabin on the left side of the road, the side she would have to go through. Perched on a high stool, he watched projected images flicker on the inner cabin wall.

Ana stopped beside the open window. 'Hello?' she called.

The guard jumped, spilling his coffee. 'Ow!' He shook his scalded hand, then mopped up the spillage with his elbow. He turned to see who'd spoken and flinched again. 'Blimey! It's you.'

'Sorry, I didn't mean to make you jump,' Ana said. The security guard tugged out his earphones and waved a hand in front of his interface. The images ahead of him froze and blurred into slowly shifting patterns.

'Where's your car?' he asked, puzzled.

'No car. I'm on my bike.' She wiggled the handlebars to draw attention to them. 'You're Neil, right?'

'Bike?' He looked at her blankly. Slowly, he took in her jeans, confirmed the lack of a chauffeur-driven car. 'Oh right. I've never seen you on a bike before . . . Yeah, I'm Neil,' he said, turning red. Ana smiled. She handed him her ID stick.

'What's that for?'

'Uh . . . to get through?'

'But who are you with?'

'Nobody, just me.'

Neil seemed totally baffled.

'Listen,' she said, leaning forward, suddenly coming up with an idea. 'You heard the news this morning about Jasper Taurell's abduction, right? And you know I was bound to Jasper yesterday . . . Well, Emily what's-her-name – you know, the TV presenter – is meeting me on the other side. She's been in contact with Jasper's kidnappers, and she's organising a special live broadcast offering them a chance to be interviewed about their cause, in exchange for bringing Jasper back.'

'Cool,' Neil said.

'It's all totally secret. No one can know, or the kidnappers will get cold feet. You have to let me through, OK?'

'Er . . .' Neil rubbed the back of his neck. 'You could get me in big trouble for this.'

'It's not illegal for me to leave the Community by myself, is it?'

'Not illegal, but I'll have to flag it up,' he said.

'Flag it up?' Ana didn't like the sound of that.

'Yeah, and then we'll both be questioned and it might mean forms to fill in.' Neil began to frown.

'Forms?' Ana echoed. She leant into the window, opening her eyes wide and pouting. 'Jasper's life is at stake here, I think that's worth a little form or two, don't you?'

Neil turned away blushing. He fumbled about with Ana's ID stick then, avoiding her gaze, handed it back to her unscanned.

'Go,' he said, gesturing towards the hill. 'But you've only got a couple of hours. You gotta be back before I clock off at six.'

'Thank you, thank you, Neil.' Ana jumped on the narrow bike saddle, squeezed between the booth and the barrier, and pedalled like crazy.

At the roundabout she glanced back. The two security guards still sat in their cabins. Neil wasn't panicking and chasing after her. Ana smiled, but at the same time the adrenalin flowing through her turned sticky with anxiety.

She wheeled her bike out of sight and extracted her bag from the metal carrier basket. She changed her blazer for her mother's leather jacket, then retrieved a bell-shaped hat she'd found in the attic. Once she'd pinned her hair to the top of her head, she pulled the hat over to hide it. Lastly, she put in brown contacts, turning her distinct grey eyes a murky taupe. She'd be stuck with the colour for a few days, until the contacts dissolved, but that was no big deal. There were other teenagers in the Community who used them.

Feeling a little more prepared for the City, she launched off the pavement, keeping to the left of the road as she joined the growing flow of pedal-powered contraptions.

Mobile food huts spilled into the street. As people waited to be served they checked mail and web-surfed against boarded-up shop fronts, stall sides and pubs. Every eye-level surface had been whitewashed to facilitate the interface projections. A stench of rubbish mixed with burgers and fried onions saturated the air. Ana pulled out the sleeve of her blouse from beneath her jacket. She cycled holding the material against her mouth and nose. The crowd of people invaded her space, making her feel claustrophobic. Anxiety washed over her in waves. Her eyes darted left and right, expecting an attack at any moment.

After another hundred metres the village street descended into Highgate Hill. Ana felt safer as she picked up speed and turned right at the domed church, down Dartmouth Park Hill. The wind pressed into her clothes. Her nervousness began to transform into a sense of excitement and exhilaration.

At Tufnell Park, she veered right following the same road for several minutes, until she reached a bridge over the canal into Camden. The slow-moving masses forced her to walk her bike, once again swamped by the crowds. Alert and wary, she wound her way to Camden's main artery. She headed for an old railway bridge over Chalk Farm Road, trying to avoid the most demented people who argued with invisible adversaries and jerked or shouted without warning. Oncoming pedestrians jostled and shoved. Her foot acquired a soggy paper bag from the litter-strewn pavement. As she shook it off, somebody thumped into her. She stumbled. A muscular man with a bell dangling from his lip elbowed past without glancing her way. His interface projected the word 'Chaos' on the world walking towards him.

Rubbing where he'd bashed her and glancing around to pre-empt trouble, Ana ploughed onwards, past the last of the brightly painted buildings which rose above jumbled shop fronts, towards a converted market warehouse. Ahead, in the glow of the low orange sun, a dozen creatures floated above the crowds. She squinted to see better. The nine-foot tall people wore white garments that billowed in the wind. They had small faces and long, silvery-white hair. Their interfaces projected something that made the air around them sparkle and glitter. Ana attempted to veer around the eerie street performers, but one of them caught her eye and stopped advancing. The stilted woman crouched before her. In the palm of her hand she carried a translucent ball. Ana gazed at the bubble. Words projected from it. The glittery air somehow held them and made them clearly legible.

'*Things are not what they seem.*'

The woman's dark eyes gazed deeply into Ana's. Ana shrunk away. The woman smiled then rose. With a few skilful leaps, she caught up with the others.

Ana loosened her grip on the handlebars and wiped her

clammy hands on her jeans. *Everything in Camden has been turned inside out*, she thought. The inner turmoil and instability of the Crazies was splattered across the town.

At the Gilgamesh building she found a parking rack for her bicycle. She programmed in a code to lock the metal release pin between the frame and the back wheel, and stopped to examine the strange hybrid construction. The ground floor of Gilgamesh was a continuation of the market stalls. The next six levels were glossy mirrored windows. A canvas awning hung from the first floor. Beneath the awning, neon shop signs and torn posters littered the walls.

Ana took a deep breath and headed for the stone-clad entrance. She knew exactly where she was going. Cole Winter had a website advertising wind chimes, which he made and sold. It was located somewhere inside the stone passages.

Oriental takeaway huts lined the tunnel walkways. A smell of noodles and spices wafted on the air. Gradually, the food stalls gave way to booths selling bags, jewellery, and rugs. Ana stopped beside a cylindrical display case and ran her hand over its intricate wood carvings. She didn't recognise the strange symbols and shapes, but she noticed the walls too were engraved with the same magnificent detail.

As she traced the shapes, she focused on the touch of her fingertips, the way she did when she played the piano. For a moment she tried to empty her mind and absorb the coded language. It was beautiful, even though she didn't understand it.

A disjointed tune broke her state of mild concentration.

Wind chimes! She tried to slump her shoulders but her whole body went rigid. Tension buzzed through her.

A girl, not more than sixteen, perched on a stool at the back of a narrow alcove. A dozen mobiles of various sizes hung from the alcove's black velvet ceiling. The girl's dark clothes and bobbed, jet-black hair merged with the backdrop, so that for a moment it seemed as if she was emerging from a shadow world, face luminous as the moon. A band of eyeshadow, like a superhero mask, streaked the girl's blue eyes. Her hennaed fingers plaited strands of colour into a bracelet.

As the browser who'd set off one of the wind chimes moved away, Ana entered the nook.

She blew against a mobile, sending it gently swaying. Notes of the D-minor harmonic reverberated at random. As they faded, Ana tried another – a pentatonic scale, evoking a distant time when people were more connected to the earth and the seasons.

'Perfect pitch,' she muttered, amazed at the clarity of the notes. The girl looked up from her foot-bracelet.

'My brother makes them.'

'He's got a good ear,' Ana said.

'He's got two good ears,' the girl quipped with a grin. Ana pulled her mouth into what she hoped resembled a smile. The girl continued plaiting.

'He must be very musical,' Ana said. The girl nodded. Ana looked closer at the pretty, heart-shaped face beneath the makeup. The girl probably wasn't even sixteen. A lot of City children left school early to help their families make a living.

'Does this one have a name?' she asked.

'Earth Song,' the girl said. 'It's an ancient melody.'

'Are there any others in A minor?'

'A what?' the girl asked.

'I might like one in a Dorian scale. Does your brother make them to order?'

'I expect he could.'

'Perhaps I could talk to him?'

The girl stopped plaiting. Ana slouched and tried to make her body language appear open. She was used to being scrutinised, but not when she was in disguise. For almost three years, she'd been consciously perfecting the art of passing as a Pure, constantly suppressing any negative thought patterns or behaviour that could be deemed inconsistent or irrational. And now she was pretending to be no different from the other Crazies. She wondered if they could sense she wasn't really one of them. She tried to put aside the self-conditioning and tune in to her genetic make-up. But it scared her.

The girl stared at Ana for a moment as though looking for something. Abruptly, she smiled, the smile lighting up her blue eyes.

'I'll ask him about the B–Borean scale. If you can, you should come by tomorrow and I'll let you know what he says.'

Ana nodded, not bothering to correct the girl's mistake. She knew she wouldn't return. Neil would hardly let her through the checkpoint a second time.

'Thanks,' she said, barely holding back the disappointment. She turned and trudged towards the tunnelled exit.

'See you tomorrow,' the girl called after her.

In the bustle and noise of the market outside the Gilgamesh building, Ana typed in the code for her bike and pulled off the release pin. Fluorescent and neon lights from the street stalls pulsed in the dwindling daylight. She checked her watch. It was only five p.m., but thick cloud smothered the sky, promising rain.

Lifting her bike from the rack, it became obvious the tyres badly needed inflating. Ana sighed. The uphill marathon home would be a nightmare unless she found someone to lend her a pump. She crouched down, delaying the moment she'd have to ask a Crazy for help.

A whirling siren, the sort you'd expect to hear during a prison break, stormed up the main street. The crowd scattered. An instant later, a black van veered on to the pavement. The back doors swung open and two men climbed out followed by a third in a doctor's coat. Ana clasped the handlebars of her bike. *The Psych Watch!* She straightened her shoulders and raised her chin, willing herself not to be intimidated.

The siren crushed her ability to think. The men strode towards her, the eye emblem of the Psych Watch projecting from their interfaces. She held her breath. For a wild moment, she thought they'd come for her. But they marched right past.

People darted out of their way, clearing a path to reveal a hunched, middle-aged man only fifty metres away, swinging a hammer and lunging towards anyone who dared come close. A second man already lay knocked out on the ground in front of him.

Without any preliminaries the male nurses approached the hunched figure from two sides with electric-shock Stingers. As the man took a swing at one of them, the other nurse leapt forward, prodding him in the rib cage. The man's body jerked wildly, as though he was having a fit. The nurses each took hold of one of his arms. A third man – the psychiatrist – strolled up and thrust a needle into the deranged man's leg. The man struggled until his body grew limp. Then the psychiatrist tore the hammer from his fingers.

Shocked, Ana stepped backwards and bumped into someone behind her.

'Sorry,' she stuttered. Her voice didn't carry over the siren. She glanced around to gesture her apology to the person behind and saw the wind-chime girl – Cole's sister – standing a little further to her left.

The girl didn't notice Ana. She too watched as the nurses carried the deranged man to the van and threw him inside. The doors slammed shut. The siren broke off, leaving a silence as intense as darkness.

Ana felt nauseous. They'd taken the guy having the mental fit, but what about the unconscious man – he needed help too – why had they left him?

'Never to be seen or heard of again,' Cole's sister said.

The van receded into the empty road. As people resumed their activities, Cole's sister bolted in the opposite direction to the Gilgamesh building. With a glance back at the injured man, Ana scrambled after the wind-chime girl. The girl's sharp, determined movements were nothing like the laid-back teenager minding the stall. She resembled a missile. Perhaps Ana hadn't fooled her, after all. Perhaps Cole's sister recognised Ana from all those pictures of her and her father in the news three years ago, and was rushing to warn her brother.

Ana hurried through the crowds, pushing her bike. Cole's sister threaded a path towards the brightly coloured buildings of the main high street, then veered off at a converted warehouse. For a moment, Ana lost sight of her in a confusion of secondhand clothes stalls. But then she reappeared, jogging across a canal footbridge. There were fewer people around the canal, making it harder to pursue discreetly. Ana hung back as much as she dared. From the footbridge she watched as the wind-chime girl leapt on to a black barge, one of several boats tied along the bank.

The girl entered the boat's wooden wheelhouse and descended through a hatch. Ana edged closer. She scanned the hull, searching for movement in the portholes.

She was still in shock from Jasper's abduction, from being in the City and seeing the man carted off by the Psych Watch. She had to be, because at first the red capital letters on the narrow band at the top of the boat's exterior didn't make any sense: $E \ldots N \ldots K \ldots I \ldots D \ldots U$.

It took several seconds for her mind to join the letters together, to form a word, to realise that Enkidu was not the name of a person but a boat.

8

Noodles and Giants

Ana barely noticed the uphill ride home, she was too distracted with thoughts of *Enkidu*. *Enkidu* belonged to Cole's family and Cole was an ex-member of the Enlightenment Project. Finding the boat seemed to confirm that Jasper was mixed up with the sect, and also suggested there might be some kind of organised group helping others escape it. Why Jasper would become involved in the first place, and why Warden Dombrant was looking for 'Enkidu' but didn't know *Enkidu* was a boat, were questions she couldn't answer yet. It was possible the Wardens' 'no interference agreement' with the Enlightenment Project went much further than most people in the Community thought. If the Wardens were actually protecting the Project in exchange for – well, it sounded farfetched, but something like getting rid of Pures the government didn't want around – it would explain why Jasper hadn't turned to them for help, and why Dombrant was now tracking down Enkidu in the hunt for other ex-members.

Ana considered going to see Jasper's parents and explaining to them what she'd discovered. But implicating the Wardens in dark dealings with the Enlightenment Project probably wouldn't go down very well. David would require more than speculation. He'd want hard proof, especially considering the improbable information was coming from her.

No, she needed to pursue this herself. Tomorrow, if Nick was around, she'd persuade him to drive her to Camden, hide the car, and watch over her while she questioned Cole.

Ana cycled up Highgate High Street. Wisps of grey streaked the gloomy sky. In the Community, the street-lights would be coming on around now, but out the in City, government cuts meant that the only unnatural sources of light came from interface projections and roadside fires burning the day's rubbish. Motion advertisements, government slogans, music videos and tweets rippled and shuddered on passing cyclists and traders as they packed away their stalls. *It's like an electronic ghost world*, Ana thought. A distorted, empty reflection of real life, which took over as the day seeped away.

She stopped just before the roundabout and hunched over to catch her breath. Then she switched her mother's leather jacket for her school blazer. She pulled off the bell hat and shook out her long hair. Keeping to the inside of the pavement where it was darkest, she wheeled her bike towards the checkpoint. Neil's cabin glowed blue. He had his back to her; a dark figure bent over the coffee machine. She propped her bike against the wall and sidled to the window facing the hill. She was about to knock when headlights swung on to Hampstead Lane. The saloon car climbed the rise towards them. The security guard straightened.

In a heartbeat, Ana dropped out of sight. Back pressed

against the wall, her legs shook so hard she thought she'd fall. She was in trouble. Big trouble. That was *not* Neil. It was only twenty to six, but the night shift had already arrived.

From the shadows, she watched the Pure car pass through security. Once it had disappeared into the City, she got back on her bike and pedalled with only one thought in her head – to put as much distance as she could between her and the checkpoint. The wind zigzagged through her unbuttoned blazer. Her heart hammered painfully. Her legs and arms trembled with fright and adrenalin. That had been too close. Far too close.

One thing was for sure, she couldn't go back. At least not until 9 a.m. tomorrow morning when Neil's shift started. Otherwise, Neil would be fired for helping her, and her father would snatch away what small freedom she had in the Community. It wouldn't be beyond Ashby to lock her up for the next four weeks until the joining day or, in the likely event that didn't happen, until the day after, when she turned eighteen and the Board came to escort her out of the Community for good. She wasn't about to sit staring at walls while Jasper was being beaten, drugged, reprogrammed. But where could she go?

Halfway down Highgate Hill she approached the right-hand turning at the church with the green dome and giant petal-shaped windows. Earlier that afternoon she'd turned right down Dartmouth Park Hill. She did so again now. As she cycled, she struggled to surmount the fear and think things through. Tonight, if her father followed his usual routine he'd be late home from work and he would do what he'd done countless times. He would climb the stairs, discover her light off, hover for a minute or so outside her door, then go and lock himself in his office for a couple of hours. He wouldn't knock for her until morning.

She dipped a hand inside her tote bag to check for the fist of rolled-up notes. At least she had the wad of cash she'd taken from her father's sock drawer before setting out. Though illegal, cash remained popular among the Crazies. They didn't like the government keeping track of everything they bought, everywhere they went. She'd always thought it a bit paranoid of the general public to think the government would bother with ordinary citizens, but now she felt grateful. She would use it to pay for a room. And if worst came to worst, she could probably track down Nick and stay at his. But she didn't like to do that. Nick wouldn't refuse to help her, but she didn't want to risk getting him into trouble.

Half an hour later, Ana huddled out of the wind under the awning of a takeaway van in Camden, fist curled around a ten-pound-note as she waited for a cup of tea and a carton of noodles. Nearby, a troop of street performers finished constructing a platform in the middle of the road. The crowds had thinned and people seemed to be milling about now, rather than going places. In the twilight, as the performers embarked on their mime act illuminated by giant fire torches, Ana watched, amazed at how good they were. She felt on edge and was anxious about finding a hotel for the night, but the buzz in the atmosphere excited her too. Nothing untoward had happened since the Psych Watch episode. She was beginning to hope the City wasn't as bad as the news always made out.

'Ten,' the dark-haired woman behind the counter said. Ana handed over the note and took the tea and carton. Her stomach growled with hunger.

'You don't know anywhere I can get a room for the night, do you?' she asked, taking a sip of her tea.

'You could try the hostel, Greenland Road. Six to twelve bunks in a room, but clean.'

'OK, thanks.' Ana pulled apart the wooden chopsticks and gulped down several mouthfuls of food. She paused as an after-taste of curdled milk, grease, and unwashed beans filled her palate. Tilting the noodles towards the counter strip light, she picked through them for a better look. A painful spasm gripped her stomach. Deciding she'd rather be hungry than poisoned, she reached over and threw the carton at the bin hanging off the side of the van.

A large hand caught the noodles as they fell.

'Waste not, want not,' a gruff voice said. Ana felt warm breath on her bare neck. It smelt of days-old sweat and boiled cabbage. She lowered her head, avoiding eye contact. The man's large bulk boxed her in. She edged up against the van, trying to put more space between them.

The man slurped and sucked. Revolted, Ana glanced up. Noodles spat from his mouth. Sauce dribbled down his bristly chin. But it wasn't his manners that made her queasy, it was the size of him. Well over six-and-a-half foot, he had broad shoulders, a long neck, and a giant head. His biceps bulged against his short-sleeved T-shirt. Around his waist hung a frayed blanket. His hair looked like it had been cut by a blind person.

'Excuse me,' she mumbled, crushing her shoulders up to her ears so that she might slip through the gap without touching him. He moved back to let her pass. She slackened her facial muscles, careful not to show her fear.

Head down, she began walking away, when the woman running the fast-food van called to her.

'Hey, you're the one said she wanted a room, right?'

Ana turned and nodded.

The woman pointed at the giant. 'You've got something haven't you, Mickey?'

'Sure, I've got something.'

Nerves began to pinch Ana's stomach. She didn't fancy following Mickey down some dark alley. The woman behind the counter laughed.

'Got the looks of a wolf,' she said, 'but he's a puppy dog.'

Mickey pulled a mad grin, which didn't help boost Ana's confidence in him.

'I've got a couple of hotels to try, thanks,' she said.

'You wanna watch out. Things get pretty booked up around here, specially that youth hostel I was telling you about.' The fast-food woman turned to serve another customer.

'Place I know is cheap and comfortable,' Mickey said. 'It's two minutes from here. Nice barge on the canal. I take you and you give me ten pound cash for my trouble.'

Ana's stomach did a little somersault. 'Where is it?' she asked. He pointed south, roughly in the direction she'd walked when she'd followed Cole's sister. A barge on the canal near *Enkidu*. It was the perfect opportunity to find Cole Winter. She nodded, indicating she'd go with him. *He's a puppy dog*, she thought in a feeble attempt to reassure herself. *A puppy dog dressed as a wolf.*

Mickey strode ahead, a dark giant merging with the night. Ana followed, wheeling along her bike. They turned down a street and approached a row of warehouses. Several broken windows flickered with firelight. Ana quickened her pace to catch up.

Beyond, in a dark alcove, she caught sight of a glow-in-the dark cat. She watched it slink around a collection of discarded wine barrels. Genetically engineered pets were popular in Asia, but they were illegal in England. The nose, mouth, ears, and eyes of the Siamese shone phosphorescent green. The white whiskers were like luminous sticks.

I've slipped through a crack into a whole other world, she thought.

Passing under a small bridge between two warehouses, they entered a large courtyard encircled by derelict buildings. Electronic music emanated from a circus tent in the yard's centre. As the tent flaps caught in the wind, Ana saw people inside dancing like they'd been hypnotised. She stared at them as she hurried along, unable to draw her eyes away. She didn't see the woman with the burnt face, until she felt a hand close around her wrist.

Crying out with fright, Ana pulled back. But the woman grasped her tightly. Instead of cheeks the woman had taut red patches. Her eyelashes and eyebrows had been burnt away. Rumples of skin gathered at the edges of her face. Her eyes were the most frightening thing of all. In the shadowy light from the tent's fire torches, the irises looked black.

Ana pushed down her fear. 'Let go.'

'Such smooth skin,' the woman said. 'Hard to find these days.'

Ana tried to pull away again, but the woman was stronger.

'There's someone I'd like you to meet.'

'I can't,' Ana said. 'My friend's waiting for me.'

'I don't see anybody.'

Ana peered up ahead. For a moment she couldn't see Mickey either. But then a voice called out to her from the darkness. 'Hurry up!'

The women relaxed her grip. Ana tugged back her hand and hurried after her giant escort, bike wheels flicking up dirt. Mickey disappeared down an alley. Ana ran after him and came out at the edge of a canal.

Light from a moored barge rippled on the oily water. Mickey jumped up on the boat's curved roof and knocked on one of the portholes. Something wooden clattered and scraped along the deck. A flickering lantern appeared in the wheelhouse.

'Mickey?' a woman said. The giant loped along the centre of the barge and pressed his face up to the wheel-house window.

'Got a customer.' He signalled to Ana. She laid down her bike and traversed the slippery gangplank.

'Come here,' the woman said. Ana stepped inside the wheelhouse. 'You're shivering. You're not sick, are you?' she asked.

Ana shook her head.

'What meds are you on?'

'Nothing,' Ana said.

'Show me your eyes.' The woman demonstrated what she meant, pulling down the skin beneath her eye to show the white. Ana copied. The woman stood on tiptoe and raised her lantern for a better look.

'All right. Hurry up and pay Mickey so we can go down.' Ana dug inside her tote bag and retrieved the roll of notes. She pulled off the top one and passed it out to Mickey. Mickey grinned at her and pocketed the money.

'I've only got a hundred,' she told the woman.

'It's enough.'

'What should I do with her bike?' Mickey asked.

'Put it under the awning at the front with the others. I'll lock it up in a minute.'

Before Ana could thank him, he jumped off the boat. The woman jostled her towards the trapdoor and down a vertical ladder.

Ana stepped into a panelled cabin infused with the smell of burning logs. A closed stone fireplace dimly illuminated the living area. Heat radiated from the aluminium chimney, which stretched up through the ceiling. Ana reached out her hands towards it.

'Come on,' the woman said, inclining her head towards the only door at the other end of the cabin. Ana followed her through the small living space, noting the cartography drawings on the walls, the rickety old-style television, and to her surprise, an upright piano tucked behind a sofa.

The area extended into a kitchen, the two spaces divided

by a couple of bookshelves. Beyond the kitchen lay a narrow corridor with a door off either side and a third straight ahead. Ana followed the woman to the door on their right. The woman passed her the lantern and produced a stick the size of a headless match. She lit the stick with the lantern flame and entered the cabin. A moment later, the berth brightened as a second square lantern on a night table began to glow. A low double bed took up most of the room. Several wooden storage racks lined the walls.

All the tension in Ana drained away. Her body sagged.

'Thank you,' she said, stuffing her roll of cash into the woman's hands. The woman took off the elastic band and began to count the notes. In the soft lantern glimmer, Ana realised the woman was younger than she'd first thought, closer to twenty-five than thirty-five. She had neat, shoulder-length hair and wore dark lipstick. A shadow of hostility lay etched in her oval face.

The woman finished counting and gave Ana back a ten-pound note.

'I'm in the berth across from you,' she said. 'Don't touch anything. And lock your door.' With that she turned and disappeared down the corridor.

Ana closed the cabin door and pulled the metal latch across. She sank back on to the bed. Her thighs ached from all the cycling. Her fingers and toes were numb. She kicked off her shoes, stripped away her jacket and jeans, and crawled under the covers. The cabin was cosy. Her duvet smelt clean. Exhaustion swept through her. She hadn't realised how much the stresses of the day and last night's broken sleep had taken out of her.

She closed her eyes. Raindrops began to gently patter on the roof. She lay listening to them, thankful she wasn't still outside searching for a room. She would sleep now and get up at dawn. There were bound to be more people around to chat to then. Before returning home, she'd find Cole and convince him to talk. She had to.

9

Lila

Light fell on Ana's eyelids, forcing her to surface from a deep sleep. After a minute she roused. The low ceiling rippled with sunshine reflected up from the canal through the porthole. Water lapped against the hull. She felt sleepy and comfortable, until she tried to move. Her whole body resisted. She raised an aching arm and found her hair tangled up in her interface chain. As she twisted around to pick it undone, she caught sight of an alarm clock fixed to the wall.

06.48!

She bolted upright. Her forehead collided with part of the storage rack above the bed.

She yelped and clapped a hand over her mouth, at once aware of other man-made noises. The deck above her creaked with people moving around. Distant voices travelled through the porthole. She scrambled out of bed and checked the lock across her door. It was still securely bolted. Hurriedly, she gathered her clothes and dressed. She pinned up her hair as best she could and pulled the hat down over it.

After she'd made the bed, she stood by the cabin door to listen. She couldn't hear anyone in the corridor or the kitchen beyond, so she put her tote bag over her shoulder and unbolted the door. The living area felt deserted. Last night's fire had burnt out. Cold air blew down through the open hatch.

Ana grabbed the ladder rungs and climbed into the wheelhouse. A smell of coffee and bacon wafted across the water, along with the sound of chattering voices. She peered through the wheelhouse window. To her left, several metres up the bank a group of people mingled around a campfire, stomping feet and rubbing hands. A few of them sat on plastic crates, rugs drawn up to their noses. Nearby, two children messed about tying a piece of rope to a low tree branch.

'Hey!' A deep voice called out. Mickey, the giant who'd brought her there last night, waved. All eyes turned and looked at Ana. She lifted her hand in a small, embarrassed gesture of acknowledgement and pulled her hat further down on her head.

'Subtle,' she mumbled. 'Very subtle.'

Mickey bounded up the concrete path and reached out to help her jump the awkward step down from the gangplank.

'The girl who throws away food,' he grinned. 'What about tea?'

'I usually prefer to drink it,' Ana answered. Mickey barked with laughter. They walked along the footpath, past another barge, towards the campfire.

Soon Ana's father would be rising and getting ready to go to work. At first, he'd wait for her to come downstairs. He'd drink espresso in the kitchen and check his interface messages. In a few minutes, she'd send him one letting him know she'd got up early and gone out for a walk. He'd be annoyed because he'd want to discuss her interview yesterday with the Board. But it would also work in her favour; he'd think she was avoiding him. She would aim to be back at the checkpoint at 9 a.m. when Neil's shift started, just in case her father deemed their talk important enough to wait around for her, or the Board arrived for their follow-up interview. She could spend an hour and a half with these people. She hoped it was enough time to discover which one was Cole and find a way of getting him to talk about the Enlightenment Project.

Mickey scooted a girl along one of the crates so that Ana could sit down. Ana held her hands up to the fire. Strips of bacon sizzled on the large grill. A pregnant woman sprinkled tea leaves into a pan of water. Ana tried to squeeze some life back into her fingers, while discreetly studying the men in the gathering. The eldest of them was busy hooking up a white sail to a tree where the children were playing. The sail cracked in a gust of wind and ripped from his fingers. The children laughed and jumped about, leaping to grab the snapping ropes.

Cole Winter was in his twenties, not his sixties.

That left Mickey and three others. A guy in a bobble hat and yellow ski jacket, who kept an eye on the bacon; a skinny man hunched on a crate; and a man with spiky hair who paced back and forth as he talked to the woman Ana had met the night before.

'Your lips are blue,' the girl beside Ana said. Shivering, Ana dropped her gaze to the smoky fire. She wondered if the girl had noticed her examining the men. The girl's arm opened like a wing. She wrapped her blanket around Ana's back. When she took her hand away, they were left joined beneath the cover, shoulders touching. A strange nervousness crept through Ana. The intimacy of the girl's gesture unsettled her.

'You don't recognise me, do you?' the girl asked. Ana turned and was about to say 'no', when the girl spoke again. 'It's the eye make-up, see?' She covered her face with her fingers, spreading the middle two of each hand to peek out.

Cole's sister.

'You look pretty different without the mask,' Ana said, trying not to let her surprise show. The wind-chime girl laughed with a snort.

'Mask!' she said. 'Where are you from anyway?'

Ana hugged her arms tighter around her chest. 'Around,' she said.

The girl grinned as though Ana had said something funny again. 'Not around here though,' she said. 'You don't have an accent, but you talk weird.'

So much for blending in, Ana thought.

'I'm Lila,' the girl said.

'Oh, right. Hi.' Ana wriggled on the crate. The hard ridges dug into her thighs. Her stiff legs felt like they might freeze, bent at the knees. 'So, did you talk to your brother about the wind chime?' she asked. But before she'd finished getting the last word out, Lila jumped up.

'Tea's ready!' she said. 'You can't do that, Si,' she scolded the pregnant woman. 'Put it down.'

'Oh, stop your fussing, Lila,' the woman said. But she

lowered the pan of boiling water back on to the grill and let Lila take over.

Ana suddenly noticed a slight boy of about four clinging to the pregnant woman's long skirt and poncho, like a bulky fold in the fabric. The boy readjusted himself to his mother's position. Just before he disappeared again, Ana glimpsed his face. He had odd eyes. Haunted. Deeply sad. She felt a sudden, cutting jab to the heart. The boy was sick – Active.

'Here.' Lila passed her a mug of tea.

'Thanks.' Ana cupped both hands around the mug for warmth and wondered how many others in their small gathering were Active. It wasn't always easy to spot. Especially if a person didn't take any meds, because then they didn't have the telltale side effects like spasms and hair loss.

She dipped her nose into the steam of her drink. The tea smelt strange – bitter herbs, mint and sugar. Blowing on the watery liquid, she peeped at the barges moored along the canal inlet. At the far end, a black-painted boat was moored directly beneath a warehouse façade, which rose four storeys sheer from the quay. It was the boat Ana had slept on. *Enkidu*.

She jolted. She'd actually slept on *Enkidu*, the one clue to Jasper's abduction. Was it Cole's boat? And if so, who was the girl who'd shown her to the cabin last night? Ana decided she would wait a few more minutes, then say she'd forgotten something below deck and return aboard to have a quick look around.

Lila sat down and snuggled in beside her, adjusting her rug so it lay across the two of them again.

'That's my brother Nate's wife,' Lila said, gesturing to the pregnant woman she'd called Si. 'She's due in three months.'

'Do you all live together?'

'Not my mum. Just me and my brothers, Nate's wife, their son Rafferty, and Rachel.'

Rafferty had to be the little boy hiding in his mother's skirts; Rachel, the woman who'd shown Ana to her sleeping quarters last night.

'So is that one of your brothers?' Ana nodded in the direction of the moody-looking guy with spiky hair. His discussions with Rachel looked like they were turning into an argument.

'Yeah, that's Nate,' Lila said. 'He and Rachel are always arguing. They practically grew up together.'

Electronic voices crackled on the air. Ana spun towards the sound. Above the footpath, the cut-up canvas sail now hung taut from the tree, like a cinema screen. The grey-bearded man sat in a chair two metres away. His interface projected on to the canvas, which had been strategically angled to avoid the morning sun. Either side of the man stood two cumbersome speakers.

'Here he goes,' Lila said. The gathering began to amble away from the fire, across the bank. 'Come on.' Lila pulled Ana up from their crate. 'Gary gets upset if we don't all join in.'

Ana forced her stiff knees straight.

'It's not very long,' Lila said. 'But he thinks it binds us together. Like praying or something.'

Ana trailed Cole's sister up the concrete steps towards

the patch of grass. Away from the fire, her feet felt icy and the wind bit the bare skin at her throat. She peered at Nate from beneath her bell-shaped hat which now sat so low it cut across her eyes. His body jerked slightly as he walked. He halted beside the pregnant woman, wrapped a hand around her waist and kissed her neck. But his small eyes and mouth remained puckered with tension.

Only the yellow-ski-jacket guy who handed out crunchy bacon in foil wrappings, and the skinny man who'd moved his crate up the hill to the screen, were unaccounted for. Neither bore a family resemblance to Nate or Lila, and they both seemed a bit old. Perhaps Cole wasn't there this morning. She wondered if anyone else among their group had been involved with the Enlightenment Project. She needed to find a way to broach the subject, without alerting them to the fact she'd run a search on Cole.

Stuffing her hands in the side pockets of her leather jacket, Ana stopped beside Lila. The gathering formed a hotchpotch semi-circle. Once they'd settled, Gary turned up the volume on the speakers.

A BBC newscaster reported live from the old US capital, Washington or something. It was a city razed in the twenties by Kuwait or Iraq – Ana couldn't remember – over the Middle East and US Petrol Wars. The Petrol Wars had finished ages ago now, but anarchy still plagued the East Coast of North America. The UK was working with the Central United States on a Pure Separation Programme to help re-establish order in the worst-affected areas.

Lila shook her head and sighed. Ana glanced at her,

noting how the sparkle vanished from her pretty eyes and a hardness set over her face.

Ana's father watched BBC News. It was the only live broadcast to survive the internet after the 2018 Collapse and the Global Depression. Ana had never understood the attraction of watching live when you could select the programme you wanted, when you wanted, and forward fast or pause at your own leisure. Now she wondered if a large part of the appeal lay in the shared experience.

'And now the home news,' the reporter announced. 'There has been a traumatic new turn in the abduction of Jasper Taurell, son of David Taurell, CEO of the giant pharmaceutics company, Novastra.'

Fear buzzed through Ana.

'Oh, what now?' Nate said scathingly. His pregnant wife, Simone, shushed him. Ana coughed nervously. A new turn in his abduction? Had the Wardens found him? Had a ransom been made?

The reporter's eyes narrowed. He frowned into the camera.

'The girl he was bound to, daughter of Nobel Prize-winning scientist Ashby Barber, has disappeared. The Wardens believe Ariana Barber was snatched from her home yesterday evening.'

10

Drowning

At the sound of her own name, darkness crept across Ana's vision. But she could still see the photograph of herself on the screen, larger-than-life. And so could Cole's brother and sister, and all the others in their gathering.

Afraid she would drop her mug, she gripped it tightly, overcompensating. Tea slopped down the sides, burning her skin, which was already raw with the cold. She swayed. The earth pushed against her feet. She pressed into it in an effort to steady herself, as though they were two people back-to-back propping each other up.

'At least they can't blame Cole this time,' Lila said. Ana stared at the mud seeping into her pumps. Her breath wheezed in and out of her chest. Any second now, the blatantly obvious truth would smack Cole's sister in the face.

She raked her surroundings for an escape. She could head for the alley between the warehouses or jump a low barrier further up the canal to a car park full of tents. She prepared to drop the mug and run.

'Ariana is a sweet, fragile girl,' her father's voice continued. 'Though she was thrown into the limelight three years ago, she really has no life experience. She is still a child and has already suffered greatly.'

Ana's jaw tightened. Her body grew still – everything but her eyes, which slowly climbed the screen.

'We are deeply concerned,' her father continued, 'that she will be unable to cope with this stressful situation.'

Her father addressed a dozen different cameras and journalists from a podium. He wore his serious, trustworthy media face. The one he'd used for the Pure Separation Survival campaign before Ana even knew Pures and Crazies existed. The one he'd flogged to death rather less successfully when he'd been accused of altering her Pure test.

'If you have any information, please, please contact the Warden hotline.' He shifted his weight to look directly into the BBC camera. 'Ariana,' he said, 'if you can hear me, hold on. We'll find you.'

A shudder ran up Ana's spine. Furious wouldn't begin to describe her father's mood when he found out what she'd been up to. Thank goodness she hadn't sent him an interface message yet.

'What a phony,' Lila muttered.

Ana heard nothing of the rest of the news. Instead, she stared blankly at the screen, aware of her teeth chattering, her fingers as cold as icicles, her mind an empty igloo.

As the gathering dispersed, Lila took her by the arm and dragged her to the red barge moored alongside *Enkidu*.

'This boat and the one you slept on are twins,' Lila said, as she urged Ana down through the wheelhouse hatch. '*Enkidu* belongs to Cole. *Reliance* is Nate's.'

Ana entered the living area. She could see the resemblance between the boats, though *Reliance* felt smaller because there was far more furniture and clutter. It was also warmer. She made no objection when Lila pushed her on down the corridor and into a tiny bathroom with an offer to use the shower.

Standing in the handheld spray, Ana cocked her head to one side because she was too tall for the sloping roof. The water stung her frozen skin. Heat sizzled through her body, and feeling slowly returned to her. She wished it hadn't. She'd rather feel numb than desolate. Her father had no idea what he'd just done. By making her disappearance national news, the Board would know she'd sneaked out of the Highgate Community when she returned home. They'd think she'd snapped. Whether Jasper was found or not, the Board would never let their joining go ahead now. It was over.

She put her fist in her mouth and bit on it hard. *You can't fall apart*, she told herself. *It's not over. Your life isn't over.* If Lila and hundreds of thousands of other girls could survive in the City, so could she.

But why bother? Why struggle to endure the horrors of life in Crazy-land? Things could only get worse once her illness activated.

Because you don't have a choice. Because Jasper needs you. Yes, Jasper needed her. He had been willing to consider joining with her despite the risks to himself; he'd been abducted for trying to help an ex-Enlightenment Project member escape the brainwashing sect. Her life would not be crushed into worthlessness, because she was going to rescue him. The

99

guilt she'd carried for two years eight months and seventeen days – ever since her father was acquitted of altering her Pure test and she officially accepted Jasper's binding invitation for a second time – vanished. She wouldn't be responsible for ruining Jasper's life. She would be the one giving it back to him.

As the water grew tepid, Ana quickly finished washing, then stepped out and rubbed herself dry with a towel. She caught a glimpse of herself in the mirror above the sink and abruptly stopped. Even wet, her long hair shone white-blonde. Her eyes were too big – like a doll.

If she wanted to get by in the City, she needed to stop looking so sweet and fragile. Swiping up a pair of nail scissors from a mug on the sink, she hacked off a strand of hair. Then another and another. A feeling of freedom and defiance flooded her heart. She would rescue Jasper!

She cut her hair as short as a boy's. Then she drained the remains of her cold tea and rubbed the leaves into the tufts to dull the shine. She could do this. She could find out if Jasper was in the Enlightenment Project. She could save him and by doing so, save part of herself.

Not yet done, she picked through a pile of make-up shoved in a cardboard box beneath the sink and painted a smoky stripe of eyeshadow across her face. Then she attacked the gel, spiking up her hair so it made her forehead look giant compared to the rest of her features. She gazed at the stranger reflected in the mirror. Brown-tinted eyes swam in shadow. Her hair looked like it had been butchered. Her face seemed more pointy. A pleasing result.

In the cool light of her decision, Ana considered her

father. Afraid of the consequences, she'd done everything he'd asked to win the approval of the Pures in her Community. Yet nothing had been enough for them or for him. They still made her feel like she was contagious, as bad as the defect she was carrying. At least in the City there would be no one to constantly analyse everything she said and did. She could be obstinate, impulsive and tempestuous; she could behave any way she liked.

'Hello?' Lila called from the other side of the bathroom door. 'Are you still in there? Are you OK?'

Ana folded the cut hair in a tissue and hid it at the bottom of her tote bag. Then she rinsed the sink.

'I'm coming,' she said.

'Hurry up. If you're any good at maths, there might be a job for you.'

Ana stared at her reflection. With this hair, the contacts and the eyeshadow, you'd have to be really looking for similarities to recognise Ariana Barber.

*

By lunchtime, Ana had fifty pounds cash in her pocket, had got rid of her cut hair and had received two more offers of work. It turned out there weren't many people in Camden capable of reading instructions and doing the necessary maths to fill out a tax return form. The satisfaction of the job, coupled with the money, gave her a new sense of confidence. Her father was wrong. She could handle herself, even out here if she had to, starting from scratch.

She and Lila sat on a bench near a footbridge overlooking the canal. In the distance, *Enkidu* and *Reliance* rocked side by side on the water. It was strange. Looking at the City from where she was now, it didn't seem as dreadful or scary as it did from inside the Community, where all you heard about were Crazies attacking each other, bombing monuments and going on killing sprees.

'So where are you really from?' Lila asked, spearing a strip of chicken from the salad Ana had bought her and chewing enthusiastically.

'Another world. At least it feels like that right now.'

'What about your family? Where are they?'

Ana poked her own chicken with a plastic fork. As she lifted it to her mouth, a smell like dried pee wafted up her nostrils. She scrunched her nose.

'I'd rather not talk about them,' she said. Holding her breath, she bit the chicken in half and checked the piece still on her fork. The off-white meat appeared dry, but at least it was cooked through.

'I'm lucky I've got my brothers,' Lila said, through a mouthful of salad. 'Nate's a bit of a pain sometimes, but Cole's amazing.'

'The wind-chime maker?' Ana asked. Lila nodded, cramming more chicken and parmesan into her mouth.

Ana explored the deeper layers of grit-sprinkled lettuce in her carton.

'You'll meet him soon . . .' Lila said.

'Where is he?'

Lila straightened her shoulders. Sensing the sudden tension in her new friend, Ana focused on keeping her own posture casual.

'We're not supposed to be advertising it,' Lila said, 'but Cole's been arrested.'

Ana remained silent, giving Lila space to continue.

'Well, not exactly arrested,' Lila went on. 'But they've detained him for questioning and he's not allowed to leave. You remember the news this morning about those Pures that have been abducted?'

Ana nodded. Lila paused again. Ana's mouth grew dry. The inside of her lips stuck against her gums. Lila took a deep breath, but then her gaze shifted over Ana's shoulder towards the canal.

She jumped up and squinted into the distance. 'What's that?'

There was shouting and a commotion. A small crowd edged towards a figure on the front of the red barge. As Ana watched, the man tore off his shoes and jacket, then dived into the water.

Lila broke into a run. Ana dropped her salad and sprinted after her. Over the footbridge, down a flight of steps, to the canal. She leapt on to the narrow footpath below, and ran to the crowd gathered at the water's edge.

'Rafferty! Rafferty!' Simone wailed.

'Take her!' Rachel shouted, firmly guiding Lila's pregnant sister-in-law into Lila's arms.

'What's going on? Where's Rafferty?' Lila had to shout to be heard above Simone's lamenting and the panic and curiosity of passers by. For a moment Ana couldn't think who Rafferty was. Then it came to her – the four-year-old boy tucked inside his mother's skirts.

Rachel kicked off her shoes and tore away her coat. A

sound of gushing water split the air. Nate broke through the canal's surface, gasping. His blood-shot eyes looked wild.

'I can't find him!'

Simone began sobbing and clawing through Lila to get to the water. Rachel didn't hesitate. She jumped straight in. A beat later, Nate bobbed back under.

Lila looked at Ana, tears brimming in her eyes. 'He can't swim,' she mouthed.

Ana's mind changed gear so fast it buzzed. Anything she did was going to call unwanted attention to herself. And most likely the Psych Watch would get involved. They'd probably already been called . . . But she couldn't simply stand there. She fixed Lila's gaze.

'Find me goggles or a diving mask,' she ordered. Lila squeezed her arms tighter around Simone and whispered something. Then she let go. Simone fell into a sobbing heap. Lila hurtled up the gangplank on to *Reliance*, then leapt across to *Enkidu*.

Ana crouched down beside Simone.

'Did you see him go in?' she asked gently.

Simone nodded, pointing to the front of *Enkidu*. 'He went straight down.'

Ana stripped off her leather jacket and removed her pumps. The human brain could survive between four to six minutes without oxygen. At least two had already passed. And if the boy had panicked his oxygen supply would be cut off even faster. Ana had one dive – about two minutes – to find and recover him.

Barely aware of the goose bumps on her arms, she strode

up the gangplank, crossed the back of *Reliance* and leapt the gap to *Enkidu*.

Lila appeared in the wheelhouse and tossed her a diving mask. Ana fastened it over her face. She ran up the centre of *Enkidu*'s roof, breathing deep and fast. In and out, in and out. In one fluid movement, she reached the edge of the bow and dived in.

The freezing water hit her hard, driving the breath from her lungs. Shock disorientated her thoughts. She held her plunging body still, suppressing the desire to flail about and grapple for the surface. Blood flowed through her arms and feet so fiercely it hurt. She honed the small part of her brain that wasn't frozen on to the rhythm of her heart – imagined one beat for every two.

The canal bed came into view. Rolling her arms to stay down, she counted, waiting for the roiled water to settle. Sediment fell around her like dirty snow. And then, through the murky green, a child's tennis shoe loomed.

Ana resisted the urge to shoot forward and snatch at it. She swam to the foot with long, slow strokes. The boy's legs were almost in arm's reach. His face was turned towards the canal bed, eyes closed. His arms dangled at strange angles from his torso. Ana wrapped her arm around his waist and kicked her legs, lifting him towards the surface.

His limp body didn't budge.

She scanned the child's figure. A thick rope clung to his left foot. She grabbed it and gave a tug. The rope loosened off, then grew taut again. It had to be caught on something. Ana pulled herself along it until she reached a boulder. The rope seemed to be snagged beneath the rock. She drew her legs into her chest and with all her force kicked out. The boulder shifted. She flipped forward and snatched the free rope. Began to gather it up. The boy dragged through the water towards her.

Then he halted. Ana checked to see if the line had caught again. The end of the rope was looped through something rusty and metal. Searching through the gloom, she made out an iron stage weight the size of two bricks. It had been tied to the boy's foot.

No way. This couldn't be happening.

The air ran out of her lungs. In fifteen seconds she would pass out. Jerking wildly at the boy's foot, she knocked off his shoe. It drifted away.

Come on! Come on!

She yanked the looped rope so hard against his ankle, blood began to colour the water. And then the foot popped out of the coil.

She hugged her arm around the boy's chest and kicked.

Light refracted in the water above. Tiny rainbows of colour shimmered like jewels. Ana's mind wandered. For a moment she forgot what she was doing. The bright yellows, purples and blues mesmerised her. She jerked back to reality with a sense of panic.

Kick and count. Kick and count.

The numbers became muddled as she counted. Her vision became a wash of mushed-up colour. Suddenly, warm air slapped her face. Oxygen hurled into her lungs. Relief poured over her. But then she was sinking again – the boy too. A snatched breath of air had bought her a few more seconds, but she felt the will to fight slip away. She was tired. Too tired. Too cold.

II

A Higher Plan

The first thing Ana became aware of was the pain. It burst through her lungs, her shoulder, her arms. She rolled from her back to her side and threw up. Coughing followed, every spasm piercing her insides. The numb extremities of her body began to burn. Her skull felt as though it had been ripped open and stretched apart. Her jaw juddered fiercely.

A muffled cacophony of voices pounded against her. She became aware of light. Her eyes stung with the brightness of it, and her vision returned in popping circles of colour.

The boy!

She tried to sit up. A wave of dizziness rushed in on her. Her arm collapsed beneath her weight and she dropped on to her back. Above, sunshine bleached out one corner of the sky. Nearby, a female voice counted. The rhythm and familiarity of the numbers relaxed her. Her body trembled, but the pain receded, enough for her to become conscious of the cold and for her thoughts to regain some semblance of motion.

A scorching hand pressed on to her forehead. Ana squinted and saw Lila's face, surreal against the scattered clouds. She tried to speak, to ask about the boy. But she could only cough. Foul-tasting water spluttered from her. As she turned her head, she saw a figure kneeling on the towpath. The figure swayed forward and back as she counted, as though chanting or praying.

'Lila—' Ana croaked. She tried to lift herself up again and failed.

'You shouldn't move.'

Ana drew a fist into her chest where the flames still licked. 'You . . . must . . . get . . . him . . . warm,' she managed. 'Blankets. Fire.' An awful heaviness pulled at her. She struggled to stay alert, but it was too hard. Letting go, Ana collapsed into the emptiness.

*

She was running through a jungle of car wheels, windows, doors, bonnets, searching for Jasper. He was supposed to be there. A car engine hummed. She thought if she could locate the source, she'd find him. But each time she seemed to be growing close, the quiet thudding changed direction. Her lungs began to burn. She gasped in pain and woke up.

Wood smoke stung Ana's nostrils. A smell of mildew lurked beneath it. Ana scrunched her eyes into slits and saw her cream blouse hanging on a wooden chair in front of an iron furnace. Her tote bag, leather jacket and jeans lay beneath them. Cartography drawings decorated the walls and an old-style television sat on a wooden shelf. She was back on *Enkidu*, semi-naked, chugging away from Camden.

Above, feet padded across the roof. Hushed voices murmured. The ladder into the living area creaked with the weight of someone descending. Ana couldn't rally herself to sit up. She couldn't even keep her eyes open. Her body felt as though the canal water had osmosed through her skin and filled her cells with dead weight. She lay on the couch, an itchy blanket tucked around her naked arms and legs. Her hair stank of pond scum.

'What are you doing?' Lila's voice hissed through the hatch. Light steps scuffed the ladder, as she followed down whoever now stood in the cabin.

Ana persuaded her eyes half-open and saw Lila's brother, Nate.

'Sshh!' he said. His hands were in Ana's tote bag. She frowned. Her thoughts were fuzzy, but that definitely seemed wrong.

Then Nate picked up her jeans and shook them. Her ID stick fell out. He swiped it up and put it in his pocket. Shock pinched Ana's sluggish mind.

'What do you want that for?' Lila whispered.

'It's about time we found out who she is.'

Ana dug her nails into her hands. *Wake up.*

'She's not going to tell anyone about Rafferty,' Lila said. 'I'll talk to her.' She stepped in front of the couch, as though protecting Ana from her brother. From the way they were behaving, Ana decided the little boy must be OK. Her eyes welled with emotion. She'd heard of this sort of thing before – children as young as four or five trying to commit suicide because the Pure test only identified a category of illnesses, and the child had never been diagnosed correctly, or their parents objected to giving them the proper medication. It made her heart ache with sadness.

'She turns up out of the blue,' Nate hissed, 'and pays only in cash and never switches on her interface. She's obviously

110

hiding from someone. You can let her know that if she reports Rafferty's accident, I'll use her ID stick.'

Ana remembered the hair she'd hidden in the bottom of her tote bag. Thank goodness she'd got rid of it. Her thoughts turned to the weight wrapped around the boy's ankle. Nate was scared. He obviously believed she might call the Psych Watch.

'No,' Lila said. 'She's not like that. I'll explain.'

'I'm keeping the stick,' Nate said. In the silence that followed, Ana's heart leapt so wildly against her chest, she was sure they'd hear it.

'Fine,' Lila answered eventually. 'But let her think she lost it. I'll keep an eye on her. If she makes any sign of contacting the Watch, I'll let you know and you'll do what you have to.'

Nate didn't respond.

Inwardly, Ana lurched with foreboding. If Nate had her ID stick, her identity wasn't safe. And obviously he didn't trust her. She'd saved his son and instead of gaining his confidence, she'd made him suspicious. He would be watching her every move from now on. How was she going to bring up Cole's arrest and the Enlightenment Project if they were questioning everything she did?

'You should have left her on the quay,' Nate said, clumping up the ladder.

For a long time afterwards, Ana lay quietly, listening to Lila clean up the kitchen. Roaming around the City with her interface switched off so that she couldn't be traced was one thing, but being without an ID stick was totally different. She had no fall-back if she ran out of cash or faced an emergency. Nothing to prove who she was. In the event of an injury or accident, she would be taken to an insanitary, germ-infested hospital for Crazies. She'd have to wait to be operated on by second-rate medics who were overworked and always striking. And what would Nate do if he used the stick and found out that she was the missing girl bound to Jasper Taurell? He wouldn't like the fact she had half of London's Wardens out looking for her, that was for sure. Not to mention the way she'd infiltrated his family to try to obtain information on Jasper's whereabouts.

Ana considered going home. Perhaps she could use her father's and the Wardens' assumption that she'd been kidnapped and pretend she'd escaped her abductors or been freed. When the Wardens hauled her aside and detained her for hours of questioning she could lie, say she'd been sedated, left in a room, sedated again. And then, for no explicable reason the Crazies had brought her back. But what if Neil, the security guard, confessed the truth?

Anyway, even if the Wardens believed her, even if she could fool the Board, her father would see the truth – he'd taught her how to lie – and he would probably lock her up safe and sound until Jasper's return, or the Board came to throw her out of the Community. No, there was no going home. Not without knowledge of where Jasper was. She'd known that this morning.

Ana closed her eyes and found herself remembering last New Year's Eve at the Taurells'. With only four months until her eighteenth birthday, she'd been too old to hang around in the children's quarters and too awkward to socialise with the young, recently joined couples.

She'd ended up outside by the pool, lying on a sun lounger in the dark and the cold with a foam mat wrapped around her shoulders. Jasper had eventually found her. He came out carrying an enormous fake fur coat belonging to his mother and offered it to her without a word. He watched her put it on.

'You're staring,' she said. 'Like I might burst into tears and have a breakdown. I won't. You might as well know I'll never fit in. Even if we did get joined.'

He sat down beside her on the sun lounger, leaving a respectable distance between them.

'Has it ever struck you,' he said, 'that what's going on with the Pures and the rest of the population is like a kind of scientific racism? The Pures think they're better, think they have a divine right to rule, because, according to them, everyone else isn't in their right minds. It's like the use of science to sanction a belief in biological superiority.'

'Science isn't racist. Science is just an understanding of the physical workings of things. It's how we interpret and employ the knowledge that can turn it into something corrupt.'

'Ah, but if there's a goal behind a scientific discovery or development, surely that colours the expected results?'

Ana shook her head. 'Scientific fact is scientific fact, whether discovered by induction or deduction.'

Jasper smiled. 'You might be too clever for me,' he said. Then he stood and held out a hand to help her up. 'We should go inside. If we wish the Board to let the binding go ahead I guess we should start following protocol. Don't want to give them any reason to change their minds, do we?'

Ana took his hand. It was warm and soft. Dipping her

113

chin into the fur collar of her coat, she smiled to herself. Jasper was intelligent and provocative. He might have his faults, but he had great strengths too. They walked side by side without touching. Before they entered the living room through the wall-to-wall glass doors, he stopped. Coloured lights glowed in the flowers and shone up at the house.

'This is for you,' he said, reaching his arm around her and removing an envelope from his mother's coat pocket. The closeness of their bodies sent a hot flush through her. She held her hands to her cheeks to cool them. The party lights tinted the Board's gold seal on the envelope green. Beyond the glass doors, Ana could hear people counting down. Only seconds remained until the hour struck midnight.

She took the envelope from Jasper and her fingers fumbled to open it. The last time she received an envelope with a gold seal was when the Board came to school with her redone Pure test results.

'Five . . .' people shouted. 'Four . . .'

Ana read the card.

A binding between
Jasper David Taurell and Ariana Stephanie Barber
is scheduled for
Friday 21st March 2041
at the Hampstead Community Hall
at 5.30 p.m.

'Three . . two . . . one!' Great cheers erupted from the house. Party crackers popped and from the far side of the pool, a Catherine wheel began to spin, lighting up the water with yellow and pink sparks. The doors to the living room opened. Sound burst forth as people poured into the garden, shouting at each other to mind the pool.

Jasper had finally set a date.

Ana couldn't speak. He leant towards her as though about to whisper something in her ear, but instead his lips brushed gently against her own.

'I should probably stay away from you now,' he murmured. 'Or I'll just keep breaking protocol.'

He slipped off into the crowd, leaving her rooted to the spot in his mother's coat, her frozen fingers clasping the envelope, the Catherine wheel spitting and fizzling against the night sky.

She'd spent so much time worrying about Jasper ditching her, and feeling guilty about what sort of life she'd be taking away from him, she'd never really seen how happy they might have been together.

Ana blinked back the sting in her eyes, then strained to lift herself up on one elbow. She cocked her head towards the kitchen and saw Lila, sitting at the narrow table with paper, scissors and glue.

'Hey,' Lila said, looking over. 'How are you feeling?'

'Could I . . .' Ana clutched her palm around her throat, which felt as if it had been scraped raw, and motioned for a drink.

Lila fetched a glass of water and came to sit beside her on the sofa. Ana sipped slowly.

'Aspirin?' she asked. Lila nodded, got up and went to rummage through a kitchen cupboard. She produced a packet of cereal, shook out the contents and popped a pill from a silver packet at the bottom of the box.

'We have to keep them hidden, because . . .' Her voice broke off.

Because of Rafferty, Ana thought. Because they were living with a suicidal four-year-old.

Lila sat down beside Ana again and fiddled with her fingers. Ana forced herself to swallow the aspirin and gulp some water.

'You saved him,' Lila said. 'Thank you.'

'Where is he?' Ana asked. Her voice cracked.

'On Nate's boat.'

'He should be in hospital.' Ana sipped more water to ease her throat. 'There could be complications.'

Lila shrugged uncomfortably. She flicked back her dark hair and looked away. 'He's fine.'

Even if the boy was bleeding to death, Ana sensed these people wouldn't take him to a hospital.

'A doctor then,' she suggested.

'You should have a shower.' A warning lurked in Lila's tone. 'You don't want to get sick from the water.'

Ana nodded, but she hadn't saved the child so that he could die from hypothermia later. 'Cold water exposure can cause organ failure,' she said. 'You have to get him checked.'

Lila turned and stared at her for a long moment. 'I'll try,' she said.

*

Warm water dribbled across Ana's back. Crouched on her haunches, she tilted her face towards the shower head, gratefully washing out the rotten-cloth smell from her hair and scrubbing away the possible toxic waste clinging to her body. She could hardly believe that only yesterday morning, she'd showered in her own pristine power-shower, unaware of the luxury as spray pummelled her from all angles. This morning she'd been too preoccupied to think about the creams, soaps, hair products and the hairdryer she didn't have here. Now their absence felt like another layer peeled away, along with the hair she'd always worn long, her piano, her interface, and her ID stick. She couldn't even risk checking her interface to see if after her dive into the canal it still worked. The Wardens would have tagged her by now, which meant the moment she powered up her interface or Nate checked her ID, the activity would be reported and her whereabouts traced.

Ana shut off the shower, slicked back her hair with her fingers, and dabbed herself dry. Lila had leant her a loose sweater and bottoms. She put them on. The shapeless, cotton trousers rippled as she moved, lightly touching her stiff thigh muscles. Adolescent Pure girls rarely wore trousers, and these made her even more self-conscious than her tight jeans.

Arm pressed against the ache in her chest, she exited the bathroom and crept barefoot down the narrow hallway. In the kitchen, a female and a male voice were disputing something. Ana reached the half-open door and saw Nate and Rachel. She wondered if Nate had tried using her ID stick yet. Hearing her, both of them stopped talking and turned. Rachel carried on slicing potatoes. Nate shoved his hands in his pockets.

117

'You look . . . uncomfortable,' he said. 'Something you're not telling us?'

A pang of anxiety contracted Ana's chest. She winced, and suddenly the pain made her furious at his ingratitude.

'And you don't look uncomfortable enough,' she replied. 'Or wasn't that your four-year-old son I just fished out of the canal with a stage weight wrapped around his leg?' She glared at him, heartbeat drumming in her ears. *Forget trying to get on his good side*, she thought. Nate clearly only responded to aggression. You probably had to fight him to gain his respect.

Nate flushed. Rachel put a hand on his shoulder.

'Now hang on,' she said. 'You don't know what you're talking about.'

'I know what I saw.'

'It's hardly his fault,' Rachel said.

'Well there's a lot of people that would disagree with that. When was the last time you took the boy to a Mental Watch Centre?'

Nate's nostrils flared. Even Rachel started to look charged up. Ana was pushing it too far. She didn't even believe in the check-ups, but she couldn't rein in her anger. 'Is he receiving his free monthly psychiatric evaluations? Have you registered him with a local psychiatrist?'

Rachel's hand slipped from Nate's shoulder. A taut silence strung across the cabin.

'You have your reasons for keeping out of the way of the Watch,' Ana continued, careful to use their word for it, 'and I have mine.'

Wood creaked. Lila descended the wheelhouse ladder, stepping into the living area, breathless and buoyant.

'He's OK,' she panted. 'The doc's given him a very thorough examination and he says Rafferty's fine.'

Ana glanced at Nate. So his sister had managed to persuade him to call a doctor. That was something. Nate caught her eye, his expression unforgiving.

Lila passed through the waist-high walls that delineated the kitchen and seeming to sense the tension, pushed between her brother and Rachel to grab Ana's arm. She drew Ana into the living area.

'Glad to see you're not blue any more!' she laughed. Ana's lips twitched up at the sides, but with her adrenalin starting to drain away, she felt weak. Feeble. 'You can sit and relax if you want,' Lila went on. 'Watch a film. We've got discs for the screen. We're going to pamper you. It's the least we can do. And tonight you'll stay in the cabin again, no charge.' She smiled, but Ana noticed her eyes shift towards her brother.

'Yeah,' Nate said. 'It's the least we can do.'

'Thanks.' Ana wondered if this was part of their plan to keep an eye on her, or if Nate had checked her ID stick and had something else lined up.

Don't lose your nerve, she told herself. He believed she was on the run, so he'd know there was a high probability that she was tagged. If he had any sense, he'd avoid checking the stick.

Lila switched on the screen, but Ana went over and hovered by the piano.

'Impressive, isn't it?' Lila asked.

'May I sit?'

Lila nodded.

Ana perched on the piano stool. 'Whose is it?'

'Cole, my oldest brother, the one I was telling you about.'

'The one that was arrested?' Ana asked, itching to play something.

'It's not exactly an arrest. It's called detention,' Lila explained. 'When somebody's suspected of a terrorist or politically subversive act, they can be held up to forty-two days for questioning.'

'The 2017 Terrorism Act – pre-charge detention,' Ana nodded. There'd been a paper about it on the Oxford first-year law syllabus.

'Right,' Lila said, trying to suss out why Ana might know this. 'It's the third time they've picked him up. A Pure is abducted and so they take him in for questioning. They don't have anything on him. It's discrimination. Just an excuse to try and grind him down.'

Ana became aware of Nate and Rachel in the kitchen. They'd stopped talking in low voices and though they were pretending not to, they were obviously trying to listen in. Did they suspect Lila was saying things she wasn't supposed to? Ana raised her chin. This was it. She had to push, to find out what she could before Nate silenced his little sister.

'Why would they target your brother like that?'

'Lots of reasons,' Lila said, waving away the question with her hand. 'I suppose mainly because he was at the concert.'

Shock and excitement fizzed through Ana.

'He was there when the Pure was abducted?' she asked, fighting to keep her voice steady.

'Uh-huh,' Lila said. 'The justice courts have given him the same lawyer as the last time to turn over the forty-two-day detention rule, but the guy's totally useless.' Lila bit her lip. 'I don't think Cole can do another forty days,' she said, almost to herself. 'It isn't the solitary confinement that's so bad. It's what they do to them. He never said anything, but I'm sure they tortured him last time.'

Ana straightened her shoulders. Torture was obviously illegal. It went against the 2020 Torture and Inhumane Treatment Act. Would the Psych Watch break the law to get a suspect to talk?

'Why do they think Cole's involved?' she asked.

'The Pure guy was snatched from a car park under the concert hall,' Lila said. 'There's video surveillance of Cole getting in a lift that goes down there at the time of the abduction. And Richard Cox, the leader of the Enlightenment Project, practically raised my brother. When they found Richard guilty of the Tower Bridge explosion five years ago, they tried to get Cole too. They've been after him ever since.'

Images of the collapsed, smoking monument filled Ana's mind. The Tower Bridge explosion had been on every news site for a week. Eighteen people died in the bombing, another sixty were injured.

'So they think your brother's still involved with the Enlightenment Project?'

Lila frowned and pinched her lips together. 'What have you heard about the Project?'

121

Ana shrugged. 'The usual, I guess. A group of people living on the heath like they're out of the Middle Ages. Anyone that goes inside the wall doesn't come out. The followers are starved and tortured until they break down. Then they're brainwashed into accepting the Project's teachings and carrying out abductions and massacres as part of a divine prophecy to banish evil from the world. That sort of thing.'

Lila's gaze dug into Ana. 'How original.'

Ana coughed and began twisting the longer strands of hair from the top of her head down into her eyes. If Cole was still involved with the Enlightenment Project, he could be really dangerous. They all could.

'So, um, what do the Wardens think your brother and anyone else involved have done with the Pure guy?' she asked. 'Theoretically . . .'

'Theoretically, they haven't got that far. There've been no demands. No one even knows if Jasper Taurell is a political hostage. Maybe he wanted to disappear.'

Lila fiddled with the pretty key on her necklace, then glanced furtively back at Nate and Rachel, who had now resumed their own heated discussion.

'Cole's pre-charge hearing is tomorrow,' she murmured. 'The court will decide whether he can be locked up for another thirty-nine days while they investigate the missing Pure guy's case. Nate thinks we should ask for another lawyer, but then the actual hearing could get pushed back weeks and by that time Cole will have almost done the forty-two days and they'll have to let him go anyway.'

'What about hiring a lawyer?'

'Yeah,' Lila said. 'You couldn't lend us a thousand credits could you?'

Ana looked away. If she got back her ID stick she could get them five thousand credits. Her ID was linked to her father's current account. But if she touched that money, he would know. And he would find her.

There had to be a way of getting Cole out without giving herself up. He was still her best bet for obtaining information. Either he was involved with the abduction, or – and this seemed far more likely given everything else she'd learnt so far – he'd known Jasper was in trouble and had been trying to help him. One way or another, Cole would have answers.

Ana closed her eyes. She had to surmount her fear. She would think through the problem. There had to be a way.

'Two years ago,' she said, 'a man called Peter Vincent was taken in for the third time under the Terrorism Act. The first two times they kept him the full term but never charged him. The third time, the court over-ruled the Wardens' request to hold him for up to forty-two days on the grounds of unfair discrimination.'

Lila sat up on her knees. 'That's what I was saying. It's discrimination. So you think there's a chance of getting Cole off because it's already happened twice before?'

'The law works on precedents. If they've conceded the possibility before, and Cole's case is similar, the judge is more likely to go the same way again, otherwise it's inconsistent.'

'My God, this is brilliant!' Lila leapt off the couch, clasping her hands in front of her. 'I knew you being here – I knew it wasn't just coincidence.' She reached out and pulled Ana up, squeezing her hands so tightly they hurt. Then she pulled Ana into a hug and whispered in her ear, 'There's a bigger plan.'

A bigger plan . . . The words sizzled inside Ana like frost touching fire. Religious people talked about 'bigger plans'. Belief in a higher power was a form of psychosis. Everybody knew religion had destroyed every culture that ever existed. That's why the Board fought so hard to ban public acts of worship. That's why there were twin billboards everywhere warning people:

> DOES GOD SPEAK TO YOU IN MYSTERIOUS WAYS?
> DON'T BE A VICTIM OF YOUR ILLNESS.

Ana suddenly remembered something else she'd heard about the Enlightenment Project. They were conspiracy theorists. They taught that mental illnesses didn't really exist. They claimed that none of their followers ever became sick.

She scrutinised Lila for signs of Personality Faith Disorder. The key on the chain around the girl's neck could be a religious symbol. Lila's pupils seemed larger and darker than before.

'Will you do it?' Lila said, clasping Ana's hands in her own.

'Do what?'

'Well, you clearly know a bit about law. You can help with building the case to get Cole off. You could drive the argument in court.'

Ana shook her head.

'Listen,' Lila continued, 'it's obvious you're on the run, hiding from someone. So you could do with some new ID, right? My brother can get you the best there is. It would pass under a normal police check. And when Cole gets out he could get someone to hack into the Wardens' network files, so that even they wouldn't know the difference. You could officially become someone else. No more running.'

'I'm not barred. I don't even look old enough to have a degree. I can't go into a court hearing with fake ID and pose as a lawyer. That's ridiculous.'

'You could be a lawyer's assistant,' Lila said. 'If I styled your hair and did your make-up you could pass for at least twenty. You could help Cole's crap lawyer make a proper case.'

Ana thought about the security checks there would be to enter the courts. It might be easy enough to get through, but even with contacts and short hair, it didn't rule out the possibility of someone recognising her.

And what if she failed to free Cole? Would his family lay the blame on her?

Lila followed Ana's gaze to her brother and Rachel in the kitchen. 'I'll take care of those two,' she said. 'Will you do it? Will you help?'

Ana bit the insides of her cheeks. The wild city seemed to be bleeding her of all her good sense. She felt like she was on a ride she couldn't get off. No going back. Whatever happened, wherever it took her, she was on it until the very end. She huddled her arms around her bent legs.

'OK,' she said. 'I'll do it.'

Lila squealed.

Ana smiled, but deep down she wondered who she needed protecting from the most – the Wardens, Cole's family, her father or herself.

12

The Defence

A thump sounded on the cabin door. Ana startled from troubled dreams. She'd been in a car park again, frantically trying to find Jasper as the concrete cavern filled with water. Disorientated, she rolled on to her back and tried to open her eyes. Pain jabbed her eyelids. Her head throbbed from lack of sleep.

'Time to go,' a rough voice shouted.

Nate! Ana's body jerked wide-awake. Pre-dawn light washed the berth in grey shadow. Hurriedly, she scrambled for her clothes, pulling on jeans and Lila's sweater. Her heart raced as she unlocked the cabin door.

Dressed in a T-shirt and jeans, despite the early morning chill, Nate had evidently been up long enough to shower and shave. He was alone.

'What?' she said.

'Get dressed,' he ordered. 'I'll wait for you up top.' He looked Ana in the eye a moment too long. She nodded once. As she closed the door and leant back against it, needles of anxiety rolled up her arms and legs.

In the bathroom, she splashed cold water on her face and pushed back her hair. Then she grabbed her leather jacket and clambered up the ladder to the deck.

She emerged to the smell of freshly ground coffee and decaying rubbish. In the distance, a couple of pink tower blocks glimmered in the dim half-light. Nate and Rachel leant against the exterior wooden panelling of the wheel-house. Rachel passed Ana a paper cup and without a word started across the gangplank. Ana relaxed a bit. *This obviously wasn't about her ID stick then.*

She followed them across the plank, coffee burning her through the flimsy cup. Safely on the narrow bank, she pulled her sleeve down to buffer the heat and took a sip. Instantly, she felt better. The coffee tasted as good as it smelt.

They walked alongside a high black fence. The map projected by Nate's interface shimmered in the early morning fuzz. For as far as the eye could see, barges of various sizes and colours lined the canal, two, sometimes three across. Occasionally, a stench of bad drains wafted from the litter-strewn waters. Birdsong filled the morning quiet.

Ana wondered where they were going. She walked fast to keep up. Though lacking sleep and still recovering from diving into the canal, her body was used to early-morning physical exertion, and she soon fell in with Nate's stride, leaving Rachel to pull up the rear. They followed the canal wall along for two hundred metres then climbed steps, passing through an opening in a fence, on to a street.

At first glance, the row of whitewashed Regency houses and parked cars reminded Ana of British movies set in London at the turn of the millennium. Romantic comedies with bumbling lead characters that fell in love but were kept apart by insecurities and misunderstandings. But as they strode past several vehicles, she realised the cars weren't empty. People slept on backseats and in gutted boots. A canvas tent hung from a large estate car. Further along, two vehicles had been rolled back to back, doors torn away to make a single shelter. The tranquil, leafy suburbia was an illusion. As Ana examined the street, she noticed a labyrinth of tents and shelters behind the white walls and iron railings of boarded-up houses.

She'd driven through this sort of neighbourhood before. She knew about the Global Depression and how in the late tens and early twenties the banks reclaimed over fifty per cent of people's homes. Tent cities had sprung up. Pockets of England were abandoned, while others became over populated with the jobless searching for work. In the end, when the Depression was officially over and the slump in the economy became the norm, the National Bank, a conglomeration of several English investment and high-street banks was the only one left standing. They had total control over the remaining oil reserves in the North Sea, ownership of over ninety per cent of the country's agricultural land – land that was heavily policed – and legal possession of millions of homes.

'You could comfortably house four to five families in each of these.' Nate scowled.

'There are plenty of other streets where people squat,' Ana said. 'Why not here?'

'You'd have to knock down a wall to get into one of these places,' Rachel answered. 'The windows and doors are boarded from the inside with steel sheets. And then, even if you did get in, after a night or two you'd be going to hospital. National's not messing around with their property. They've got a deadly deterrent. No one knows what they're using, but you see a house with steel boards, you're better off on the outside . . . Where you from, anyway?'

Ignoring Rachel's question, Ana stared up at the windows. The rising sun began to catch and reflect off the metal. If you narrowed your eyes, the sheets looked like ordinary windows on a bright day.

They continued to weave through back streets, until they came to a Victorian house with sash windows and a wooden front door. A sturdy fence surrounded the front garden. Nate wound his hand through a gap in the gate and unhooked the lock. They trod the wide path up to the door. On either side of the path long grass swished in the breeze.

'Who lives here?' Ana asked.

'Cole's lawyer,' Nate said. He lifted up the letter box and peered into darkness. After a moment, he quietly let it drop shut. 'Wait here. I'll just let him know we've arrived.' Nate jogged down the steps, vaulted over a picket gate at the side of the house and disappeared through a passage.

Ana didn't know much about how things worked out in the City, but she was pretty sure entering unannounced through a back door at such an early hour meant they weren't invited. She glanced up and down the street.

Rachel leaned back against the porch wall, watching Ana sceptically, making her feel self-conscious. Rachel was far older than Ana, probably in her mid-twenties, and she had an edge to her. As though if you got too close you risked getting mangled.

At last, there came a dull thud from the other side of the

door, followed by a click. Nate poked his head around the corner. He scanned up and down the street, then ushered Ana inside.

'Have fun,' Rachel said.

The hallway stank of bleach. Two doors lay ahead of them. The one on the left stood open; the one on the right had been boarded over. Nate waved Ana through the open door and followed her in, closing it behind them.

Floorboards creaked underfoot as they passed an empty living room. Up ahead lay the kitchen. Nate guided Ana through a door on their left, into a dark space that smelt of bad breath and body odour. Heavy curtains blocked the window light. Something unseen whimpered in the folds of darkness. Ana held back, pinching her nose, waiting for her eyes to adjust. Nate switched on a small bedside light. Just an arm's length away, a naked man sat tied to a kitchen chair.

Ana cried out in alarm and tumbled backwards.

A sock gagged the man's mouth. A large, pink moon of skin shone in the centre of his patchy black hair. Bushy eyebrows stuck out from the edge of his face like a misplaced moustache.

'Mr Jackson,' Nate said, 'I present you with your new assistant.' Ana's heart felt like it had jumped right out of her. Nate was definitely deranged. He must have some sort of Aggressive Personality Disorder because he'd tied up his brother's lawyer and was threatening him, instead of conducting a normal conversation.

Nate bent over the man so that their heads were almost touching. 'This afternoon,' he said, 'when you walk into court to have my brother's pre-charge detention overruled, she'll be with you. You will carefully follow her instructions as to how to proceed. Clear so far?'

The man's low whining turned into a frantic effort to speak. Ana recoiled in disgust – at Nate, at the lawyer, at this ridiculous plan.

'I haven't got a frigging clue what you're saying,' Nate told the man. 'To be quite honest, I don't care. There's only one rule. You do exactly what she tells you to.'

Ana swallowed down her horror as best she could. 'Surely we could have this conversation without the violence?' she said. Nate folded his arms across his chest, face screwed up tight. She shook her head. What had she got herself mixed up in? 'So how will he know what I want him to say?'

'He'll wear an earpiece and we'll give you an interface set to vocal. Whatever you type he'll hear through his piece.'

'That won't work,' she said. 'Someone will notice.'

'We'll extend his sideburns so they cover the ears,' Nate said. ''Course, it would help if you could touch-type so you weren't constantly looking down at your lap.'

Ana stared at him. *He's demented.* But how could she back out now? She tentatively stepped forward and squatted in front of the lawyer. She ripped off the tape plugging his mouth and removed the dirty sock, almost gagging at the smell.

'Don't do that!' Nate said. She shot him a scathing look. The lawyer's frightened eyes flitted back and forth between them. He exhaled a puff of stale air. Ana backed up, breathing through her mouth. Nate clenched his jaw but remained silent.

'What do you think of this plan, Mr Jackson?' she asked.

The man's head whipped up to Nate and back down again. 'I'm a tax lawyer,' he stammered. 'Not a people person. You should ask for reassignment.'

'Take too long,' Nate said.

'I only get put on the cases they want me to lose.'

'Why?' Ana asked.

The man broke eye contact. He stared down at his pasty thin legs. 'Because I never win.'

'Will they allow you to bring an assistant?'

'If you've got an LLB degree.'

Ana looked over at Nate. 'Will I have an LLB degree?' she asked. Nate nodded. 'OK.' She held her breath and began to untie the lawyer. 'Mr Jackson,' she said, 'I'd like you to transfer all the information you've got concerning the charges against Mr Winter on to his brother's interface so that I may study it later.' The man rubbed his wrists. Red cord lines lay grooved in his skin. He hesitated before getting up.

'May I?' he asked, pointing to a dressing gown draped across the floor at the foot of his bed.

'Of course.' Ana turned aside. She had no desire to see more of the crêpe-like skin stretched over angular bones, the mottled chest and arms, the wrinkles of flab at the waist, the droopy bump underneath his stained Y-fronts.

'How can we be sure he's going to go along with this?' she said quietly to Nate. 'He could easily talk to someone between now and this afternoon.'

Nate laughed nastily. 'Oh, you don't have to worry about that. He knows who he's dealing with.'

'Threats don't work well with everyone,' Ana said. She turned to the defence lawyer. Slumped in an armchair by an oak wardrobe, he seemed slightly less pathetic in his navy dressing gown.

'How are you regarded among your work colleagues?' she asked him.

'My work colleagues?'

'Yes. And your boss who puts you on these losing cases?'

Jackson looked at her bleakly, as though expecting her to twist the knife. 'How would it feel,' she continued, 'to show them that you can win?'

He shrugged. Obviously, winning lay beyond the realms of possibility.

'Think about it,' Ana said feigning confidence. 'This afternoon, all you have to do is follow the script. Nobody will know and you'll win the case.'

'You're just a child,' he said.

'I can win it.'

Jackson shook his head forlornly. No wonder Nate despised him. He was hopeless.

'There's a lot to do before this afternoon,' she said turning to Nate. 'I'll see you outside.' She nodded at the lawyer, desperate to leave before he totally demoralised her. 'See you in court.'

Outside, the rising sun bathed the terrace houses in lemon light. Rachel was nowhere to be seen.

Ana steadied herself against a white wall and gulped

down the fresh air. The hearing was at 3 p.m., less than nine hours away. They couldn't possibly be ready in time.

Nate slammed the front door. He looked ghostly pale in the light of day. His short, spiked hair needed a wash. Dark circles ringed his eyes.

'What was all that about?' he said.

Ana shrugged. Looked like she wasn't the only one who wasn't sleeping well.

'You better be sure about this,' he said.

She gazed at him keeping her expression flat. She had enough to worry about without Nate doubting her ability.

'So where did you study?' he asked.

She didn't answer.

'Aren't many Crazies our age who've studied law.'

'Guess not,' she said. He frowned at her and then, to her surprise, let it drop and turned away.

*

They descended into Warwick Avenue station and picked their way over sleeping bundles strewn around the ticket hall. They scanned cards across a ticket barrier, waited in a crowded tunnel that smelt of ozone and were carried by a rattling Tube under the heart of London.

They resurfaced at the Cross. The exit came up near a six-lane road, divided down the middle by antiquated railings. A brownstone building with giant arched windows stood opposite them, bearing the station's old name: King's Cross. Behind them, the gothic steeple of St Pancras Station clock tower pierced the sky.

Ana recognised the Victorian railway terminus. Any time

a committee of government officials crossed into Europe for international negotiations, they were filmed arriving at the Eurostar terminal. It was the only open passenger access to Europe and heavily restricted.

The hands on the clock-tower faces ticked towards seven. A smell of scrambled eggs and sausages from a nearby van caught the breeze. Further up the road, a uniformed man unlocked the glass door beneath the golden 'M' of a fast-food restaurant. A flock of people huddled in blankets and perched by railings rose and hurried towards the establishment. A small fight broke out. A man in a puffa jacket and shorts head-butted a second guy. Fear knotted Ana's chest. She shrunk inwardly, glad she and Nate were headed in the opposite direction. As they turned down Cresterfield Street she glanced over her shoulder. A dozen men now brawled, throwing punches, stumbling and striking innocent bystanders.

To distract herself, Ana focused on their new surroundings. Unlike Highgate High Street – the road outside her Community – the red- and brown-brick Victorian houses and factories here hadn't been whitewashed. Few people projected or even seemed to be wearing interfaces. In the poorer London areas, advertisers obviously didn't bother buying up the wall space.

She followed Nate down into the basement of a building that would have housed factory workers a century ago. Harsh fluorescents lit the low-ceilinged room. A work surface skirted three of the four walls. On it, evenly spaced out, were a dozen archaic computers. Ana wrinkled her nose at the stink of wet paint.

'Alex?' Nate called out. A man holding a roller emerged from a door at the far end of the underground room. He approached grinning. His woolly hat sat askew on his head and blue paint flecked his T-shirt.

'So this is her?' he asked. Nate nodded. 'You didn't mention she was young and pretty.' Ana blushed and went to smooth her hair down the sides of her cheeks before realising it was no longer there. 'Let me just finish up and I'll be with you,' he said, retreating. 'Take a seat. Make yourselves at home.'

Ana pretended to inspect the equipment. Being alone with Nate made her uncomfortable.

'You can use your interface,' he said. 'Plug it into the black pad linked to the PC and it'll be untraceable. No one would even know you're online.'

Ana shrugged, but her hand reached covetously to her silver pendant with the sapphire centre. She hadn't powered up for two days, and she was beginning to feel like she'd literally lost one of her senses, gone deaf or something.

Nate plugged his interface into one of the pads. The wall map he was projecting vanished and reappeared on the computer screen he'd linked up to. Like at home with the flatscreen. Ana copied him with her own interface. Relieved to discover it still worked, she quickly turned it off again.

Nate straddled a stool in front of the computer. His hand rested on an object shaped like a stone. When he moved the oval object, the arrow on the screen moved. He opened up the downloaded file from Jackson.

Ana forgot about the giant computers and examined the

list of documents from Cole's lawyer. There appeared to be four arrest reports, three under the 2017 Terrorism Act for Pre-charge Detention and one, the first of them, for assaulting an officer at a protest rally. There was also a psychiatric assessment dated from the time of Cole's first arrest, and a police report describing what had been registered by the concert hall's surveillance cameras the night Jasper was abducted.

Ana opened the police report first. Nate fiddled with his retro mobile. Occasionally, he glanced over her shoulder at the computer screen while she read.

Jasper had been filmed taking the stairs down to the Barbican's blue car park, an underground lot of three levels that no longer had any functioning cameras. At the same time a Volvo with one man driving and no passengers had entered the car park. Four minutes later, the Volvo departed with two unidentified passengers. A search of sixty-two surveillance cameras in and around the arts centre revealed no other trace of Jasper leaving the premises. Thus it had been assumed that Jasper left the building in the Volvo.

Alex, the guy running the internet café, reappeared, wiping his hands on a bit of cloth. The intoxicating smell of white spirits clung to him. Ana pressed her fingers into her temples to ward off a headache. At least Alex was relaxed and friendly, unlike Nate.

'So,' he said. 'Let's see.' He perched in front of a computer beside her and plugged his interface into another black pad. Code raced over the screen. Ana watched as he manipulated the information in ways she'd never seen before, using hand gestures to dive through the code and pick out text like he was collecting up loose stitches in a strange weave of fabric.

'Here we go,' he said. 'Race: Caucasian. Eye colour —' He stopped and peered at Ana. 'Are those contacts?'

'No,' she said.

'Oh, well I guess your eyes are a grey-brown. Kind of hard to say.'

'Just put brown.' She shrugged, trying to smooth over her hostility.

'Brown it is then,' Alex said. 'Now, hair. Mmm . . . I see you've got a rather talented hairdresser . . .'

'I'll get Lila to cut and dye it properly this afternoon. Just put down brown.'

'I'm sensing a pattern here,' Alex said playfully. Ana ignored him, hoping Nate wasn't paying attention.

Alex went through all of her defining features – small nose, pointy chin, oval face, five foot seven and skinny. He set an age range between eighteen and twenty-two.

'Sorry, no way anyone would believe you're older,' he said. 'Just have to pretend you're a genius. Besides if the picture is a good fit a court security guard won't be bothering to work out how old you are. Now, all we have to do is send the system on a search for girls in the database matching your description. Then we'll check the photos and see who you could most easily pass for. As long as you don't buy anything on the ID, the person you're doubling will never know. Unless you're unlucky enough to get ID'd in two places at exactly the same time, this will stand up to almost anything.'

'What about the law degree?'

'I'll hack in and tag it on. Obviously a university check would come up negative, but court security won't be doing that.'

Ana nodded. Letting him get on with it, she opened up Cole's most recent arrest report.

Cole's current pre-charge detention depended on circumstantial evidence and inductive reasoning. The first assumption that Jasper had left the Barbican involuntarily in the Volvo, led to a second; the driver of the Volvo must have had an informant keeping him abreast of Jasper's movements. Cole, who'd been captured riding the lift down to the blue car park shortly after Jasper, fitted the profile. Additionally, during the wide video surveillance search to see if Jasper had left the Barbican by some other means, the Wardens had scanned for Cole. He wasn't seen again, which pointed to the strong possibility that he was the Volvo's second passenger.

Ana checked the other arrest reports. Cole's first detention under the 2017 Terrorism Act occurred simply because he'd been caught on video surveillance camera taking snapshots around the Tower Bridge area several months before the bombing. Two years later, a fast-food restaurant's surveillance camera filmed him drinking coffee beside a Novastra employee who disappeared a week later, and Cole became a suspect for the second time.

Flimsy evidence. Clearly what counted against Cole was his relationship with the Enlightenment Project leader, Richard Cox. Lila had said it herself. Cox practically raised him. Without that connection Cole wouldn't have stood out from the crowd. But this time was different. His presence in the car park when Jasper vanished wouldn't be so easily explained to a courtroom. And for all she knew, the Wardens might now have discovered *Enkidu* was the name of Cole's boat.

A shard of doubt cut through Ana. For the first time, she seriously considered the possibility that Cole still operated for the Enlightenment Project and was involved in Jasper's abduction. The evidence might be circumstantial, but there was a pattern, and Cole was at the centre of it. He was the invisible eye of the storm. Dread swamped her. She began biting her fingers, an old nervous habit.

Catching Nate's eye, she blushed, hoping that in her distraction she hadn't done something to reveal her Pure upbringing. But then she realised why Nate's look struck her as odd. The hostility had fallen away. Anxiety lined his face.

'So?' he said, the defiance instantly returning. She moved aside to let him see the screen. 'Don't want to read all that legal jargon. Summarise, why don't you?'

'I don't know,' Ana replied.

'But there was that other guy, same thing right?'

'The case of Peter Vincent, yes.'

'And?'

'And the blue car park is unused except for Level One where all the Pure chauffeurs wait. There's no reason for your brother to go down there, but there's evidence showing he took the car park lift at pretty much the same time the Pure disappeared, and neither were seen leaving the Barbican afterwards.' Nate squeezed a hand over his knuckles. The bones cracked.

'Yeah, we know that. What else?'

'Peter Vincent didn't have your brother's connections. His mother was just foreign.'

Nate rose abruptly. 'Hurry up,' he said. 'I'll wait for you outside.'

Ana pretended to continue reading as Nate crossed the basement and headed up the concrete stairwell. The computer beside her whirred, scanning millions of IDs to find her a physical likeness. Once she was alone, she clicked open Cole's psychiatric assessment from seven years ago and read a brief summary of his background, lifted from a second 'unavailable' report from his infancy.

Born twenty-four years ago to Samuel and Jennifer Winter, a drunk driver killed his father when his mother was pregnant with her second child. Cole became disruptive and problematic at nursery school. Teachers referred Jennifer Winter to a local psychologist. A preliminary examination diagnosed Cole as ADHD. The nursery refused to accept him back unless he took the advised medication. Opposing the medication, his mother pulled him from the establishment. A year later, when school became compulsory, welfare services got involved. A subsequent investigation deemed Mrs Winter unfit to care for her two boys. Cole and Nate were placed in a foster home. Within the space of a year Cole moved to three different homes and finished in a boy's orphanage. At ten years old, he ran away, and became a missing person. He didn't resurface until his assault on a police officer seven years later, at a protest rally against compulsory Pure testing to all school children. Up until then it had been voluntary, though you could only move to a Pure community if you'd had the test.

Ana stopped reading. She glanced at the high basement windows facing the stairwell. Nate must have been about a year old when social services took him from his mother. Had he been shipped from foster family to foster family too? Had he ended up in the Enlightenment Project with his brother? Lila had said Nate and Rachel grew up together. Were they all from the Project?

These weren't the sort of people she was used to dealing with. She didn't know the first thing about growing up in the insane City with Psych Watch and welfare constantly breathing down your neck. She didn't know what people like Nate and Cole had to do to survive.

Cole's psychiatric report concluded with a diagnosis of Aggressive Anger Disorder, Impulse Personality Problems and a diagnostic impression of Hidden Personality Disorder.

In a courtroom, none of that would mean much. Ana could argue that eight million Londoners had similar records. Hidden Personality Disorder just meant the examining psychiatrist thought something was wrong but couldn't back up his judgement with anything specific. And the Aggressive Anger Disorder diagnosis would simply be a result of his one-time arrest for assault.

She closed the computer file and sat for a few minutes. She wondered if what she was doing proved more than any suicidal mother or DNA tests that she belonged among the Crazies. The deceit, the danger, her curiosity – surely a normal Pure girl would be running for her life right now?

But Ana was still there. Because, beneath her determination to help Jasper, there was also the fact that she'd been waiting years to take control of her future. Because like a wooden puppet in a fairy tale, when she'd ventured into the City, the strange, dark place had brought her to life.

Court

Ana and Nate met Cole's lawyer two blocks from Acton Magistrate's court. Jackson looked marginally better with clothes on, but even a clean shirt and suit trousers couldn't conceal the seedy neglect that pervaded him. As they approached, the lawyer combed in the bristled tufts around his bald patch. When he saw them he stopped and began chewing on a finger.

Ana kept her distance as Nate set up the lawyer's interface, configuring it to the control pad she would be using to type on. The pad meant Ana could type from her lap, without an interface camera needing to track her hand gestures.

'Put these in,' Nate said. He thrust a set of headphones at Jackson. Jackson's hands trembled as he fixed the soft globes into his ears. Nate glued a bit of extra fuzz on to the lawyer's sideburns, then they tried a practice run. Ana typed, getting a feel for the pad's touch screen, adjusting her finger gestures to the keyboard which was smaller than the virtual one she usually used. Jackson spoke her words out loud like a child learning to read. As they practised, it didn't seem possible, but the lawyer's delivery got worse. She looked askance at Nate. He ignored her.

When they'd finished, Jackson began to fiddle with the hidden headphones. Sweat patches bloomed under his arms despite the cold.

'We should go,' she said. Nate nodded, but for a moment no one moved. Finally, Ana put Jackson's greasy interface chain and housing over her neck, and they trudged down Ave Road, stopping at the corner of Winchester Street.

The magistrates' building lay up ahead, a red-brick, one-storey structure, reminiscent of the Victorian industrial era. The grey slate roof sloped back on all four sides. Sash windows ran the length of the two visible walls.

'You'd better not mess this up,' Nate said, scowling at thin air, so Ana couldn't tell which of them he was talking to. Without another word, she and Jackson stepped off the kerb, leaving him behind.

At the stone-carved gable above the entrance, Jackson nervously twisted his headphones. Half the fuzz of his left sideburn dropped, dangling down at an angle. Ana stopped him just before they reached the metal detector. Blocking him from the security guard's view, she fixed the hair back in place.

'You'll be fine,' she whispered. 'Just promise me you won't do that in the courtroom.' She turned and smiled at the guard, took off both the interfaces she was wearing and put them, along with the pad, on the automatic roller mat to be scanned. The guard returned her smile, raising an eyebrow at the equipment as though to say, *travelling light?* She grinned, fear and excitement jostling inside her.

They passed through a double doorway and turned left into a courtroom. Half a dozen rows of slim tables faced a raised platform. Wood panelling enclosed the judge's podium. Centred directly below the platform stood the transcriber's beech-wood desk. The transcriber's interface was already synched up to a projection screen. The dock lay on Ana's right-hand side, level with the transcriber's desk. Before the bench, on the left of the courtroom there was a locked glass booth.

Ana settled into the front row beside Jackson. It was strange that after nearly three years of following Jasper's studies, it was her and not him putting it all into practice. She breathed in the smell of polished wood. Her insides tingled with anticipation.

The counsel for the prosecution arrived and took his seat at the other end of the front bench. He placed a silver pad on the table and slicked back thick hair with a large, steady hand. He glanced her way but showed no interest.

The courtroom stirred with the defendant's arrival. Handcuffed to a guard, Cole Winter entered the glass booth from an external doorway. A second guard sealed the booth behind them. The first removed the cuffs, then un-locked the door into the courtroom.

Ana watched Cole as he crossed to the dock. Despite the shabby suit and bruises on his face, his smooth movements conveyed deep self-assurance. His shorn hair was dark, his eyes deeply set, and his muscular frame towered above the guard. Everyone in the courtroom rose, looking left as the Bench arrived, but Cole turned his gaze to their table. His eyes met Ana's and locked on her. Heat rose to her cheeks. She struggled to disengage but found it impossible until he looked away.

The Bench stepped up to their raised seats. As two of the three judges sat, everyone but Cole and the prison guards on either side of him, did likewise.

'The court requests the defendant gives his full name for the records,' the standing magistrate said.

'Cole Alexander Winter.'

The deep, smooth quality of his voice surprised Ana. She found herself looking at him again, noticing a tattoo the size of a postage stamp peeping out of his shirt collar. He seemed to sense her. His eyes flicked to where she sat. She looked down immediately, staring at the pad on her lap.

'We are here to discern,' the standing magistrate said, 'whether the court has the right to hold you under the pre-charge detention of the 2017 Terrorism Act. This will be a plea before venue.' The magistrate pushed horn-rimmed glasses up his nose several times as he spoke. 'We wish to know,' he continued, 'if you are later arrested for the abduction of Jasper Taurell, how will you plead.'

'Not guilty,' Cole said.

'Prosecution, you may stand to outline your reasons for holding the defendant.'

The prosecution rose and recounted the circumstantial evidence weighing against Cole: his presence the night of the abduction in the same car park as Jasper; the formative years Cole spent with the Enlightenment Project; his close relationship with the terrorist Richard Cox.

Ana switched the pad to mute and practised touchtyping with the screen lying flat on her lap. As she focused her breathing, entering the light zone of concentration she used for her piano-playing, she decided she would not look at Cole again. He totally unnerved her.

The prosecutor outlined Cole's prior conviction for GBH and his arrest two years ago in connection with the abduction of a Novastra employee.

'Jasper Taurell,' the prosecutor said, 'is the son of Novastra CEO, David Taurell. In each of Mr Winter's prior arrests, Novastra was the target. This alone, I'm sure, is enough to convince this court that Mr Winter's presence in the car park, under no circumstances—'

'Objection!' Ana fumbled to her feet. Jackson squinted warily at her. 'Mr Winter was questioned, but never charged in either of his prior detentions,' she said, hoping the wobble in her voice wasn't too obvious. 'His prior arrests should not be counted against him.'

The female magistrate scowled. 'This isn't a trial, miss, sit down.' Ana plonked into her seat. The magistrate's eyes slid across to the prosecution. 'Stick to the point,' she instructed.

The prosecution straightened his tie and cleared his throat. 'A look at Jasper Taurell's telephone bill will remove any doubt from this courtroom as to whether Mr Winter's presence in the car park can be considered a mere coincidence.'

At that moment a digital phone bill came up on the double-sided projection screen. 'This is Jasper Taurell's phone bill, dating from 1st February of this year until March 21st – the night of his abduction.'

The prosecutor, Ana realised with a small stab of frustration, had his interface linked up with the courtroom screen.

He flicked a finger in front of his tie and the last number came up highlighted.

'This is the last number Jasper Taurell phoned on March 21st, 8.45 p.m., approximately seven minutes before the car we believe abducted him was caught on camera leaving the blue Barbican car park. The recipient number of this call is registered to Mr Richard Cox, who is currently serving a life-sentence for the Tower Bridge bombing. The man who pays his telephone bills however, is sitting right here in this courtroom.'

A bank statement flashed up on screen, confirming the prosecutor's statement.

Shock fluctuated through Ana, radiating from her stomach into her feet and her hands. Cole paid Cox's phone bill. Which meant he still had to be involved with the Enlightenment Project. But why would Jasper ring Cox the evening of the concert? Why would he even have his number?

The prosecutor smoothed his tie and sat back down. Jackson bustled to his feet. Ana flicked her forefinger twice to reactivate the interface vocal response and then remembered she'd disconnected the pad. Her heart flipped into her throat. Her eyes raked over the touch-responsive screen but the mute symbol had disappeared. Jackson stood beside her, waiting. The silent courtroom also waited.

She peered down at where the mute symbol had been only moments ago. Her hands trembled. Her breath sounded raspy and loud even to her own ears.

There it was! She touched a clammy finger to the symbol and began to type.

We draw the judiciary's attention to the case of Peter Vincent.

Despite herself, Ana glanced at Cole. Their eyes linked for a second. She shivered. Jackson began to speak, his words flat, stilted. Cole wouldn't be the only one questioning what was going on if the lawyer didn't deliver his lines better than that.

Ana closed her eyes. Blocking out Jackson and Cole as best she could, she set forth the argument of Peter Vincent. The words flowed from her, but splattered from the defence lawyer. He bled them of all meaning and significance, until it became excruciating to listen to.

Reaching the close of her argument, Ana peered at the Bench. The female magistrate stared at Jackson with contempt. The two men seated either side of her shuffled papers as though readying to leave. Jackson didn't even have their attention, there was no way he could influence their decision.

Jackson realised he'd finished, abruptly halted and sunk down. The woman looked at the two men. Both nodded. Without conferring further, the female magistrate stood to give their decision.

Ana scrambled to her feet. 'Excuse me, sorry . . .' she said. 'I know it's unorthodox in a pre-trial hearing, but in light of the telephone bill the prosecution omitted to show us prior to today, we would like to ask Mr Winter a couple of questions.'

The younger male magistrate looked surprised, the other two bored.

'All right. Keep it brief,' the elder of the men said.

Ana brushed out the black skirt Rachel had leant her,

smoothed her hazelnut-dyed hair and straightened her shoulders. The questions she had were for her own benefit and would more likely incriminate Cole than help him. But she had to know.

'Mr Winter,' she said, bracing herself to meet his gaze. But he was looking down at his lap, as though he knew he unhinged her and was trying to make this easier. 'Why did Jasper Taurell phone Richard Cox the night he disappeared?'

'No idea.'

'Do you know Jasper Taurell?'

'No.'

'What were you doing in the Barbican underground car park on the 21st of March?'

Cole's gaze flickered up with interest. It felt like a match struck in the centre of her mind, destroying her thought process.

'I'm a musician,' he said. 'I was at the Barbican for the concert. Just before the end, I saw a student from my academy leaving the concert hall and I followed her out to talk to her.' Ana thought of his perfectly pitched wind chimes. She shouldn't have felt surprised that he was a music student, but for some reason it threw her off. Like everything else about him.

'Was she a friend?'

'No, we'd never officially met.'

'Get to the point,' the female magistrate growled, 'or sit down, miss.'

'The defendant has a clear, innocent motive for attending the concert,' Ana said, putting on an authoritative voice

152

like her father's. 'If we can show the court that he is, as he claims, a music student, and that he was following a fellow student out of the concert, we have established a motive for his presence at the Barbican on the night of Jasper Taurell's abduction, leaving the prosecution's only case against Mr Winter that he was taken by the state from his mother when he was four and put in one inadequate foster home after another, until he ran away from an orphanage and ended up spending his teenage years hiding from the authorities in the Enlightenment Project. Will Mr Winter be discriminated against for a third time, because the government was unable to provide him with a secure upbringing?' She paused, wondering if Cole was telling the truth. If he was lying, he'd just made his own bed.

The younger male Bench member put down his papers and leaned forward.

'As this is not a trial,' Ana continued, 'if any other evidence is brought to bear against Mr Winter concerning Jasper Taurell's abduction, the court will of course still uphold the right to detain him again.'

'Objection,' the prosecution said. 'We have Jasper Taurell's phone bill linking him to Mr Cox and Mr Winter.'

'But there is nothing linking the Enlightenment Project to Mr Taurell's abduction,' Ana argued. 'The Wardens currently state it could have been any number of religious or fanatical groups.' She paused, taking her time, anticipating the moment she would twist the facts around in her favour. 'As far as I'm aware, it is not usual practice for a victim to call their kidnappers several minutes before an abduction. It actually strikes me as rather preposterous. Unless

153

the prosecution can explain to this court the logic of Mr Taurell attempting to contact his kidnappers before he vanished, I don't see how Mr Taurell's telephone bill bears any relevance to the issue at hand.'

The older male magistrate conferred with his colleagues, then nodded for Ana to go on. She assumed he wished her to prove Cole's claims of being a musician and following a fellow student.

'If it's possible,' she said, 'we'd like to call up the surveillance footage the prosecution submitted in evidence against Mr Winter, claiming he followed Mr Taurell down to the car park.'

The transcriber checked with the bench and received an affirmative nod. A few seconds later, the surveillance recording appeared on the screen. A black and white image showed an overhead shot of Jasper furtively entering the blue alcove by the concert hall bar, and exiting through a stairwell off to the right marked CAR PARK. The transcriber forwarded through the next two and a half minutes of footage until a man, strongly resembling Cole, approached the silver lift door next to the stairwell exit. At the base of the man's neck was an empty square tattoo, making his identity indisputable.

A girl already stood at the lift, waiting.

Ana gaped at the projection, speechless. It was her! She was standing right beside Cole. He said something and her screen-self nodded. The lift doors opened. They entered.

Ana clung to the courtroom desk. *Think now, freak out later*, she warned herself.

The night before last she'd been so determined to find

Jasper, she'd barely noticed the man in the white shirt and scruffy suit trousers beside her. She'd thought he was one of the Pure chauffeurs going down to Level One where all the drivers gathered at the end of the evening. She'd felt uncomfortable riding alone in the lift with him, but she'd been too worked up to worry about it.

'May we roll back the surveillance tape, please?' she said. Her tongue felt heavy and uncooperative, making it hard to get the words out. The images reversed showing Cole backing through the bar, and several seconds later she was striding backwards too.

'Is it possible to access the camera from the balcony corridor of the concert hall so we can see if, as Mr Winter said, he followed the girl out and not Mr Taurell?' she asked.

The transcriber nodded and within a minute the dim corridor leading down out of the concert hall to the bar, filled the screen. Ana saw herself exit the hall in a hurry. About twenty seconds later, Cole came after her. What was he doing in the balcony seats? And more to the point, why was he following *her*? Fortunately, the specifics of where they'd both exited – seats allocated only to Pures – didn't seem to matter to anyone else.

From across the courtroom, Ana felt the heat of Cole's eyes on her. Instinctively, her hand rose to her cropped brown hair.

'The music school where you and the girl attend?' she asked, though of course she knew the answer.

'The Royal Academy of Music.'

'Would it be possible to access the Royal Academy of Music's student list?' she asked the court.

155

The transcriber set to work again. Cole cleared his throat. She purposefully ignored him. Rather theatrically, he cleared it again. She turned slowly, struggling to meet his gaze.

'I'm not a student,' he said. His eyes twinkled. She pressed her fingers into her forehead, hoping she wouldn't faint. 'I'm a teacher. I go in from time to time and help with the composition class.'

'Here it is,' the transcriber said. She'd pulled up a list of Academy departments and professors. Cole's name was among the visiting professors for composition.

'Well,' the elder male magistrate said, 'it looks as though Mr Winter had as good a reason to be at the Barbican on Thursday evening as anyone else. As the young lady here so rightly points out, this is not a trial. The Wardens have already had Mr Winter for two days of questioning and if they wish to detain him any longer they'll either need to charge him or come up with more evidence indicating his involvement.'

The prosecutor jumped to his feet. 'But what if he runs?'

'No charges have been brought against Mr Winter. He is free to come and go as he pleases. Case dismissed.'

Cole looked over at Ana and smiled. Her whole body began to shake.

He'd been following her the night Jasper was abducted. He paid Richard Cox's phone bills. He'd recognised her even with the brown eyes and brown hair. He knew who she was: a part-time music student at the Royal Academy; the girl Jasper was bound to; the daughter of the man who practically invented the Pure test the Enlightenment Project preached against. She was probably the back-up plan in case they had any problems with Jasper. And she'd just got him off the hook.

14

The Rescue

Within minutes the only people remaining in the courtroom were Ana, Jackson and Cole. Slumped in his seat, Jackson looked neither victorious, nor relieved, just humiliated.

'Sorry,' Ana said, handing him back his interface.

'Why?' Cole asked, sweeping over to them and standing square on to her. 'You did it because he couldn't.' He stretched out an arm to shake her hand. 'Thank you.'

Ana stared at his open palm, afraid of touching him, afraid of looking into his eyes. She swayed and gripped the table to steady herself.

'Are you all right?' he asked.

She clambered out from behind the long desk and ran into the aisle. She didn't look back as she flew towards the double doors. She had no idea if Cole would follow. She just knew she had to get as far away from him as possible.

Outside, she slowed to a brisk walk and checked behind her. Beyond the stone gable a security guard lounged beside the metal detector; the hallway lay empty.

Ana stalked down the path to the street. She'd come all this way only to have her plan ripped out from under her. Cole would hardly help her find out if Jasper was in the Enlightenment Project when it seemed likely he'd been sent to kidnap her if Jasper became a problem.

A hundred metres up the road on her right, Nate and Rachel saw her and began hurtling forward. Ana put her head down and turned left, heading for the junction with Ave Road. Nate shouted and burst into a run. The patter of his trainers grew louder. Then suddenly stopped.

She shot a look over her shoulder and saw Cole swagger out of the courthouse. Nate punched the air with his fist and whooped with joy.

Ana turned the corner into Ave Road and began to run. Cole had turned the situation on its head. All this time she thought she had been tracking him, when in fact he had been coming after *her*. Perhaps Lila was in on it too. Hadn't she hinted that Ana was part of some big plan?

After several random turnings, Ana slackened her pace to a fast stride. Litter strewed the long, quiet road she now walked up. Plastic cups, paper flyers, and bits of orange peel crunched and squashed underfoot. She passed shabby brownstone and whitewashed town houses. The stream of rubbish became a hoary sea, swallowing up the tarmac. Not content to claim the pavements and roads, toilet paper, plastic bottles, food cartons and chocolate wrappings climbed the walls and hedges, and ran through gardens like rivulets. An acidic smell pervaded the air, growing stronger as Ana pushed on. There was something not right about the place.

Not only were there no pedestrians and no cyclists, but there were also no parked cars. This was the first City street she'd been into without encountering the neglected

159

or recycled vehicles. There were no shanty shelters either, and no tents erected in the gardens.

She ground to a halt. Her body resisted entering any deeper into the oppressive emptiness. From a high window, a distant drumbeat broke the silence. She looked up. The windows of these houses weren't boarded up. They were glazed, though many were broken with jagged, open holes.

A feeling gripped Ana and became unshakable – she had to go back. She tried to rationalise with herself that back meant towards Cole, Nate and Rachel. They'd seen the direction she'd left the courthouse. If they'd split up at the two junctions she'd passed, there was a strong chance that one of them would run into her.

Up ahead she saw a male figure swimming in the shadows of a first-floor window. She shuddered at the sight of him. Turning, she began to slip and stagger over the uneven ground, back the way she'd come. Her foot twisted on a glass bottle. Pain shot through her ankle.

Deriding herself for over-reacting – it was just a man – she glanced back at the house and saw someone exiting the front door. Adrenalin buzzed down her arms making the tips of her fingers ache with energy. She clenched her teeth and began to move faster. From the corner of her eye, she saw a second figure appear at another door. Closer this time. And then her heart stopped dead. Almost every door up and down the street behind her had people pouring out of them, like creatures from a disturbed nest. Their eyes watched her as they ventured off porches and down paths on to the pavements.

She began to sprint. Fear obscured the pain in her ankle,

obscured everything around her. She didn't hear the throb of a motorbike biting through the eerie drumbeat, didn't see it until it was practically on top of her. The bike pulled up beside a lamp post.

'You look like you might need a ride,' the driver said.

Cole! She stared at him, panting. Her ankle was agony. Behind her, the motley crowd bore down. For the most part they moved dreamily, like they'd come out to see a strange light in the sky, like they couldn't quite believe their eyes. But four young men in hooded tops and dark combat trousers had zoned in. They only hesitated now, at this unexpected complication.

Ana climbed up on the seat of the bike. Whatever Cole might do to her, he didn't make her skin crawl like these people. She circled her arms around his waist. He revved the engine and spun the bike in a semi-circle. From the safety of her moving seat, she watched the sleepwalkers recede. Their strange eyes seemed to pull the outside world into them, like dark matter. Without thinking, she drew closer to Cole.

Acton High Street teemed with fruit and veg market stalls, street vendors calling out prices and deals, customers balancing over-full carrier bags of food on their handle bars, and infants splashing in puddles. The presence of so many ordinary Carriers and Sleepers comforted Ana. The bustle and activity made things seem almost normal again as Cole threaded his motorbike down the centre of the street and veered into a road with no pedestrians and fewer bicycles, e-trikes and rickshaws. The engine spluttered as they pushed forwards at thirty miles per hour. Ana wondered what it ran on. There was no way he could afford pure petrol.

They passed under a wide highway, suspended above the streets. It was part of the London ring road used by Pure chauffeurs to circumvent the City. Five minutes later, they traversed a canal bridge. In the distance, Ana could hear hollering and a crowd chanting. Cole pulled up and cut the engine. He wheeled the bike under a bush, then turned to her. His eyes held a mixture of curiosity and warmth.

'Are you coming?' he asked. Without waiting for her response, he slipped over a crumbled wall. If she was going to make a run for it, now was the time. Ana hesitated. The chanting masses were getting closer. She squinted towards the end of the street. A swarm of jerking, limping people approached. Ahead of it, several women fled as though trying to outrun a natural catastrophe. She didn't want to get caught up in a Crazy protest march. She'd have to move fast, quickly put some distance between herself and the crowd.

But she didn't. Because if she ran, she might never find Cole and his family again. And Cole was the only person she knew who might have answers to her questions. He'd startled her in the courtroom, but she didn't feel so afraid of him now. Not that she trusted him. But if he meant her harm, surely he wouldn't have walked away from her just now.

She turned and followed where she'd seen him go, over the wall and down a steep, overgrown incline to the waterway. High banks sheltered the canal from street view. Only two boats coloured the brown water – *Enkidu* and *Reliance*.

As Cole headed towards them, Lila scrambled along the side of *Enkidu* shouting, 'They're here!' Simone popped out of *Reliance* followed by Rafferty. Lila jumped on to the canal path and ran into her brother's arms. Rafferty, Simone and her bulge joined the embrace. Ana hung back awkwardly.

From the bridge above came a strange howl. The yelling and hooting grew louder. Ana looked up to see burning pieces of paper flying through the air. Ash fluttered down like black rain.

'Come on,' Lila said, pulling her towards the boat. 'We should get inside.'

*

Two hours later, dusk settled across the canal. On the horizon, tower blocks cut black fingers against the deep-blue evening. A March wind gusted through Ana's jacket and the skirt she still wore. She was sitting on *Enkidu*'s roof, legs hugged to her chest. Inside *Enkidu* it had been warm. Her cheeks were still flushed from the fire. She gazed at the skyline and wondered why Cole hadn't told the others who she was.

She'd felt increasingly uneasy watching him laugh and celebrate with his family – Nate and Rachel had arrived an hour and a half ago. She couldn't understand what he wanted her for. Why was he letting her in among them when he knew who she was? And why had he been following her the night of Jasper's abduction?

Adding to her agitation were thoughts about the hooded men and the zombie people. She felt as though the zombies were still watching her, their strange black eyes looking straight into her mind.

The wooden ladder up through the hatch creaked, followed by footsteps. Ana turned to the pale light of the wheelhouse and saw Nate, Simone, Rafferty and Cole filter out. Simone held her son's hand across the gangplank.

'Night,' she called, as they passed Ana, walking up the bank to *Reliance*'s mooring.

'Night,' Ana said.

Cole and Nate embraced. Ana heard the rumble of their low voices, but couldn't make out their exchange. Then Nate crossed on to land and Cole pulled up the wooden plank. He tucked it down the side of the wheelhouse and disappeared inside. A minute later, he re-emerged with two steaming mugs. The nervousness Ana had felt looking at him in the courtroom crept over her again. He came up the barge and sat down, taking off the thick knitted sweater he was wearing.

'You're cold,' he said, pushing the sweater into her hands.

'Freezing.' Tentatively, Ana shucked off her leather jacked and pulled Cole's jumper over her head. It smelt of sunflowers and cut grass.

'Lila said you don't take sugar.'

A tang of black tea began to blanket the faint odour of summer. Ana rolled up the jumper's long sleeves, put her jacket back on, and took the hot mug Cole was holding out to her.

'Thank you,' she said.

'You're welcome.'

Her hands trembled, so she quickly placed the mug at her feet.

Cole lay down, arms folded behind his head. He sighed contentedly. 'The first stars are out.'

Ana tilted back and looked up. For the last three days, while she'd roamed the City with an illicit sort of freedom she'd never known in her life, Cole had been in prison. From the corner of her eye she examined the prominent bruising to his face and wondered if the Psych Watch had tortured him for information.

He was different from what she'd been expecting. Not less dangerous. No. She'd never felt such concentrated energy in a person. It was bound to be volatile, explosive. But he was also open, unguarded and totally unpredictable.

'Lila told me you pulled Rafferty out of the canal,' he said. 'It seems two of us wouldn't be here right now, if it wasn't for you.' He caught her eye, and she looked quickly away, gripping her knees tighter to her chest. So that was why he hadn't told the others who she was yet. He owed her. But how long would his debt keep her safe? Would he still try to use her as collateral if the Enlightenment Project didn't get what they wanted from Jasper's abduction?

'When Simone had Rafferty in the hospital,' Cole continued, gazing at the sky, 'he was diagnosed a Big3 Active. The nurses put Taxil in his bottle. Nate and Simone weren't even told. They were forced to keep him on it, partly cos of all the follow-up health visits, partly cos a newborn can't handle the withdrawal. At six months Rafferty couldn't sit up, couldn't do anything. By one year . . .' Cole paused, rubbed his chin. When he spoke again, she could hear the pain in his voice. 'By one year he had never smiled. Nate has tried weaning him off the Taxil a couple of times, but Rafferty's too young. The mood swings, the depression, the flood of emotions he's never learnt to handle . . . how do you explain what's happening to a four year old?'

The sadness Ana felt after pulling Rafferty from the canal returned to her, compounded by confusion. The meds were supposed to help Actives live balanced lives. But a one-year-old baby who'd never smiled? No parent could accept that was the best they could do for their child. No parent could be expected to live with such heartbreak.

She sat quietly, knowing she would have done what Nate and Simone had done. And yet yesterday she'd practically accused Nate of child neglect. After a couple of minutes, she grew conscious again of Cole beside her and grew uncomfortable.

'So,' she said, twisting a strand of her short hair and shifting her feet. 'I've been wondering, why were you following me at the Barbican?'

Cole rocked his head to look at her, then perched up on one elbow. 'And I've been wondering,' he said, 'how you ended up in that courtroom today. You're not a lawyer.'

'I've studied law – sort of.'

He stared at her, his lips curled in a slight smile. 'I saw you once at the Academy,' he said. 'Your hair was different and you've changed the colour of your eyes, but it was you.'

'So?'

'You're the only Pure girl I've ever seen there. And now you're the only Pure girl I've ever seen in the City. And not

166

just out in the City, but posing as an assistant lawyer, and doing it rather well I might add.'

'I'm not really Pure.' Ana challenged his probing gaze with one of her own.

He laughed. 'You live in the Community and you're bound to Jasper Taurell. Trust me, you're Pure.'

She broke eye contact and looked out at the canal, trying to buy herself time to think. He must know she was Ariana Barber, the Crazy girl who'd been mistakenly raised with the Pures, mustn't he? After all, he knew Jasper was the son of the CEO of Novastra, and anyone who'd done their homework would know about Jasper's contentious decision to bind with a Crazy.

'I notice that you haven't answered my question yet,' she said, sounding calmer than she felt. 'Why were you following me that night?'

'I'm not sure you're ready for the answer.'

'Really? And how do you think you know me so well?'

Cole stopped, looked down and laughed to himself.

'I didn't realise I was funny,' she said.

He shook his head. 'I didn't think a Pure girl could be so feisty.'

She hesitated, unsure if she was been complimented or insulted. 'What were you expecting? Timid, sweet, naïve?' She stared at him fiercely, but her eyes snagged on his blue irises and her heart back-flipped, landing askew in her chest. 'Anyway, don't try to tell me you don't know who my father is.'

'I've no idea who your father is.'

'I don't believe you.'

167

His eyes shifted towards the wheelhouse. She rocked back, as though he'd literally let go of her.

Rachel stood at the stern of the boat watching them. Flicking back her dark bob, she brushed along the deck, leapt to the bank and slunk into the dwindling half-light.

Cole lay back down, arms behind his head. Ana wondered if he'd told Rachel who she really was. Ever since Rachel had returned with Nate, she'd been giving Ana nasty looks.

'So, what are you saying? You think I'm involved in Jasper's abduction, and that I was following you as a back-up plan?' he asked. Her face began to burn. It was as though he'd plucked the words right out of her head, but for some reason it sounded ridiculous coming from him. 'It wasn't exactly the first impression I was hoping for.' He frowned, but his eyes were smiling.

Ana's throat closed up. She wrapped her hands around her mug. Warmth leached through her fingers.

What does he mean, the first impression he'd been hoping for?

'Did you know I was going to be at your pre-hearing?' she asked.

'No. That was an extremely random and unpredictable move on your part.'

She was losing the thread. He'd mocked her for thinking he was part of some abduction back-up plan, and now he was practically admitting he'd been following and pre-empting her movements.

'Why did Jasper call Richard Cox minutes before they took him?'

'The number he rang is a kind of emergency hotline for

people who need to disappear right-frigging-now before they get bagged.'

'Bagged?'

'Shot with some insane dose of LSD, so they flip out and the Watch rocks up to take them away, no questions asked.'

Ana stared at Cole, lost for words. 'Shot by who?' she said finally.

'The Watch, the Wardens . . . it depends.'

'Fine.' She was having a hard time making sense of any of this. 'What's that got to do with Jasper?'

Cole pushed himself up on both elbows and looked at her hard, as though gauging whether to say something. For a second time, Ana managed to hold her own. But then a terrible feeling slid through her. She already knew the answer: The morning of Jasper's abduction, his acquaintance – the ex-Project member – had suddenly gone nuts in the street and the Psych Watch had turned up in record time, as though they'd been waiting for it to happen. He'd been *bagged*. Had Jasper thought he was next?

'Jasper was involved in something big,' Cole said. 'A couple of months back, I heard a guy from your Community had got his hands on information that proved the DNA Pure tests were a scam.'

Ana baulked like a horse reaching a ten-foot-high jump. 'What guy?' she said. But again she knew the answer. She knew he meant Jasper.

Cole just looked at her.

'My father was seminal in developing those tests,' she said. 'But you know that, don't you?'

Cole's eyes narrowed as though he didn't understand, as though he was trying to figure out what she meant.

'You expect me to believe that the boy I'm bound to has been plotting to discredit my father and the whole mental health system that's holding this country together?'

'Listen, I . . .' The concern in his voice made everything worse.

She sprang to her feet, fury making her wild and invincible. He was obviously trying to manipulate her, confuse her. Perhaps this was one of the Enlightenment Project's brainwashing techniques – pretend to be caring and kind to a new recruit and then make them believe they'd been betrayed by the people they cared about most. She might still be Jasper's insurance policy, but let Cole try to stop her from leaving. Then he'd see how submissive and fragile she really was.

Lies

Ana stormed down the side of the barge to the stern. She faltered at the dark four-foot gap where Rachel had leapt ashore. Behind her, something knocked the wheelhouse. She spun about and saw Cole with the gangplank. He gently brushed her to one side and laid the plank across from *Enkidu* to the shore.

In the semi-darkness, he lifted his palm to her. For a moment, she thought he was offering her the chance to change her mind – to stay with him – but when she looked down she saw an ID stick glinting in the faint light from the porthole. Her ID stick. He'd retrieved it from Nate. He was letting her go.

She snatched the ID and marched over the plank. On the towpath, she strained to see the lay of the bank where they'd come down earlier. She sidled towards the slope of grass. Behind her, footsteps brushed the path. She scrambled for purchase on the incline. Her pumps slipped and slid. Something sharp scratched her right hand. She cried out and let go, skidding back down to where Cole's six-foot silhouette waited. Mud soaked through her skirt and tights.

Cole took a step forwards.

'Stay away from me,' she shouted.

He stopped.

'Where's Jasper? What have you done to him?' A sob split her chest. The pressure and confusion of the day descended on her. 'Were you following me to get to him?'

'I knew Jasper was in trouble,' Cole said. 'He was being closely watched by the Wardens. I slipped him a piece of paper with the hotline telephone number. I was trying to help. When I saw you with him, I recognised you from the Academy. You got up to go after him and I followed to make sure you were OK.'

Ana shook her head. No, Cole was the bad guy. He was mixing things up so that she'd trust him.

'Why didn't you follow Jasper to make sure *he* was OK?'

'There was nothing more I could do for him. I was more concerned about you.' The tenderness in Cole's voice confused her. Curious, she looked at him and sensed he was telling the truth.

She slumped down on the edge of the muddy slope, groaned and wrapped her hands over her head. She felt like an idiot. No wonder he found her so amusing.

Cole squatted down beside her. 'So,' he said, 'you *were* in court today because you thought I was involved in Jasper's abduction?'

'No, not at first,' she sniffed. 'At first I thought the Enlightenment Project had taken him. I thought because you're an ex-member you could help me find out where they were holding him. But when I saw you're paying Cox's phone bills and following me . . .' She trailed off.

'But if you didn't know about Jasper's phone call to the hotline number before today, why were you looking for me?'

'I knew the day Jasper disappeared he'd met an ex-Project member. He'd talked about it when he told me he was in trouble. And I knew the Wardens were searching for someone called "Enkidu". It all led to you.'

Cole let out a huff of annoyance. 'Jasper wasn't very careful. No wonder they pre-empted him.'

Ana rubbed her face with the sleeve of his woolly jumper. 'They? They who?' she said.

'Whoever knew what he'd got his hands on.'

'That's mad. How could the Pure tests be fake?'

'Have you heard of the Human Genome Project?'

Ana shook her head.

'The Human Genome Project,' he said, 'was an international research effort to map all the genes that make up the genetic blueprint for a human being. It was completed in 2003. Afterwards, there was a huge race in the global scientific community to be the first to use this information to isolate gene patterns responsible for different diseases. Personalised preventive health care was a pharmaceutical's wet dream. Imagine being able to provide medication before something even went wrong with a person.

'Then came the Collapse and the Global Depression. Hundreds of thousands of people lost their homes, their jobs, the Petrol Wars started, and all over the world things were falling apart. You said your father helped develop the Pure test?'

She nodded. 'My father's Ashby Barber.'

Cole's eyebrows shot up. But his surprise was quickly usurped by understanding.

'There was all that stuff a couple of years ago about Jasper binding with Ashby Barber's daughter, Ariana,' he said. 'I didn't realise. It didn't register.'

Ana shrugged. If Cole had stepped in at the last minute to try and help Jasper, there was no reason why he should know.

'Well,' he continued, 'your father's work and everything to do with the Pure test research was funded by one of Europe's largest pharmaceuticals at a time when the average person had lost any sense of security or hope for the future.'

'Novastra,' Ana muttered.

'Exactly. They saw an opportunity. They capitalised on it. But rumours have always flown about that they never found any of the mutated-gene patterns that could be considered responsible for the Big3, let alone any of the others. It didn't stop them. They had an idea, and they weren't about to give it up.'

'But how could they fake something so big?'

'"The bigger the lie, the more people believe it." Hitler's right-hand man said that. It's happened all through history. Human sacrifices, witch hunts, Nazis.'

Ana lay back and crossed her arms over her chest. Mud slipped around her neck, and up into her hair.

Could it all really be a lie? Was that why her father had been so determined she cheat the system? Was that why he'd forbidden her to take any preventative medication?

Because of the Pure test she'd spent nearly three years squeezing every irrational thought out of herself, crushing her emotions into a well-contained hollow where her heart should have been.

And all this time, Jasper had believed there was nothing wrong with her and never said a word. Had he been using her to get to her father?

'Ariana?' Cole's voice drifted through her awareness. But she might as well have been at the bottom of a cave full of water, and he might as well have been calling to her through a crack in the earth high, high above. 'Are you all right?'

She didn't bother to answer. If she just lay there, in time her body would wear a hole in the ground, decay, disintegrate, meld with the earth.

'Ariana?'

She felt light-headed. In the starlit blackness of her mind, someone else spoke, as clearly as if they stood in the same room.

'You shouldn't trust him.'

Tamsin.

They were sitting in the school theatre, legs propped up on the backs of their auditorium seats. It was the last week of Ana's Year 11 summer term, fourteen months before Tamsin vanished. The school variety concert had ended half an hour ago. Pure boys and young men from all of London's eleven Pure communities were drinking juice in the gym with Ana's peers. Except for Jasper. Jasper had left moments after the final song.

'He told you,' Tamsin continued, 'that he's going to transfer from Oxford to Durham and do the second year of his law degree there – Durham, where it'll be too expensive for him to come back until next summer. He's avoiding you.'

'You can't expect him to get over his brother's death just like that.'

'It's been more than a year, Ana. I'm sorry but either he's stringing you along, or he's messed up big time.'

'Pures can't get messed up big time.'

''Course they can,' Tamsin said.

'But they don't get proper diseases.'

'In Shakespeare's day, people went crazy cos of broken hearts and lost loved ones. Why would it be any different now?'

'Because now we know those things are just triggers. A broken heart can only trigger suicide if you're a Big3 or bi-polar or . . .'

Tamsin shook her head. 'You should know better than anyone else. How many girls in our class would pass one of the Board's tests you have to do every month?'

'They don't have to.'

'Why not?'

'Because even if they have symptoms they don't have the genetic structure which will lead to the disease, so it won't develop.'

Tamsin sighed. 'Whatever,' she said. 'You're better off without Jasper.'

'Better off in the City with all the lunatics stabbing each other and starving to death?'

'You're exaggerating.'

'How would you know?'

Tamsin was quiet then. It made Ana wonder about her

best friend. She knew Tamsin sometimes accompanied her father into the City to purchase goods for their shop, and once or twice Tamsin had implied she was allowed to wander around alone. But Ana had never understood why anyone would want to.

As it turned out, Tamsin had been right about Jasper. Ana shouldn't have trusted him. She'd been naïve; and vain enough to think the handsome, rich, eligible Jasper Taurell would give up his perfect life for her. Except he obviously didn't think it was perfect.

Ana roused when she realised Cole had picked her up and was carrying her. She pushed him off, insisting she could walk. They boarded *Enkidu*. Relieved to discover there was no one else about, she lay down on a sofa and Cole covered her with blankets.

As much as Ana didn't want them to, all the pieces fitted Cole's explanation. Whoever had taken Jasper – the Psych Watch or the Wardens – were probably doing the Board's bidding to protect the Pure test, and were unlikely to ever let him go. Ana saw herself middle-aged, living a ghost life in the City. Alone. Surrounded by people who acted crazy whether they were or not. Living in fear that one day the Psych Watch would come for her, because she knew what they had done to Jasper.

As she lay there, consumed by misery, a small part of her registered music. Woolly, hollow notes. They fluttered against her like the beating wings of angels. They poured into her, as warm as sunlight.

A wet stick crackled as it caught alight in the glowing furnace. She breathed in wood smoke and gradually allowed the music to thread her back together, each note like a tiny pricking stitch. When the melody turned darker and more mysterious, she rolled on to her front and pulled herself along the sofa to peer around the edge.

Cole sat at the upright piano with his back to her. A lantern glimmered on the case top, softly shaping his face and casting shadows over his fingers as they swept up and down the keys.

She examined him. Despite everything that was happening, she couldn't help wondering how on earth someone raised in foster homes, an orphanage and a secluded sect, could play the piano like that.

The piece guttered like a candle in a draught, notes flickering unsteadily. A final chord struck, lingered and then burnt out. His hands lowered. He sat for a moment, unmoving.

'You still there?' he asked finally, breaking a strange and powerful silence.

'Yes.' She sat up and pulled the blankets tightly around her shoulders. She didn't feel ready to look at him. She was too overcome by the music and embarrassed about her earlier little breakdown.

'I've never heard it before,' she said. 'What's it called?'

'"Second Sight".'

'"Second Sight",' she repeated, committing the name to memory. She knelt up on the sofa and looked over Cole's shoulder at the sheet music. A strange form of coded notes marked the page. He put down the piano cover and turned so that they were face to face, only a foot between them. Up close, she could see the scar through his left eyebrow, the dent in his chin, the square tattoo on his neck. Involuntarily, her eyes rested on the curve of his lower lip. The lip rounded into a smile. Suddenly realising she was staring, she pulled away.

'So,' he said. 'What did you think of it?'

She twisted towards the fire and watched the flames behind the blackened furnace door.

'When I hear a piece like that,' she said, 'I find it hard to believe that there isn't something more than this.' She waved a hand at the cabin, at all the material things surrounding them. 'Something we haven't begun to understand, but it's captured in the music. It's there. You can feel it.'

'Yes,' he said. 'Exactly.' Behind her, the piano stool creaked and something rattled. He began rummaging through a wooden storage shelf nailed into the wall and retrieved a thumb-sized disc case. 'It's a recording of "Second Sight",' he said passing it to her. 'You can keep it.'

His dark pupils were holes, pulling her into him. She stood up and reached out to take the recording.

'You . . . you wrote it,' she said, suddenly understanding.

Their fingers touched. He smiled. For a second she gazed into the black holes and gravity abandoned her. She was falling. She was falling and it was the scariest and most thrilling feeling she'd ever had.

'You should give it to someone who can do something with it,' she stuttered.

'That's why I was giving it to you.'

'Me?' *Why her?* Cole must know plenty of proper pianists that could perform it for him. 'I—' She curled her fingers around the disc case, skimming his skin. 'I'm not sure I understand. But thank you.'

Cole gathered the sheet music and shoved it inside the piano stool along with a large messy stack of similarly drawn-up pages.

She stepped closer, resting her hand across the closed piano case. After three days' withdrawal from her piano practice, and with so many emotions and 'Second Sight' bubbling inside her, the desire to play was overwhelming.

'May I?' she asked. He nodded. She opened the key cover. He moved aside, giving her room to perch on the piano stool. Gently, she struck a key and began to pick out his melody.

'Do you still plan on trying to find Jasper?' he asked.

Ana tinkled on the keys, considering. There were at least sixty loony bins in the Greater London area. The Psych Watch or the Wardens could have dumped him in any one of them. Or they could have done something else with him entirely.

Jasper must have been out of his mind to even consider going up against the Board. But maybe that's why he'd chosen to bind with her, to remind people the Board could make mistakes and if they could make mistakes then they weren't infallible.

Jasper had as good as lied to her by not telling her about his brother's evidence. He'd also risked his own life in an attempt to pass on evidence he thought proved the Pure test was fraudulent; evidence that affected over fifty-five million people.

'I can't leave him rotting in some psych dump,' she said. 'This evidence he supposedly has. Where's it meant to have come from?'

'His brother,' Cole said. 'Tom Taurell had a degree in biochemistry.'

Ana thought of Tom's accident. Tom had just begun working in Novastra's research department before he fell off a cliff in the abandoned county of Dorset and drowned. Had he discovered anomalies in the Pure test? Had he been killed for trying to expose them?

For a moment, Ana pushed aside her anger with Jasper and instead tried to put herself in his shoes. He'd wanted to avenge his brother's death by undermining the Board. Granted, his relationship with Ana had facilitated that – binding with the girl whose original Pure test had somehow been faulty – but deep down she felt sure it wasn't the only reason he'd gone ahead with it. In the handful of times they'd seen each other after her fifteenth birthday, he'd never pressed her for information about her father. And he must have believed he could hand over the evidence to the member of the Enlightenment Project (or ex-member) without being caught. If things had gone to plan, at some point in the days leading up to their joining, the 'truth' would have become public knowledge and the Board would have come under attack. Jasper had never intended to join with her under false pretences. She would have known the truth about the Pure tests, perhaps he'd have confessed to her what he'd been up to.

'Are you and the guy Jasper met with still part of the Enlightenment Project?'

'Yes.'

'But I thought you weren't allowed to leave the compound.'

Cole raised an eyebrow. 'And yet here I am.'

Ana flicked her eyes away from him. She wished he wouldn't look at her and speak to her like *that* – it made goose bumps appear on the tops of her arms, the back of her neck; it made it impossible to be normal around him.

'So, I guess the Psych Watch who spiked Jasper's contact must have taken the evidence,' she said, directing her gaze at the piano.

'I believe there are two copies. Jasper had a second one.'

A wall of energy slammed into Ana. *Another copy!* Perhaps the evidence was still out there. Jasper knew they were coming after him; he'd have had the time to hide the disc. If she found Jasper, not only could she tell his mother where he was but she could help him get back the disc proving the Pure tests were fake. Then she would know for sure that she'd never get sick.

'We have to find him,' she said. 'We have to find out what they've done to him, so that his father can make a stand against the Board and get him out.'

Excitement buzzed through her as she began to play the part of 'Second Sight' she'd already unravelled. Without the Big3 hanging over her, she'd be a new person; she'd have a future; she'd never have to worry again about the day her own mind turned on her. The bitter-sweet melody tumbled from her fingers. Absorbed by the feel of piano keys she played until she'd woven each element of the piece back together, until the fire embers died and the cabin grew cold. When she stopped, it was long past midnight and Cole had gone.

16

Benzidox

Hours later, Ana woke in her cabin, hungry and apparently alone aboard *Enkidu*. In the kitchen she found a piece of bread from the evening meal. The fridge and the cupboards were empty. She ate the chewy baguette, then showered. Dressed again in her jeans and Cole's chocolate-brown sweater, she ventured up on deck and was surprised to find they were moored back near Camden market. Across the water, she could see stalls jammed with people milling about, browsing, buying, selling. She could hear oriental music and the faint base beats of something electronic.

She returned to the living room and began searching for a key to close the wheelhouse hatch. She planned to head out and buy herself a late breakfast, then a large coat.

'Hey!' Lila called breathlessly into the cabin. She clattered down the steps carrying a pizza box. Her interface projected animated gremlins. They ripped through the top of the cardboard box and audibly gobbled up the pizza. 'Cole said you'd sleep late, but I wasn't sure if I'd miss you. I've brought lunch.'

Ana took the warm carton and the creatures disappeared. As Lila jumped off the last ladder rung the box burst back to life with a jingle. Lila closed her thumb and forefinger together across her chest. The hand gesture muted her interface sensor.

'I was just about to go out, but I couldn't find a key for the hatch,' Ana said.

'Oh, you don't need to worry about that. People know us around here.' She went to the bookshelf and dug out a key from a ceramic owl-shaped pot. 'But here,' she said. 'For next time.'

'Actually,' Ana said, 'I was going to ask you about that. Um . . . when do you think I'll need to find somewhere else? I get the impression that whoever usually sleeps in the cabin will be back sometime soon.'

Lila laughed. 'Don't you know?' she said.

'Know what?'

'It's Cole's cabin. This is his boat.'

'Oh.' Flustered and embarrassed, Ana turned to get glasses from a rack beside the kitchen sink. 'Yeah, I knew it was his boat, but I kind of thought he and Rachel were together. He didn't say anything about the bed. I didn't realise. I suppose I'd better try that youth hostel then, what was it called? On Greenland road or something . . .'

'Absolutely not,' Lila said.

'But I couldn't—'

'Yes, you could. Cole will sleep on the couch.'

Ana cringed. Not only had Cole evacuated his cabin for her last night, but her playing had prevented him from using the sofa. She felt awkward accepting the arrangement. She'd assumed Cole and Rachel, living together on the same boat, were an item. The prospect of Cole being single made her uncomfortable.

Lila dropped the cardboard box on the kitchen table and tossed back the lid.

'Did you two argue about something?' she asked. A tangy odour of tomato sauce and tinned mushrooms drifted off the pizza. Ana's stomach churned. No one in the Community ate fast food, especially not girls of her age who had to think of their complexions and the health of their soon-to-be-child-bearing bodies.

'Argue?' she asked. Lila removed a slice of pizza and offered it to Ana on a plate. Ana prodded it.

'Oh, maybe he's just worried about tomorrow night,' Lila said.

'What's happening tomorrow night?'

'Well, now he's no longer in detention, he's back to helping a Pure from one of the Communities get into the Project. A guy that wants to disappear.'

Ana remembered the three Pures working for Novastra who'd all vanished, reportedly abducted.

'Why does he want to disappear?'

Lila shrugged and stuffed more pizza into her mouth. 'He's a minister. He's got this ancient recording proving Novastra, the government, and the Chairman of the Board came up with the whole idea of Pures before that Nobel Prize-winning guy ever came close to discovering a genetic pattern for schizophrenia. Do you know what a Glimpse is?'

At the mention of her father, Ana's cheeks flushed. But Lila didn't seem to notice. 'Uh, a brief look at something?'

'No, I mean an Enlightenment Glimpse.'

'As in the Enlightenment Project Cole's a member of?'

Lila nodded, chewing her pizza. 'But it's not what you think.'

'I don't know what I think any more.'

'Well, that's a start,' Lila said, smiling. 'Originally, the Project was one of the temporary camps set up by the government after the housing crash. Except that summer a flu virus spread through it. The media overdramatised the problem and the government ended up putting the camp under quarantine for six months. The government ensured the walls were impenetrable. They stopped anyone entering or leaving the camp. Finally, nine months later the camp got a clean bill of health and the government announced that they were relocating everyone up north. A lot of people in the camp wanted to stay. There were big protests, et cetera, et cetera, and finally the government gave in and left them alone. Any of this sound familiar?'

Ana shook her head.

'Well, the camp worked on becoming self-sufficient. Animals, crop farming and their own small mills for electricity and wells for water. Several years later, when a documentary crew came to do a follow-up story on them, they were living this idyllic life compared to the chaotic madness of the City. This was all before the Pure Genome Split Referendum. It was the media who dubbed the camp the "Enlightenment Project". Many of the things the people living there advocated went against what the government was doing. As the voice of the Project grew and became more political, Richard Cox, the Project's spokesperson was attacked and defamed. They tried to make out he was a charlatan, anti-establishment and only interested in power.'

'Richard Cox, the terrorist bomber?'

'If you believe what the government want you to believe. He was innocent. Anyway, the media got hold of Richard Cox's past – stock trader, lost millions, walked out on family and kids – he almost had another breakdown. But this Nganasan shaman turned up inside the Project. Came out of nowhere. I mean, we're not simply talking about scaling a wall – the country's borders were heavily restricted by then. You couldn't just decide to go on holiday somewhere, or come into the country to visit long-lost relatives. Aside from the fact that the guy came from Siberia!'

Ana put down her pizza and folded her arms across her chest. Maybe the Project wasn't as dangerous as the media made out, but clearly there was some weird stuff going on there.

'Anyway, this shaman was able to enter the spiritual plane. He healed Richard, and showed him there was a boy he'd been looking out for, who could potentially become part of a very important event in the future. As long as Richard continued to protect the boy and keep him out of trouble.'

'And Cole's supposed to be that boy?'

'You said it.'

Ana bit the insides of her cheeks, annoyed with herself for jumping to the conclusion Lila was clearly trying to foist on her.

'OK, so what's an Enlightenment Glimpse then?' she asked.

'It's a fleeting vision of a likely future.'

'Oh right, so the Project leaders *do* say they can see the

future.' *No wonder they have a dodgy reputation if they go about spouting that sort of stuff.*

Lila leant back in her chair. 'The problem with a Glimpse,' she said, 'is it's fractured. Like looking in a broken mirror with missing pieces.'

'It doesn't sound any different to all the other Beliefs,' Ana said. 'You just have to have faith in what you're told. You've never actually experienced one of these Glimpses for yourself, have you?'

'No, not *me*,' Lila said.

A tingle ran up Ana's spine. The implication sat between them like a challenge. Ana narrowed her eyes.

'Cole,' she said. It wasn't a question.

Lila nodded.

'Cole's seen the future . . . How?'

'Well the shaman was able to help him enter a plane of the spirit world by appearing to him in a dream and showing him a door. When Cole walked through the door it was as though he'd walked into the future. As real as you and me sitting here.'

'I thought you said it was fractured.'

'Well, imagine you were lying in your bed nine years ago and you suddenly found yourself here now. You wouldn't know anything about what had happened to get you here. So it's like being given a piece of a puzzle, but you've no idea how it all fits together.'

'And Cole told you this?'

'No. Cole doesn't speak about it. Richard told me.'

'The terrorist bomber?'

'Why do I get the feeling we're going round in circles?'

'Perhaps we're on a time loop.'

'Ha ha.'

A thump resounded on the roof as someone jumped aboard.

'I've got to get back to the stall,' Lila said. 'If you don't finish the pizza, can you put it in the fridge?'

'Sure.'

'OK. See you later.'

She bounded into the living area and waited by the ladder as Cole descended. 'Hi, bro.'

Ana got up from the table and self-consciously ran a hand through the short strands of her shower-damp hair. As if she hadn't felt tense enough around Cole before – now he was some kind of clairvoyant.

You don't believe what Lila told you, she reminded herself. Mystical Experience Disorder was a temporary disturbance in a person's perceptions that they then attributed to some higher force. Simply put, a hallucination.

But nothing seemed straightforward any more.

Cole swept through the living room like he was riding a wave of fresh air and energy. He dumped a manila bag on the kitchen table and cleared aside the pizza box.

'Have you eaten?' he asked, pulling down a chopping board.

'Lila brought the pizza, but no, not really.' His scent of summer, washing powder and something spicy like cinnamon, overwhelmed her. She had to physically stop herself from stepping closer to guzzle it up. As she stood with her hands pressed to her sides, she noticed he hadn't actually looked at her yet.

'I'm juicing. You want apple and banana, or orange and lemon?'

'Apple and banana would be great, thanks.'

He rolled his sweater sleeves up to his elbows. The muscles in his forearms flexed as he took the fruit from the manila bag and cut the apple into eighths. Then he plugged in a blender and began juicing.

'I er . . .' Ana had to shout to be heard. 'I'm sorry about last night.'

He cut the power. Her voice seemed to echo in the sudden quiet. His eyes finally drank her in. She felt pleased, but disconcerted at the same time. There was something in his look she didn't understand.

'I didn't realise I was sleeping in your cabin,' she said, 'and by staying up I left you with nowhere.'

'Oh that.' He shrugged, flicking the blender back on.

She wondered where he'd ended up sleeping. With Rachel? Lila had said they weren't a couple, but Ana knew things in the City weren't as strict as they were in the Community. In the Community everything was black and white. Here, romantic relationships took on shades of grey; they were full of uncertainty, maybes, broken promises.

Ana watched Cole from the corner of her eye, wondering what drove him; what sort of awful things had made him run away from the orphanage and seek refuge in the Project.

Finally he turned off the blender and they could talk again.

'Where did you learn to play piano?' she asked.

'The orphanage.' Cole poured out two glasses of fruit

juice. 'There was an old piano there. I didn't have much else to do and none of the kids had interfaces or pods or anything to play music on, so if I heard something in the street or on the radio, I'd go back and try and work out the notes. By the time I left I could play a bit and then Richard got me my piano.' He gestured to the living room.

Ana rubbed the tight pressure across her chest. She'd had years of lessons. For the last twelve months she'd studied under one of the country's most gifted teachers, yet she was just a mimic. She couldn't even interpret a piece of music, let alone write something. She simply copied others who'd gone before her.

'How much original material have you got?' she asked.

Cole shrugged. 'No idea,' he said. 'Ten or fifteen hours of stuff I guess. Here . . .' He passed her a glass, then took out a roll of paper from his back pocket and laid it flat on the kitchen table. 'These are the admissions to the loony dumps on the night of the concert.'

Still thinking about the unbelievable fact that Cole had ten to fifteen hours of original compositions lying around, Ana struggled with the change of subject.

'Loony dumps?'

'Psych bins . . . They're your best bet.'

She fell silent. Last night she'd accused him of abducting Jasper, and now he was helping her find him. 'Thank you,' she said eventually. She drank her juice slowly, purposefully making herself savour the flavours and not look at Cole. Then she began scanning the sheets of paper.

'Those are all the dumps within a hundred-mile radius of London – a conceivable distance if they were driving,'

Cole said. 'But I think it's best to start closer to home. I've taken a look and I reckon there are two strong probabilities. Here.' He pointed at two names that had been circled. 'They've both got John Doe entries for the night of the concert.'

Ana read the names. St Joseph's in Putney and Three Mills in the East End.

'If we can find out the exact time of admission,' Cole continued, 'then factoring the driving time and the probability that whoever abducted Jasper took him straight there, we might be able to identify where he's being held.'

His music, the vision, and now this. Ana felt baffled.

'Thank you. I—'

Cole nodded, then glanced at his watch. 'I have to go,' he said, finishing his juice in one glug.

'Go?'

'I won't be long.' He gathered up his keys.

'I could help you.'

His blue eyes raked through her. For a moment she didn't quite know who she was. Or rather, she didn't feel like the same person she had been a week ago.

'Help me what?'

'Whatever. I won't get in the way.' She pushed her hands into the back of her jeans.

Cole bit his lip. His gaze became appraising. 'OK,' he said finally.

Her heart leapt. Perhaps she should be trying to stay away from him, but despite how nervous he made her, she didn't want to. A strange feeling sprang up inside her; an

192

instinct she knew she had to follow: as long as she stuck with Cole from now on, everything would work out.

*

They rode to Archway on his beaten-up Yamaha and parked in a pedestrian walkway flanked on either side by a towering maze of council flats. Ana followed Cole up a foul-smelling stairwell to a long corridor with endless blue doors. After a couple of minutes, they passed through a suspended tunnel into another corridor.

Cole knocked at a door with a silver eight tacked over flaky paint, and a white mark where another number had fallen off. After a long wait, a heavy-set woman in a tracksuit answered. She mumbled a greeting and shuffled back to let them in. From the moment they entered, she didn't stop scratching her bloated face. Tufts of hair sprang up from her bald head in patches. Her light-blue eyes were milky and glazed.

Ana felt repelled by the claustrophobic ambience and stuffy smells as she followed Cole into the gloom. A narrow kitchen area lay off the main room to their right. On their left, a miniature archaic television that wasn't even flat flickered. Straight ahead, a door led into the back of the unit. All the curtains were drawn.

The woman scuffed into the kitchen, put on a kettle, twitched and jerked for a moment, then returned to the sofa. Cole, who'd followed her into the kitchen, opened a small window releasing the stale air. Then he took off his black rucksack and began to unpack noodles and rice, tinned fruit and vegetables. He didn't put anything away.

He left it out on the sideboard, replacing a clutter of empty baked-bean tins and soup cartons, which he swept into a plastic bag.

Afterwards, he crossed the living room and checked behind one of the closed curtains. From the front window, he peeled off a Neighbourhood Watch sticker and pressed it on to some material he produced from his jacket pocket. Tucking it away, he looked around as though checking he hadn't forgotten anything.

Sensing they were about to leave, Ana let out her breath and edged towards the front door.

But Cole turned off the telly and crouched before the woman, taking both her hands in his.

'You've got food for the next four days,' he said, trying to fix the woman's attention. After a couple of seconds, she nodded. Cole activated his interface. He held up a piece of white plastic in front of his projection. 'Look,' he said. 'It's Rafferty, he's going to be five soon.' The woman nodded again. Her eyes wandered over Cole's face. He switched to another image.

'Simone's due in three months. Look how big she is.'

'Are they coming?' the woman asked.

'Nate's going to try, when the baby's born.'

'OK,' she said.

Cole nodded, then stood up. 'I'll be back soon.' He leant over and kissed her on the cheek. Then, after a moment, he put his arms around her and pressed his face into her shoulder. She waited for him to finish.

In that motion, as he embraced the woman – his mother – Ana understood something: Cole thought he might not see her again. This business tomorrow night, helping the minister disappear, was more risky than he was letting on.

They left the flat, showing themselves out, and stood in the brick corridor, as though they'd both had the air knocked out of them.

'Your mum?' she asked.

'Yeah. It's the Benzidox. She's been on it for a long time.'

Benzidox. The 'miracle drug' had appeared on the market about fifteen years ago. It reportedly delayed the advent of every diagnosable mental illness and slowed down development of the Big3. It was so effective and so broadly useful, more people took Benzidox than all other medications and anti-depressants put together. And now Novastra were in the middle of negotiating a one-billion pound deal with the government, so they could provide Benzidox free to every Sleeper or Active Big3 under the age of eighteen: BenzidoxKid.

'She seemed . . .' Ana wanted to say 'vacant', but didn't want to offend Cole.

'The drug's got a four- to six-year peak,' he said. 'After that the mind often deteriorates so rapidly it's like it collapses. One day she was there and the next she'd gone.'

A memory flashed over Ana. A green barn door. Car fumes poisoning clean air. Messy morning hair hanging in tangles across her face. Mud seeping up the bottoms of her white pyjamas. A gentle throb of a car engine. Her heart crashing against her chest.

She gasped and doubled over. Her arms flailed the air, searching out an alcove to her left. Reaching it, she vomited. A whiff of urine and sick struck her, making her heave again. Her throat burnt. Her head pounded. She wiped the corner of her mouth with trembling fingers, then stumbled back towards daylight.

In the narrow corridor Cole stared at her, eyes dark with concern.

'What's wrong?' he asked.

'I . . .' Ana shook her head. She held her knuckles against her heart, fearing the stabbing pain would return. 'My mother—' she managed. Her eyes swam with tears. They dropped down her cheeks. She swept them away with her sleeve, but they kept coming. 'My mother was on Benzidox. I remember now. She didn't want to take it. She said it made her feel like the Unliving. But my father, he insisted. He—' she faltered. How had she forgotten all this? 'He ground it up in her food. So she starved herself. For days. At first I tried to sneak her stuff from the kitchen, but my father locked the kitchen door and instead of going back to London, he spent the week working at home. After about four days she came and ate dinner with us. He was pleased. He produced her special plate and watched as she spooned it all in.'

Ana battled to inhale and exhale. Cole stepped towards her. Gently, he put an arm around her back. She leaned in towards him. He smoothed his hand over the tufts of hair at the nape of her neck. A racking sob built deep within. It lashed out from her in uncontrollable spasms. But in spite of the pain, she felt like she was finally being released.

17

Revelations

Jack Dombrant didn't like complications. Nor did he like travelling on the Underground or mixing with the crowds that glutted City high streets. But here he was, stepping out of Camden Tube on foot, into the stench and mayhem of North London, to check out an anonymous tip that Ashby Barber's daughter was staying on a barge in Camden Lock.

Side-skipping a half-crushed carton of puke-coloured noodles, he headed up the main street, sticking as close to the central flow of bicycles and as far from the sprawling market stalls as he could manage without getting run down.

He checked his projected map and turned left down Jamestown Road leading to Gilbey's Yard. Several things irked him, which is why he hadn't told Ashby what he was up to. Ariana Barber was more astute and intelligent than her father gave her credit for. Her composure the morning after Jasper's abduction showed an unusual amount of self-control; a reminder to everyone involved that this was not the first devastating blow life had dealt her. Additionally, she'd been suspicious of Jack, when she should have felt trust.

But Jack hadn't foreseen anything like this. It begged the question, how much did she know? Had they underestimated her relationship with Jasper Taurell? Why the heck would she be sneaking around the City, if she didn't have the faintest inkling of what Jasper had been up to?

It was complicated all right. He didn't like it at all.

Just as the informer had described, Jack found two boats moored a hundred metres up the canal, in the direction of Gilbey's Yard. He strolled towards them, flicking through scenarios, mentally preparing himself for a myriad of possibilities, so he wouldn't be caught off guard.

Bending into the black barge, he scratched fresh mud off the hull. Both boats had recently been moved. The varying watermark striations indicated regular moorings in several different places. Then he noticed the name – a name he'd been chasing for the last four days like an idiot trying to catch his shadow. He might have laughed at himself, if it wasn't for the fact that he'd mentioned 'Enkidu' to Ariana.

From somewhere behind and to the left, gravel crunched underfoot. Jack deducted a short lone male heading towards him from the market. He swivelled to his feet and smiled at the sight of the young man with spiky hair. It felt good to have his powers of deduction proved right time and again. It was one of the things he loved about his job.

'Can I help you with something?' the man asked. Jack had set his interface on profile mode, yet nothing projected on the boy's grey sweater. He glanced at the interface hanging from the boy's neck. The power light shone green. Which meant either the guy had no blog, no face page, no website, no frequently visited sites and no memberships to any online organisation, or he knew one heck of a talented profile blocker.

'I'm looking for a girl,' Jack said amiably. 'Young, five-foot-seven, very attractive. I heard she's staying here.' The boy shrugged as though he didn't know, didn't care.

'Why don't you try Barry's. There's lots of pretty girls there.'

Jack smiled. 'This girl's special,' he said, loading the word 'special' with undertones even someone as unsubtle as this guy wouldn't be able to miss.

The boy's left eye twitched.

'A lot of important people are worried about her. Here.' Jack extracted his hand-sized pad and held it up. 'Perhaps I could show you some video of her. You tell me if she looks familiar.'

Something moved on the red boat. Jack looked up and saw a dark-haired teenager with black lipstick, heavy eye-shadow and bright blue eyes, peering from the wheelhouse. The girl folded her arms across her chest and walked across the rear of the barge. She jumped on to the dock and joined them, never breaking eye contact.

Jack swallowed his annoyance. She was a child, nothing to worry about. He connected his interface to his viewing pad and pulled up the video he'd prepared of Ariana playing piano at last year's school variety concert. As the thirty-second segment began, he noted the girl and the boy's reactions. The boy's level of discomfort instantly rose, but the girl didn't bat an eyelid.

'She looks like a Pure,' the girl said. 'What would someone like her be doing around here?'

Jack's mood darkened. What was it with this assignment and clever young girls who looked deceptively sweet?

'Recognise her?' he asked the boy.

'No.'

'She could have changed her hair, or eye colour, or make-up.'

'I don't recognise her,' the boy answered.

'Because, you see, the problem is, she's supposed to be joinin' with that abducted Oxford student Jasper Taurell in a couple o' weeks and—' The young man flinched. 'And, we think she may have seen somethin', may have information about the abduction, but she's scared of comin' forward.'

The boy's eyes darted from the dark-haired girl to the red barge, then across the towpath and back again.

'Her father, Ashby Barber, is extremely concerned,' Jack continued. Now even the girl paled. Despite Ashby's renown in educated Pure circles, it was surprising to find two young City kids who'd heard of him. Most Sleepers, Carriers and Actives under the age of thirty paid no attention to the news or politics. Half of them couldn't even name the prime minister.

Jack took out his wallet and flashed his badge.

'Can I see some ID?' he said.

The boy swallowed, hands now rigid in his pockets. He blinked, but didn't move, like prey suddenly recognising it's in the sight line of its pursuer. The dark-haired girl handed him her ID stick.

'If this person you're looking for was afraid,' the girl said, 'why wouldn't she go to you, the Wardens? Pures don't exactly hang around in the City, do they?'

Jack felt his patience wear thin. He ignored her question,

flashed the girl's ID in front of his interface and examined her details.

Lila Aimes. Born October 2026. Fifteen years old. Daughter of Simon Aimes, 54 years old, whereabouts unknown, and Jennifer Winter, 47 years old, 84 Burbary Estate, Archway.

Jack stared at the data, scarcely believing the coincidence. He'd installed a hidden surveillance camera at that address only last month when it had come to light that the Secretary of State for Trade and Industry could no longer be trusted. The minister visited the Archway estate weekly. Jack hadn't paid it too much attention; he'd thought the Secretary was simply paying an old debt – his son had killed the woman's husband in a drunk-driving accident twenty years ago. But maybe there was more to it than that. If these people were connected to the Secretary of State for Trade and Industry for other reasons, this went beyond complicated. The Secretary and Jasper Taurell were the Pure Protection Unit's prime concerns right now, and Ariana was linked to both of them. Ashby would be furious if his daughter had discovered what Jasper was involved in.

Lila Aimes had no judicial or psychiatric history. Jack thrust her ID back at her.

'Yours?' he said, glowering at the boy.

The boy's gaze snapped forward from somewhere off to the left. He'd been looking at something. For a fraction of a second, there'd been fear in his eyes. Jack turned. A pregnant girl waddled towards them. Jack scanned the boy's ID, keeping an eye on the latest arrival.

> Nate Winter, born January 2020, twenty-one. Son of
> Samuel Winter, deceased, and Jennifer Winter, 47 years
> old, 84 Burbary Estate, Archway.

So the dark-haired girl and this boy were half-brother and sister. Unlike his sister, however, what followed the boy's headers looked like a dissertation on a dysfunctional childhood in the system. Taken away from his mother by the health services when he was fifteen months old; moved foster care homes three times before he was six; ended up in an orphanage before his seventh birthday. Six months later, he disappeared. The authorities had him filed under missing persons until four years ago, when he applied for official ID and declared the birth of a son, followed by his marriage to Simone Janet April.

Out of the corner of his eye, Jack saw the pregnant girl veer away from them. Nate Winter was signalling her with his eyes.

'Excuse me,' Jack called. The girl ground to a halt. Nate and his half-sister froze. Jack strolled over to the boy's wife.

'Six months? Seven?' he asked smiling. The girl's hand moved over her stomach.

'Six,' she said.

'You're carrying it low. Looks like another boy.' He paused. 'Strange, I just checked your husband's ID and it didn't come up that you were expecting another child. Can I see the pregnancy permit?'

The girl twisted her plain silver wedding ring, which sat tight around her bloated fingers. She didn't deny she was Nate Winter's wife. *Spot-on as usual*, Jack thought.

202

'I . . . er . . .' She blew her fringe and flipped open her shoulder bag. Practically dipping her head inside it, she rummaged through the contents. Meanwhile, Nate and his sister approached.

'What seems to be the problem?' Nate said.

'Your ID doesn't show you have a second child registered,' Jack replied. 'Your wife is just looking for the permit.'

Nate gazed at Jack evenly.

'It's on the boat,' he said. 'Why don't you wait here, while I find it?'

'Sure.' Jack nodded.

Nate strutted towards the boat moored alongside *Enkidu*. The girls backed away. Jack didn't fancy his chances of getting out of there unscathed if he pushed any harder. He needed back-up. He needed concrete confirmation that Ariana was with these people. And then he'd figure out how they were connected to Jasper Taurell and the Secretary of State for Trade and Industry.

Pretending to receive a call on his interface, he plugged in an earphone and hand gestured picking up. 'Yes . . . ? Yes . . . Straightaway.'

'Looks like we've found the girl elsewhere,' he said to Nate's sister and the pregnant girl. 'I apologise for bothering you.' He arranged the pad in its leather case and slipped it into the inner pocket of his jacket. 'You make sure you sort out the permit, though. Home births are dangerous, and you'll need it to be accepted into any hospital.'

He smiled and turned towards the warehouses, stretching out his awareness behind him in an effort to discern whether Nate was following.

*

After leaving Cole's mother, Ana and Cole rode a short distance to Tufnell Park. Ana waited with the bike, while Cole vanished into a town house and emerged several minutes later apologising for having left her on her own.

'I thought we could go and get a coffee before we go back,' he said. 'If you're up for it.'

Ana nodded. 'I'd like that.' She felt drained and wanted to recharge before she faced anyone else.

They headed in the direction of Camden, turned right off a long road and travelled west, weaving through the backstreets. Cole drove slowly even where the roads weren't crowded. Exhausted, Ana rested her head on his shoulder, aware of the exact places their bodies met and breathing in the smell of soap and summer on his jacket. He hadn't said anything, but she knew he understood the guilt and the helplessness which would stay with her always.

They pulled up at a huge round monument constructed from antique brick. Cole cut the engine.

'Here we are,' he said, nodding at the building. A glass, rectangular extension jutted out from the sandy-coloured structure. The three-storey addition bore scruffy letters on the windows. 'The Roundhouse', Ana read.

'Long, long time ago it was a steam-engine repair shed,' Cole said, alighting. He reached out to help her down. As her hand slipped into his a hot shiver flushed through her.

She pulled away, wondering why she couldn't control the way her body reacted to him.

'Where do you get the petrol from?' she asked, trying to cover up her embarrassment.

'Actually, it's ethanol, a form of alcohol. They make small amounts of it in the Project from overripe fruit. A few modifications to the bike and I don't even have to mix it with petrol.'

'Really?'

'Sure. If you know what you're doing there are several ways around the petrol issue. For example, you can make a diesel car engine run on pure vegetable oils . . . Smells like someone's having a fry up.' He grinned. She smiled back, her embarrassment almost forgotten. They pushed through the glass doors and entered a large reception area. A girl behind the counter batted her eyelashes at Cole.

'This the latest one, then?' she asked, flicking a fake smile in Ana's direction. 'She looks younger than your sister.'

Ana grew self-conscious again. Staring at her pumps, she tucked her hands in her pockets.

Cole ignored the girl's innuendos. 'Is Rob around?'

'No, but you can wait for him upstairs till he gets back.'

Placing his hand on the centre of Ana's back, Cole guided her to an arched doorway. She lengthened her step to break contact. *You have to stop thinking of him like that*, she warned herself.

'Denise is rehearsing,' the receptionist called after them. 'Sure she'd *love* to see you.'

Denise . . . Rachel . . . Apart from the fact that Cole was clearly the kind of guy who played the field, he was also involved in the Enlightenment Project and followed a mystic shaman, whose vision had him doing God-knew-what in the future. Besides, she had Jasper. Once Jasper was free, he would need to go away until the evidence against the Pure tests was in the public hands. She would go with him; support him. Perhaps they'd return to the farmhouse where she'd lived as a child.

Resolving to keep her distance from Cole, Ana strode ahead through the arched corridor.

'You all right?' he asked as they entered a circular room with six arched corridors leading off it.

'Fine.'

'This way.' He took the lead. Ana followed him down a brick passage, nerves tightening around her insides. She needed to remain on guard. It wasn't normal the way Cole had managed to penetrate her defences in such a short period of time.

He opened a door into a white area with a glass desk, huge flatscreen, microphones and recording equipment. She paused on the threshold.

'We can go if you want,' he said.

'I didn't know this sort of place still existed,' she said looking around in amazement. 'I thought with the record companies all bankrupt, recording studios were a thing of the past and everyone did this sort of thing on their interfaces.'

'Nope, there are still a few places like this hidden around London. There'll always be a market for good music.'

'I suppose. So this is where you record your stuff?'

'Not the classical. Just the fusion bits and pieces I'm working on.' He vanished into one of the tiny side rooms. Ana peered around the corner. A kettle, cups and instant coffee were set up on a low shelf. He shook the kettle. Water sloshed against the plastic sides. He plugged it in and flicked the button. 'Would you like to hear something?'

She nodded. *Not a good idea.* She folded her arms across her chest. *It's just music*, she argued with herself. *I think I'm capable of resisting him, even if he is a musical genius.*

Cole showed her to a swivel chair in front of a dark panel. As he booted up his interface, the computer synced with the desk and the panel began to glow. A spectrum of colour projected from it, like a foot-wide, foot-deep and five-foot-across rainbow. She inhaled sharply. It was beautiful.

'You can virtually do everything on this,' he said. 'Composing, mixing . . . Use your hands to blend the colours and shape the notes.'

Ana gazed at the machine, stunned. She'd never seen anything like it.

He put the chain of his interface around her neck. The rough pads of his fingers grazed her bare skin. She flushed. From now on, she thought, they should definitely avoid touching. The effect it had on her was far too disturbing.

He began arranging giant earphones on her head.

'I'll do it.'

He backed off. 'OK, you're all set. Have a go.'

She dipped her hand into a haze of dense blue light and the colour around her fingers rippled like water. A deep discordant jumble of notes resounded in her ears. She smiled, tried stroking a finger down and to the left, as though plucking a harp. A rich bass G vibrated. Intrigued, she placed her other hand in a band of sparkling red and purple. A dark swirl of sound crashed in her headphones. Carefully, she spiralled one of her fingers in the crimson air. An electronic pulse began to loop back on itself.

Cole appeared next to her with two steaming mugs. She pulled the headphones half back from her ears.

'It's amazing,' she said. His eyes sparkled, reflecting her enthusiasm. 'How does it work?'

He set down the mugs and angled in beside her. 'Each strip of colour does something different. But it's also kind of organic. It adapts to the way you play. You can't just learn it technically, you have to feel it. Here,' he said. Gently, he placed her hand on top of his. 'Follow what I do.'

So much for not touching.

She attempted to flow with the diving and weaving of his fingers, relaxing her body as far as it was possible in such close proximity to him.

'Close your eyes,' he said. 'Don't try to make anything happen. Just go with it.'

At first there was so much extraneous noise, she couldn't be sure 'Second Sight' lay beneath it all. But as her movements tuned into Cole's, his melody took shape, sculpted by their hands from a sea of colour.

Her breathing became erratic. The hairs on her arms stood up. An ominous electronic shudder appeared beneath the notes. She wondered what was causing it and, in a sudden flash of understanding, realised it was her. Her hands were shaking.

She opened her eyes and snatched back her arm.

'Sorry, I . . .' She blundered to her feet, sidestepping away. 'I guess I'm still shaken up about my mum.' Things between her and Jasper were confused, complicated, but they were still technically bound. She shouldn't be here like this with Cole.

'You look pale. Can I get you something? Water?'

Ana shook her head, 'I think I just need to lie down. I haven't been sleeping well recently.'

'I'll take you back to the boat,' Cole said. 'We can listen to the fusion stuff another time.'

She smiled weakly. It might help if he wasn't so damn understanding. Avoiding his gaze, she waited for him at the edge of the room while he drained and washed their mugs.

As they strode down the corridor back towards the reception, she began to feel silly. She'd totally overreacted. Nothing was going on between them. Cole wasn't interested in some innocent Pure girl who was six years younger than him and had no idea what she was doing.

18

Betrayal

Ten minutes later they were back on *Enkidu*. Ana followed Cole down the hatch, desperate now to lie down. So much had happened in the last twenty-four hours, she was floundering mentally to keep up. Stress and exhaustion were probably intensifying the muddled and overwhelming sensations she was having around Cole. She needed sleep. She needed time to recover and reorientate herself.

Stepping off the ladder, she saw Nate, Simone, Rachel and Lila standing shoulder to shoulder, facing the hatch.

'What's going on?' Cole asked. His voice made her snap to attention. He sounded way too calm, almost icy.

Ana frowned at Lila in an unspoken question. Their eyes met momentarily, before Lila tilted her head away.

'The Wardens came here looking for *her*,' Nate said, jabbing a finger in Ana's direction. 'That's what's going on.'

Heat spread over Ana's face and down her neck. The Wardens had found her!

'When?' Cole asked.

'She's Ashby Barber's daughter,' Nate growled.

'He doesn't care,' Rachel said.

Ana looked pleadingly at Lila, but Lila avoided her gaze.

Cole reached for her hand and drew her towards the kitchen.

'Get your stuff together,' he said.

Nate blocked their way. 'She's not going anywhere until we know what she's up to.'

'I'm going to get her somewhere safe,' Cole said. 'She needs our help.'

'She's Ashby Barber's daughter,' Nate spat. 'Ashby Barber. The man who practically invented the Pure test. The man who's helped this government make unthinking morons out of half the population. What, she's just turned up here by coincidence? I don't think so.'

'There are no coincidences,' Cole said.

Ana's insides prickled at his tone and intensity. It reminded her of Lila's talk of bigger plans. Cole didn't believe she was part of a bigger plan too, did he?

'Don't give me that bollocks,' Nate said. 'What's she doing here?'

'She's looking for Jasper Taurell,' Cole said.

'Well, why did she come to us?'

'She knew about Spike getting bagged by the Psych Watch the morning Jasper met him to give him the disc. She came here looking for me.'

'For all we know, Jasper Taurell was a set-up to weed out guys like you and Spike. I mean who's actually seen this evidence?' Nate shoved a finger into Cole's chest. 'You knew about her yesterday, didn't you? That's why she bolted outside the courthouse. You should have told us who she was.'

'I didn't know she was Ashby Barber's daughter until last night and I didn't mention it, cos for some reason I didn't

211

think you'd take it that well. And I might remind you that without her, I'd still be inside.'

'It was probably a set-up,' Rachel jumped in. 'A way of getting us to trust her and let her stay. How much have you told her about tomorrow night?'

Cole gave Rachel the full force of his laser-sharp attention. 'You shouldn't have tipped off the Wardens,' he said.

Nate's eyes twitched. He cocked his head towards Rachel. 'What?'

'Why do you think they came here?' Cole asked.

'You told them?' Nate shouted at Rachel. 'Are you insane? That foreign geezer asked for a pregnancy permit! I was thinking I was going to have to find someone to do him in!'

Ana felt a slap of shock. It wasn't just any old Warden who had been snooping around. Jack Dombrant had been here. Had he seen "Enkidu" written on the side of the boat? He'd come looking for her, but what did he know about Jasper's abduction? Was he involved?

'Listen,' Simone said. 'We all need to stay focused. Let's not forget what we're doing. We have a real chance of stirring up enough public outcry that they'll have to open an enquiry into the Pure test.' Her hand moved over her large belly and stayed there. 'I'm sorry, Cole,' she said, 'but she's high risk. We need to keep her under close watch until after tomorrow night, then get her as far away from us all as possible.'

'She's part of this,' Cole said firmly.

'Be reasonable,' Simone said. 'She could be spying and informing on you.'

'This isn't a group decision. Ariana's coming with me. I'll keep her safe.'

'What will happen to her when you go off tomorrow night?' Lila asked. It was the first time she'd spoken and there was something strange about her voice. Ana could hear the hurt, yes, but something else too.

'I'll only be gone a couple of hours.'

'Something could go wrong,' Lila said. 'You could be delayed. I think she should go to the Project.'

'The Project!' Nate scoffed. 'They won't let her in.'

'I think they will,' Lila said. 'Richard spoke about her too.'

Rachel huffed and stormed from the cabin.

Ana froze. *Oh my God*, she thought. *They think I'm part of some Glimpse into the future where Cole will heal the world.*

Cole chewed the side of his lip, considering.

'You may be right,' he said to Lila. 'OK. We'll go to the Project. In fact, I think we should all go. The Wardens will come back here and try to apply pressure. It'll be the safest place for all of us right now. You two always planned to go back there to have the baby.'

Simone looked at Nate. As he met her gaze, his eyes softened. She nodded. He took her hand and helped her up the ladder.

'Right, we'd better get moving,' Cole said. Ana didn't budge. Mentally she was still at the precipice looking into the abyss. She wanted to trust Cole, but an uneasy, creepy feeling roiled inside her. Growing up in the Community, the evil camp beyond the wall had been like the bogeyman – sinister, dangerous, terrifying. What if her illness had activated? What if all this was some complex hallucination and she was about to voluntarily enter the Project to save herself when actually it was tantamount to suicide?

'Ariana?'

'I can't,' she said. 'I'm sorry.' The puzzlement in Cole's eyes for some reason saddened her. She dropped her gaze. 'I have to find Jasper.'

'I know a guy in the Project who should be able to hack into the psych rehab home records.'

Ana shook her head. 'I know you're trying to help, but I can't go to the Enlightenment Project. Your vision . . . your Glimpse . . . you believe in higher plans and I – I don't.' There was a pause. Cole turned and stared at his sister.

'I told her what a Glimpse was,' Lila said, 'I didn't . . .'

'OK,' Cole said to Ana. Their eyes locked. The turmoil deep inside Ana was growing unstable, threatening to break through her years of carefully mastered composure. 'Let's forget the Project.'

'Hang on—' Lila objected.

'No,' Cole said. 'I agree Nate, Simone and Rafferty should go, but I won't take Ariana against her will. You can go back to the Project with them or you can come with us. Up to you.'

Lila glowered at her brother.

'Let's get moving,' Cole said, turning his back on her.

*

Ana waited on deck as Lila and Cole packed clothes, food, cooking utensils and sleeping bags. She shifted her tote bag on her shoulder, keeping a look-out for Warden Dombrant

214

and regretting the way Cole had looked at her when she'd told him she didn't believe in his Glimpse. But she'd only spoken the truth. And she was not going to let them all be misled into thinking she was some sort of sign or saint sent to help their cause.

After a few minutes, Lila and Cole appeared, hauling camping rucksacks up the hatch. They crossed the deck and threw their bags on to the bank. While Cole secured the hatch, Lila jumped aboard Nate's boat and vanished into the wheelhouse. Ana gazed down at the dirty water. Metal clanked against metal, then a hammer banged as Cole tacked lightweight boards over the Perspex windows. Lila returned just as he was finishing. Without speaking, the three of them disembarked.

Cole removed the gangplank and dropped it in the lock. It hit the water with a slap. Ana watched it sink with a sense of regret. She'd driven them from their home. Cole and Lila had gone out of their way to help her and yet she didn't trust them enough to follow them into the Project.

Cole chained his motorbike, covered it with tarpaulin, and he and Lila set off down the towpath without looking back. Ana caught up. They headed east along the waterway, passing beneath the busy markets and following the weave of the river until they cut north through a block of flats, a playground, and a park. They came out on a narrow street and turned left down an alley that led to Camden Road station. At the ticket machine, Lila slotted in her ID and purchased three tickets. Then they stood on the platform until the next southbound train arrived.

The journey to Forest Hill in South-East London was

agonisingly slow. There were lengthy waits for the electric, crowded trains. They had to change three times and the silence between them grew leaden, until it was impenetrable. Most of the time, Cole stood apart from the girls, making calls and sending interface messages. The rattle of the train drowned his voice. Once or twice, Lila attempted to smile at Ana, but the strain and sense of disillusionment in her eyes only made Ana feel worse.

Ana decided to risk powering up her interface for the three seconds it would take to switch offline. Undoubtedly the Wardens would have her tagged; they'd receive a flutter of activity somewhere between Shadwell and Wapping. But she couldn't take any more of the heavy silence. Besides, Warden Dombrant would already know she was on the move. A train in east London wouldn't help him find her.

Offline, she selected a compilation of Chopin and Schumann and let her head drop back against the seat. Jumbled images filled her mind. Her thoughts drifted, and she found herself back in the Barbican car park where she'd looked for Jasper after the concert.

Water dribbled down the walls. A strange light pulsed. She tried to lift her feet, but slime pulled at her shoes. At once, she realised she wasn't alone. A shadow moved, pulling itself inwards, gathering up the darkness like folds of cloth. From its inky centre a figure emerged. Ana gazed at the dark holes where eyes should have been. Glacial terror spread through her. She was being attacked by zombies!

Frantically, she began running for an exit. All around her shadows amassed themselves into black doorways for zombies to step through. The first creature closed in on Ana. Throbbing light sent forks of pain into her head. Her dream self cried out for Cole. At the same time, her head knocked against the train window.

She blinked awake. They were clattering over a bumpy part of the tracks. Chopin's 'Goutte d'eau' floated through her earphones. Beyond the window, rows of squat houses flew past, their narrow backyards overgrown or deluged with junk.

'We're there,' Cole said. Ana looked up and gulped in his presence with an uncomfortable mixture of relief and self-consciousness. Opposite her, Lila stood up. The train crawled into Forest Hill station and they alighted.

A simple portico lined the station building on the platform side. Hanging baskets dangled from the shelter, their plastic flowers so old, the greens and reds had faded and ripped. They crossed a footbridge and came out on a busy street. It was almost six o'clock. Vendors had begun packing up their stalls and people hurried home. Ana trudged behind Cole and Lila, vaguely taking in the disorderly array of Victorian and Georgian houses on either side, sprinkled with modern, concrete architecture. The uphill hike tired her, but at least it was something to focus on; something to distract her from Cole's broody reticence.

Finally, they veered into a driveway, climbed three steps, and knocked at a 1930s house that had been divided into a dozen flats.

The front door opened at once. They were ushered into darkness and the door closed behind them. In the glimmer of candlelight, a man led them past stairs and through a second door. He bustled them into a room and went around lighting other candles to reveal a ten-foot-square bedroom with two single beds, a dresser, and a wardrobe. A faint pink glow from the sun sinking on the horizon spilt around the closed curtains. Cole slipped the man cash and told him they were expecting someone. Then he closed and locked the door, and the three of them were alone.

The absence of conversation compounded the bleakness of their surroundings. The dream Ana had had on the train came snaking into her thoughts. She thought of yesterday afternoon, running from the courthouse. She wondered again at the zombie people, at what might have happened if Cole hadn't arrived when he did.

Lila began to scour the wardrobe, which took her all of a minute because it was small and empty. Cole unpacked a camping stove, a pan and some tins of food.

'That's a waste of fuel,' Lila said when she saw her brother intended to heat up their supper.

'Tomorrow night you'll be in the Project,' he said. 'You won't need to worry about fuel.'

'What about Ariana?' she asked.

Ana plumped down on the corner of a springy bed and looked at Cole, curious to hear his answer.

'Hopefully we'll know where Jasper is by then, and she'll be talking to his father about getting him somewhere safe.' He twisted a metal opener across a giant tin of beans.

She wondered if he really believed that. She felt strangely empty at the notion of making contact with Jasper's parents. And now she was uncertain whether Jasper's father would be willing to wage war for a son who'd jeopardised his own empire – without scientific evidence of mental disease, many people would stop their preventative and prescriptive medications and Novastra would lose millions.

But she would have to go back and explain everything to them in the hope that Jasper's mother could convince her husband to save their son. She would have to face her father and answer everybody's questions. She wondered what would happen if once Jasper was released, he confronted Ashby with the evidence. What would her father do? After all, it was his research, his reputation that was on the line.

Lila's angry voice broke through her ruminations. 'Don't say that!' she hissed.

Ana wondered what she'd missed.

'The future isn't written,' Cole answered. He poured sloppy orange beans into a pan. 'That's the point. A Glimpse is just a possibility.'

'The most likely possibility,' Lila argued.

'A possibility,' Cole said.

'But everything—'

'No.' Anger lined Cole's voice. The conversation was over. Inwardly, Ana shrunk, not quite understanding why. She didn't like being the cause of Cole's bad mood. And she felt guilty. He'd been supportive and helpful. She missed the closeness she'd felt with him earlier that afternoon after visiting his mother's, even if it had been unnerving – the way he'd held her.

'Yesterday, after the hearing,' she said, changing the subject, hoping to ease the tension, 'when you picked me up on your bike, who were those people?'

Cole shook his head, evidently not in the mood to talk about it.

'What people?' Lila asked.

'When I discovered Cole had been following me the night Jasper was abducted,' Ana explained, 'it scared me. So I ran away and wound up in this street where all these zombie people were coming out of the houses.'

'Arashans?!' Lila gasped. Her head whipped across to Cole, then back. 'You walked into a street of Arashans and managed to leave?'

'What are Arashans?'

'They're an army experiment,' Lila said.

'Nobody knows exactly,' Cole said.

'There's something transmitted in the air where they live,' Lila ran on, 'that immobilises thought and movement. After living with it for a while, the person can act and think again, but they're disconnected, slow, dreamy. The experiments are being run by a special Psych Watch unit.'

'Nobody knows exactly,' Cole repeated. 'It could be some type of new drug that makes them like that.' He lit the portable stove with a match and set the pan on the metal ring. The flame danced beneath it.

'There's tons of stuff about it on the net,' Lila said breathlessly. 'There are documents suggesting that the government has pumped millions into financing a new army 'peace' weapon. They say the Board plans to use it in the loony dumps too.'

'There were four guys that didn't look affected at all,' Ana said.

'I bet they were wearing hats, right?'

Ana thought back and remembered they had, in fact, been hooded.

Lila took her silence as a yes. 'They have some special kind of deflector that goes over the brain and stops the electromagnetic waves.'

Cole pretended to concentrate on their dinner, but in the dim light of the candles Ana could see his interest rising.

'Cole and I both went in and out of the street,' she said, 'and nothing happened. So it can't be anything to do with wavelengths.'

Cole stopped stirring the beans. 'Actually,' he said, 'I didn't enter.'

'Yes, you did.'

'No, not past the posts.'

'What posts?' Ana asked.

'There were two grey posts at either side of the road. Like lampposts without the lamps.'

Ana tried to think back but couldn't remember them. 'Well,' she said, 'I walked about two hundred metres up the street and nothing happened to me.'

Lila pulled the key on her necklace back and forth across its chain. 'Whatever they transmit,' she said, 'it makes thinking like trying to wade through treacle. And it disables the body's motor-cortex.'

'Didn't you notice anything odd at all?' Cole asked. Ana began to feel uneasy. She didn't like the way he was looking at her, but at least he was talking to her again.

'The street felt emptier than it should have done,' she said. 'There were no cars. Then I noticed a man in a window. He gave me the creeps. So I turned around and started to make my way back.'

'You didn't feel any desire to, I don't know, to stay?' Cole asked.

'No way. Did you?'

He observed her for a beat then puffed air through his nose and returned to stirring the beans and buttering bread.

'You felt it, didn't you?' Lila asked her brother. 'Even from behind the posts it was trying to lock you down!' Cole didn't answer. Ana's mind began to buzz. She thought of the zombie eyes, the sensation she had even now that they were still looking into her mind. How come she hadn't been affected?

Neither Lila nor Cole said anything more.

After they'd eaten, Lila rose to wash up. Ana, anxious about remaining alone with Cole, offered to help. Using a candle to light their way, they left the bedroom and passed through a door on their right. It led down a cobalt-blue corridor to a second, open door.

In the bathroom, Lila rinsed the plates, using the water sparingly. She chatted as she did so.

'Once,' she said, 'a house like this would have been for one family. Then maybe eighty years ago each floor was divided into flats. And now every room is a separate unit and everybody has to share a bathroom. I suppose the whole housing crash wouldn't have been so bad if it weren't for the petrol crisis. Only a small percentage of the railways had already switched to electrical so commuting to the City

222

became impossible from certain areas. Did they teach you about the 2018 Collapse in the Community?'

'I'm sorry,' Ana cut in.

Lila stopped the running tap. 'Sorry?'

'We only met in Camden Lock that day because I was looking for Cole. I thought he was an ex-member of the Enlightenment Project and that he could help me find Jasper. When Mickey told me there was a free room on a barge, I took it hoping to get closer to you all, and I helped you with Cole's pre-charge detention because I thought he'd be able to give me inside information about the Project.'

'It's OK. You got Cole off. You saved Rafferty. Besides you could hardly say, "Hi, I'm Ariana Barber, my father's the mad scientist responsible for the Pure tests and I'm looking for the Pure guy that was abducted yesterday".'

'Thanks,' Ana said. A lump of anxiety inside her softened. 'I prefer Ana.'

Lila nodded. 'No problem.' She scrubbed a plate and put it on the side beside the bath to dry. 'Are you in love with Jasper?' she asked.

Ana swallowed. Out of habit, she lifted her arms to pull back her long hair and found it all had been cut off. 'When I was eleven I thought Jasper was the most amazing boy I'd ever met. I barely knew him, but I daydreamed about him all the time.' She laughed at herself, then picked up a tea towel. Lila handed her another washed plate and she began to dry. 'I used to secretly watch the stars at night from my window and wish that I would have my chance – that he wouldn't be joined before I turned fifteen. And then

223

on my fifteenth birthday he sent me a binding invitation. I thought my dream was coming true. Three weeks later the Board came to my school and told me I wasn't Pure. It was like my world had been blown to pieces and nothing could make it right again. Not even Jasper.'

Ana leant back on the edge of the bath, brushed a hand up the back of her neck. 'After that everything got complicated. I was suspended from school until my father's investigation had been concluded and a fortnight later, Jasper's brother died. It was all a mess. And the only way to fix it was to bind with Jasper and hope he'd want to join with me. I stopped knowing what I wanted after that.'

'Perhaps it wasn't meant to be,' Lila said.

'I don't believe in destiny. I don't believe something's meant to be or not meant to be.'

Lila put aside her scrubbing brush and smiled. 'What about Cole?'

A prickly sensation rolled across the inside of Ana's stomach. 'What about him?'

'He's been waiting for you.'

'What do you mean?'

'The Glimpse!' Lila said, as though it was obvious. 'He never said it,' she continued, grabbing Ana's hands in her own wet ones, 'but I know you're the reason he left the Project and got into all this political stuff in the first place. And then six months ago he came back from visiting Richard in prison and it was like he began preparing for you. He knew the time of the Glimpse was catching up with him. He split up with Rachel and took on more risky assignments because he knew you had something to do with disproving the Pure tests.'

Ana's heart skipped in her chest. Her grip on the plates turned slippery. 'He knew I had something to do with disproving the Pure tests? What are you talking about? Cole told me he didn't know who my father was. He told me he didn't even know I was going to be bound to Jasper until he saw us together at the concert. And what's this got to do with him splitting up with Rachel?'

'Don't you feel it even a little bit?'

'Feel what?'

'The connection between you and Cole.'

Ana put down the plate she'd dried three or four times over. It clattered as it hit the shelf by the sink. Was *that* why her body felt so out of control around him? She'd always been attracted to Jasper, but with Cole it was like being with an oppositely charged magnet. A force she couldn't resist drew her to him. But he was so cool and calm around her. Surely if he felt the same way, she would know?

'What happened in this vision? What did Cole see?'

'I don't really know. You should ask him.'

Ana blew air through her nose and shook her head. If the Board heard them talking like this there wouldn't be any need for creative or free-association tests; they'd both be certified Active.

'Did you ever have the Pure test, Lila?'

'Sure, I lived with my mum until Cole left the Project four years ago. You had to have it to go to school. They did it when I was five, around the time the whole country was getting it done.'

225

'And?'

Lila shrugged. 'No idea. School put it on their files. My mother burnt my envelope without opening it.'

Ana felt as though there was a glitch in time. For a moment, everything seemed to freeze. Her own life had been ruined by a test that meant nothing to Lila.

'You decide who you are, Ana,' Lila said gently. 'Not some test.'

Ana's lower lip began to quiver. Was that really how it was for them? Could it be like that for her?

Lila stacked the washed plates and cutlery. She smiled warmly, then shook her head and slunk into the corridor.

Ana thumbed hot wax dripping from the candle on the bath ledge. Lila's claim that Cole had seen her in a vision and had been waiting for her was absurd. Impossible. But a week ago, everything about her life now would have seemed impossible too – she'd never have believed Jasper could be in a psych dump for trying to expose the Pure tests as phony. She'd never have believed that Crazies from the Enlightenment Project would be helping her to find him or that she could feel incomprehensibly, wonderfully, dangerously drawn to someone the way she was to Cole. He made her feel as though until now she'd only been living half a life. It wasn't anything like her crush on Jasper – Jasper had been a fantasy; like falling for a movie star, when what you'd really fallen for was the character the actor was playing. But Cole was real, solid. He made her want to explode out of herself, let go of everything she'd held back for so long.

She ran the bath tap. Steam drifted off the water. She

vaguely wondered how much it might cost to have a hot bath. Picking up the candle, she rose and went to find out. As she walked down the corridor, she heard the front door slam. From back in their bedroom, Lila's voice penetrated the walls.

'She's confused. You can't give it to her! She doesn't know who she is.'

'Stop it, Lila.'

'You can't!'

Ana reached the bedroom door and paused on the threshold. Cole and Lila fell silent.

'Give me what?'

'This.' Cole slotted a mini-disc into the side of his interface. He walked over to her and put his interface chain over her head. She swallowed, steeling herself to look at him. But when she did, the expression in his eyes made her forget her awkwardness. What he was giving her had something to do with Jasper. She could sense it. Cole continued to go out of his way to help, despite the fact it never seemed to be what he wanted.

'Have you looked at it?' she asked.

He shook his head. 'It's just been dropped off.'

Ana set down the candle on the mantelpiece and turned to face the wall. Projected in front of her was a copy of the London Mental Rehab Home admission records for the evening of March 21st and early hours of the following morning.

'We've managed to get more details from eleven institutions in the London area,' Cole said. 'Not just the names,

227

but exact times they were signed in, who signed them in and what they were diagnosed with on admission.'

Ana searched the entries looking for the John Does Cole had mentioned before – there had been two the night of Jasper's abduction, one at St Joseph's in Putney and one at Three Mills in the East End. The St Joseph's John Doe had been signed in at 8.44 p.m. *Too early*, she thought. She skipped over the rest of the submission data – 'Last Name, First Name, Legal status of admission, Date, Time, Diagnosis impression at admission, Doctor Admitting patient' – down to the information from Three Mills. As she did so, she noticed that nine admissions for St Joseph's had all been signed off by the same doctor, which was odd because most institutions had at least half a dozen psychiatrists attached to them, to say nothing of the fact that the admission process was supposed to take at least an hour.

In the silence, she could hear Cole's soft breathing. He read over her shoulder. His closeness was like heat from a fire. She thought of Lila's claim. He must have seen her in one of those awful news headlines three years ago, and her face had subconsciously stuck and melded over time with a girl he'd had in some vivid hallucination as a teenager. But why did she feel such a pull? Like he was the moon and she was the sea.

She inhaled deeply and returned her focus to the admissions list. The Three Mills John Doe had been signed in at 7.07 p.m. while she and Jasper were still at the concert.

Cole took back his interface and studied the list again, systematically crossing off names. He quickly covered the forty-or-so entries and by the end there were only five left un-struck. He looked over at her, cocking an eyebrow.

'It seems the insane keep office hours,' he said. 'Look, out of forty-three admissions here, only five happened between 9.15 p.m. and 7 a.m. the next morning.' Ana moved closer, noticing his fingers, the strength in his hands as he gestured to his interface projection. The first admission that hadn't been ruled out was for a psych dump in Barnet. The admission time was 9.19 p.m. That would have given the abductors less than thirty minutes to get out of the Barbican, travel fifteen miles north to Barnet and get Jasper signed into the hospital. Even with clear roads it was unlikely, if not impossible.

Cole scrolled down the page to St Lazareth's in Elephant and Castle.

'This time is feasible,' he said.

Ana shook her head, acutely aware of the way her body angled towards his. 'The diagnosis is "Undifferentiated schizophrenia and psychoneurotic depressive reaction".'

'You what?' Lila said. 'What would that be when it's at home?'

'It's as complicated as it sounds. But for our purposes, it means the guy must have been admitted voluntarily. If Jasper was supposedly voluntary, he'd have been drugged or unconscious and incapable of answering any questions. Because if he wasn't drugged he'd have been labelled with paranoid persecution disorder, or something along those lines. Not schizophrenic and depressive.'

'These next two are female,' Cole said. He scrolled past

them, to stop on the only one remaining: Scott Rutherford; 11.05 p.m.; admitted to Three Mills.

The diagnostic impression was schizophrenic with grandiose persecution disorder; admission involuntary. That made sense. If Jasper had been struggling against his admission, if he was trying to convince the assisting psychiatrist of the truth – there were always two present to sign in any admission – then this could easily be a preliminary diagnosis.

If she had managed to acquire fake ID so easily, she imagined the Wardens or whoever had incarcerated Jasper could have done the same. Skimming along the rest of the admission details, her gaze settled on the psychiatrists' signatures at the end.

Her heart bumped to a stop. The room swam before her eyes. She reached out to steady herself on the bed's footboard, but missed and plunged towards blackness, reality shredding around her.

Milliseconds later she regained consciousness. She lay on the floor not moving. Lila panicked. Cole lifted her up and drew her limbs into him, so her head lounged against his chest.

'I'm fine,' she murmured.

'Get some water,' Cole said to his sister.

'I'm absolutely fine.'

Cole and Lila fussed until Ana forced herself to sit up and told them to leave her alone. She spent the next hour by the curtained window, watching the twilight turn to dusk, dusk to night, staring at the driveway and the street beyond. Cole and Lila packed away the remains of supper, pushed the beds together – Ana would sleep on one side, Lila in the middle, Cole on the other side. They cast furtive glances in her direction, which she felt rather than saw and wholly ignored. She thought of nothing; her father's signature had burnt a hole through her mind.

19

Three Mills

Hours later, Ana woke with a start to find the numbness had passed, replaced by an intense headache. She rolled off the edge of her bed and crept to the window. Outside, the world had spun into the deepest centre of night. Nothing moved in the pitch blackness.

Still dressed in jeans and one of Lila's borrowed T-shirts, she slipped on her pumps, pulled Cole's brown jumper over her head and borrowed his puffa jacket. She lit a candle and tiptoed towards the door.

The corridors between their room and the steps outside were frozen and eerie. She fumbled for the latches, leaving both doors resting against their locks so she could get back in. The crisp air burnt her throat as she crept out into the night.

On the porch, she gazed at the stars. Once there'd been so much light pollution in London you wouldn't have seen the stars, even on a clear night. But now hundreds of glinting, silver flecks spangled the sky.

Ana shivered and hugged her arms tightly around herself. The cold chased away all remnants of her earlier unconsciousness and lethargy. She sat down on the curved steps and begun rubbing her hands.

A scuff sounded from inside. She twisted towards the noise and saw Cole's six-foot frame in the doorway.

'Hey,' he whispered.

'Hey,' she whispered back.

He came and sat beside her. 'Couldn't sleep?'

'No,' she said. 'Sorry, I borrowed your coat. Do you want it back?'

'No, no, it's fine, you keep it.'

'Thanks.' Ana squeezed the jacket around her waist and dipped her chin into the collar.

'Do you want to talk about it?' he asked.

The pressure in her head moved down to sit on her shoulders as well. She cleared her throat.

'My father,' she said, 'programmed me into thinking joining with Jasper Taurell was the only way I could have a safe and happy life and then he . . . he discovered Jasper was going to expose his dodgy research and he got rid of him. Incarcerated him in a psych dump under a false identity. Then he had the gall to promise me that if I just sat tight, we'd get Jasper back.'

'I'm sorry.'

'Everything I thought was wrong. Everything I've valued . . .'

'It wasn't your fault.'

'I just accepted what I was told. After I realised what happened when you asked questions . . .' She remembered the awful morning in the Head's office; the first time she met the Board. It seemed like a million years ago. How she'd regretted writing to the Guildford Register's Office for her mother's death certificate.

Cole sighed.

'That's the way it's been set up,' he said. 'It's dangerous to ask questions. Instead we have the Board, the fix-it-all pill, the endless bombardment of new distractions. It's just the same in the City. It's like a magic trick. Our attention is directed one way, while a sleight of hand conceals what's really happening.'

Ana drew her knees to her chest and rocked herself.

'All these years I've been carefully watching myself, terrified of when, or where, or how I might crack. Now I'm finding it hard to believe there's nothing really wrong with me.'

Cole squeezed his hands together and blew on his fingers.

'You're not the only one,' he said. 'Look how many people out here are convinced they're sick. Most people believe and trust those in authority. We're conditioned to as kids and we don't expect them to lie to us.'

Ana breathed out, watching the white cloud of breath just visible before her eyes.

'The morning after my mother gave in to my father and started taking the Benzidox again,' she said, 'I woke up really early with this terrible feeling.' Her mouth grew dry. She'd never told anyone this before. For years, the memory had been hazy and broken, buried beneath the lies she'd told the Board. But seeing Cole's mother had brought the morning flooding back in excruciating detail.

'I went to find my mother but she wasn't in her bedroom. I passed my father's study and saw the light on beneath his door. He was always up reading half the night and falling asleep on the sofa. I searched for my mother downstairs and then I went outside.

'I could hear an engine running. So I crossed the overgrown lawn to the barn and I stood outside, listening. My father rationed the petrol. When he went off to London for the week, he left the spare car with just enough fuel in it to drive a couple of miles to the nearest neighbours in an emergency. So the engine being left on like that wasn't just weird, it felt deeply wrong. And I could smell the fumes. They leaked under the double doors. I tried opening the doors, but couldn't. I ran back to the house and got my dad. He made the girl that was with us at the time keep me inside, while he went to see what was going on. I heard him chop through the door with an axe.

'From the kitchen window, I saw him carrying my mother, limbs dangling, to his car parked at the side of the house. I broke away from the girl and ran to them. He laid my mum on the back seat and closed the car door. He told me she was fine. "She's had an accident, Ariana. You're not to worry. I'm taking her to the hospital." I never saw her again; never got to say goodbye.' The grief settled over Ana like an ache, like flu.

Cole took her hand and held it between his own. His palms felt warm. She liked their roughness, it made them seem solid and reassuring. She felt him watching her. Staring through the shadows at his hands cupping hers, she brushed a finger across his wrist.

She had a plan. It was the only way forward. The only path open to her.

'I need proof Jasper really entered Three Mills as Scott

Rutherford,' she said. 'I'm going to get myself committed. If he's there, I'll find out what he's done with the research evidence and I'll get him out.'

'That's the most insane thing I've ever heard,' said Cole. She could hear a smile of disbelief in his voice. 'Anyway, he won't still have the evidence. If your father didn't take it, the orderlies will have frisked him. It's pointless.'

'Jasper knew he was being followed. He could have hidden the disc before they took him.'

'Listen.' Cole's grip tightened around her hand. 'Even if he'd managed to hide it, he's been institutionalised for almost a week. They have ways of extracting information.'

'My father isn't affiliated with Three Mills. He wouldn't have been able to go back there to interfere with Jasper's treatment, especially if he thought someone might start asking questions about Scott Rutherford's background. Perhaps he thought it wouldn't matter if Jasper had hidden the disc. Because Jasper was the only one who knew where, and who would he tell? Who would believe him?' Vocalising her argument increased Ana's certainty. Posing as a patient was worth the risk. 'Besides, how else will we know if it really is Jasper?'

'There are other ways. Anyway, Jasper obviously hasn't been able to get out, so how do you think you're going to?'

'After admission, there's a routine evaluation that has to be done within twenty-four hours: an interview with one of the resident psychiatrists and a sanity test of a hundred questions. If you pass, you're released.'

Cole withdrew his hand. 'And if you don't pass you're

kept for another month of involuntary treatment before the next assessment.'

'I'll pass,' she said.

'Nobody passes. If you're too normal they think you're abnormal. If there's nothing apparently wrong, then it's deeply hidden and that's even worse.'

'I've taken that test ever since I was fifteen,' Ana said. 'My father coached me on it. I know exactly how to respond. I can't fail.'

'There are other things that could go wrong. It's too risky.'

'What about you?' She turned to face him. 'This minister you're helping has information that backs up Jasper's, right? Something that proves the government and Novastra came up with the idea of Pures before my dad even began his research. What's going to happen if the Wardens know about the minister? You're taking the same risk. I saw the way you said goodbye to your mum.'

Cole stared at her. She angled away to face the street. Across the road, the blue LED street lamp softly shaped the iron railings of a park.

'You're in shock,' he said finally.

She shook her head. 'You're the one who thinks I'm part of all this. That I have something to do with disproving the Pure test.'

'Not by getting yourself locked up in a loony dump!'

'What then?'

Cole's eyes narrowed, his face compressed.

'What did you see?' she asked.

He shook his head. 'I don't know how to explain.'

'Try.'

He turned away as though it hurt him to look at her. 'I saw us.'

'What were we doing?'

'Kissing,' he said.

Ana's stomach flip-flopped. Nerves fizzled inside her. For a moment she thought she was going to laugh. She pressed her fingers together and tried to continue breathing.

'Well, that was part of it, anyway,' he said.

She nodded.

'The better part,' he added.

Her hands shook. She had no idea how to respond. Her heart felt like it was going to pump itself so hard it would burst through her chest. She glanced at him and saw he was grinning.

'You're joking?' she said.

'I'd never joke about kissing you.'

Heat rushed to her cheeks. Thank goodness he couldn't see her properly. She shot to her feet, trembling.

'I've never really kissed anyone,' she blurted, instantly wishing she'd kept that piece of information to herself. *Idiot*, she thought as she scampered quickly back inside. In the bedroom, she kicked off her shoes and lay down beside Lila. Cole returned a minute later. She heard him stretch out on Lila's other side. In the darkness, she imagined she could hear him smiling.

*

Three Mills was formerly part of a group of tidal mills on Three Mills Island. Vehicles could access the psych dump from Sugar House Lane, a long, isolated road to the north. Pedestrians entered by a street to the west which had been closed off to cars. Beyond the first bridge, on the left, a row of brownstone houses led up to a blue gate, which dated back to the mill's conversion into film studios. On the right-hand side stood a pretty, industrial mill with a clock tower.

'This time tomorrow morning,' Cole said, holding Ana's shoulders, fixing her gaze, 'you get on at Bromley-by-Bow and go to Whitechapel. From there you take the train to Forest Hill. You go straight back to the room. You wait for me, until I come for you. The room's all paid up.' Ana nodded. But every time she looked at him, she thought of them kissing.

They were standing outside a boarded-up Tesco on the edge of the long pedestrianised lane.

'This is crazy,' Lila said for the hundredth time.

'If the psychs don't give you back your money, jump the barrier and get on the Tube without a ticket. No one will stop you.'

Had he been teasing her about his Glimpse?

'Ana, concentrate. What I'm telling you is important.'

'Get on the Tube without a ticket,' she said. Her heartbeat accelerated as she imagined jumping barriers and riding through London alone. She should be more worried about a night in the psych bin than Cole's Glimpse and ticket evasion, but that part of what she was doing seemed too alien to even contemplate.

'Lila's going back to the Project,' Cole said. 'But I'll be there for you tomorrow night.'

Ana unfastened her interface from the silver chain around her neck and gave it, along with her real ID, to Cole. 'If I don't get out,' she said, 'I want you to send this to my father and tell him where I am.'

Cole took the ID and interface dubiously. She could see he was thinking that if her father was capable of putting Jasper in Three Mills to protect his reputation, he was probably capable of leaving Ana there too. But Ana knew Ashby Barber wouldn't let his daughter rot away in a loony dump. He would come for her. His pride, if nothing else, would insist on it.

'I'll see you tomorrow night then,' she said, the uncertainty in her voice leaking through.

'Tomorrow night,' Cole repeated. He held her gaze.

Ana longed to reach out for him, but she only smiled. 'Besides,' she said, 'you've seen the future. And we haven't . . . you know.'

Cole smiled back, then reached out his fingers to lightly touch the short hair at the back of her neck. She closed her eyes, wanting to engrave the feeling on her memory – the tingling sensation where their skin met, the electricity that flowed between them, setting her on fire.

Lila shook her head. 'Madness,' she said, kicking a fizzy drinks can and sidling off to examine a poster on the boarded-up Tesco shop front.

'I want to understand,' Ana murmured. 'What makes you so sure this Glimpse wasn't a trick?'

Cole's hands dropped around the curve of her shoulders, down her arms. 'Don't you ever just know something?' he asked.

Ana searched his eyes. *No*, she thought, *not really*. Ever since she'd been told she was a Big3 Sleeper she'd questioned everything, especially herself.

'But it happened so long ago.'

'Yeah. I was only sixteen.'

'I barely remember things that happened before I moved to the Community. Sometimes, I think if I didn't have a photograph, I wouldn't remember what my mum looked like. What makes you think I'm the girl?'

Cole dug his hands in his pockets and took a deep breath. They stared at each other for several seconds, until Lila came and stood between them.

'Just for the record,' Lila said, 'in case anyone is actually listening, I think Ana voluntarily getting herself committed to a loony dump is a really bad idea.'

Ana tore her eyes away from Cole and hugged Lila. It was the first time she'd initiated physical affection with anyone since Tamsin disappeared. She drew back embarrassed, but Lila pulled her close.

When Ana let go, she absorbed Cole's presence one last time, memorising the iceberg blue of his irises. Then with nothing but the fake ID stick and forty pounds cash, she strode, head down, towards Three Mills.

Her legs trembled as she crossed over the footbridge towards the clock mill. She stopped by the gate. A security guard appeared out of nowhere.

'Got an appointment?' he said.

Ana allowed her fear to express itself as a general nervousness. She scratched beneath her hair at the back of her neck.

'Er, the Mental Watch Centre sent me.' In her mind she recalled the signatures of the psychiatrist who'd admitted the John Doe patient on the same night as Jasper. Cullen, or Cohen perhaps. 'They told me to ask for Dr Cullen.'

'You must mean Gudden,' the guard said.

'Oh.' She nodded and ducked her head.

The security guard backed up to the last house opposite the clock mill, once the home of a foreman or a factory official. He disappeared inside then reappeared behind a latticed window, holding an intercom phone. A moment later, the blue gate opened. Ana shuffled through. As it closed, she glanced behind and caught sight of Cole and Lila. It was too far to see their faces. But their bodies were still and she could tell they were both watching her.

Inside Three Mills, she shambled along a cobbled street with built-in railway tracks, anxiously casting about for an indication of how bad the place was. To her right a large field of tarmac, broken up into faded white boxes, lay empty. On her left sat a long, utilitarian building that didn't look inviting. But at least it had windows.

She followed an arrow painted on the ground, tripped up steps to the reception and entered flustered, which under the circumstances, she decided, wouldn't hurt. A lady behind a circular desk met her eye. She nodded at one of the seats pushed against a bare wall. As Ana sat down, a man in a three-quarter-length doctor's coat appeared.

'Good morning,' he said. 'I'm Dr Dannard. I'm afraid Dr Gudden isn't available this morning.' He held out his hand to shake Ana's.

'Emily,' Ana said, using the name Nate's contact had matched her to.

'May I?' He reached over her and took off the chain carrying her fake ID. His intrusive proximity made her instantly wary.

'Nice chain,' he said. 'Follow me.' The door ahead sensed their approach and swished open. Ana followed him down a brightly lit corridor. Dr Dannard pushed open the second door they came to and stood back to let her in. She shambled forward, the twinges in her stomach going berserk.

He gestured for her to sit in a low chair on the patient's side of his wooden desk. Then he settled into a high-backed leather seat opposite her and inserted her ID stick into his interface pad.

'You've dyed your hair,' he said.

Panic stabbed Ana's chest. Had he recognised her?

'You've cut your hair like a boy and you've dyed it because you don't want people to think you're pretty.'

She relaxed, realising this was all part of his 'astute' assessment. Dr Dannard was obviously happy to do all the talking, so she didn't bother to answer.

'Got a boyfriend?' he asked.

'Not exactly,' she said.

'Dumped you, has he?' He nodded in agreement with himself. 'Low self-esteem. Nervous too, mmm?' Again, it wasn't a question. He reached into his top desk drawer and pulled out some papers.

'You need a break,' he said, folding his hands together

and resting them over the papers. 'A bit of time to relax, unwind. Let somebody else take care of you.'

He was making a stay in the dump sound like a luxury holiday.

'Wouldn't you like to forget about all the stresses and strains of everything *out there*?' His eyes gleamed. He pronounced 'out there' with an edge of disgust, simultaneously waving his hand as though brushing reality away. Ana nodded, wondering if the outside world could be so easily dismissed here.

'Good,' he said. He got up, belly bumping over the top of the desk, and left the room. Internally, Ana began to question whether if she walked out now, the security guard would open the gate. Dannard was clearly unhinged. Anyone who merely looked at another person and saw a catalogue of mental illnesses in the way they cut their hair had to be.

He returned with a second, younger doctor, who seemed irritated.

'Boyfriend's dumped her,' Dannard said by way of introduction, 'and she's not taking it too well, are you?'

'Suicidal?' His colleague snapped.

'No,' Ana replied. She certainly didn't want something like that getting written down on her form.

'She's got self-esteem problems,' Dannard went on. 'Nervous too.' He leant into the younger doctor and said something Ana couldn't make out. Probably going on about her hair.

'Fine,' the other doctor said. He strode to the table, picked up the form and scribbled something illegible in the box, *Diagnostic impression at admission*. He signed at the bottom and hurried back out.

She was in.

Now she really understood why her father had made her learn the test answers by heart, had made her swear she would never improvise or try to answer any of the Board's questions truthfully.

Dannard lounged back in his chair. The pupils of his tiny eyes shone brightly as he signed the forms.

'Well that's that,' he said, handing her a pen. 'You just have to sign here.' Ana took the biro. Her hand shook. 'If you can't write,' he said, 'just make a cross.'

'When do I get the full evaluation?'

The beady eyes in Dannard's large head blinked.

'So you've stayed in a Mental Rehab Home before, have you? I didn't see that on your ID. A few years back, was it? Well, you're in safe hands now.'

'I heard there was a big test. One hundred questions.'

'Oh, yes, that. Nothing to worry about. Now sign the form and I'll call someone to come and collect you.' He picked up his phone.

Ana's hand hovered over the space where she was meant to sign. She fixed the pen on the page but didn't move her hand.

Dannard hung up. The clang of the receiver on the desk made her jump. She drew the pen hard down and up, making an X.

'Well, there we go,' he said. He retrieved his hand-held scanner and scanned the document into his interface. Perhaps they were legally required to have hard copies in case there was ever a virus or a power cut that wiped out the home system, she thought.

She sat as still as she could. Fear crawled up her skin like spiders' legs.

Two women arrived with a wheelchair. The one pushing wore loose green trousers and a plain green top. A large, jagged scar ran from the corner of her mouth to her chin. She had a truncheon on the belt around her waist. The smaller woman wore a blue three-quarter-length coat buttoned up over her clothes.

'Morning, Dr Dannard,' they sang. He nodded at them and then pretended to be very busy with paperwork. It looked to Ana as if he was trying to hide.

'Sit,' the orderly said. Ana scooted across to the wheel-chair.

'Roll up your sleeve,' the nurse said, retrieving a syringe from a box in her pocket. She held it up, flicked it and let a colourless liquid dribble out the end.

The spasms in Ana's stomach came together in one hard fist. *It's most likely a sedative*, she told herself. But who knew if they'd sterilised the needle properly.

'I, um.' She swallowed. 'I—'

The orderly reached for her truncheon. 'Not a trouble-maker, are you?' she said.

Ana shook her head once, rolled up her sleeve and held out her arm.

20

Jasper

Ana woke in a vast black hangar. She gazed up at the ceiling. It was at least three storeys high. Slowly, she became aware of a mattress beneath her, an itchy rug covering her body. She felt sleepy, satisfied. A distant part of her brain told her it was the drug, told her she had to get up and find Jasper, but she didn't feel like listening. Rocking her head sideways, she saw the filming studio had been converted into a dormitory. Dozens of mattresses were strewn across the floor. There were no other furnishings. Grey daylight shafted through the gap of a heavy sliding door; a door large enough to let a truck through.

Close by someone sniffed. Someone else hummed. The black, squidgy walls gobbled up sound, making it impossible to glean how many others were lying in the old film studio with her. The dozen beds she could make out lay empty. From beyond the door, a constant burble of voices ran on and on.

An unpleasant stink of vomit floated on the air. A reminder that everything was not all right. *Get up*, she told herself. Who knew how long she'd been lying there, how much time she'd already lost?

Ana pushed up on her elbows. Her head spun, and then

her brain settled, hovering inside her skull. Gauging that she wasn't hungry, she felt an element of relief. At least they'd only used a light sedative, something to knock her under for an hour, rather than a day.

She slapped her legs to see how much feeling she had. Her thighs tingled on impact. She rolled off the mattress on to the cold concrete floor and wrestled her limbs into a kneeling position. Then she flexed her right leg and leant hard on it. As she pressed down, the muscles in her thigh shook. Concentrating, she lifted up her other leg. With both feet planted on the ground, she slowly stretched out her body. Her legs trembled. Just standing took enormous effort. For a moment she felt her resolve crumble. She wanted to curl back up and drift in the hazy borderlands of her mind.

But then she looked down. A long-sleeved, shapeless robe hung over her hands and brushed her bare knees. They'd taken her clothes. They'd left her without shoes or socks. She had to get moving. There was no knowing when they would come for her test. It could be any time within the first twenty-four hours of admission. She needed to find Jasper fast.

She shuffled towards the doors, hugging her arms around her chest in a futile attempt to conserve body heat. The cold stiffened her elastic limbs. Her mind felt like sludge the whole world had walked their dirty boots through.

She passed through the hulking doors into a courtyard reminiscent of a school playground. Except the kids were

248

too old, their robes too skimpy for anywhere but hospital beds and their bodies crooked and jerky.

Ana grew nervous at the sight of so many volatile young people clustered together. Her shaky legs buckled. She slouched against the blue studio door. Fortunately, no one was paying her the slightest bit of attention. She breathed in deeply and tried to absorb her surroundings.

Flat-roofed hangars lined the wide yard. One of the blue doors across the way had been left closed, revealing faint white markings of a number five, encircled twice like a target. The yard was around sixty-foot long. To her left lay a brick wall with narrow passages running off both ways. To her right, a grey building with walls either side plugged up the other end. Her gaze fluttered over the sixty or so patients. A dozen boys, most of whom looked younger than her, threw dice and bet coloured bits of plastic. Another mixed group sat bunched up on a low wall. The rest of the various cliques appeared to be girls.

Inhaling deeply, Ana shambled left towards the passageways. They had to lead somewhere. The other entrances on to the yard seemed to be hangars, like the one she'd come from. And she wasn't going to try searching those dark interiors, not until she felt steadier and understood how the psychs kept everyone under control. So far, she'd seen no doctors, nurses or orderlies.

She was almost at the high wall and about to turn down one of the alleys, when a girl shouted.

'Oi! Get back here!'

Ana flinched and swivelled around. Nearby, a huddle of girls watched her. One of them, with a tattoo of a vine twining down the side of her neck, stepped forward. She glared at Ana through straggly hair. Ana dropped her gaze at once. She wobbled away from the wall, back in the direction she'd come. She didn't fancy her chances against a bunch of medicated, hostile Crazies.

As she reached a queue for the grey building, which from the smell had to be the toilets, a second smaller yard became visible on her left. At the end of it, a flight of steps led up to a closed door. To the right of the yard stood two more doors, the furthest of which was ajar. Ana tottered towards the hissing noise which came from it.

Inside a luminous room with a thirty-foot-high ceiling and four arched windows, patients crowded around folding card tables. The luckier ones were seated, playing dominoes, board games and chess. The rest stood watching. Fierce whispering buzzed around the room. By the unanimity of their sibilant communications, Ana decided talking had to be against the rules.

She searched the room, looking for signs of how the orderlies monitored them, and noticed two surveillance cameras high above, beating back and forth along old gantry tracks. Conscious of the cameras, Ana padded into the hall. The springy wooden floor was warmer than the studio concrete, or exterior tarmac. Her feet began to tingle as the blood circulated through them again. Her hunched shoulders dropped a little, thawing. Unlike the dark hangar where she'd woken, sunlight from the high windows heated the room without letting in the cold.

In an aimless fashion, she wound around the games room. The agitated clusters pushing against the tables, watching and waiting for a turn, obscured the few patients actually playing. After Ana had circled a couple of times and was sure Jasper wasn't among those standing, she toured the tables for glimpses of those seated. She was patient, waiting until someone bobbed their head, scratched or jostled forward to reveal the players.

She'd traversed one side of the room and was scrutinising a table near a round distillery barrel from the mill's industrial days, when she caught sight of Jasper. She almost cried out in astonishment. Emotion swelled around her, too high and moving too fast to escape. All she could do was let the wave break and hope she was still standing afterwards.

In an effort to calm herself, she focused on the strange copper barrel to the left of Jasper with a chimney-like top. Snippets of infantile banter trickled through her awareness.

'It's my go.' – 'You're cheating.' – 'That's not fair.'

They were like overgrown children. She wondered why everyone looked under twenty. The psychs must separate patients according to age and put the older ones in some other part of the institution.

The emotion and adrenalin finally ebbed away leaving one clear thought – she had to get Jasper's attention without shocking him. She took a step back and craned over several other patients for a better look at his face. It transformed before her; the memory and the reality two different things entirely.

His skin looked grey. Darkness rimmed his eyes. Bristly stubble and pockmarks from where he'd cut himself shaving with a blunt razor covered his chin. His sandy hair hung limply. The last five days hadn't been kind to him.

Ana tunnelled through a group of girls and positioned herself behind the chair of the teenage boy playing with Jasper. The boy shook dice, clucking and sucking his breath between his teeth. He kept shaking, shaking. The dice thumped around inside a stiff, leather pouch. Jasper, legs crossed, hunched forward with his hand plugged over his mouth, counting under his breath.

'He's cursing it,' the boy said. Jasper smiled sneakily and carried on counting.

'Throw the dice,' someone whined. The dice fell. Silence descended over the group as they rolled to a stop. Then a grin broke across Jasper's face. The boy banged a silver dog across the board spaces, counting out four, then six. The dog toppled on to a purple stripe, barely visible beneath a sprawl of big red houses.

Jasper fanned a wad of colourful play cash in front of his opponent.

'Six multiplied by four hundred and eighty is three thousand and eighty,' he murmured. 'Time to pay.'

'You cheated,' the boy hissed.

'Of course I didn't.'

'You put thoughts into the dice.'

'That's ridiculous,' Jasper objected.

'You were counting.'

'Pay or lose!' The lively exchange stirred up the onlookers. They pressed closer. From the corner of her eye, Ana noted one of the ever-moving surveillance cameras had stopped and was pointing over them. If Jasper was the source of some commotion, he might get carted off. She needed to attract his attention and stop him from causing a scene.

'You've got too many houses on there,' she said. Jasper's eyes shot up to see who'd spoken. He looked directly at her without a glimmer of recognition. 'It's against the rules,' she continued, losing confidence. He'd either become amazingly good at bluffing, or he didn't know who she was. 'Besides,' she said, 'six times four hundred and eighty is two thousand eight hundred and eighty. You overcharged him.'

'And you are?' he said.

Ana swallowed, barely able to get the next word out.

'Emily.'

The teenage boy leapt on to the table. He kicked the board. Tiny red and green houses went flying. 'You lying cheat!' he shouted, lunging for Jasper.

A heartbeat later, an alarm blasted. Ana clamped her hands over her ears, but still the sound shook her skull. Pandemonium broke out. Patients scrambled for the door, pushing each other aside, stomping over those that had fallen or lain down in terror. Jasper stuffed the play money into his robe pocket and darted with an uneven gait through the crowds. She followed, barely able to see straight the noise hurt so much. Jasper headed for Studio 5 – the hangar opposite the one Ana had woken in. All around them patients dashed back and forth.

Out in the yard, she grabbed his arm. 'Jasper!' she screamed.

He circled around, afraid. When he saw who it was, his shadowed eyes filled with annoyance. He tried to shake her off. She leant towards him.

'Where can we talk?' she shouted. He yanked back his shoulder, releasing her hold on his gown and was about to stumble away, when uncertainty flicked across him.

'Do I know you?' he shouted.

Ana's heart lurched. 'Don't you?'

'Don't you?' he mimicked. They gazed at each other for a moment. And then around her she sensed a renewed flurry of desperation. Below the high-pitched alarm sounded the stomp-stomp of boots. The orderlies, truncheons carried between their arms like rifles, were filtering into the compound from the narrow passages by the far brick wall.

Ana tore to the studio where she'd woken and smacked down on the only free bed in the doorway. This time she had no blanket, someone had taken it. Most girls lay with their hands over their heads, muffling sobs and moans or the sounds of others.

The alarm stopped abruptly. Ana's ears continued to ring. Boots tramped. She clutched her arms together to try and stop the trembling. She couldn't believe what was happening. This was a nightmare. The insane were in charge of the insane, and nobody, not even Jasper, knew who she was. Did they know how to wipe people's minds now? Had her father had years of Jasper's memories erased to protect himself?

Two orderlies entered the studio. They stood like prison guards on either side of the blue doors, sneering in disdain at the smell. The vomit odour hit you when you came in from the outside. That was the silver lining of having a bed by the door, Ana supposed.

Beyond, something rattled across the tarmac. A nurse

entered pushing a huge plywood and metal trolley. Hundreds of tiny plastic containers shaped like eyes lined the trolley's two shelves, their coloured beads rattling within transparent casings. The nurse wheeled the contraption up the edge of the hangar. With a distilling sense of horror, Ana realised why the other girls were all lying on their fronts. Large white numbers had been sewn on the backs of their blue robes; the nurse was matching up the numbers one through to eight with the eight different types and quantities of pills inside the transparent eyes.

No one voiced any objection to the medication, though several girls snivelled and cried as they swallowed their capsules. The nurse passed Ana without pausing. But once everyone had been administered their meds, she returned to Ana's bed pushing a wheelchair. Head bowed, she didn't so much as catch her eye, let alone speak as she waited for Ana to get up. Ana glanced at the orderlies posted by the door. She recognised the one who had brought her from Dr Dannard's office. The scar was unmissable. The orderly stared at her.

Thinking better of making a fuss, Ana clambered off the bed and lowered herself into the chair. The nurse in charge of medication retrieved a needle. Ana shrivelled. Sedation seemed to be standard routine for getting moved around the compound, but that carried no reassurance in a place like this. Being knocked unconscious while Dannard and the scarred orderly were in charge chilled Ana to the core. Her only recompense was that they were probably taking her for the twenty-four-hour assessment. Perhaps she wouldn't even have to spend a night in Three Mills. She exhaled and held out her arm.

*

Giant trees stretched up towards the sky. Raindrops dripped through leaves the size of old paper fans and umbrellas. No sooner had Ana opened her eyes and marvelled at her surroundings, than she knew something was wrong. She was hallucinating or dreaming. She needed to wake up. The cold drops turned into a torrent of gushing water, sinking into her skin, choking her.

She shook her head and blinked. A hoary tiled wall appeared three feet in front of her. Something hard pressed into her back. Disorientated, water still pouring so she could barely breathe, she wiped her face.

She was slumped on the floor in a shower cubicle big enough for seven or eight people. And she was naked.

'There you go,' someone said.

She struggled to draw her legs to her chest. They wobbled and thumped back down like dead animals. Her arms at least were cooperating. She crossed them over her breasts, squinting through the water and the fuzz in her head to see who was out there, standing several feet back from the open showers, observing.

'Hello. I'm Dr Cusher,' a female said. 'How are you feeling today?'

'She has low self-esteem,' a man said.

Dr Dannard. Wake up! She screamed inwardly at herself. *Time to wake up!* She smacked her lips together. Her cheeks felt as though they'd been stuffed with cotton.

'Good heavens,' the female voice said. 'Could someone turn this off? We can't hear ourselves think in here.' The shower reduced to a dribble. Ana felt a surge of gratitude. Thank goodness it wasn't only Dannard again. Somebody sane.

'So,' the female psychiatrist began. 'You've been institutionalised before. But it's not on your records. You must have been . . . Let's see – Emily Thomas, eighteen years old, eight years ago everything was put on the same system, so that would have made you ten, at most. A childhood trauma.' She said nodding. 'Death in the family?'

Ana began to shiver uncontrollably.

'Towel – p-ple-ase,' she said. Her jaw juddered so hard she almost bit off her tongue.

The psychs conferred over a clipboard. At the edge of the shower room, the orderlies that had brought Ana stood in an alcove, smoking cigarettes and gossiping.

'She cuts and dyes her hair,' Dannard said.

'Identity disturbance,' Cusher said, jotting something down.

'And low self-esteem,' Dannard added.

'Not fat though,' Cusher said. 'Bulimic?'

'I'll have the nurses keep an eye on it.'

'Yes, good. Cuts, bruises?'

'No,' one of the nurses said, puffing out smoke and waving it away.

'Why did you come here, Emily?' Cusher asked, her face a mask of impartiality. 'You look troubled. Why don't you tell us what's troubling you?'

All vestiges of hope that Cusher wasn't as insane as Dannard vanished. 'C-c-ol-d,' she managed.

'Anything else?'

Ana stared at the woman through strands of dripping hair. Her lethargic mind could only compute the cold, the embarrassment of her nakedness, the insanity of being interviewed in a shower.

'When's the tessst?' she asked.

'What did she say?'

'She wants to know when the test is,' Dannard said. 'She's obsessed with the Personality Diagnostic Analysis Test.'

'Ah,' Cusher nodded. 'You're afraid of our little test, are you? Tell me about that.'

'I jus wanna do the tesst,' Ana said.

'Tell me about that,' Cusher repeated. Irritation wound through Ana, twisting her in its grip. 'What will the test tell us about you that you can't tell us yourself?' Cusher asked. 'You prefer machines to people? You don't like people, do you, Emily? You don't trust them.'

'I jus wan ta do the frigging test!'

'Got a temper,' Cusher said to Dannard.

Ana suddenly remembered her father's Golden Rules. When speaking to a psychiatrist, never show any emotion but polite attentiveness. Never improvise. Never use sarcasm. Never joke. Never admit guilt. She clamped her mouth shut. But it was too late.

Cusher made a note. Dannard peered over her shoulder and nodded.

'The usual,' Cusher said. 'Two milligrams of Diopaxil

and four of Benzidox, to be upped to a maximum of six and eight until our review next week.'

Ana flushed with panic. 'No!' She lunged forward to grab Cusher, her useless legs dragging behind her. Cusher's boot struck her hard. She yelped.

'For goodness' sake,' Cusher said. The orderlies on standby crushed out their fags and charged forward. Something warm trickled into the corner of Ana's left eye, blotting out her vision. In a last-ditch attempt, she flung up her arms and wrapped them tightly around Cusher's black-trousered leg.

'Pleeease, the tesst!'

A blow to the back winded her. She collapsed, falling face down on grimy tiles. As she gasped for air another blow struck. Pain swept through her skull. Rivulets of burning ice. So bright the hoary room flared snow-white.

21

Cole

The Right Honourable Dr Peter Reed wasn't late, but something felt wrong. Cole scanned the Gospel Oak checkpoint again with his infrared binoculars. The checkpoint cabins lay fifty metres beyond the entrance to Gospel Oak station, where Gordon House Road turned into Mansfield. Usually at this time of the evening, the straight two-lane highway saw a regular flow of chauffeur-driven saloons, one or two every few minutes.

Cole had been watching from under the railway bridge for a quarter of an hour and nothing had gone in or out. He focused his binoculars on the guy sitting in the booth on the right-hand side of the road. The guard forked up a microwave dinner from a cardboard container. The light of a reality TV show glowed on the cabin wall. Cole couldn't see the security guard in the left-hand booth.

He shook his shoulders inside his puffa jacket to keep warm. His mind wandered to Ana. She was strong and resourceful, but he was worried about her. An institution run by the Board, whether a prison, an orphanage or a psych dump, was a dangerous place to be. The Board's objectives were always the same – a quiet, subservient population, who cost as little time and effort as possible. Invariably, their methods of attainment included sedation, medication and demoralising conditions. And when those weren't enough, brutal punishment.

Cole tucked away his binoculars and blew on his stiff fingers. Nothing was working out the way he'd imagined. He realised now how little he'd actually seen in his Glimpse, and how his efforts over the years to remember everything about it had only watered down the memory. Now all he had was a vague impression of events and the words he'd used over and over to describe the moment to himself.

I kiss her and the whole universe slots into place. Music plays in my head. Music so beautiful, I think I'm listening to the stars singing.

Directly after the shaman had left the Project, Cole had written the melody of 'Second Sight'. But as often as he tried, he'd never been able to finish the piece, not until he'd seen Ana leaving the Academy of Music a couple of months ago and something in him had clicked. He'd tried following her and had been thwarted by her chauffeur-driven saloon. Shocked and disheartened to learn she was Pure, he'd wondered how on earth their paths were ever going to cross. He'd asked after her at the Academy but no one seemed to know who he was talking about. Then he'd gone to the concert to help Jasper Taurell. He'd come face to face with Ana and the overwhelming feelings he'd had for the girl in his vision came hurtling back. He hadn't doubted the girl whose hand was bound to Jasper was *the girl* for a second. Eight years ago, when he'd woken from the Glimpse, he'd felt galvanised, as though all the negative charge from the losses and pain of his childhood had been stripped away. When his eyes had met Ana's in the Barbican lift, he'd felt that same sense of electrification, like he was being given a fresh start.

Cole struggled to remember as much detail from the end of the Glimpse as he could. It was the part he'd never liked thinking about. He and Ana were near a Community checkpoint, surrounded by men who wanted her to stay. She'd been afraid of something; she'd persuaded him to leave her behind.

A Glimpse isn't immutable, he reminded himself. When the time came, if Ana chose him, he wouldn't leave her no matter what.

Movement flitted in the centre of the road beyond the checkpoint. Cole retrieved his binoculars and adjusted the focus. A man lumbered up the street, landing with greater weight on one leg than the other. A ponderous man with a limp. Cole's pulse accelerated. He edged out of the bridge's shadows.

The minister had abandoned his car and veered from the plan they'd spent months finessing. Unless the Secretary of State for Trade and Industry had panicked and lost his nerve, there had to be a good reason for it. Either his car had been sabotaged or he'd been forced to make a quick getaway without anyone seeing.

Cole watched the old man's progress through his binoculars. If the minister had come from his house, he'd jogged over a mile. Cole would have been impressed if the situation didn't make him so anxious.

Within a hundred metres of the checkpoint, the minister staggered to a halt.

Come on, Cole thought. *Don't give the security guard any time to think about this. Keep going.*

Under the cabin's blue LED lighting, the minister's face burnt purply pink and contorted with pain. The security guard stood up. The minister limped to the booth, unclipping his ID stick from his lapel.

Cole watched as the guard scanned the ID. The minister's information flashed up on the white cabin wall.

Name: The Right Honourable Dr Peter Reed.
Birth: 6th Sept 1970
Employment: Secretary of State for Trade and Industry.

'Come on now,' Cole muttered. 'You don't want to flag up a government minister, do you?'

The security guard smiled uncertainly. Peter said something and the guard laughed.

Cole clenched his hands together and sucked in his breath. 'That's it,' he muttered. 'Tell him you had a spot of bother with the wife. Domestic tiff . . . Now get out of there.'

The guard held out the ID and Peter, chest heaving, re-claimed it.

Just a little bit further. Cole resisted the temptation to step forward and wave the minister on. Peter knew roughly where Cole was hiding. If he'd brought the car, as they'd agreed, he'd have driven under the bridge past Cole and they'd have met up at the nearby Lido ruins. From there, they'd planned to ride together on Cole's bike, following the Heath's border half a mile until they ran into their escorts from the Project, who would take them over the wall.

The minister limped from the checkpoint up the centre of the road. Cole trained his binoculars on the guard who had let him through. The man poured a flask of water into a tea urn. Reassured, Cole refocused his vision on to where he'd first seen Peter jogging, searching for signs of anything amiss, anything scuttling in the shadows.

The soft rumble of a hybrid closed in from behind. Cole backed up against the bridge wall. A split-second later, the bridge's arched underbelly flared with light from the vehicle's headlights. The car flew forwards. Too fast. Too loud. A screaming contrast to the eerie quiet of the last twenty minutes. All wrong. As it whooshed by, the world blazed white, then fell black.

Cole swung to check Peter's progress. Still a hundred metres off, the minister stumbled right, fleeing for the pavement.

'Peter!' Cole shouted. He sprinted forwards. The car headlights swerved across the minister's path, lighting him up for an instant. Then he disappeared. A crack split the air.

Cole's knees weakened. He gazed in disbelief at the dazzling shafts of light. The car slowly reversed revealing the minister's crushed head, brains and blood smattered across the road.

Cole clutched his stomach. His skin burnt. He was about to vomit or pass out.

A door clicked open. A bulky figure got out of the car and strolled around it to the minister's body.

'Is he dead?' A voice inside the car said, carrying on the night air.

'Course he's bloody dead,' a second voice answered. Metal glinted in the man's outstretched hand. 'Brains everywhere,' he added, prodding Peter with his foot.

'You sure you shouldn't shoot him?' the voice inside the car said.

Cole fumbled towards the pavement and heaved. His eyes watered. His hands wouldn't stop shaking.

'Near the bridge!' a voice shouted.

For a moment, Cole was falling through cloud – everything soft, hushed, grey. Then with the pop of gunfire, he was back. A man wearing night-vision goggles sprinted towards him. The hybrid switched gear, swinging around. A siren wailed in the distance. Cole's arms and legs kicked with adrenalin.

He flew thirty metres to his bike, mounted, flipped the key and stepped on the gear pedal. As the bike jerked forward, another shot echoed through the darkness. It impacted in the arched wall behind him. Shattered brick rained down, covering him in a cloud of dust as he revved on to the empty road.

Hunkered low against the wind, he pushed his bike faster than it had ever been before. The archaic engine roared and jounced with the effort, choked by the diluted ethanol fuel. Cole's skin was on fire. The night breeze cooled the sweat on his face, making him shiver.

Beyond Gospel Oak station, the streetlights died. The road waned into the moonless night. No pedestrians. No cyclists. No bonfires or shanty houses. Only Pures had reason to travel this way.

Cole passed the station and cut his headlamp. Darkness enveloped him. The slip road towards the Lido ruins lay two hundred metres up ahead.

A Psych Watch siren whirled in the distance and two police sirens grew closer. Pale yellow light crept up behind Cole as the car that had run over the minister gained on him. In a few seconds, they would have him in their sights.

Squeezing his brakes, Cole swung hard left. The back wheel skidded across the road. Burning rubber stung his nostrils. The front wheel thumped the kerb. He accelerated. The bike bounced up the pavement, now a grey silhouette in the bleed from the headlights. A second later the pavement ran out. He slammed down on to uneven ground, disappearing into blackness. The bike juddered through long grass and bush. Cole shielded his face with one arm as brambles slashed his face.

Up ahead, sirens flashed. He held his course, cutting a line to the slip road. Headlights flooded the bracken further off to his right, as the pursuing vehicle overtook. Everything lit up and then went dark again.

Cole let go of the throttle. The bike ground to a halt in a thicket of high shrubs. It took several shaky attempts for him to kick out the stand. As his adrenalin ebbed, shock wrapped over him. He couldn't breathe. He couldn't move his limbs properly. He vomited again into the bushes. The Psych Watch van with its prison-break siren drowned out the sound. The police sirens came next.

Cole managed to flip his headlamp back on and slowly rode the bumpy terrain towards the ruins. Alone.

They'd killed Peter. A government minister. And it was his fault. The minister would never have got involved if Cole hadn't emotionally blackmailed him to hand over the incriminating government recording.

*

Ana lay curled up on a mattress in Studio 8. The pain in her head shut out all thought. Her body was sore and bruised. Only her left eye opened, letting through a narrow slit of day. She watched as the day faded and night crept in around her. Others came to lie quietly on their beds. Occasionally, she heard whimpering and groaning. Once she thought it might be coming from her.

After what seemed like hours, but might have been minutes, a distant bell broke the spell of lethargy cast with nightfall. Girls stirred from their beds.

A slight girl came and crouched beside her.

'Here, take this,' she said, pushing something small and round against Ana's lips. Ana grunted. 'It's just aspirin, for the pain.'

Ana opened her mouth. A bitter taste hit her tongue. She crunched, which made her head hurt even more.

'Looks like your interview didn't go too well,' the girl said.

'They didn't give me the test with all the questions.'

The girl shook her head. 'Never heard of anyone having a test before,' she said. 'Come on, you need to eat.' She hooked an arm around Ana's waist and pulled her to a sitting position. Ana's head spun from the sudden movement, but she didn't protest. She was starving. She hadn't eaten since she'd left the flat at Forest Hill. That morning?

'What time is it?' she asked.

The girl chuckled. 'It doesn't make any difference. In here, we're always in the Twilight Zone.'

The girl helped Ana across the courtyard to the door at the end of the smaller yard, which now stood open. They blundered inside and down a maze of dimly lit corridors, up some stairs and into a crowded dining room. Slouched against a wall, chin resting on her chest, Ana waited as the girl fetched them supper.

The meagre meal consisted of soup and bread. Ana ate slowly, hunched over, eyes closed. She flinched as cutlery clanged and chairs scraped. Her head pounded. She focused her efforts on getting a few spoons of sustenance inside her without throwing up – the soup smelt of duckweed and tasted mouldy. No wonder half the patients were bones sticking out of blue robes. And now Ana wore a blue robe too, instead of the white one. The nurses must have dressed her in it after her interview with Cusher. She imagined it had a number on the back denoting what meds she should be given.

Twenty minutes later, she returned to Studio 8. The girl managed to acquire another blanket for her from somewhere and helped Ana lie down on a mattress close to the door but out of the draught. Sleep came eventually. Deep and empty. When Ana woke, it was to the grating of the giant doors as they opened.

Morning crept into the dark interior. With it, the girls

around Ana twitched to life, pacing, whispering and picking at their beds and robes. No one left the studio. They were waiting for something. Ana, however, could barely move. The combination of the sedative and beating had stiffened her body and left her too sore to want to try. She wheezed, forced by the bruising on her back to take short, shallow breaths. At least tonight Cole would be waiting for her at the Forest Hill flat, and when she didn't make it, he would contact her father. She had a way out. But all the other boys and girls were stuck in Three Mills for months, maybe years. How did they live with that?

Thoughts of Cole sneaked through Ana's defences. For a few brief seconds she felt the warmth of his presence, comforting and strong. She imagined him holding her the way he'd done outside his mother's flat. Then a dozen trolleys rattled across the courtyard, bringing her sharply back to reality. Girls scampered to their beds and lay face down, numbers to the ceiling.

The trolleys rumbled in various directions. One grew louder, approaching Studio 8. Ana listened as it crashed over the metal door rails and into the dorm. She caught a whiff of cigarette smoke and suspected her least favourite orderly was, once again, posted on guard duty.

The nurse began distributing medication. The trolley wove between the girls, squeaking and clanking. When the nurse reached Ana, she stopped, held out a small toothbrush, a tube of toothpaste, a tiny bar of soap and a plastic container. Ana heaved her prostrate body high enough to free an arm. She took the goods, tucking the toothpaste, toothbrush and soap against her cheek. Then she squeezed the seal of the eye-like container. It popped open. She tipped the contents into her mouth, accepted the cup of water and swallowed.

With a final effort she extended her arm to return the plastic cup. Nothing happened. Her chest tightened. She lifted her head and squinted at the nurse. The nurse didn't look at her, didn't move. From the corner of her good eye, Ana saw movement in the entrance. She wavered. They couldn't know she'd pressed the pills against her top gum. She caught the eye of the girl that had helped her the night before. The girl stared at her unblinkingly, a warning lay buried behind her impassive expression.

'Water, please,' Ana croaked. The nurse gave her another thimble of liquid. This time Ana tipped it into her mouth and swallowed the pills. The nurse moved on.

Once all patients had received their meds, a bell sounded. The nurse and orderlies retreated. Girls rushed out into the chill morning.

Ana struggled to her feet. Her muscles ached with each small gesture, but she had to get to the toilet. She had to throw up.

Doubled over, clasping her blanket around her shoulders, she staggered into the yard. Her heart sank when she saw the queue for the toilets. It curled back on itself twice. At least sixty girls were waiting. The boys' queue was shorter, but that didn't help.

Ana peeked in the opposite direction. By the far wall on her left where the alleys ran on either side, several girls crouched, gowns lifted high on thighs, pee trickling through legs. Keeping close to the studio walls, Ana lurched towards the passageways, planning to dip into the left-hand alley just long enough to jam her fingers down her throat.

At the end of the yard, she steadied herself against the gravel wall, checking quickly about for nurses, orderlies or surveillance cameras. Tension built inside her skull. She pressed her hands to her head. Soon the chemicals would enter her stomach, would be absorbed by tiny capillaries and carried through her bloodstream to her brain. She breathed in deeply, let go of the wall and tossed herself into the passageway.

'Whoa . . .' Mid-manoeuvre, two firm hands caught her shoulders. 'Steady there.' It was a voice Ana knew well, even if everything else about the girl had changed beyond recognition. Stunned stupid, Ana could only blink. The girl with the vine tattoo pushed her back into the yard.

'Slow learner huh?' Ana narrowed her semi-good eye to examine the skinny teenager. A black fringe cut a jagged line high on the girl's forehead. Long lashes framed dark eyes. A mole sat on the right, sallow cheek. Yesterday, Ana had been too dosed up and disorientated to recognise the girl with the vine tattoo. Today, as Ana absorbed her former best friend's features, her mind hurtled back through time. She saw Tamsin impersonating their home economics teacher the day Ana was called to the headmistress's office; she saw Tamsin challenging any girl in their class to make fun of Ana after it came out she was a Big3 Sleeper; she saw Tamsin pouring her heart and soul into Portia's monologue from *The Merchant of Venice* at their Year 10 school variety show.

Ana bit a hole in her lip in an effort to come back to the present. Blood trickled into her mouth. She wondered if Tamsin recognised her even though she was covered in bruises, and had short hair and brown contacts that were dissolving day by day and would soon be gone.

They were standing along the back wall in full sight of the yard. The acidic tang of vomit and urine, along with the blood and Ana's confusion, set her head spinning.

'Pull down your knickers and crouch like the rest of us,' Tamsin said. Ana did as instructed. Her thighs shook under her weight, her chest heaved, but she couldn't stop gawking at the vine tattoo. 'Wait . . . Wait . . .'

Ana held back her retching reflex.

'OK.'

Perhaps Tamsin meant for Ana to pee, but Ana turned sideways and threw up. Two pills dribbled down the brick wall coated in brown liquid. Without pausing a beat, Tamsin doused the sick with a bottle of water. The liquid mix washed away, joining a foul-looking, yellow rivulet at the foot of the wall. Relieved, and unable to restrain her bladder, Ana peed.

'Don't know why they bother to put newcomers in the white gowns and pretend there's some sort of twenty-four-hour evaluation,' Tamsin said. 'Everybody gets a blue one with a number the next day. No such thing as passing the interview. How can anyone prove they're not insane to people that are?'

Ana hoisted her knickers back on and stood up. In the alley beyond, something moved. A blurry boy jerked backwards and forwards, obscured by another boy, who stood with his back facing the yard and whose body sagged under some heavy weight. Ana struggled to untangle the image, her mind still floundering over Tamsin. She caught a slither of white flesh. Then a handful of long hair. An extra arm.

She choked on her own breath. The heavy bulk was a girl – a barely conscious girl. And the boys were . . . they were raping her. The picture burnt itself on to Ana's retina. She held out an arm to stop herself from falling. A hand coiled around her waist.

'They're—' She wanted to tell Tamsin what she'd seen, but she couldn't form the words.

Tamsin dragged her from the wall. 'Better move it,' she said, leading Ana to a throng at the edge of the smaller courtyard. 'Breakfast is on a first-come-first-served basis.'

A bell rang. The crowd pressed forward. Carried on the wave, Ana let the tears of anger and shock slide down her face. She didn't know how much more of this madness she could take. How on earth could Tamsin be here at Three Mills? How could Jasper not know who she was? How could boys do something like that in a place where the girls were patients? They were supposed to be safe. The nightmare had no limits; it was as wide and black as the space between stars.

*

After breakfast, orderlies corralled patients into a giant, white-padded room with an arched roof. Three horizontal structural beams strung out across the ceiling. Metal poles hung from the beams, rigged with a dozen flatscreens. Ana shuffled towards a group of patients huddled beneath one

273

of the screens and discovered that the accompanying sound became audible from a metre and a half away. Otherwise, the padded walls muffled the quiet drone.

A long, eye-level window ran along the left-hand wall of the old rehearsal studio. Instinctively, Ana crossed to it and gazed out. A cobbled street lay directly below. When she pressed her nose to the window she could make out the blue security door which she'd entered by. Dannard had been right. Inside Three Mills the real world was lost. The blue door might as well have been a porthole linking two different planes of existence.

Ana searched the drawn, sickly faces of boys and girls coming in from breakfast. If Jasper had queued for a morning shower he could still be a while. She moved away from the window, entering the nearest screen's sound radius. A news report filtered through her awareness.

'The Right Honourable Dr Peter Reed,' an anchorperson was saying, 'Secretary of State for Trade and Industry, formerly Secretary of State for Health, was killed yesterday evening close to his home at the southern boarder of the Hampstead Community.'

Ana stopped and cocked her head at the image of a septuagenarian government minister. 'The Wardens are looking for Cole Winter, who is wanted for questioning about the murder.'

A police-arrest photograph of Cole from a couple of years ago filled the screen. His shoulder-length hair hung in straggly clumps. Dark stubble made his face look gaunt and menacing.

Ana stared at the haunted eyes. Her arms hung limply at

her sides. She felt the blood drain from her face. Felt herself plunge headfirst into fear.

'Cole Winter,' the reporter continued, 'a disciple of Richard Cox, the mastermind of the 2036 Tower Bridge bombing, was seen leaving the crime scene. Mr Winter had personal ties to Dr Reed. He is considered dangerous and should not be approached. If you have any knowledge of his whereabouts please report it to the Warden's hotline.'

The screen image cut to a mountain of smoky rubble.

'The collapse of the US Middle East peace process has resulted in another night of heavy bombing over the eastern coast of the United States.'

Ana couldn't move, couldn't even twist her neck away from the flatscreen. The reporter's words floated around her meaninglessly.

'Another 20,000 are estimated dead and a further 140,000 reported missing. This is the third air raid since the collapse of the peace process last week . . .'

She sucked in deeply. *There are people who will hide him*, she told herself. For all she knew, the Crazies in the City hated the Wardens and wouldn't contact the hotline. Cole could just hole up somewhere until things settled down, then go to the Project. As she grew calmer, her train of thought shifted. If the whole of London's Wardens were on the lookout for him, he couldn't possibly risk going back to the Forest Hill flat. He wouldn't be there tonight. He wouldn't know she hadn't made it out of Three Mills.

She bent over, passing her head through her legs and forced herself to breathe. Her face tingled feverishly. How was she ever going to get out of here?

After a moment, she staggered back to the window. She had to try speaking to Jasper again and jog his memory, so they could figure out what they were going to do.

Minutes dragged by as she waited for him to come in from breakfast. Finally, as the orderlies divided the patients into groups to herd them back to their respective studios, Jasper appeared. Seeing her approach, he warded her off with the sign of the cross. Whatever decisions had to be made, she realised, whether she should confess to the psychs who they really were, or find some other way out, she couldn't count on Jasper. She was on her own.

22

The Tanks

Back in the studios, the atmosphere sparked with tension. From snippets of conversation, Ana gathered they would soon be free to roam the inner compound. They were waiting for the orderlies to collect those few who would be taken off for morning therapy.

A bell rang and boots tramped through the yard. The scarred orderly and her usual dour companion entered Ana's dormitory. The orderly read six names, 'Emily's' included, from a clipboard. Five girls edged towards her, holding out wrists and they were shackled to a link of metal chain.

Stunned, Ana rose. She stepped forward, the fear around her palpable. Most girls kept their eyes lowered. The scarred orderly jangled a pair of cuffs.

'We're not going to be having any trouble today, are we, Emily?' she said.

Ana held out her wrists, arms weightless like in a dream. The metal hoops crunched down on her hands, linking her to the other five patients.

The chosen girls skittered across the yard like leaves blown in a gust of wind. They passed through the grey building with toilets and shower facilities to a back door.

The door led out of the compound into a wide cobbled walkway; the walkway Ana had looked down on only an hour ago.

The line of girls bunched up, grinding to a standstill. Though no one looked at it, Ana knew they were all conscious of the blue gate lying in full view beyond the reception.

She lowered her eyes and squeezed her shackled hands into fists. She would divulge her true identity to whichever psychiatrist they were now taking her to. She would make them listen. She would be persuasive. Her father could end any one of their careers. What would one day's difference make to verify her story when their job was on the line?

They crossed a cattle bridge to a cluster of warehouses. A river ran alongside the thirty-foot-high studio walls. From time to time, a girl ahead stumbled or tripped, yanking Ana's arm from its socket.

The scarred orderly stopped and detached Ana and one other from the group. They stood before an entrance of a loading bay with a roller-shutter half open. The second orderly took up the other four girls and tussled them away. The girl beside Ana stopped crying and began to shake. Ana gazed at her feet, tinged blue from the cold. Liquid trickled across the dirt path towards her. She looked at the girl, and saw the girl stood in a puddle.

The scarred orderly laughed. 'What doesn't kill you makes you stronger,' she said, lighting a cigarette and pushing them towards the accordion-like studio entrance. 'It's time. Hurry up.'

Ana obediently ducked under the roller-shutter and

found herself on a dark, concrete stage fifty metres long and half as wide again. The girl tumbled in beside her, letting out a cry of terror. Five glass tanks lined the sparse stage, lit up internally like they were in an aquarium. The shutter clattered down. The studio disappeared into pitch-black nothingness. Except for the eerily glowing tanks.

Ana wrung her hands together until the bones cracked. She closed her eyes and set herself the task of finding a logical answer to what was going on.

Tubes travelled in and out of the tanks. A metal frame, like a bed, had been welded to the bottom of each man-sized casing. And each one had its own control panel on a separate pedestal.

A century ago, the psychs used to strap their patients into baths and douse them with icy water. It had become popular again recently when a respected psychiatrist 'proved' it successfully altered chemical imbalances in the brain. Or perhaps the tubes pumped gel into the tanks and this was a new form of ECT, administering electric shocks to all zones of the body. Ana began to shake. Either way, she was totally screwed.

'We haven't got all day,' a voice said.

From the furthest end of the stage, a figure strode towards them silhouetted by the closing door through which she entered. A petite nurse followed.

Cusher. Ana's hope shrivelled. Cusher hadn't listened to a word Ana had said in the shower interview.

'Hurry up,' Cusher admonished. 'No need for false modesty.'

Neither Ana nor the girl beside her moved. The door at

the back of the studio sucked shut. A dim red light came on at either end of the stage. Pumps skittered across the hard floor. The nurse reached them and breathlessly began to disrobe the girl beside Ana. The girl submitted at once. When the nurse reached for Ana, Ana slapped her hands away.

'My name isn't Emily,' she said, wrestling to keep her high-pitched voice steady. 'There was a mistake. I'm not supposed to be here.'

'Good God,' Cusher sighed. 'Mrs McCavern!'

A harsh grinding sound followed by the clatter of metal scraping across metal rang through the studio. Ana flinched. The roller-shutter ascended. Daylight poured through the jaw-like opening. The scarred orderly ducked through.

'Mrs McCavern,' Cusher said. 'I told you not to leave me alone with the new one.'

'Sorry, Dr Cusher.' McCavern didn't sound sorry, she sounded furious. Ana cringed.

'Get her into tank four,' Cusher ordered.

McCavern prodded Ana in the back with a truncheon. Ana stifled a cry as one of yesterday's bruises flared up. She tumbled forward to the nearest tank, then limped up the three steps. When she reached the top, McCavern knocked her over the edge.

She fell on to the metal bed-frame, her left side crashing against the sharp rails, her knees scraping the sides of the tank and starting to bleed. McCavern clambered down the short stepladder into the narrow gully beside the bed, cursing under her breath.

'Troublemakers don't do well here. No, they don't do well at all. I'm going to keep a special eye on you.'

'You're making a big mistake,' Ana stuttered.

'Lie down,' McCavern growled.

'My father is Ashby Barber.'

McCavern's hand twitched towards the truncheon tucked in her belt. Tears swelled in the corner of Ana's good eye. She lay down on the metal frame, face up. McCavern leant over her and drew a plastic strap tightly across her chest. Then she pinned Ana's wrists with metal half-circles and fastened a second strap over her legs.

'Please,' Ana choked. 'Please. My father is Ashby Barber.'

McCavern regarded her for a moment, before climbing the small stepladder and disappearing into darkness.

Liquid gurgled. Ana heard it slosh below her, gathering in the bottom of the tank. Her chest heaved against the strap. She gasped at the air, starting to hyperventilate. Blackness edged across the corners of her vision. She was about to pass out when a scream pierced the old film stage. A split second later liquid oozed around the edges of her feet, calves, thighs, back and neck. She wiggled her toes. The texture and lack of smell indicated it was only warm water. Ana grew still, not understanding.

They weren't going to be shocked with ice, or electrocuted through specially designed body gel. It had to be some sort of immersion therapy.

The tension in her limbs unravelled. She slackened her muscles, allowing the adrenalin to work its way out of her. She tried to ignore the other girl's screaming and focused on relaxing her feet, then her legs, her thighs, her buttocks, all the way up through her body until she'd almost regained a sense of calm. In a few more seconds, the water would fill her ears. Then there would just be the sound of the pump and the liquid slopping back and forth against the tank walls.

The average person couldn't hold their breath for anywhere near sixty seconds, especially not when they were panicking. As Cusher surely didn't intend to drown them – Ana hadn't noticed any resuscitation gear – she would be fine. Stilling her mind, she did her best to evoke herself at home, sitting at her piano, fingers running up and down the keys. But as the water closed over her head, instead she imagined herself descending a curved staircase. It was strange, she could actually feel her hand trailing along a banister. A door stood at the bottom of the stairs, blocking her way. She reached out. It felt solid, even though she knew it couldn't be. She twisted the handle. The door swung back and an infinity of stars greeted her. In the distance, suspended on the edge of the horizon, lay a spiral galaxy.

She almost gasped and swallowed water. It was so vivid and beautiful, it seemed impossible that it was only in her mind.

Entranced, Ana floated through the door, feeling as though she'd hopped across the folds of space and time to the most magical place in the universe. Young stars swirled around the spiral galaxy's golden centre. Silvery-blue light trailed behind them, as though the galaxy had just been stirred by a giant spoon.

Cool air blew across the tips of Ana's face. She blinked,

was back in the tank. Water gurgled as it drained. The young nurse jumped down beside her prostrate form. Water splashed around the nurse's waist, but she didn't seem to care about her uniform getting wet. She laid two fingers on Ana's windpipe, checking for a pulse. When she felt one, she grappled for an oxygen mask attached to a long hose wound along the side of the tank.

'No,' Ana said.

Startled, the nurse's finger shot to her lips, signalling for Ana to be quiet. She attached the mask over Ana's head. Just as it snapped on, Cusher loomed over the side.

'Well?' she said.

'The pulse is faint,' the nurse answered, looking at Ana warningly.

'Once you've checked her vitals, bring her to my office. I'll see her first.'

The nurse nodded, then began to undo the strap across Ana's shoulders. The stage echoed with the click-click of Cusher's shoes and the sound of the other girl coughing and retching. Ana strained to sit up, but the nurse gently put a hand on her chest and shook her head. She began to rub Ana's legs with a towel.

As Ana lay there, an icy feeling of anger and power coursed through her. When a far-off door banged shut, she pulled herself up. The nurse stepped back. Ana swung off the metal frame into ankle-deep water, then climbed the stepladder. At the top of the tank, she jumped the five-foot drop on to the stage floor. Her hair and gown dripped water everywhere. The nurse appeared behind her at the top of the tank.

'Give me that,' Ana said, snatching the towel. She stormed over to the next tank where the girl she'd come in with now lay curled up in a ball on the floor. Puke dribbled down the girl's lips and around her cheek, which pressed flat against the concrete. Gently, Ana lifted her blonde head of hair and began mopping up the vomit. She moved the girl away from the puddle of sick, pulled tight the towel already draped over the girl, and began to rub. The girl burst into tears.

'What's your name?' Ana asked.

'Helen,' the girl cried.

'How old are you, Helen?'

'Thirteen.'

The stench of vomit twisted up Ana's nostrils and seethed down her throat. She'd done nothing as boys took advantage of an unconscious girl, nothing as McCavern cuffed her and led her here, nothing as Cusher drowned them.

The anger grew so dense, she thought it would choke her.

*

Ten minutes later, Ana sat on Cusher's tweed sofa in a bland room, short hair drooping over her eyes, gown clinging to her damp skin.

'Tell me, Emily,' Cusher said, after a drawn out silence. 'What was going through your mind while you were trapped under water?'

'Tell me, Dr Cusher, do you enjoy drowning your patients?'

Cusher's left eye twitched. 'Let's stick to me asking the questions, shall we?'

'Contrary to popular belief,' Ana said, 'they actually drowned more women for witchcraft in the age of Enlightenment than in the Middle Ages. Trials by drowning.'

'Tell me how you felt, Emily.'

'The Age of Reason.'

Cusher bristled with irritation. Her finger curled back the short hair already combed behind her ear.

'Why don't you tell me about the last time you were institutionalised?'

'Because you don't listen.'

'I'm listening.'

Ana held Cusher's gaze. Cusher smiled, dropped her eyes and began shuffling through the papers on her desk.

'I was never institutionalised.'

'Really?'

'My name is Ariana Barber. My father is Ashby Barber. He won the Nobel Prize for identifying the mutated set of genomes responsible for schizophrenia. When he finds out I'm here, you're going to lose your job.'

Cusher sniffed and pinched her nose. She noted something down while stifling a yawn.

'Well, let's see if you're still feeling that way tomorrow, shall we?' she said.

As though on cue, the door opened and McCavern entered with a wheelchair. Seeing Ana, surprise flickered across her gaze, quickly followed by contempt. She groped for her cuffs, obviously not used to needing them after the tanks.

Ana got up and stood looking down on the psychiatrist. Cusher stopped tidying up and met her gaze, trying to appear amused, an effect that was undermined by the spasm in her left eye and the lip tremble when she smiled. Ana turned, strode to the wheelchair and plumped down.

23

Shockers

McCavern wheeled Ana alongside the river, over the cattle bridge, and past the empty car park. They rolled to a halt outside the wash-block door to the compound. Ana waited. McCavern's eyes drilled into the back of her head. Ana clenched her jaw and sat up straighter. The tight manacles gnawed at her wrists. But she sensed any effort to alleviate the pain would be taken as a sign of weakness. Perhaps exactly what McCavern was waiting for now.

She held her hands still in her lap. Finally, the orderly produced a chain of keys from her belt, unlocked the wooden door, and pushed Ana into the grey building. The stink of excrement assaulted Ana's senses. She'd been too scared to notice on her way out, but faeces smeared the corridor walls and piles of vomit rotted in dark corners. Resisting the impulse to gag or cover her nose with the sleeve of her gown, Ana focused on the square of yard beyond, bathed in daylight. Only one day in Three Mills, and she was actually glad to be returning to the compound.

In the main yard, patients milled around, twitching, fidgeting, arguing with each other, or themselves. A group of girls fought over blankets. Registering Ana, they quietened and shushed each other, though most didn't dare look over.

McCavern removed the cuffs. Ana stood up without prompting, ensuring the three inches she had over McCavern were felt. McCavern didn't move. She was obviously still thinking about taking matters into her own hands. Such an unruffled countenance after a trip to the tanks couldn't be good for morale.

Ana held her head high. She felt the orderly's presence behind her and was determined not to flinch or duck away. The wind tugged at her flimsy robe and swept through the damp strands of her cropped brown hair. She breathed in, letting the cold burst through her lungs, noticing Tamsin, who was leaning against Studio 8's brick wall.

The wheelchair creaked. Rubber rolled across tarmac. McCavern retreated.

Ana remained still and poised, taking in her audience. Tamsin met her roaming gaze with a fixed, appraising stare. Ana gave a small smile and strode towards her. The yard sprang back to life.

Tamsin frowned. 'You had hydrosynthesis this morning,' she said.

'So that's what they're calling it?'

Ana had heard of narcosynthesis, where patients were given narcotics and then put through analysis. But hydrosynthesis was a new one.

A hush fluttered over the yard. Ana turned to where everyone was looking. Someone else was being wheeled out of the wash-block. The male patient's head draped over his body.

'Most people don't have your stamina,' Tamsin said.

Ana gripped Tamsin's arm, scrunching her good eye to see better.

The orderly tipped up the wheelchair. The patient flopped forward, smacking face-down on the tarmac, one arm twisting around his back. Ana broke into a lopsided run. The orderly quickly turned and disappeared back into the wash-block.

Ana knelt beside the sprawled figure. She stroked back the tangled, sandy hair. 'Jasper?' she whispered. 'Jasper?' His name stuck in her throat.

He groaned. She looked up helplessly. A huddle of girls stood several metres away, watching.

'Give me a blanket!' Ana ordered. The girls clung to the precious covers around their shoulders. Ana jumped to her feet and hurtled towards the group. She snatched the nearest blanket, meeting no resistance. Returning to Jasper, she wrapped the cover over him and lifted his head on to her knee. He moaned when she moved him, hands protectively coming up over his ears. She stroked his hair, hummed his favourite Miles Davis jazz piece. He dropped his hands and slumped against her. He smelt awful; unwashed, metallic, a faint trace of chemicals sweating through the skin.

After a couple of minutes, Ana became aware that the persistent background clamour of the yard had not resumed. If anything the murmuring had grown quieter. She looked up. A hundred faces stared at her. Boys and girls crowded into the main court from the games room. Tamsin lingered among those who stood closest. Ana gazed at her imploringly.

'He needs to lie down,' she said, wrapping an arm under his shoulder. After a moment's hesitation, Tamsin stepped forward and took up the other side.

'Where to?' she asked.

'Where I can keep an eye on him.'

They staggered across the yard to Studio 8, Jasper's torso flopped over their hunched shoulders, his legs dragging behind. The crowd parted with looks of amazement, confusion and fear.

Inside Studio 8, they lowered Jasper on to a mattress. He groaned again, barely conscious.

'Why isn't he wet?' Ana asked.

'He didn't have hydrosynthesis. He's a shocker.'

'Shocker?'

'Electric Shock Treatment. One of their better ones. Wipes out memory, messes up the neurological system, causes permanent brain damage. Your difficult patient syndrome is totally cured. 'Course there's no future in being a vegetable, but at least it's not a corpse, right?'

The dust from the mattresses, coupled with Jasper's odour scratched the back of Ana's throat.

'Shock Treatment is safe,' she said feebly, repeating the advertising slogans she'd heard again and again growing up but knowing as she said it, she didn't believe it. 'Ninety per cent successful. Immediate relief for depression.'

'Yup,' Tamsin said. 'I suppose that's one definition of relief, an actual inability to have a clear thought about anything.'

Ana sank on to the mattress by Jasper's feet. It would be

her father's fault if Jasper wound up brain damaged. She had to get them both out of there.

She spent the next hour by Jasper's side in the dim half-light of the studio. At lunchtime a bell rang and girls began to trickle out into the yard. Tamsin, who'd gone off, now reappeared in the doorway.

'You need to eat,' she said.

'I can't leave him.'

'He needs to eat, then.'

'We can't carry him all the way up there.'

'No, we can't. But you can come with me and sneak him back your bread roll. He'll be OK. No one bothers the shockers.'

Ana rubbed her swollen eye, which had started to itch, then got up reluctantly. She stretched her stiff legs. Her stomach grumbled at the thought of food.

'He'll be fine,' Tamsin repeated, retreating.

Narrowing her good eye against the brightness, Ana followed.

Only a handful of patients still loitered in the yard. Ana drifted towards the main building where they'd eaten supper the previous night. Six bodies now lay heaped in front of the wash-block, like debris tossed ashore. Three covered their heads with their arms, two were curled into balls, one lay lifelessly. Ana stopped, thinking one of the balled-up girls was the thirteen year old from the tanks.

'Hurry up,' Tamsin shouted over her shoulder. Ana edged towards the girl, but it wasn't Helen.

'There isn't time,' Tamsin said, coming back and yanking her away. 'Move it!'

In the dining room, Ana hurried through her lentils and mashed potato, wondering what had happened to Helen. She hid her bread roll in a fold of the blanket Tamsin had given her. The orderlies prowled up and down the aisles between the tables. Once Ana had finished her meal, she waited for an orderly to pass before rising and following in the same direction. As she moved by Tamsin, her arm shot out and snatched Tamsin's half-eaten roll. In a flash, Tamsin's hand clamped over hers.

'There are six of them out there,' Ana whispered.

Tamsin studied her for a moment, then let go. Ana tucked the roll away. She walked the aisle behind the orderly, appropriating the rolls of every girl in Tamsin's posse.

Back in the yard, she handed out the bread. After checking on Jasper and getting him to eat a few crumbs, she searched for Helen. She eventually found the girl tucked into a far, dark corner of Studio 3, snivelling and muttering to herself.

'Helen?' Ana said, walking towards her.

The girl screamed and lashed her arms in the air, as though fending off a monster.

Ana took a step back, crouched down and talked to her in soothing tones.

'Remember me? I was in the tanks with you. It's OK. You're OK now.'

Crying and trembling, Helen held up her fists like she was still expecting some kind of attack.

Ana inched forwards, keeping her movements small and unthreatening. 'Are you hungry? I bet you missed lunch. Not that there's much to miss. Overcooked, mushy lentils.

Old mashed potato. I have bread. Do you want some bread?'

Helen's raised fists sagged. Her eyes finally seemed to focus on Ana. Ana broke off a piece of the roll Jasper had barely touched. She held it out. Tentatively, Helen took it, clasping the bread in shaky fingers for several seconds, as though waiting to see if this was a trick.

'It's OK,' Ana said.

Helen brought the bread to her lips and nibbled. When Ana didn't stop her, she pushed the whole lump into her mouth. Ana held out more. Helen looked at the bread, then at Ana. Her eyes filled with tears, glistening in the semi-darkness.

'Why are they trying to kill me?' she whispered.

Ana shook her head. 'They're insane,' she said. She crouched down near the girl, breaking off bread and passing it to her until the roll was finished.

Several minutes later, when she rose, Helen trailed after her into the courtyard, sticking to her like a shy shadow all afternoon, as Ana sat keeping vigil over Jasper.

Jasper stirred back to life at around 4 p.m. He rambled about a country house his parents had owned when he was a child; about crowding into the family car with his golden retriever and driving two hours to the rustic retreat with its outside toilet and log fires; about his brother Tom teaching him to snare rabbit and pitch a tent. Speaking about his childhood seemed to help him. Ana listened, an aching sadness occasionally sinking her heart. He'd never opened up to her like this before. It made her happy and miserable and guilty, at the same time. Because he didn't know who she was. Because while she was with Jasper, sitting beside him, holding his hand, all she could think of was Cole.

Several of Tamsin's posse helped Jasper to supper. Ana let Tamsin take charge, not wishing to draw any more attention to herself and Jasper than she already had done. When the orderlies rounded them up before returning them to their studios for the night, Ana saw Jasper go with a feeling of relief. He'd be safe until the morning. And she wouldn't have to look at him any more and think, *I'm in love with someone else*.

Helen returned to her allocated Studio 3 to sleep. Ana returned to her own studio, and discovered Tamsin's group was also in there. They'd bagged the best-placed mattresses behind the studio door where the air was fresh, but the draught didn't reach them. Tamsin had saved Ana a place beside her.

Night orderlies waited for the girls to settle, then roamed the compound, checking through the ajar door every half hour or so, to make sure no one was trying to hang themselves with bed sheets or slit their wrists with blunt supper knives. Endangering the girls' lives was obviously a privilege the psychs liked to keep for themselves.

*

At daybreak, orderlies stomped across the compound, trolleys rattled, studio doors ground back, and McCavern and her colleague appeared, flanking the nurse who began to distribute everybody's meds.

Ana had slept off and on through the night, woken often by the cold and the aches and pains in her body. She was wrapped up in her blanket on the bed, head under the cover, meds lining her stomach, when the bell allowing them to leave the studio rang.

Tamsin sprung up. 'Move it!' she shouted.

The girls from her group dashed to the door. Alarmed, Ana jumped up and tore after them, blanket flapping behind her. Out in the courtyard, she saw Tamsin sprinting towards the wash-block. She ran hard to catch up. Patients swarmed the building from all sides, rushing to get there first. The closer studios were at an obvious advantage. Tamsin's group linked hands and began pushing through the narrow entrance. Ana ducked under a couple of guys and bumped aside several teenagers to grab a dark-skinned girl's wrist – the last of Tamsin's posse. In a chain, they veered from the main toilet queues down a left-hand corridor. The corridor led to three large cubicles, each with its own yellow door. As they arrived, two doors slammed closed and locked.

'Come on,' Tamsin said. Seven of them bundled through a swing door into the remaining cubicle. They pushed out three stragglers who'd arrived first. Tamsin leant back against the door to stop others from entering, while the dark-skinned girl swivelled a flat bar into place top and bottom. Locked inside, the girls cheered.

Dazed and breathless from the run, Ana took a few seconds to register what was going on. The dirty shower cubicle was similar to the one Cusher had interviewed her in. The girls weren't wasting any time. They'd all stripped off and were now hanging their gowns on hooks at either side of the door. Ana fumbled to remove her robe. She retrieved the bar of soap stored in her gown pocket. The showers came on automatically. The girls leapt into the tepid spray, scrubbing hard at their bodies, rubbing soap into their hair. Ana copied, thankful her hair was short. After two minutes, Tamsin shouted, 'Time!' and the girls turned their attention to cleaning soiled knickers and grubby bras.

After three minutes the showers cut out. A wooden hatch scraped open in one of the side walls. Six small threadbare towels appeared. Tamsin handed out the towels to her girls, excluding Ana from the count. The youngest-looking girl offered Ana her towel. Tamsin watched with a look of amusement.

'She'll probably be back in the tanks today,' the girl said defensively.

Ana shivered, partly at the thought of being strapped down underwater again, partly because the wash-block wasn't heated and it was freezing. Winter at Three Mills had to be hell. Hurriedly, she patted herself dry and returned the towel to the youngest girl.

They left the damp rags in the hatch, donned their robes, shoved wet underwear in their pockets and gripping each other's hands, returned the way they'd come, pushing through the shoving hordes. Ana glanced back and saw a dozen boys pack into the shower cubicle they'd just exited. A girl who'd been swept into their midst, struggled to break free. Ana turned to help, but the dark-skinned girl pulled her back. 'Lost cause,' she muttered.

They entered the main corridor, where there were still more crowds. 'Sorry, folks,' the dark-skinned girl said, 'you're too late. The water'll go cold on the next one and run out on the third.'

To Ana's surprise, their group didn't return to the courtyard but veered the other way, down the corridor towards the faeces-smeared walls and the boys' toilets.

'Hold tight,' Tamsin warned. A group of boys whistled as they jostled past. They fell into a door on their right. A second set of girls' toilets. Situated past the boys' block it was obviously seldom used. Ana had been in there last night, when an orderly escorted several of them before lights out.

Inside, the girls let go of each other. Two of them headed straight for the motion-sensor hand driers at either end of the row of sinks and began to dry their underwear. Tamsin and the rest of them disappeared into the cubicles. Ana heard them throwing up. She glanced around and saw a fixed camera high in a far corner. Shutting herself in the last toilet, she checked for hidden cameras, then stuck her fingers down her throat.

When she came out, Tamsin was leaning against the doorjamb.

'You needn't have bothered,' she said. 'Yours were placebos today.'

'What?' Placebos were fake pills, used to make a patient or someone on a drug trial believe they were receiving medication. What was Tamsin talking about?

'You can always tell,' Tamsin continued, 'cos they're just one colour and they're bigger.'

'Why would they do that?' Ana asked.

Tamsin shrugged. Ana moved to a sink and washed out

the sides of her mouth. Then she took her toothbrush and toothpaste from her robe. The young girl who'd given her a towel came and stood beside her. At first Ana was too distracted to notice, but then she saw the imploring look, the extended hand holding a toothbrush. Ana squeezed out toothpaste on to both their brushes and began cleaning her teeth, barely noticing as the girl skipped away.

Had Cusher reconsidered? Did she believe Ana might be who she said she was? Had she cut out the medication as a temporary precaution, until she'd verified Ana's story? But then why maintain the farce of giving her the medicine at all? Perhaps she'd wanted to conceal her uncertainty. Ana felt a thrill at the possibility of having got under Cusher's skin.

Tamsin came and stood beside Ana at the sink. She spoke quietly, dipped over the sink, the water running so no one overheard.

'What the shite are you doing here, Ana?'

'Jasper was abducted. A friend helped me track him to Three Mills.' Ana blushed as she said the word 'friend', but Tamsin had her head down and didn't notice. 'I thought I could confirm it was really him and the psychs would let me out after the twenty-four hour test.'

'They don't let anyone out – not until right before your nineteenth birthday.'

'Why nineteen? And what are you—'

'Shhh . . .'

Two of Tamsin's posse joined them, chatting about hair-styles and plotting to get their hands on a pair of scissors.

Tamsin caught Ana's eye in the mirror reflection above the sink. Ana wiped a rogue tear and moved away.

They were late to breakfast, which meant by the time they entered the white-padded TV lounge they'd missed the national news. Desperate for information about Cole, Ana became agitated and annoyed and kept to herself as they separated into groups to be taken back to their studio dorms.

As the orderlies rounded up the first group of boys, she caught sight of Jasper. Her shoulders dropped a little. It was good to see him walking about with a bit more colour to his face. She shuffled towards the doors with a cluster of girls. McCavern stepped forward from the row of orderlies and stuck out her truncheon.

'Not you, missy,' she said. 'You're to wait here. You've got a special appointment today.'

24

Dr Frank

McCavern trundled Ana, who was strapped down in a wheelchair, past the river and therapy stages towards a huddle of nineteenth-century town houses. Ana tried to worm her hands from the cuffs but it was no use.

'In some places,' McCavern said, 'getting noticed might be a good thing. Not here though,' she laughed. Ana's stomach churned.

They stopped before an open front door. McCavern pushed her through a salmon-papered hallway and dumped her in a parlour room furnished to fit the Victorian setting. The door slammed closed. Ana turned towards it and caught sight of her reflection in a gilded mirror hung above an oak sideboard. One large grey eye and one hooded purple eye stared back at her. The last of the brown gel contacts had dissolved. She looked a wreck.

The parlour door creaked. A man in his mid-twenties with long sideburns and layered glasses, one layer currently in the up position, entered.

'Good morning, Emily,' he said. His voice crashed against the stillness. 'I'm Dr Frank.' He undid the strap around Ana's waist but kept her hands cuffed. Then he sat down on the edge of an armchair and folded one leg over another, trying to get comfortable. He shifted to balance his clipboard on his leg. Unhappy with his position, he got up, perched on the arm of the chair and peered down at her.

'Let's see, Emily,' he said, unable to stay the excitement in his voice. 'Yesterday, you told Dr Cusher that you were Ashby Barber's daughter. How do you feel about that today? Still think you're Ariana Barber?'

'Time doesn't change who we are,' Ana muttered. There seemed to be no shortage of idiot psychiatrists at Three Mills. She wondered where Cusher was.

'Apparently you asked Dr Cusher to contact Ashby Barber,' Frank said. 'You wanted us to get in touch with him and tell him his daughter was in our care.' Ana felt a jolt. Her guard went up. Was Frank offering her an opportunity, or a trap?

'Did you contact him?'

'I'm curious,' Frank continued. 'If Dr Barber was here, what would you say to him?'

'I wouldn't have to say anything,' she answered warily.

'Why not?'

'Because he would see the mistake with his own eyes.'

'Tell me about this "mistake", as you put it.' Frank leant back, enjoying the sound of his own voice. 'Didn't you come here of your own free will?'

'I don't remember.'

'Tell me about what you do remember.'

Ana concentrated. She had to make this plausible. This is what they'd tell her father, if they followed up her claim.

'I woke in a strange room in a block of flats,' she said. 'My head hurt so bad I couldn't think straight. I just needed

301

something to stop the pain. So I went to the nearest Mental Health Centre I could find and they sent me here.' She wondered if the MHCs kept records of their visitors. Unlikely. Besides, they'd never know which centre to check up with.

'And why did you sign in as Emily Thomas?'

'That was the name they said was on my ID.'

'You didn't remember your own name?'

'I was confused.'

'Well, how do you suppose you got this ID?'

'I don't know.'

'There is no mention of headaches on Dr Dannard's form when you registered.' Ana pursed her lips. The story had holes, but it was the best she could do. 'And now you're not confused?' Frank continued. 'And you want me to call Ashby Barber because you think he'll take you home?'

It was a rhetorical question, but Ana answered anyway. 'Yes.'

'So tell me how you got to the strange room.'

The puffed up bits of her eye itched. She tried not to scratch.

'I think I received a message,' she said.

'A message . . .'

'Asking me to meet someone who said they knew where Jasper was. They said they would tell me at a price. I thought they wanted money.' Frank frowned for a moment and then his face broke into a wide smile.

'Ah, Jasper,' he said, delighted with the extent of her delusion. 'You mean the man Ariana was supposed to join with, the abducted Taurell boy? And what did they want in exchange for this information?'

Ana bristled. 'How old are you?' she asked.

Frank shifted position and flipped down the second layer of his glasses. 'Continue,' he said.

'You look a bit young. Are you even qualified? You grew up in the City, didn't you? You're a Carrier – one of the lucky ones allowed to study to become a doctor or a lawyer or a psych. Carefully ironed shirt, a cheap suit, an esteemed psychiatric post. You're very pleased with yourself because you think you've really cut your way in the world.'

Frank snorted and clipped the lid on his pen. Ana smiled, relishing his discomfort.

'You've struggled,' she continued, 'and now you think you've made it. In a couple of years you'll realise that there's no satisfaction in talking to a bunch of neurotic teenage Crazies. You'll grow bitter and that faint light pulsing at your very core will go out for ever.'

'Enough!' Frank shouted. He pounded his clipboard on a coffee table with filigree legs. One of the legs snapped. The clipboard slid off, papers spilling loose on to the floor.

'Forever is a very long time,' Ana said.

'Emily Thomas,' he snarled, 'admitted to Seven Sisters' Mental Rehab Home in May 2031 after the death of her parents in a house fire that left her catatonic.'

Ana tried not to alter her body language, but instinctively she sat up straighter as the alarm bells began to go off.

That was an extremely unlikely coincidence. A decade ago the Mental Rehab Homes were only starting up, like the Communities. The chances of the real Emily Thomas having been institutionalised as a child were slim to none. She stared at Frank.

'What do you have to say?' he asked.

'Dr Cusher is more creative than I gave her credit for.'

Frank flipped up the second layer of his ridiculous glasses and grinned. 'A conspiracy,' he said.

She wanted to slam her foot into his stupid mouth and smash that smile. Instead, she smoothed out her face and relaxed her body, the way she'd always done with the Board.

'Just call my father and let him see me with his own eyes.'

'Well, I'm sure that would be a fascinating encounter.'

Ana was worried now. Frank was too certain of himself. He knew something. She trembled, cold in her flimsy robe.

'You see,' Frank said, bending over to gather up the papers, 'the eminent Dr Ashby Barber was Emily Thomas's physician at Seven Sisters for the five months she was there.'

Ana's mouth popped open. She couldn't stop it. Clearly someone had fabricated Emily Thomas's psychiatric history because there was no way the real Emily Thomas could have been treated by her father. He'd had all of a dozen patients while he trained to become a psychiatrist as part of his research into schizophrenia. But why would Cusher bother? They had plenty of other, much better ways to torture boys and girls. An invented file to break down a patient's delusion seemed far too subtle for any of the off-the-wall psychs at Three Mills.

'Not so verbose now, are you?' Frank said.

Ana managed to close her mouth. She kept her facial

expression blank, but she knew if he looked close enough he'd see the fear.

'Well,' Frank said, stretching. 'Now I've got your attention, I'd like to show you this news clip I found on the net this morning.' He waved a hand in front of his chest and his interface booted up, projecting coloured light into the air in front of him. From his suit pocket, he extracted a wireless speaker and set it down on the oak sideboard beneath the mirror. Then he turned Ana's wheelchair to face the parlour door. He stood behind her, the light from his interface automatically focusing on the white surface ahead.

A reporter stood outside the iron gates to Ana's home. Frank pointed his finger over the virtual arrow key and the reporter began to speak.

'Ariana Barber, daughter of Nobel Prize-winning geneticist Ashby Barber, was returned to her father's home in the Highgate Community early this morning.'

The image cut to a limo door opening in the dusky half-light. A tall girl emerged. Her long hair flicked out beneath the coat she was using to shield her face. Ana's father took the girl's arm and guided her away from the cameras, towards the house.

Ana stared at the screen. She couldn't think, couldn't move, couldn't breathe.

One time, years ago, when Tamsin watched all the old films she could get her hands on, they'd seen a 1950s thriller about a private investigator who was afraid of heights. During the film the investigator was forced to climb up a tower. When he looked down, the camera zoomed in and pulled away at the same time, making the building's perspective shift unnaturally. Ana's head felt like that now, simultaneously expanding and contracting as she attempted to grasp what she was seeing.

'Dr Ashby Barber and all of the small Highgate Community are deeply relieved by this unexpected turn of events,' the reporter concluded.

The image flickered and vanished. Ana looked at the space it left behind, the gears of her mind locked down. Frank wheeled her chair around. Triumph lit his face.

'It's something of a conundrum, wouldn't you say, *Emily*?'

Ana gazed straight at him, though she barely saw him now. Why would her father pretend she'd been returned home?

It came to her like the slow forming image of a photograph dipped in developer. He knew where she was. He planned to leave her in Three Mills. Just like Jasper. Her limbs seized up. Excruciating pain sliced through her chest. Her organs felt as though they were collapsing.

25

Tamsin

Ana lay on a mattress. Around her people spoke. But she didn't care about words. They prodded and snapped fingers. But she was too tired to tell them to stop. Sometimes others lay down too. Sometimes it hurt to breathe. All the time she felt a crushing emptiness.

The earth turned from the sun in tiny jolting fragments. She began to believe it would never turn back.

Then a bell hurtled through time towards her. And something changed. The people stopped coming.

Her body unfurled from its ball and found its way inside the main building. It dragged her upstairs. It bumped into things. It sat down. The hand paddled a plastic spoon through brown liquid. Something scorched her throat. She let out a cry. A spoon clattered into watery soup. She blinked and looked down in amazement. She hadn't even realised she was eating. A bread roll lay split in two by her bowl, large air holes gaped through the dough. She pressed a finger into the crust. It was as solid as dry earth. She wondered how she'd managed to halve it.

Girls and boys around her muttered to themselves, chairs scraped, mouths moved behind scabby hands. Everywhere there was staring, crying, lost and empty looks.

After lunch, she returned to Studio 8. Sat on a mattress in the dark. Watched grey phantom girls wander in and out, vanishing into the blackness each time the hazy sun dipped behind cloud, reappearing in the doorway, silhouettes haloed by afternoon light.

She became aware of burning sulphur tickling her nostrils. Tilted her head towards the smell. Saw a flame in the darkness. A pale, patchy hand held a match.

She followed the flame as it glided back and forth. A black vine tattoo flittered in and out of the light. Close by, so close she could feel warm breath on her ear, Tamsin spoke.

'Oh good,' she said. Her words formed slowly. 'You are there. I was beginning to wonder.' The flame loomed towards Ana's nose. Suddenly, it withdrew and extinguished, leaving behind wisps of smoke. 'It's easy to tell which ones are going to fall to pieces in here,' Tamsin continued, still speaking slower than normal. 'Almost always happens within the first twenty-four hours.'

Tamsin sat cross-legged on the mattress beside Ana, though Ana had no idea how long she'd been sitting there.

'That's when they get a taste of what they're really in for,' Tamsin said. 'Psychs know they got to start the therapy fast. Just to groove you in, make sure you know where you stand. You listening to me, Barber?'

Ana observed the spectral figures in the doorway. Ghosts had it better off than these girls. Here, bodies were trapped in loony dump hell, while their spirits were broken into pieces and scattered in the past.

'You, though,' Tamsin continued, 'you come back from

your first time in the tanks as though you've just been on an invigorating jog around the block.' She grinned. 'You always were a bit odd. That's part of the reason you and I became friends – me the poor girl in the Community with parents who were barely able to scrape by and you, the quiet, motherless country girl. I used to wonder whether, if you'd had normal parents and hadn't spent your first eleven years home-schooled in the middle of nowhere, you'd be like all the others. Now I know. You wouldn't. You're different, Ana. In the whole ten-year history of the Pure test, you're the only person who the Board has ever retested – except for the batch that they *had* to do after your dad got off the hook. And when they found out you were a Big3 Sleeper they gave you a reprieve until your eighteenth birthday and officially broke the rules of Pures and Crazies so that you and Jasper could be bound. And then you get yourself committed here looking for him.' Tamsin laughed. 'And I thought of the two of us, *I* was the wild one! '

She peered at Ana, waiting for a response. 'The important thing is to get through the therapy,' she said. 'Once you're through that, it's not so bad here. As long as you don't get addicted to the pills.'

Ana tried to move, do something, say something, but it was like the life had been sapped from her body.

'Hey, remember that time we cat sat for a friend of your dad's, and we locked ourselves out of her house? We had to break in through the letter box to get back in.'

A vague sensation fluttered through Ana. A feeling she'd almost forgotten. The simple pleasure of hanging around in the Community with a friend she could trust, a friend who made her laugh.

'Or that summer evening we snuck into the Highgate golf course, stripped down to our underwear and swam across the lake to see if the rumours were true; to see if there was a way out of the Community without going through the checkpoint?'

Ana remembered the stench of stagnant water. The echoes of their laughter rang in her ears.

'It's things like that which keep you going in here.'

No, she thought. *It's things like that which make this place unbearable.*

A cold hand gripped her chin, twisted her face so she was looking into Tamsin's brown eyes.

'Ana, please. Don't give up. Otherwise you'll drift away. I've seen it. I've seen it happen a hundred times. The special therapy is the worst bit. You only have to get through a couple more days.'

Ana blinked. She suddenly thought of Helen. Helen would have faced the tanks alone this morning.

'Is Helen back?'

Tamsin let go of Ana's chin. 'The girl trailing around after you yesterday?'

Ana nodded.

Tamsin shrugged and angled away.

'What?'

'No,' Tamsin said. 'She won't be back today.'

A hard ball of trepidation appeared in Ana's chest. 'Why?'

'Rumour has it she totally flipped out when she got to

the tanks. The lovely Dr Cusher put her under anyway. I heard they had to resuscitate her, so I guess she's been taken to hospital for overnight observation. You'd be amazed how often that happens around here.' Tamsin struck another match against the floor. 'Or maybe not. They normally return, though. Eventually.'

Ana stared at her old friend. It was hard to believe that this was really the same girl she'd thought about and missed more than anything, for the last seven months. The girl she'd once spent every waking minute with when they were fourteen, fifteen, sixteen years old.

'You disappeared,' she said.

Tamsin's free hand began to trace the tattoo vine on her neck.

'Not on purpose,' she laughed. But the bitterness in her voice was like a seam of hard metal through rock. 'One day, not long after your dad packed you off to the country for the summer, I snuck out of the Community. I always wanted to go to the cinema. Remember?' Her pale lips rose in a genuine smile. 'Remember how I dreamed of being an actress? Anyway, I was in East Finchley, buying toffees from one of those pick-and-mix stalls and this two-year-old kid came by with his mum. Started crying cos he wanted sweets and she couldn't afford any. Fell on the pavement, kicking, screaming, thumping his hands. Just a tantrum. But the Psych Watch turned up. The mother began to panic. Soon she was kicking and screaming too. Some big bloke arm locked her. A guy in a white coat stuck her with a needle. I couldn't just stand there and watch—' Tamsin broke off. In the dim light Ana saw tears in her friend's eyes. 'Been here ever since. No word from my family . . . The Watch took my ID. I heard they can sell a Pure ID for a fortune in certain circles. At first I tried to tell the psychs, but it was useless. The more I insisted, the more they put me into special therapy.'

Of all the strange things Ana'd imagined about Tamsin's disappearance, nothing had come close to this.

'But what did they do with your parents and your brother? How did they stop them from going to the Wardens? How did they make them leave the Community?'

'Leave?'

'When I came back at the start of term,' Ana explained, 'your whole family had gone. Someone was running your dad's shop. I asked just about everybody where you all were and the only answer I got was that your family had relocated.'

Tamsin pushed a palm hard against her forehead. 'I always wondered why nobody came,' she said. Her lips began to tremble. She plugged her hands over her mouth but a sob broke through.

Sadness rose over Ana like the tide. Her cheeks itched and she realised they were wet with tears.

Tamsin gulped down air in spasmodic gasps. She sniffed, hopelessly trying to pull it together. 'Does your dad know you're here?' she asked.

'Yeah.'

'Oh shite.'

Ana laughed and cried in the same breath. She reached out and took Tamsin's hand. They sat side by side, no longer trying to hide the gasps and sobs that racked their bodies. After a minute, Ana rubbed her nose with the back of her free hand.

'I'm going to get out of here,' she said.

'That's the spirit.' Tamsin sighed, letting go of her last tears.

'Next time they take me to the tanks,' Ana continued, 'I'll make sure they drown me.'

'OK, it's official. You're mad.'

'Will you look after Jasper for me? If I make it to one of the City hospitals, I'll find a way to contact his mum. I'll get you both out of here.'

Tamsin inhaled deeply and shook her head. 'Not that I don't appreciate the offer, but that's totally mental.'

'Will you keep an eye on him for me?'

'Ana, you could kill yourself trying to do that.'

'I'm not like you. I won't survive here.'

'Everyone feels like that at first.'

Ana shook her head. Tamsin looked away, bit her top lip, considering. Finally, she spoke.

'On one condition.'

'OK. What?'

'If you make it, you don't do anything stupid or dangerous to try and get me out.'

Ana frowned and folded her arms over her chest.

'You have to promise me, Ana. You risked too much coming here for Jasper. I won't have you doing anything so risky for me.'

'But you can't stay here.'

'Maybe Jasper's worth it, but I'm not.'

'What's that supposed to mean?'

'He's the son of the executive director of Novastra. His brother mysteriously died three years ago and now he's supposedly been abducted by terrorists while his dad's in the middle of negotiating a major deal with the government for BenzidoxKid. Get him out. Get him to talk. Concentrate on the big picture.'

Ana shook her head. The tears welled up all over again. 'You always knew it, didn't you? Even when we were fifteen, you knew there was something weird about the Pure test. You never bought into it.'

'You have to promise me you won't take any stupid risks trying to get me out . . . Promise.'

Ana stared at her friend. The devastation she'd felt seven months ago as every effort to discover Tamsin's whereabouts failed, came thudding down on her. She finally nodded, then reached over and clutched her best friend in her arms. 'I missed you,' she choked.

After a moment, Tamsin hugged her back. The two of them held each other as though it was all that kept them from being torn away into oblivion.

*

The following morning after breakfast, Ana waited anxiously for the orderlies to call her name. Of the thirty or so girls who slept in Studio 8, she was one of only four summoned for extra 'treatment'. Eyes on her feet, butterflies in her stomach, she offered her wrists to be cuffed. Once Orderly McCavern had linked the girls together, she led them out into a mild, late March morning.

Ana stopped short, blinking at an expanse of summer-blue sky. Sunshine warmed her hair. Spring had arrived to say goodbye. The chain tugged Ana's wrists, propelling her across the yard. Once again, they passed through the wash-block and came out near the empty car park. They crossed the cattle bridge and turned towards the riverside ware-houses.

Reaching the door to the hangar with the tanks, McCav-ern removed Ana's cuffs. Ana lurched forward, ducking under the roller-shutter before McCavern could jab her with a truncheon. Inside, she heard a click and a buzz of electricity, followed by the clattering descent of the shut-ter. The tanks glowed dimly in the darkness. Ana stood absolutely still, worried the slightest move might make her throw up. Eventually, a far door opened. Soft-soled feet scurried across the studio. The nurse from Ana's previous trip to the tanks appeared at her side, cautiously reaching to remove Ana's gown. Ana limply submitted.

Dressed in the bra and knickers she'd left home in an eternity ago, Ana climbed the steps to the nearest tank and dropped inside. Without prompting, she lay on the freez-ing metal bed. A strap tightened around her chest. She closed her eyes. A distant click of high-heeled shoes echoed off the walls.

Cusher.

Cold metal bars curved over Ana's wrists. The nurse locked down her thighs and feet. The low hum of a water pump began. Liquid gushed into the tank, spattering against the hard plastic floor. Ana breathed in. Chill air mixed with bleach filled her lungs. She relaxed her feet, her fingers, her neck, allowing her body to sink into the metal frame beneath her. Water tickled against the underside of her body. Goose bumps broke out on the tops of her arms and legs.

'I think we might see some improvement today,' Cusher said. Inside the tank, with the splattering and sloshing of water, Cusher's voice had no direction, no origin. It was everywhere at once, possessing the air.

Water grew over Ana like a second skin. She kept her breathing steady and light, determined not to inhale deeply. But when the time came, her body involuntarily closed her airways and she sucked in her breath. Fully immersed, she tried to relax. Pockets of oxygen in her lungs quickly burnt away. Pressure built in her head.

Let go, breathe in, she told herself. But she didn't. Her head began to feel like it would explode. She thought it couldn't get worse. But it could. It did. The pain widened and deepened. Fog seeped around the edges of her mind. She tugged against the bars holding her feet and wrists. Metal bit her skin. Her muscles sucked up the last vestiges of remaining oxygen.

She gasped for air. Water poured down her throat. Into her lungs.

I don't want to die. Please. I don't want to die.

Panic. Thrashing. Trying to scream.

Her thoughts became indiscernible shapes. Like objects covered in snow. Everything muffled. No visibility. No horizon. Whiteout.

26

Ashby

Ashby had spent the last forty-eight hours supplicating Charlotte Cusher to meet with him like he was a bloody door-to-door salesman. Not today. Today he had a letter from the Secretary of State for Health, officially permitting him to oversee Emily Thomas's mental rehabilitation. Today Ana was coming home with him, one way or another. Screw the Board and their three-month discharge procedure. He'd fight his way into the compound, use the Paralyser, immobilise everyone in a twenty-metre radius if he had to. Hell, he could get the place closed down in a shot. A simple call to Felix Post on the Mental Health Investigation Committee would do it. Ashby knew the rumours – missing attire, meagre meals, government funds lining staff pockets while the children went barefoot. He'd chosen Three Mills for Jasper precisely because of its reputation for easy admittance and patient neglect.

Ashby's saloon car, driven by Jack Dombrant, turned into Sugar House Lane. Barren wasteland lay on either side of the road up to the old tidal mill. Metal rattled beneath the wheels as they drove over the cattle bridge. Ashby gazed at the gloomy landscape. When he'd realised Ana had sneaked out into the City, he'd never in his wildest dreams thought she would wind up here.

Four days ago, Jack had informed him that Ana was staying with a crowd connected to the Enlightenment Project. Ashby had scarcely believed it. Then they'd connected a flutter of activity from Ana's interface to travel tickets purchased by Lila Aimes. It had taken almost a day, but they'd traced Lila Aimes to Bromley-by-Bow train station. A team had searched all the local CCTV cameras until they'd found pictures of Ana looking God-awful and doing the most bizarre thing Ashby had ever seen – entering Three Mills of her own free will.

Since then, he'd been applying pressure on Charlotte, pooling his resources, pulling in every favour he could think of to get Ana out. Charlotte, the bitch, hadn't even come to collect Emily Thomas's psychiatric file when Ashby had delivered it in person to the reception. And she hadn't responded to any of his requests to see Ana/Emily.

The car pulled up at an iron gate. A security guard approached. Ashby lowered his electric window and produced his permit.

'Sorry, sir,' the guard said leaning in. 'Power cut. Should be back on any minute now.'

'How long's it been out?'

'Ten minutes,' the guard said. 'They're working on the back-up generator.'

Over the last decade, despite a continual decline in national power consumption, the power surges and blackouts were steadily getting worse. Ashby took out his permit and held it up before his interface. Down the right side of the white card a list of hospitals and clinics he was associated with appeared. He touched his finger to the Three Mills header. An icon spun beside the header as the computer began searching. He unzipped his case, took out his pad, and linked it up to his interface. A moment later, he had the Three Mills home page on his portable screen. He typed in his six-digit pass code. The mainframe opened, providing him access to everything on the database, from financial records to staff log-in times. The records had cut out at 10.04.24, almost fifteen minutes ago. He checked the file for Emily Thomas. She'd been logged into a tank at 10.02.42. Less than two minutes before the power cut.

The tanks were automatic. They ran on the main power grid like everything else. Ashby began to calculate. Forty to fifty seconds for the tank to fill up, thirty seconds under water, forty to fifty seconds to drain totally . . . He rubbed his locked jaw. It would have been close. He exhaled, trying to relax. Could have been worse though.

A distant siren disturbed his returning calm. He glanced out the rear window. Though he couldn't see anything, he could hear the siren approaching.

Jack reversed the car and pulled over on to the grass. A battery-powered ambulance emerged on the horizon, kicking up dust. Ashby alighted from the car, leaving the passenger door dangling in the wind. He strode to the outhouse where the security guard now peered from his bulletproof window.

'What's going on?' he demanded.

'It's here,' the guard said into his interface mic. With a loud clunk, the steel security door released. Using his shoulder, the guard thrust open the usually automated door so that the steel back hit a magnetic wall grid. The door stuck in place. At the same moment, brakes squealed, and a whiff of burning tyre filled the air. The passenger side of the ambulance opened. A paramedic jumped out.

'The power's down,' the security guard said, trailing the paramedic to the rear of the ambulance. The paramedic mounted. From inside the ambulance he grabbed a medical kit with defibrillator, oxygen masks, and other resuscitation paraphernalia. 'You'll have to come through the security booth,' the guard explained.

'Get someone to help you bring the gurney,' the paramedic called to the ambulance driver. 'If these gates don't open we may have to get her back through security.'

Ashby noted the gender reference. He nodded at Jack who now stood beside the saloon, and the Warden swept in to help the ambulance driver. Meanwhile, Ashby followed the security guard and the paramedic. The paramedic looked experienced and controlled; his resuscitation gear hung on his shoulder as though it were no weight at all.

The security guard stepped aside to allow the paramedic through the security outhouse, then attempted to close the door. Ashby shoved his arm in the way. The lock had to be bolted down manually and he refused to budge. The guard gave in at once. The three of them ran the length of the narrow security building out on to the other side of Sugar House Lane. The guard pointed down a driveway to a cluster of warehouses facing the river.

'Stage D,' he panted. 'Second left.'

'Is she out of the water?' the paramedic asked.

The breathless guard shrugged.

Ashby began sprinting. His hard soles slammed the tarmac, jarring his knees. He was used to running, but in trainers. He swung second left and saw stage 'D', the first studio in a long row.

'This way,' he called to the paramedic behind him. The loading access shutter hung three-quarters open.

The two men entered the dark stage. Daylight reached in ten feet before dwindling to grey. Light also shafted in from the loading access on the opposite side, at the furthest end of the stage.

'Cavalry's arrived,' a voice said. Ashby looked around and saw an orderly leaning against the stage entrance, smoking.

'Over here,' a younger voice called from thirty feet away, where the doors opened on to the river. The paramedic jogged into darkness and dropped his kit by one of the tanks. Through the murk, Ashby could make out a nurse bent over a prostrate form. The paramedic took over, checking vitals, inspecting the limp body before him.

Ashby sidled closer. He stopped a few feet away. Sweat beaded on the palms of his hand, under his arms, in his hairline.

'Unavoidable, I'm afraid.' Charlotte Cusher's brittle voice cleaved the air. Ashby startled. He hadn't been aware of her lurking nearby. Charlotte rubbed her neck. 'The girl was in the tanks when the power went down.'

The paramedic thumped down on the girl's chest. He instructed the dripping wet nurse to continue giving mouth-to-mouth; then he removed a defibrillator from his kit.

'The ties have to be very secure,' Charlotte continued.

'Not easy to undo. At least not when they're two foot under water.'

'She was the only one under when the power went out?' Ashby asked.

'She was the only one in the tanks at all today,' Charlotte replied.

Ashby grew still. No, this girl couldn't have been the only one. Because that would mean . . .

'But she was immersed over three minutes before the power went out,' he said. 'She couldn't have still been under water.'

Charlotte's cold eyes glittered. 'Perhaps you should wait outside. Visitors aren't supposed to be on any of the stages.' She held out her arms, palms upwards, as though to usher him away without making physical contact.

Ashby sidestepped her and strode to the girl. The paramedic rubbed the charged defibrillator pads together, getting them ready. Slim calves with chipped pink-varnished toenails, poked out of a towel. The nurse bent over the girl, breathed air into her lungs. When she pulled back, Ashby was waiting. But the shock hit him hard.

Lifeless eyes stared from a bruised, swollen face. Gone was his daughter's beautiful hair, her soft, pale skin. Raw, dry patches mottled her forehead. Her lips were cracked, her hair limp, short, mousy. It hardly looked like her at all.

He filled with a sense of self-loathing. How had he let this happen?

'Clear,' the paramedic said. Ariana's body jerked, flexing up, head tipping back. Then it flopped level again.

'Nothing,' the ambulance driver said. Ashby hadn't

noticed the driver arrive, but the man was now crouched over Ariana. Jack and the driver must have brought the gurney up to the stage already. He glanced around for Jack and saw the young nurse, relieved of her duties, sitting in a crumpled heap. 'Clear,' the paramedic repeated. Ariana's body convulsed. The driver laid two fingers on her throat, shook his head.

'How long was she under?' the paramedic asked.

Charlotte Cusher folded her arms across her chest.

The ambulance driver pressed his mouth against Ariana's blue lips, breathed into her.

'Around a minute,' Charlotte said.

The young nurse sat up. 'One hundred and thirty-two seconds,' she corrected, wiping away the snot and tears from her face with the back of her hand. 'Fifty-two before the power cut out and then about a minute twenty, while I was undoing the straps.' Charlotte shot her a nasty look. The nurse's bottom lip trembled, but she wouldn't be silenced. 'I couldn't quite reach, you see,' she sniffed. 'My arms aren't very long, and I had to hold my breath each time and go under to reach down.'

'Fifty-two seconds!' Ashby shouted, as he watched the paramedic now pressing forcefully and rhythmically against the centre of Ariana's chest. 'It's supposed to be thirty.'

'We've got to get her to hospital,' the paramedic said.

'The first time, thirty had no effect on her whatsoever,' Charlotte argued.

'What's happening with the power?' the ambulance driver called out.

Ashby turned and saw the security guard had appeared

in the entrance and was standing beside Jack. The guard raised his arms and shook his head.

'Could take us a couple of minutes to get back through with her on the stretcher. It's too long.'

'Too long?' Ashby echoed.

'We've got nothing,' the paramedic said, resetting the defibrillator. 'Two minutes without oxygen on top of what she's had already . . .'

'You need to bring the ambulance up here.' Ashby latched on to the problem like it was a life raft.

'Charged.' The paramedic pressed the paddles against Ariana's snow-white chest. 'Clear!' Electricity buzzed through the machine. Her body jerked up and then thumped down. 'Clear . . .' the paramedic said, getting set to go again.

'Give me a minute,' Ashby said. 'I'll get the ambulance to you.'

The paramedic nodded.

'The engine's running,' the ambulance driver said.

Heart thumping in his chest, Ashby loped towards the roll-up gate. 'Jack, let's go. You,' he pointed at the security guard, 'you're with us.'

'Ashby?' Charlotte trilled behind him.

He leapt out into the bright morning and bolted towards the security outhouse, Jack beside him. The guard galumphed behind them. 'Move it!' Ashby shouted. But with the biometric ID panel deactivated, he realised he didn't need to wait for the guard to go through security. Jack shoved back the heavy door and Ashby pushed into the control room.

'Where's the switch for the gate?' he called. The guard appeared, panting in the doorway. He pointed down the corridor to a compartment with a touch screen.

'It's all computerised,' he wheezed. 'There's a manual latch, but you wouldn't be able to do anything. It's on a pulley and weighs a ton.'

Ashby darted into the compartment. He whipped off his interface and used its sharp corner to prise away the control panel. Wires cascaded. He twined them together, then wrenched. The magnetic force holding the gate shut, released.

'He . . . he's disconnected the circuits!' the security guard said.

Charlotte swaggered through the outhouse. 'What's going on?'

Jack blocked her way, while Ashby bolted in the opposite direction. He thrust aside the security door and ran to the gate. It had inched back enough to wedge in his hand, but he needed leverage. Sprinting back to the guard, he grabbed the man's truncheon, then used it to jimmy the door. Once the gap was large enough, he squeezed in and began to push. All he needed to do was slide the metal ton across its rails. Impossibly heavy work. But he was damned if that would stop him.

Jack came to help. They laid their shoulders into the gate, giving it everything they had until it inched along. Charlotte emerged from the security building, her prudish face a pool of wrath.

'Who is she? If you've admitted someone that wasn't

supposed to be here, I'll have you charged. I'll have your licence taken away.'

'I didn't send her. One of your lot committed her,' Ashby said. 'And if she dies, I'll have you killed.'

The colour drained from Charlotte's face. She could see he meant it. Perhaps she wasn't so naïve. Perhaps she knew he could carry out such a threat. He thrust harder. The rolling door gained momentum.

'We won't be held responsible for someone that was never supposed to be here,' Charlotte said. Her voice trembled.

Too little, too late, Ashby thought. When he'd finished with Charlotte Cusher she would be petrified. She would beg for his forgiveness. She would never show such nonchalance towards the life of one of her patients again. If Ariana lived. If she didn't live . . . Well, needless to say, drowning would be a blessing in comparison to Charlotte's last few minutes in the world.

'Get me the ID she came with and the paperwork to release her,' Ashby said.

'You want to take her into your charge?' Charlotte asked incredulously. Ashby felt himself swell from his body and mentally crush the woman before him into dust. He chucked the letter he'd received an hour ago from the Secretary of State for Health towards Charlotte. Her neck muscles strained taut. The letter fell into the mud by her feet.

'You have no right,' she floundered. 'Who is she? She's – she's . . .' Understanding flashed across Charlotte's eyes. 'No, no, that's impossible – she can't be – the news . . .'

The door finally shifted along far enough for the

ambulance to pass through. Ashby rounded the vehicle, swung into the driver's seat, and yanked the gear lever into drive. Dombrant jumped in beside him. Flooring the foot pedal, Ashby accelerated through the gates. The right wing mirror clipped the outhouse buttress. But he was through. Within seconds he screeched to a halt outside the tank stage. He jumped down. The ambulance driver and paramedic came rushing from the darkness, wheeling Ariana on a gurney.

Ashby flung open the ambulance doors and stood aside, allowing the men to work. The driver secured the gurney. The paramedic pumped Ariana's heart, stopped to check her vitals, pumped again.

'OK,' he said. 'There's a flutter.'

Ashby bit his knuckles, tears of relief burning his vision. The paramedic rubbed solvent across Ariana's pale arm and stuck a needle through her raised vein. Then he prepped the tubing of the ambulance IV set.

'Anyone know if she's got any drug allergies?' he asked.

'Nothing,' Ashby said. 'And she's in my care now. Take her to the nearest private place there is. Cost is not a consideration.' The medic stopped for a second, looked at Ashby appreciatively.

'Let's move it,' the driver said. He jumped down from the back. Dombrant got out of the front and returned to the saloon. Doors slammed. The paramedic hung the IV bag on a hook and looped the tubing. Seconds later, they were hurtling away from Three Mills.

27

Emerging

She glided through streaks of sunlight, through salty spray, and waves whipped into froth. A foamy bubble stretched around her, shimmering, rising, lifting her above the sea. A bird swooped. In the spread of its wings glittering atoms vibrated. Voices whispered to her on the wind. *'Things are not what they seem.'*

And then she was submersed in water, not moving to save her breath, surrounded by a dim light. A shadow floated into the periphery of her vision. She turned her head. On the other side of a transparent wall, Jasper lay in a second tank. As though sensing her eyes on him, his face tilted. Her heart raced. It wasn't Jasper at all. It was Cole. She reached out, thrusting her hand through the thick, viscous barrier, but he was already drifting away, carried on a current towards the darkness.

And then she was flat on her back in a hospital room. A presence lurked close by. She tried to wake herself, pulling her eyes as wide as she could. Her dream self fumbled for a bedside lamp, hoping her real arm was reaching out, hitting a light switch and the light would wake her up.

For hours afterwards, she trudged through white haze across a barren landscape. She was searching for something, but all she found was a necklace of sharp metal vines that leapt to her throat when she held it high to see it better, and clung there.

The first time she knew she was truly awake, she was lying in a bed. Her father sat beside her, head bowed, holding her hand. His thoughts buzzed with remorse. She could feel them. Their shape, their weight. Like the vine necklace digging into her throat. But she couldn't feel his hand, or the duvet on her body, or her eyes when she ordered them to blink.

Look at me, she thought. But he didn't raise his head, and the notion of her own paralysis choked her with fear until white mist flooded her sight and she was walking inside it again, searching for the way out.

The next time she stirred there was the pain and nausea to contend with. A smell of disinfectant and rubber wormed its way inside her. She attempted to raise her arm, press the call button near her head, but her hands were slabs of concrete, her arms ship's anchors. Simply breathing deeply made her ribs flare with pain. She gave up trying to move. After that, she lay bound to the darkness with time in a bottleneck, the seconds feeling like hours.

Eventually, she woke to sunlight. A room with three bay windows. Gossamer curtains lapping against white walls. The luminous oblongs glowed like doors to other planes of existence, lingering remnants of the shadow world she'd been stuck in for the last few days.

Directly in front of her face, a pot of coffee percolated on a bedside table. A tang of roasted beans pricked her nostrils.

She tested her eyes and was pleased to feel the soft flutter of her lashes coming together as she blinked.

'You're awake,' her father said. He was standing near the door. He smiled, disconcertingly unsure of himself. 'You look much better.' A nurse brushed into the room behind him.

'Ah, there she is,' the nurse said. 'Let's sit you up, shall we?' She crossed to Ana, her voice bright and business-like. 'Now this might hurt a little. You have a fractured rib that's going to need lots of rest.' She efficiently lifted Ana under the arms. Ana cried out in agony. 'Would you do the honours?' the nurse asked her father. Ashby came and plumped the pillows. When he moved away, the nurse rested Ana against them. 'That wasn't too bad, was it?' she said, tucking a fallen strand of Ana's short hair back from her eyes. 'Looks like your father was right. He said the smell of roasted coffee might bring you back. Just don't try drinking any yet.' She winked at Ana, before breezing across the room. 'Buzz the red button if you need anything,' she said, and the door closed behind her.

In the nurse's absence, Ana's father loitered awkwardly between the door and the bed.

'The doctor said you've been showing signs of coming around for a couple of days. You've been in a coma for almost a week.'

A week! Ana struggled to grasp the concept. How could she have been out of it for a whole week?

Her father fiddled with a vase of sunflowers on a chest of drawers. Then he ambled over to a coarsely textured arm-chair and sat down by her bed. 'I'm so glad you're OK,'

330

he said, reaching for her hand. Her mind commanded her fingers to move. They twitched struggling to remember how. With a burst of determination, her hand jerked and slipped down her thigh.

Her father coughed. He stood up, moved away. 'They say it could be a couple of days until your motor cortex activity is back to normal.' At the nearest window he paused, lifted back the flimsy curtain and looked out. 'Do you remember what happened?'

Ana grunted. He turned to her. She dipped her chin to her chest in a nod.

'Three Mills—' His voice sounded muffled. He cleared his throat, let the curtain drop. 'Once I knew you were there, I did everything, *everything* I could to get you out. You have to understand, Ana, I couldn't just walk in and take you. There are procedures.'

Like the tanks. She shaped her mouth to form the words, but a strange noise came out. She tried again, determined. Her tongue flicked down and she spat through her teeth.

'Ttt . . . aaa . . . kkss.'

Her father hunched forward, pressed his palms into his forehead. 'If I could have stopped what they were doing – believe me I tried. I paid off every nurse to make sure they changed the medication. But the tanks involved the psychiatrists. I made up a file, pretending I'd treated you before, pretending you were the daughter of a close family friend, but Charlotte Cusher wouldn't even discuss your treatment. What on earth made you commit yourself?'

Carefully shaping her lips into the right letters, Ana blew air through her mouth.

331

'Jaa . . . ssh . . . per.'

Her father stared at her through spread fingers. Hurt filled his eyes. She'd never seen him so vulnerable. Despite everything, it moved her. She clung to her anger. She would never forget the horror of Three Mills, the place where he'd abandoned Jasper in order to protect his own reputation.

'I ca . . . n't ev . . . er for . . . giive you,' she said. The words were beginning to form more easily now. Stilted, but clear. 'You . . . haf . . . to . . . leeet . . . me . . . go.'

Her father cleared his throat again. His Adam's apple bulged as he swallowed.

'Let you go?' He frowned. 'I don't know exactly what Jasper's told you. Or what those Enlightenment Project people told you. They think my work is a fraud. They think there are anomalies in the Pure test. What they don't understand, what *you* don't understand, is humanity's capacity for destruction. Mankind's cruelty, hate, ignorance, has no limits. Every great civilisation has ended disastrously. After the 2018 Collapse this country was on the brink of self-destruction.

'My work was the start of controlling that volatility. When the first trial Pure tests started eleven years ago and people received preventive medication, crime began to go down in those areas for the first time since the Collapse. Without the test we'd be back in the Dark Ages like the US. We've had vaccines for ninety years. Containing mental diseases was the logical progression.'

Ana listened, her sense of injustice swelling. She raised

her shaky arm. Pain shot through her ribcage as her fist thumped the bed.

At last Ashby stopped looking at her and began to really see her. He flinched, recognising the rage behind her eyes.

'Suicidal chil . . . dren! Mind con . . . trol! Street ab . . . du . . . ctions!' she spat. 'How can . . . you . . . live . . . with yourself . . . knowing what . . . you know, seeing . . . what . . . you've . . . seen . . . at Three Mills?'

He gazed at her, speechless.

'Have . . . you . . . realised?' she continued. 'Have . . . you . . . realised you . . . should have . . . let her . . . go?'

'Who?'

Ana glowered, wondering if he'd repeated the lies so many times he actually believed them. Closing her eyes, she suddenly felt weary. The morning Ashby Barber had stood up on national television and called his daughter weak and ignorant, she shouldn't have taken it personally. It was the way he saw people. He thought he knew what was best for everyone.

The armchair creaked. Wooden legs dragged a couple of feet across the carpet. Hands rubbed against cloth. When her father spoke again, he sounded further away, exhausted.

'You've got no idea about the bigger picture,' he said. 'The world is heading for chaos. Total destruction. Containing people is the only way we'll survive.'

'You ground . . . the Benzidox . . . into Mum's food,' Ana said. Her eyes remained closed. It helped her to concentrate on getting the words out. 'Maybe she was . . . sad . . . depressed. But she loved me. Benzidox took . . . the good and

. . . the bad. Left her nothing. So she . . . killed herself. And you . . . stopped me . . . from saying . . . goodbye.'

Silence followed. The coffee machine hummed. Trays clattered in the corridor. Beyond the window a crow cawed.

'It was too late,' he said.

Ana opened her eyes. Her father slumped in the armchair, eyes glistening. She gaped at him, amazed. He hadn't cried at her mother's funeral. But then it had been a sham. Perhaps he'd cried the morning he'd pulled her mother from the fumes, carried her dead body to his saloon.

'You put Jasper in that place,' she said. 'Can you get him out?'

One tear dropped over the side of Ashby's high cheek and vanished into his hair as though it had never existed. He straightened.

'Jasper didn't understand what he was getting involved in. He needed a reality check. He needed to appreciate the life he has as a Pure – the life you'll both have. It was never my intention for him to stay in Three Mills for more than a couple of weeks.'

Ana's stomach twisted and rolled at her father's inhumanity. He toyed with people's lives like they didn't mean anything. But hope fluttered inside her too. If he could use his influence to have Jasper released, perhaps he could do the same for Tamsin.

'So you . . . can get him out?'

'It's all been taken care of. Scott Rutherford turns nineteen in eight days. They'll release Jasper before then. Three Mills patients are always released before they turn nineteen. Otherwise the Board goes in and does a thorough evaluation to decide whether the patient should be moved to an adult institution. There are several doctors working at Three Mills that can't stand having to answer to the Board. Even if they leave it right up to the last minute, they'll release him and Jasper will have seven days to recover, before declaring he wishes to go ahead with your joining.'

A muscle in Ana's neck clenched. Her head jerked. Her mind felt as though it had been rear-ended. Join Jasper? Her father couldn't be serious.

Ashby stood. 'That was always the plan, Ariana. Jasper just needed some sense knocked into him. A bit of a scare to put everything back into perspective. He was about to throw your future away. I couldn't let that happen.'

'He wasn't threatening my future, he was threatening yours.'

'If the disc had got into the hands of the public, the Board would have learnt about the claims Jasper was making against them. A little stint in Three Mills would have been the least of his problems. And I can guarantee, you two wouldn't have been joined.' Ashby strode to the door, all earlier hesitation pounded down beneath a new sheen of confidence.

'You're ridiculous!' she said. 'Jasper won't go ahead with the joining now. He'll probably disappear as soon as they let him out.'

'Jasper's very confused. He'll do as his father advises him. David, of course, is well aware of what's been happening. He'll be keeping his son under close watch.'

'Is David Taurell well aware of what you did to Tom?' Ana said, spitting out the last words.

Ashby stopped and turned. He shook his head like she was a silly, undisciplined child.

'Those Project people are dangerous. They warped Jasper's mind, but you're smarter than that. Don't let them warp yours too.'

Hate boiled inside her. All the Project dealt in was ideas and ideals. It was the Pure regime that ripped people's minds apart, that wrung people inside out with pills and electric shocks. Her thoughts turned to all the Pures sitting in their safe, luxurious homes, smugly congratulating themselves on their superiority: *they* would never be duped into believing something that wasn't scientific, that couldn't be proved. *They* were far too clever for that.

She tucked her fists under the bed covers and glowered at her father's receding figure.

28

Searching

Following their first conversation, her father's visits fell into a pattern. He popped in early before work, brought flowers, more coffee, fresh fruit and old paper books. Long after she'd eaten her hospital supper, he'd appear again on his way home. He never stayed more than fifteen minutes. They talked little.

Ana's fractured rib made it difficult for her to move. She spent hours sitting by a window reading or with her eyes closed, face tilted to the sun. She practised the breathing exercises she'd been shown to strengthen the fracture, and brooded over her predicament. She'd escaped Three Mills, but not her father, or the Board, or the joining. Jasper and Tamsin were still stuck in the loony dump. And Cole didn't know where she was. Didn't know she'd been held in Three Mills, or that she'd been in a coma for a week. She missed him. She felt like she'd been returned to the half-life she was living before they met. Except now she knew the way she could feel if he was around, the loneliness was unbearable.

On the fourth day after emerging from her coma, the nurse took pity on Ana and lent her an interface while she was doing her morning rounds. Ana spent precious minutes agonising over whether to contact Jasper's mother, and if so, what to say. The Wardens were undoubtedly keeping a close eye on all the family's communications. In the end, she sent Lucy a message, simply stating that she'd seen Jasper; he was alive.

Next, she trawled the net for news of Cole. Apart from his stature as prime suspect in the murder of Peter Reed, Secretary of State for Trade and Industry, ex-Secretary of State for Health, she couldn't dig up anything. She wondered if he'd escaped with the minister's evidence against the Pure test. Wherever Cole was hiding, either the Wardens hadn't found him yet, or they were waiting to bring him in. She imagined he'd returned to the Project with Lila and Nate. The authorities wouldn't storm the sect unless they were certain Cole had the minister's evidence and was attempting to disseminate it.

So that left Tamsin. Last September, when Ana had stalked missing persons websites for news of her best friend, she'd also searched for Tamsin's family in an online directory compiled from the country's electoral rolls, hoping she would find them settled in another Pure Community. From what Tamsin had told her in Three Mills, her best friend's vanishing should have been headline news, but it appeared Tamsin's parents hadn't reported it to the Wardens. Somehow, the Psych Watch managed to remove the whole family from the Highgate Community and coerce Tamsin's parents into silence. Even if Ana found them and told them where their daughter was, it seemed unlikely that they'd speak out now when they hadn't seven months ago.

Ana wondered whether her father could petition the

Board for Tamsin's early release. But what would he ask for in exchange? And how long would that take? She remembered a case on Jasper's law syllabus that had dragged out for over a year and the patient was never freed. There had to be some other way. Cole might have an idea or know someone who could help. If they could hack into the Three Mills data system, they could change Tamsin's age. But the Psych Watch had stolen her ID, and Tamsin had probably been entered as a Jane Doe – no official ID; no official date of birth.

Ana would have to be patient. She would have to get herself out of her father's clutches and then tackle the problem.

She spent her remaining time on the borrowed interface listening to Mozart's Piano Concerto in A, thinking up wild scenarios of psych dump break-ins. The music felt different to her now. It slithered under her skin and seemed to wrench her open. By the time her father arrived after supper, bearing news that Jasper had been released from Three Mills, she felt odd, off-kilter. The country had been informed by the media that an anonymous phone call to the Wardens had resulted in Jasper's safe recovery. Apparently, no one was questioning the lie.

But it was the news she'd been waiting for. At least with Jasper home, Ana was now free to escape. She tried to avoid the finer details of the situation – Jasper with his brain shot to pieces and dependent on the father he'd inadvertently been making a stand against. Travelling too far down that path of thought would probably end in her feeling obliged to stay and continue helping him. To say nothing of what might happen if Jasper ever remembered who had committed him to Three Mills, and why.

No, Ana had done what she'd set out to do. Jasper was home safe, and now while her father was under the impression she was crippled, was the perfect time to forge a getaway.

So the following morning Ana gathered her things – clothes her father had brought from home, shampoo, soaps, creams – and waited for the nurse's usual examination. Then in the knowledge that no one would come by until lunch, she put on her rucksack and hobbled to her door.

The corridor beyond lay empty, a lift visible at the end. Through the wall came the burble of voices – the nurse with her next patient. Gently, Ana clicked open her door and shuffled to the lift. The lift opened as soon as she called it. She hopped inside and rode down two floors, exiting into a ground-floor lobby. On her left lay a reception desk, on her right several sofas scattered around two coffee tables. Directly ahead stood floor-to-ceiling glass windows with a view on to a clean suburban street. Her heart began to flap inside her chest. She hadn't considered that the hospital might be inside one of the Communities. She'd never get through a checkpoint without ID. But then a man in a ratty coat and strange bald patches on his head (a side effect of Benzidox) trudged past. She exhaled with relief.

'Can I help you?' the receptionist asked. Meeting the woman's gaze, Ana smiled and continued advancing towards the glass doors.

'Thanks ever so much for everything,' she said. 'Don't want to keep my father waiting.'

'Is he here?'

As though on cue, a chauffeur-driven saloon cruised by. Ana jerked an arm towards the passing car and pushed through the doors. Outside, she shambled into a driveway and hid behind a wall.

In the ten days she'd spent bedridden, spring had flourished. Green buds adorned the trees. The day smelt of muddy puddles and raindrops. A promise of summer breezed on the air.

After a couple of minutes, when no one came looking for her, Ana asked a passerby for directions to the Tube and began to navigate her way across London, scrambling over ticket barriers, or pushing through after men and women who had passes.

It had been twelve days since she and Cole were supposed to meet at the Forest Hill flat. It was unreasonable, and considering he was wanted for the minister's murder, near impossible, but she couldn't stop hoping she would find him there, waiting for her.

In the ground-floor window of the Forest Hill house a girl bounced a baby. Ana rang the bell. No one came. She tried again. Then knocked. Eventually, a woman with wiry hair and glazed eyes emerged. Ana explained how she'd stayed in the house a fortnight ago with friends, how she hadn't been able to return when she was supposed to, and maybe they'd left a note or forwarding address. The woman shrugged. A smell of incense floated off her loose-flowing djellaba. People came and went, she said, came and went. And who knew where they came from, or where they went to?

Disappointed, Ana took the south-eastern line to Charing Cross, barely able to lift her feet, ribs throbbing. It was beginning to dawn on her that if Cole had heard the news of her release from 'abductors' and subsequent return home, if he hadn't seen Ana's long-haired double stepping from her father's car with his own eyes, he might believe she'd chosen to return to the Highgate Community rather than meet him. And if he was hiding in the Project she didn't stand a chance of finding him and putting him straight.

At Charing Cross she rode seven stops up the northern line. She surfaced into a crowded high street. Colourful buildings rose above a sea of churning interface projections. Cradling her ribs, Ana tramped towards Camden Lock railway bridge. It seemed as though she'd lived a whole other life since she'd seen the ethereal street performers rise from the crowds, backlit by an orange sun; since she'd sheltered from the wind under a fast-food hut and Mickey had scavenged her noodles. And now, even as she hunted the Gilgamesh building for the wind-chimes stall and cut through backstreets and warehouses, she knew Cole, Lila and Nate were long gone. In the back of her mind, she was hoping someone might see her and inform Cole she'd come looking for him. Then perhaps he would try to make contact.

She found Mickey on a moored barge. He told her what she already knew. The Winters had packed up two weeks ago and hadn't returned.

At sunset, she found the bench where she and Lila had eaten their Caesar salads on Ana's second day out in the

City. She drooped down, exhausted, the ache in her chest as much about Cole as a fractured rib.

Darkness inched over the canal. A figure appeared on the footbridge. He stood observing her for several minutes. She tried to ignore him. Eventually, he clapped across the cobbled stones.

'Time to go, Ariana,' he said.

She sighed. She'd wondered if her father would have a way of tracking her, even without her interface.

'I'm not going home.'

'Of course you are.'

She slumped, knowing he was right. She had no money. No ID. Nowhere else to go.

*

Ana silenced her alarm before sinking back into her pillows. Her room smelt of snowdrops and clothes freshly pulled from a tumble dryer. Her washed hair felt silky against the back of her neck. In the hall, her father's antique clock ticked. Its hourly chiming had woken her several times in the night. After only two and a half weeks away, the house seemed alien to her. Her room no longer felt like her room, even though she'd been back now for four days.

She listened for sounds of her father stirring. Once certain the alarm hadn't disturbed him, she threw on a sweater and trainers, stuffed the cash she'd hidden under her pillow in her sock, and crept downstairs.

In the living room, she inched open the French windows which led on to the patio and stepped into the twilight. A scent of cut grass drifted over the back fence from the golf course. A fire-escape ladder spanned the house's external brick wall, up to the roof. Ana turned her back on the stone table and chairs and the terracotta pots clustering around the patio edges, and mounted. As she climbed, she had to stop every few rungs to catch her breath and rest her ribs. Then she hauled herself on to the gravel roofing two storeys above the garden.

From where she crouched she could see the whole street; the mock Tudor and opulent Renaissance homes on either side; the sycamore trees lining the pavement; the road bending into Hampstead Lane. Other than herself, only one thing moved. His breath made vapour clouds on the dawn air. He stretched his arms and drew a watch face on his wrist. Since her return, Ana's father had been employing a security guard to keep an eye on 'the house' at night. Now she would discover whether the guard had a replacement. Someone who discreetly watched over her during the day.

She crept to the furthest edge of the flat roof and lay down on her front, straining her ribs. If she stretched, she could see a small, indistinct patch of brick and metal spikes. *The wall*. She had seven days until she and Jasper would make their declarations; nine until they were supposed to be joined – enough time for her ribs to heal and for her to figure out a way over the wall. Once inside the Project, she could only hope that a lone girl wouldn't be interpreted as a threat, and those patrolling the perimeters would listen to why she was there, rather than attacking. Her chest tightened at the prospect of being inside the Enlightenment Project. She might be able to convince them to let her stay, but how would she convince them to allow her and

Cole to leave? What if Cole hadn't sought refuge there at all, and the sect wouldn't let her go? *Stop it*, she told herself. *You can't believe anything the Pures taught you about the Project.* She had to trust Cole. Cole had been raised there. How bad could it be? The followers might be strange, but they wouldn't try to brainwash or imprison her.

A metal clang cut through Ana's ruminations. The gates at the bottom of the driveway buzzed open and the Warden Dombrant entered.

Ana hurriedly crawled back to the ladder. Gravel dug into her knees. Leaning on her arms put pressure on her ribs. The dull ache turned into small jabbing knives. She stopped to catch her breath. Behind her, Dombrant crunched up the drive and greeted his fellow Warden.

As the pain in Ana's chest abated, she swung over the roof ledge on to the ladder. She clambered down quickly. Back inside, she clicked the French windows shut. A high-pitched whistle came from the kitchen. She spun around.

'Tea?' her father said. He stood in the kitchen entrance, a smile twitching on his lips. She frowned, annoyed that after everything she'd been through, he'd managed to catch her out so easily. 'What are you wearing?' he asked.

'Recognise any of it?'

'Hardly. Floppy rainbow jumper and leggings. Not exactly fashionable around here.'

'No, but Mum never made it into the Community, did she?'

Her father didn't react. He was so much better at this than her.

'Up early spying on me, are you?' she said.

'I've got a meeting.'

She traced her fingers over the closed, silky top of her grand piano; his idea of compensation for a dead mother, for taking her away from the countryside and bringing her here.

'What would you have done, if she'd lived? How were you going to get us all accepted into the Community? Did you make a deal?'

Her father stared at her across the twelve-foot gap. The skin on her forehead itched. Even now he intimidated her. Even now she yearned for his approval. She looked away. Beyond the French windows, rays of a low, golden sun skimmed the top of the fence.

'You think I'm doing this all for me?' he asked.

'Enlighten me.'

'For heaven's sake, Ariana. There's nothing on the disc.'

Something in his voice made her stop. She turned to see whether the lie was written in his eyes.

'There's no way you could know that,' she said. Or was there? Had her father had Jasper's pendant all along? Had he discovered the evidence?

He strode into the living room. 'Jasper never checked the material,' he said. 'How could he have? You'd have to have a PhD in genetics to understand the first thing about genetic genome mutation. His brother Tom . . . had problems.'

'Problems,' Ana repeated. She clenched her teeth, determined not to let her father's lies mess with her mind. 'If that were true,' she said, 'if Tom was delusional then it proves the whole foundation of a Pure being infallible is flawed, and the Pure test is a lie.'

346

'The Pures,' Ashby said, 'are all that's holding this society from total anarchy. Would you prefer the total chaos that is sweeping through the US, Canada and half of Europe?'

'So you're not denying it. The Pure test is simply a means to an end?'

Ashby sighed and shook his head. 'I know you'd like to believe you're not carrying your mother's illness. I can understand how you must want that to be true, how hard it must have been to discover you were a Sleeper.'

'No. You're manipulating me.' But the doubt inside Ana began to grow like a larva spinning its cocoon; the fear a silky lump of fibrous thread, strangling her.

'The truth hurts,' he said.

Inwardly, she tore with frustration. She wouldn't believe him. Wouldn't listen. If Tom Taurell hadn't found out something potentially harming to the Pure tests, her father wouldn't have gone to all this trouble to stop him; to stop Jasper.

'You can't keep me here under round-the-clock surveillance for ever,' she said bitterly. 'Do you think I'm so weak I won't be able to resist the comforts and luxuries of the Community? How many days, weeks, months will it take in your expert opinion, before I grow to feel so safe and pampered that I'm unwilling to swop privilege and physical comfort for freedom?'

Ashby ran a hand through his blond hair. 'You'll get to choose, Ariana. When you're ready.'

'And you decide when I'm ready.'

'You've been through a lot the last few weeks. Your joining ceremony, the event you've anticipated for three years,

347

is in nine days. It's hardly the time to make rash decisions you will regret for the rest of your life.'

'At least it would be *my* life and *my* regrets.'

His eyes narrowed.

'Sorry, Ariana.'

'What if Jasper starts remembering? Maybe tomorrow, maybe in six months. You think he'll stay quiet about what you've done to him?'

'You'll be joined. You'll be able to explain it.'

Her whole body seemed to pinch shut with loathing. 'Thank goodness it wasn't left to you to teach me about love,' she said. 'I would have been the saddest, emptiest person in the whole world.'

'I think that's enough of the dramatics for one day.'

'I'll desist. Even if Jasper agrees to the joining, I'll desist.'

'I don't think you'll need to see the Board or go back to the registrar's office before the big day.'

Ana's eyes narrowed. Inwardly, she shivered. Could he do that? Could he make her declaration for her? Suddenly, she wondered how her father had managed to keep the Board away since her supposed return from the kidnappers.

As though he could read her thoughts, Ashby said, 'While you were being Emily Thomas, I found someone else to become you. Fortunately, none of the Board members sent to examine you in the last week had ever met you before. I think the new you would be delighted to accept the joining.'

'Would she be delighted to walk up the aisle too? Perhaps she could replace me permanently. I doubt you'd notice the difference. Except I'd be more cooperative.'

He smiled. 'I can't allow you to live in the City.'

'So you'd rather see me suffocate here.'

They locked eyes. It came to her at once – he'd never understand. To him, it was better to be in a cage and alive than in the wild, facing danger at every turn.

An hour later, she stood by the kitchen window and watched his saloon car leave. The chauffeur cruised to a halt as the automatic gates opened. Her father rolled down his electric window and beckoned Warden Dombrant from his tree hideout. They spoke briefly. The Warden glanced back at the house. Ana, visible in the downstairs window, met his regard coolly.

She watched them finish up. Dombrant moved away. Her father's saloon picked up speed and the gates closed.

Snatching a knife from the kitchen drawer, Ana ran through the living room, up the stairs and down to the end of the hall. She rattled the handle of her father's locked office. If Jasper's pendant was somewhere in the house, that was where it would be. Her father's sanctuary. In six and a half years, she'd never set foot through those doors.

Ana peered through the keyhole, then tried the knife. But she was no locksmith. She didn't know the first thing about manipulating the device components. She threw the blade down, furious with herself for doubting the validity of Tom's research, frantic with the realisation that her father was right – Jasper hadn't checked the disc. Because he wouldn't have understood it, even if he had.

29

Home Safe

Ana's father authorised Warden Dombrant to take her to Jasper's the following day. Ashby insisted they go in the car to avoid reporters. The double abduction and miraculous return of Ariana and Jasper was still headline news. Nick drove, but with Dombrant watching her every move, Ana barely said two words to the chauffeur who'd been strangely absent since her return home.

The Taurell housekeeper showed Ana into the hall and scurried up the left side of the elegant double staircase to fetch Jasper's mother. Lucy came down at once. She hugged Ana and stroked her short hair, clearly distraught at the sight of it. As Ana stood in Lucy's grasp, she remembered the last time she'd been there. New Year's Eve. Jasper had presented her with their official binding card; just after midnight he'd kissed her on the lips outside by the pool.

'Come,' Lucy said, sniffing. 'He'll be so pleased to see you.' She drew Ana into the vast taupe and grey kitchen.

Jasper slouched in a window-seat alcove at the far end. He rose when he saw Ana and reminiscent of his old, faultless etiquette, offered her something to drink.

'Mother?' he said, once he'd fetched them both freshly

350

squeezed lemonade from a jug in the fridge. Lucy stuttered an apology and edged out of the kitchen.

Ana and Jasper stood face to face without speaking. A crisp white shirt and shampooed hair did much to restore his old semblance of togetherness. But Ana noticed his hands shook and dark eyes haunted his face. 'My mother explained everything,' he said. 'I know who you are.'

She flung her arms around him and began to cry. He stiffened in her hold. She hugged him tightly, then forced herself to let go.

He had absolutely no idea who she was.

'Please,' he said gesturing to the window seat, embarrassed. She perched on the edge of the taupe cushion. At least he seemed a little more with it than he'd been in the loony dump.

He sat down beside her. 'The doctors say the memory loss should be short term.'

'I was there with you, Jasper. Don't you remember anything?'

A muscle beneath his eye began to twitch. He grimaced. 'The doctors advised my parents not to let me see you before the joining,' he said. His voice held the edge of a threat. Tiny needles of dread prickled up Ana's spine. She wondered if he'd received some sort of reprogramming so that he wouldn't even *want* to recall everything that had happened.

'Why would they do that?' she asked.

'They said you were finding it hard to adjust back. That to buffer yourself from the truth, you've concocted a fantasy around your abduction.'

Ana's internal temperature seemed to drop; her blood crystallised. She'd come to clear her conscience, to assure herself he would be OK when she left the Community. A part of her had been hoping he would escape with her to the Project. Or that she would at least be able to question him about Tom's evidence – whether he'd ever looked at it, whether he'd managed to hide the disc somewhere. But her father and whoever else was involved in this charade, had pre-empted anything like that by ensuring Jasper didn't even trust her.

She had to find a back door into his mind; something to make him question the story they'd fed him.

'What's the last thing you remember?' she asked.

'I don't know.'

'Do you remember your brother?'

He reeled back from her and snorted. 'Of course I do.'

'How did he die?'

Jasper lowered and cracked his knuckles. 'Why are you trying to make things worse for us?'

'Because the truth mattered to you.' She swallowed hard. 'That's why we're here like this now. You were prepared to do anything for the truth.'

'Stop it,' he said.

'If you don't trust me, why would you want to join with me?'

He winced as though her words stung. His mouth twisted in an ugly grimace.

'You and I are the same,' he said. 'We're both damaged now. We belong together whether we like it, or not.'

Ana's chest felt as though it was in a vice and the vice

352

was tightening. At least in Three Mills he was still fighting, even if he couldn't tell who the enemy was. This man before her had been clamped down, his wings clipped.

'But you want to call off the joining, don't you?' she asked.

'I'm a man of my word.'

She leant forward, searching his eyes for a shard of the Jasper who knew where they'd been.

'I was with you,' she whispered.

His mouth puckered. His gaze hardened. He obviously wouldn't believe anything she had to say about their 'kidnappings'.

'Try to remember. Try to remember what happened to Tom.'

Jasper rose. 'I'm a man of my word,' he repeated. 'I'll see you at the joining.' He stalked from the kitchen with an uneven gait. As he receded to the staircase opposite the main entrance, his head hunched into his shoulders and he began to lumber.

*

Ana spent the afternoon playing the piano she would soon leave behind. She'd reconstructed the melody for 'Second Sight' and now her soul twisted around Cole's music, fused with it, until it was a part of her. Sadness and hope expanded inside her. She couldn't wait any longer. Somehow, tonight, she would make it over the wall and find Cole. Somehow she would make things right again for Jasper and Tamsin. She had to.

Behind her, the French window leading out to the terrace clicked open. She jumped up in alarm and spun around. She blinked at a slim, agitated figure, bleary in the day's brightness.

'Nate?' she gasped. The astonishment in her voice was only marginally greater than the terror and excitement.

Nate's eyes gobbled up the open-planned living area, the low bookshelves, the photographs and paintings, the sofas around the glass coffee table, and finally the baby grand on the raised platform where Ana stood trembling.

'Nate!' she cried. She leapt the four-foot gap towards him. 'How did you get here? What are you doing here? How did you get past the checkpoint and the Warden?' She reached out to embrace him, but he leant away, glancing shiftily over his shoulder.

Adrenalin tore through her blood as though it would cleave her open. Something awful must have happened for him to risk coming to see her.

'Is Cole OK?'

He folded his arms across his chest. 'You gotta stop looking for him.'

'But he's OK?'

'Everywhere you go – Camden, Forest Hill – the Wardens are following you. They're practically living with you. Don't you get it? You're putting us all in danger.'

'I'm sorry. I'm sorry, Nate, really, but I have to speak to him. Please, tell him for me. I have to see him.'

Nate smouldered. She knew he despised her because she was the daughter of their enemy, because she lived like a Pure, because she'd brought the Wardens into their lives and driven them from their homes. She didn't blame him.

354

In fact, despite this, she felt enormously grateful – he was here.

'Cole's gone,' Nate said.

'Gone? What do you mean?'

'He wanted me to give you this and to say goodbye for him.' Nate chucked a coin-sized disc at the sofa.

'Gone where?'

He shrugged. 'Abroad.'

'How? Where? For how long?' The questions tripped over each other, each desperate to be answered.

Nate's gaze fixed on her with a look of pure hate.

'Just accept it,' he said. 'You've done enough damage. Cole wouldn't have been so pig-headed if it weren't for you and that rubbish about a Glimpse. That minister Peter Reed was a total liability. But Cole was trying to be a hero. Trying to impress you.'

'Impress me?' she echoed. Lila's words in the bathroom at Forest Hill came hurtling back. *He knew the time of the Glimpse was catching up with him. He split up with Rachel and took on more assignments because he knew you had something to do with disproving the Pure tests.*

'Please,' she said. 'Please. I need some way of contacting him. An address. Someone he's staying with. He'll be in touch with Lila, I'm sure of it. And when he does she can tell him I need to speak to him, and—'

Nate shook his head.

'What for? You're joining Jasper Taurell. Why make it worse for him?'

Ana turned her lips into her mouth and squeezed, trying to delay the tears.

'It's not—' She felt helpless. Nate wouldn't believe her if she told him she had no intention of going through with the joining. That she was a prisoner here, waiting for a chance to escape.

'How did you get into the Community?' she asked. 'Did you come over the wall? I want to go back with you.'

Nate's look was solid and unforgiving. 'Cole won't be in touch,' he said. 'Lila's gone with him. For good.'

'No—' Ana felt the hope she'd been clinging to for days, slip away. 'No, he wouldn't have—'

'Well, perhaps he thought the same about you. Perhaps he thought you wouldn't have come back here. But you did.' Nate was sneering now. He stepped backwards through the French window. 'He's probably starving on some cargo ship halfway to America by now. All thanks to you.'

Grief pulled Ana down. She sank to her knees, felt her ribs crush together as she flopped against the wooden floor. The room spun. Something cold and hard pressed into her cheek. Her body throbbed with a dull, distant pain.

It was over. Jasper distrusted her and thought she was delusional, and Cole was gone. The only things that had kept walking through the white, barren haze, when all she'd wanted to do was lie down and let the mist claim her, had been taken away.

30

The Joining

Time passed. Irrelevant. Meaningless. Just light inching across a wall as the world rotated away from the sun. Day rolled into night, night into day – the aftermath of a cloud of gas and dust collapsing under its own gravity billions of years ago, setting the world spinning.

*

A loud rap shook Ana's bedroom door. She jerked. She must have drifted off because she was standing in front of her bathroom mirror, tap running, a large blob of foundation cupped in her hand which she didn't remember squeezing out. Cole's music played on her interface. Her father had given her a spare one three days ago, with the net access disconnected. Ever since, she'd been living and breathing Cole's fusion music. The rhythms of her body felt as though they'd gradually altered, synchronising themselves with the pulses and vibrations of melodies that made her crave and pine for him.

'Ariana,' a voice called. A female voice she vaguely knew. She looked up at her reflection and winced. An unnatural tan colour streaked her face. Her eyes were bloodshot, glazed. She looked sick. She looked like an Active Big3.

Hurriedly, she wiped off the make-up with a hand towel.

A fist pounded on the door. 'Hon, open up,' the voice shouted. 'Your dad asked me to come over. Let me in.'

'Lake?'

'Yeah, it's me. Move it, before your dad gets his axe out and hacks his way in here.'

Ana stumbled across her room, tripping over plates with mouldy food and dodging a mound of dumped washing. She turned the key. The door opened then wedged on a half-eaten box of cornflakes. Lake forced her way through, crushing cereal underfoot.

'Blimey,' she said, shoving the door closed. 'Your dad wasn't joking. It's like the East Coast war zone in here.' Her eyes turned to take in Ana. 'Holy . . . Jeez . . . Shite.'

Ana bristled defensively, but then she remembered her own shock at seeing herself in the mirror. She glanced down and realised she was still in the leggings and T-shirt she'd been wearing five days ago when she'd spoken to Nate. That couldn't be helping.

'Well this little baby is gonna be about as much good as patching up a stab wound with a plaster,' Lake said, pulling a blonde wig from her handbag and chucking it at the rubbish bin. She kicked aside a trail of clothes strewn in front of the bed and began pacing. She dug out a lighter and cigarettes from her giant handbag.

'What you listening to?'

Ana shrugged.

'Do you mind?' Lake asked, lighting up.

Ana turned away.

'So,' Lake said, exhaling a ring of smoke, 'you're getting joined in three days.'

'Not if I can help it,' Ana said, flopping face down on to her bed.

'Well, that's not what your dad's saying. Either way, tomorrow you have to go down to Hampstead Community Hall and make your official declaration. There'll be photographers and reporters around, eager for the first images of Ashby Barber's abducted daughter. You go looking like that and the Board will have you declared Active before you've got home.' She puffed on her cigarette, bit her nails, flicked her lighter over and over.

'Dad'll send a stand-in. He'd do it for the joining too if he could, but I guess Jasper might not join a girl wearing a coat over her head.'

'Look, I don't know what's really going on here. I don't think you should tell me. Not if it might get you or Jasper in trouble with the Wardens or the Board. But you've got a decision to make. If you're going to go through with joining Jasper in three days' time, as your dad seems to think you will, you'll have to face the Board and the media. You might have had a taste of what's waiting for you from when it came out about your messed-up Pure test, but this is gonna be ten times worse. Everyone wants to know about the kidnapping, how you escaped, how Jasper escaped, what the kidnappers wanted you for. You and Jasper are huge news now, Ariana. And the Board will be watching your every move.'

Ana tried to muster up the energy to respond. 'So let them watch,' she sighed.

'Well, you'd better stop moping around is all I can say. The Board would just love to declare you Active after the way you and Jasper have humiliated them. Is that what you want? You want the Board to win?'

Ana felt a stab of injustice. 'This isn't about the Board winning.' And actually, yes, she did hope they'd declare her Active. Preferably before the joining ceremony. 'Whether I join with Jasper has got nothing to do with the Board.'

'Think about it,' Lake said, snapping her lighter open and shut again. 'The Board never proved your father altered your Pure tests, which means they had to admit they might have made a mistake. You're a constant and now very public reminder to them of that. And now Jasper, who asked to be bound to you, who told them he didn't care about your genetic defects and argued you shouldn't be punished for their mistake, is rumoured to have had some kind of involvement with the Enlightenment Project prior to disappearing. There's even speculation he wasn't abducted at all. He vanishes for seventeen days drawing enormous negative media attention to the BenzidoxKid negotiations, and is then found wandering in the City amnesic. What are the chances of escaping, but not remembering anything about what happened? What are the chances of both of you being kidnapped? Your stories are full of bullshit.'

Ana groaned. So much for not wanting to know what was going on. Lake obviously had a fair idea. Anyway, there was nothing Ana could do about Jasper's involvement with the Enlightenment Project becoming public knowledge. She curled up in her nest of bedcovers. 'I'm through. I'm done fighting. I'll live in the City. It's what I want.'

'You wouldn't last a minute in the City. They'd have the Psych Watch pulling you off the street within a week.'

A sliver of dread coiled through Ana. She wondered whether her father's refusal to call off the joining had anything to do with what Lake was saying. Was that the choice – the Community, or the Psych Watch and another loony dump? No, her father wasn't thinking of her, he was thinking of himself, of his need to protect and control.

'When the Board see Jasper,' Ana said, 'they'll know there's no longer a threat. They'll forget about me.'

'You're the threat, hon. Not Jasper. The public aren't about to forget you. If one test can be faulty, why not a thousand? If one Crazy can live in the Communities, why can't they all? They're backing *you*, Ariana.'

Ana felt a burst of peevish resentment. 'The Board, the public, my father . . . Everyone's trying to make me into something I'm not.'

Lake took a final drag on her cigarette, then tossed it in the bathroom sink where it sizzled and snuffed out.

'Yeah, well, the loser thing you've got going here – wow, I can see why you wouldn't wanna give that up.'

Heat rose to Ana's cheeks. 'You've got no idea what I've been through, what they've taken from me.'

'Everyone's got a story, hon. But you can give people something they haven't got. You can give them hope.'

Hope! She didn't have any hope left, what did she care about anyone else?

But her thoughts flew to Jasper and how his own mind

had been twisted against him. She remembered the way his face smacked the ground when the orderly had dumped him in the courtyard after shock therapy; the bafflement and pain in his eyes when he'd started to come around. She thought of Tamsin, imagined her friend's attempts to stop the Psych Watch from dragging away some toddler and his mother, and paying for it with her future. And lastly she thought of Cole, on a cargo boat to the US war zone, branded a murderer for trying to uncover the truth, for seeking justice.

Up until that moment, she'd had every intention of turning up to her joining a total wreck, hoping the Board would declare her Active. She'd even begun to suspect she was actually sick. Despair had been eating through her like rot, consuming her body and thoughts so that she couldn't sleep, eat or function normally.

As she lay with her head stuffed in the bedcovers, breathing the same warm air over and over, something tiny and delicate unfurled inside her. She finally understood – whether the pain that could turn to disease lurked in the cells, the blood or the mind, wasn't important. What was important was who controlled it. Until that moment she believed it was the Board – their Pure test, their diagnoses. But suddenly she knew it wasn't up to them. If despair, grief or yearning was going to take her, she had to let it. The paralysing fear she'd felt towards the Board, which had grown inside her for three years, began to vanish like popping soap bubbles. Lake was right. She couldn't let them win. She wouldn't. It undermined everything her friends had sacrificed. She was going to have to go through with the joining ceremony, whether she liked it, or not.

*

The following morning, the day Ana and Jasper were supposed to make their declarations, Ana's father left for work without mentioning her trip to the Hampstead Community Hall. She assumed he wasn't taking any risks and would be sending the substitute as planned. Lake arrived shortly after ten with a score of dresses for Ana to try on and dye to return Ana's hair to its original pale blonde.

As Ana tidied her room, the dye's peroxide giving her a headache, Lake filled her in on the morning's news from her father – the Taurells had managed to pull off a second joining ceremony on Saturday in North-West London, which meant she and Jasper were now booked into the St Johns Wood Community Hall under pseudonyms. Aside from close family, there would be no guests. And in an effort to distract the media, the Hampstead Hall joining ceremony would not be cancelled.

Without the usual guests and after-ceremony party, Lake's role had been reduced to fixing up Ana. But she didn't seem to mind. Ana got the impression her joining planner would do anything as long as it paid. And there was a fair bit of fixing to be done. Personally, Ana couldn't bring herself to care about how she looked – she tried on dresses and dutifully checked her reflection, but she couldn't see beyond her own heartache, beyond the grey eyes that resembled a washed-out, empty sky left after a storm.

They spent Friday manicuring, playing with the limited

options possible for Ana's short hair, body spraying her pale skin two shades darker, and trying different eyeshadows and lipsticks. It stole Ana's thoughts from Cole and for that at least she was grateful. But it didn't stop her from questioning over and over whether becoming joined to Jasper was really the right thing to do. She considered escaping. She could return to the farmhouse where she'd once lived with her mother. It would be sitting vacant, miles from the nearest occupied town. Perhaps the vegetable garden would have survived, would be growing wild and free. Perhaps she could trap rabbit and fish the river and survive on the land.

But it was a fantasy. She knew she couldn't run away from everything that had happened. She would do her part in weakening the Board's authority, in reminding the Crazies and the Pures that the Board was not flawless, faultless, or omnipotent.

*

The St Johns Wood Community Hall lay on the north-eastern border of the St Johns Wood Community, only one hundred metres from the checkpoint. Before reaching a small roundabout, Nick the chauffeur turned right into an arched driveway and pulled up in front of the elegant Regency-style building with a portico of four Ionic columns. Through the car window, Ana saw a bell turret rising up from the cream colonnade. Straight ahead stood the hall's pale-peach façade, two arched windows and two neatly trimmed bay trees. The journalists and photographers were either expertly camouflaged or David Taurell's ploy had worked.

Ana popped open her door. Before anyone could help her, she raised the heavy silk of her coral and ivory dress and stepped out. Her father's hard shoes slapped down behind her. Lake alighted from the front passenger seat. Nick stayed where he was. Ana hadn't seen him since the day he'd driven her to Jasper's house, and though she'd always thought her father hadn't noticed how well the two of them got on, now she suspected he'd been keeping them apart on purpose. He wouldn't have wanted Ana confiding in the chauffeur, or persuading Nick to drive her around London searching for a way into the Project.

Ana glanced up at the hazy sky. Not a patch of blue. Diffused sunshine sapped the colour and form of the trees and the road and the people passing by. She inhaled, lungs filling with dense air and flat light. Sighing, she took a step towards the building. At the tall wooden doors, she stopped. Lake squeezed past her into the sombre interior to inform the superintendent registrar of their arrival. What was once an old church had been recently redecorated in white and gold. Pillars stretched up along the outer aisles and the high ceiling arched over them – far larger and more imposing than the music room where she and Jasper had been bound. A wide limestone aisle led up to the registrar's desk. The box pews on either side could have held three hundred guests. Through the gloom, Ana couldn't make out a single person.

A trumpet blasted from a speaker, echoing across the

nave. Her father stepped up beside her, hooking his arm inside hers.

'You look beautiful,' he said.

She didn't turn or blink or show him in any way that she'd heard.

They crossed the threshold into the cool interior. Ana struggled to adjust to the low light. A gallery ran across the back of the Community Hall and up the sides. Jasper stood at the end of the aisle before the registrar's platform, head crushed down into his shoulders. Beyond him, the registrar waited behind a giant desk – once an altar – washed in soft light from a high window.

Ana drifted down the aisle like flotsam on the ocean – fragmented, in pieces, swept along by an invisible force. She wondered fleetingly if her legs would hold for the five-minute ceremony, or whether she'd have to sit down.

Jasper's mother, father, sister and a man Ana didn't recognise occupied the first pew on the right-hand side of the hall. On the far left-hand side, beneath the gallery, two members of the Board sat stiffly facing forward, their gold-striped lapels glimmering in the shadows. Ana closed the remaining three feet to Jasper's side. High up to her left, a flicker of movement caught her eye. Her eyes darted to the balcony. For a split second, she thought she saw a figure. She squinted into the murk, attempting to discern a form, but after a moment she realised she'd been tricked by the light, or her heart.

As she came to a standstill, Jasper tilted his head in her direction, opaque eyes shifting on to her face. The registrar began the opening address. Jasper didn't look forward like he was supposed to, he continued to stare at Ana.

Unnerved, she glanced back at his parents. Jasper's mother, Lucy, rose from her seat. The bald man – Jasper's psychologist? – put his hand over Lucy's to stop her. Jasper's younger sister scowled at Ana and mouthed '*Call it off.*'

The registrar sped over the introductory words, stumbling as she reached the part about the commitment to a family and the continuation of genetically Pure human species. Ana smiled bleakly, wishing she had eyes in the back of her head to see the Board's reaction. She and Jasper were forbidden to have children; it's what made their joining such a farce. It was a shame the press weren't here after all. Such a mistake would have been a huge embarrassment to the Board.

Ana pressed the back of her hand against her burning cheeks. As she grew accustomed to Jasper's stare, she let her eyes roam the gallery to her left. In her mind, she found herself running over her conversation with Nate. Her shock at seeing Nate in the Community – in her house! – coupled with the horror of his message that Cole had gone abroad, had submerged all logical thinking. But now she thought it through, she decided the music disc Nate had given her wasn't proof Cole had sent his brother to say goodbye. Nate hadn't explained how he circumvented the checkpoint, or how he'd found her home and got around Warden Dombrant.

Waves of doubt lapped over her. What if Cole hadn't really sent Nate to say goodbye? What if Ana's father had tracked Nate down, and bribed or blackmailed him into delivering the one piece of news he knew would put an end to Ana's plans of escape?

The registrar moved on to the declaratory words, not waiting for either of them to repeat the joining declarations. Ana wondered if the omission rendered the proceedings null.

Suddenly, Jasper grasped her hand.

'I've been thinking about what you said,' he hissed.

The registrar floundered and dried up.

'And I dreamt about you,' he continued. 'You were in a dark place, walking among the stars.'

Ana's mind travelled back to the tanks. *What did he mean? How could he know that?*

The registrar wiped sweat from her forehead. Jasper clung to Ana's hand.

'We will now hold a moment's silence,' the registrar said, picking up the cushion with the rings, 'while the couple reflect on the gravity of their undertaking before showing their final decision in the exchanging of rings.'

Behind Ana, in a pew by himself, Ashby sighed in annoyance. The air prickled electrically. Ana's eyes raked the gallery, hoping for a miracle. Hoping for Cole. She couldn't bring herself to pick up the ring. Jasper didn't move.

The rings on the outstretched cushion began to quiver. Beads of sweat dampened the registrar's upper lip.

'Help them,' Ashby growled at the official. The registrar put down the cushion and picked up Jasper's ring. She began forcing it on to his swollen finger. Oblivious, Jasper dug his free hand in his suit pocket and held up a wooden star on a rusty chain.

'I made this for you,' he said. The hand-carved wood was a replica of the pendant he'd worn the night he was abducted; the pendant with the disc Ana's father probably had in his office.

Jasper clipped the star around Ana's neck. The registrar snatched Ana's hand and began squeezing on her joining ring. Ana looked into Jasper's eyes. Beneath the turmoil and confusion fluttered the deeply buried shadow of truth, wrestling to get out.

'There's an inscription,' he said. She turned the star over. Engraved on the back was written:

Beauty is truth, truth beauty.

The smooth wood grew slick between her fingers. Ana recognised the quote. She'd studied Keats at school.

The registrar grunted. With one last twist the ring was on.

'I have the pleasure of pronouncing you joined,' she said.

A flash of light pulled Ana's attention up to the gallery. Distinct blue eyes aimed down on her. Galvanised by a gaze that pressed into her being, her heart sparked to life. Cole's solemn look absorbed her. But before a thought shot through her joy, he was turning, he was leaving, he had gone.

31

'Second Sight'

Ana yanked up the fish-like tail of her dress and flew down the aisle. Outside, a searing white sky blinded her. She raised an arm to shadow her eyes, whipping around frantically. The Community looked deserted; the streets and houses lifeless. A damp skin of sweat grew across her neck, her chest, her cheeks. She could feel it tingling, itching its way into her body.

'Cole!' she shouted.

She ran towards the street. Then jerked back to take in the Community Hall. Perhaps he was still inside. He would have to come down the gallery stairs. Turning back, she raced towards the doors and smacked face first into her father.

'There you are, dear,' he said. He gripped her arm so tightly she yelped. She began to tug away, but then registered two gold triangles in dazzling white circles floating through the gloom towards her. The projections grew larger until they laid themselves across the pleats and cuttings of her ivory and coral dress; the Board's emblem branded on her chest.

Ana froze. A thick blanket of numbness dropped over her. She struggled to pluck from her mind some reasonable explanation for running from the Hall. She had to get them off her back long enough to escape.

As the silence ground against her, she heard a scuffle across the limestone flags. Jasper was limping up the aisle, panting.

'Excuse me, excuse me,' he said, forcing the Board and Ana's father aside to reach her. He leaned in and kissed Ana on the lips. 'That was unfair,' he scolded. 'I'm at a total disadvantage. I can't compete.' He spoke softly, but the acoustics carried his voice. The two Board members, still puzzled, relaxed a little and stepped back.

Ana blushed. She hoped Cole wasn't hiding in some balcony or stairway after all. She searched Jasper's eyes, attempting to discern if the double meaning she'd heard in his words was intentional. His subconscious had re-membered enough to make the star necklace; did he have some inkling of what was going on?

Jasper's parents and sister joined the gathering in the doorway. Lucy Taurell, tears streaming down her cheeks, pulled Jasper and Ana to her, one under each arm and showered them with kisses. David shook hands with Ana's father. Jasper's sister hung back pouting, arms folded over her chest.

When Jasper's mother finally let go, Ana tucked her arm under Jasper's and said, 'Let me help you to the car.' They wobbled forward, each supporting the other across the gravel drive, the eyes of the Board and their parents pressing into their backs.

*

Palm held against the window, Ana scanned the streets. They were almost at the checkpoint, following the short crocodile of chauffeur-driven cars carrying her father, the Taurells, the Board and Warden Dombrant, who'd appeared outside the Community Hall just as she and Jasper were getting into their car.

Ana's mind raced. She'd seen Cole, she'd definitely seen him standing up in the Community Hall gallery, but now she questioned the soundness of her state of mind. Cole couldn't have disappeared afterwards. Besides, how would he have got into the Community? How would he have known where to find her? Why would he risk coming just to sneak away?

She thought of his Glimpse. The kiss. They still hadn't kissed. She found herself desperately praying for the future he'd seen. They could still be together. If he wasn't halfway to America, they could be together.

'Who are you looking for?' Jasper asked, cutting through her frantic thoughts.

Nick, driving Ana's father, was now moving through the checkpoint ahead of them. Jasper's driver pulled up behind, the last of the convoy. If they did a U-turn, Ashby, the Warden and the Board couldn't follow directly, they'd have to each come back through the checkpoint on the other side.

Ana turned to Jasper, guilt trickling into her heart. 'The Royal Academy's only two minutes from here,' she said, pinching her mouth into an awkward smile. 'Would it be all right if we stopped off? I forgot something. I left my um, my music.'

'Your music?'

'Of course, you don't remember. I take piano lessons on a Sunday with Professor Eidleman.'

Jasper leaned forward and slid back the glass panel between them and the driver. 'We're going to stop off at the Royal Academy,' he said.

'Marylebone Road,' Ana whispered.

'Marylebone Road,' Jasper repeated to the driver.

Ana's stomach clenched with nerves. She had no idea what she was going to do once she got to the Academy. Perhaps she could write a note for Cole and leave it with her piano teacher. Perhaps Professor Eidleman would know of some way she could contact Cole – after all, he was part-time staff.

Ana tried to remember the Project hotline number Jasper had called the night of his abduction. She'd seen it in court highlighted on Jasper's phone bill. But her mind had only a hazy recollection of the projection screen. She'd been too distracted by Cole's presence, the way his energy surrounded and pulled at her.

Jasper's driver turned about and headed south along Park Road towards Baker Street. Tension built in Ana like a crescendo. She glanced back through the windscreen. So far Nick hadn't altered the course of her father's car to follow. But he would.

Perching forward, she slid back the window divide to the front. 'Excuse me,' she said to the driver. 'Could we go a little faster? My music teacher will be leaving the Academy any minute now and I don't want to miss him.'

The driver accelerated from the leisurely twenty miles an

hour up to thirty five. Ana glanced through the back wind-screen again. She could no longer see the checkpoint or her father's saloon.

'I looked up my brother's death,' Jasper said, 'before they took away my interface.'

Ana jolted – it was as though she kept forgetting Jasper was there. But he was, and each time he reminded her of it she felt a tug of self-reproach drawing her towards him and away from Cole.

'Why would Tom have been wandering around on a clifftop in the middle of nowhere?' he asked.

Ana looked at him. Their last meeting had not gone well, but Jasper seemed to have woken up a bit since then, even if he couldn't remember a vast chunk of his past.

'It's a good question.'

'Do you know the answer?'

'Do you still believe I've concocted a fantasy about my abduction?'

Jasper drummed his fingers against the door handle. 'Nothing adds up,' he said.

'Nothing they've told you.'

He frowned and then slowly raised a short blonde hair from her head. 'Was it always this short? I have a feeling it should be longer.'

'I . . . Something happened to me out there, Jasper. I can't go back. I can't be who I was.'

'I have no idea who you were,' he said smiling, the warmth and humour of the boy she'd once fantasised about, breaking through. 'I don't think that'll be a problem.'

'It's a problem for me,' she said.

The driver stopped at the Baker Street checkpoint. They passed forward their ID sticks, neither of them looking at the other.

'I don't want to hurt you, Jasper,' she murmured. The barrier rose and the saloon plunged on to Marylebone Road into the vast crowds of grungy men, women and children, pressing in the opposite direction.

'If you didn't want to be joined, why did you go through with the ceremony?'

'I thought I didn't have a choice.'

Jasper hunched over his own window, considering. After a moment, he said, 'What are they doing out there?'

Ana glanced at the crowds. 'There's a small restaurant up the road. Everyone's waiting for the leftovers they throw at the end of the day.'

'But it's only four o'clock.'

'And there are over a hundred people queuing for a few burgers and stale loaves of bread.'

A frown returned to Jasper's face making him appear haggard. Ana fiddled with the wooden star. There was a little catch to hide something inside, but the secret pocket was empty.

'Why did you make me this?' she asked.

'It reminded me of another one I had.'

'You remember it?'

Jasper clenched his jaw and squinted, like daggers of pain were firing through his skull. 'Yes, I think it was important to me. But I can't find it. And I know it sounds odd, but I have a feeling I gave it to your dad.'

Coldness slid through Ana. Her father *did* have the evidence.

'Let's get out,' she said, popping open her door. 'We'll be faster walking.'

Jasper looked horrified. The chauffeur whipped around in his seat, gaping at her like she'd lost her mind. Ana hopped down, raised her dress up to her knees and began weaving through the crowds. Only a hundred metres and she would reach the relative safety of the Academy.

Undernourished men and women stared as she twisted and ducked between them. Some reached out to touch the silk of her dress. Others cursed and spat in her direction. Reaching the Academy's arched double doors, she pressed her ID stick into the sensor pad. As the doors clicked open, she shot inside and closed them firmly behind her.

The noise of the street crowds grew muffled. Far off, notes of a single violin cut the still air. Ana leaned against the doors breathing heavily. The familiar entrance hall, with its initial impression of grandeur and the usual signs of dilapidation and neglect slowly rising to one's awareness, calmed her. She took in the paint flaking from the cherub wall fresco; the ceiling that hadn't been painted in thirty-two years; the glass in the lamps over the unmanned reception desks which were cracked and missing.

Professor Eidleman usually taught in the Barbirolli room. Ana headed through the grand arch and up the main stairs. As she reached the third floor she heard a dreamy, lyrical refrain from Schumann's A Minor Piano Concerto. She knocked on the Barbirolli door, and then, imagining her father and Jasper and the Board gathering in the entrance three floors below, decided there was no time to waste on formalities and burst into the room.

The piano playing halted immediately. A pretty Chinese-looking girl with hair down to her waist looked up from the keys, frightened.

'Ana?' Professor Eidleman said, turning towards the door.

'I'm sorry!' She rushed over to him. His warm familiarity made her want to sit down and sob.

'Are you OK? I've been terribly concerned about you.'

'I can't explain. I need help,' she said. Her words tumbled over each other. 'Do you know Cole Winter? He's a visiting professor, teaches composition part-time. I desperately need to get hold of him before they come and get me. I'm desperate. I have to speak to him.'

'Sarah, please go on as you were,' the professor instructed. Schumann's melody floated from the piano.

Professor Eidleman waved a hand across his interface to power it up. He took the transparent plastic tag around his neck and held it in front of his chest. The interface began projecting digital information on to the card: A list of departmental professors.

'Composition you said?'

Ana nodded. The professor scanned down to Cole's name and selected contact details. Ana's chest hurt. Each heartbeat made her throb with anticipation. Professor Eidleman selected the number and hand-gestured dialling. Ana heard ringing; then Cole's voice.

'Hello?'

'This is Scott Eidleman from the Academy. I have a student here who needs to talk to you.'

'Cole?' she squeaked. Her voice sounded so weak and pathetic even the pianist girl's playing froze over. 'Cole?'

There was a pause. An aching, endless, smothering pause, which ended when the line went dead.

Shock flared inside Ana. Cole refused to speak to her. He thought she'd chosen the Community, the Pures, Jasper . . .

'I'm sorry, Ana,' the professor said, guiding her to the door. 'I'll be finished in fifteen minutes. Why don't you wait out here and we'll talk then?'

Ana floundered into the hall, barely seeing the staircase, the arched windows, the dirt-streaked walls. The door rattled closed. How could Cole think she'd chosen Jasper?

She drifted down the stairs. Voices stirred in the back of her mind. She reached the first floor, barely aware that she was moving. But now the voices were loud and intrusive. She snapped awake, leaned over the banister. There was a commotion in the hallway below. A wall of Wardens blocked the large central arch leading up the stairs. Jasper was standing behind them, along with his parents and Ana's father. Twenty or thirty people were gathered in the main entry, many of them filming with their interfaces. On the left, a professional camera crew with a reporter and boom operator thrust forward. The reporter was addressing the camera, then she turned and called across the crowds to get Jasper's attention.

Ana sank back into the corridor. Her thoughts felt as though they were spilling all over the place. She struggled to collect them together. She'd joined with Jasper to make

378

a stand against the Board. Had she made the stand? Could she go now? Or had she done it to protect herself against the Psych Watch? And what would it do to Jasper if she ran out on him now, on the very day of their joining?

But she had to find Cole. She had to explain to him why she'd done it, even if he wouldn't understand – now that she'd seen him, she barely understood herself. She didn't know what could have made her think joining with Jasper was a good idea.

She fled into the dark theatre on the first floor, past a row of blue seats and out through a fire exit. A set of stairs led down to the side of the Academy's grand entrance. She skipped down them, stepping into the main hall a mere two feet from the nearest Warden. But the Wardens' efforts were fully employed in keeping the onlookers from passing through the archway. No one glanced in Ana's direction. Another camera crew arrived. Jasper's father unsuccessfully attempted to quieten the bombardment of questions and make an announcement. Ana's father was talking to the two Board members that had been at the joining. She couldn't imagine what he would say to justify her behaviour. If she was caught now, they'd probably drag her off for an immediate evaluation.

Ana pushed open the doors leading into the percussion studio corridor. As they swung closed behind her, the opening chords of 'Second Sight' rang out. She tripped and slapped her hands against the wall to steady herself. *Cole's music*. The melody began to reach for the heavens and simultaneously delve into the earth, as though capable of drawing them together, making them one. It was coming from a rehearsal studio. Like a sign. A miracle.

The shimmering light and air in the notes filled her, knitting over the hole of loneliness, pulling her back together the way they had done the first time Cole played them. Amazed, warmed from the inside out, she shook off her heels and sprinted down the corridor towards a back flight of stairs.

The stairs led to the basement and the student common room. Professor Eidleman had shown Ana around it when she'd first started at the Academy. Though she'd never had the time or inclination to use the common room, she remembered it led to the David Josefowitz recital hall – an arched, semi-underground building that sat between the Academy's main block and the York Gate addition. She only needed to get into the York Gate basement and she'd be able to leave through the museum.

A string quartet was practising in the recital hall. Ana entered from the opposite end. The exit she needed was all the way down the front, by the stage. She coiled the tail of her skirt in her hands and crept across the oak floor, hoping they'd be so engrossed in the music they wouldn't notice her. She was halfway there, when the door by the stage opened. Her stomach rolled over. The open-plan hall offered no refuge. If it was a Warden, she was done for.

A six-foot, athletic frame stepped through the exit, chest heaving. Ana's eyes met Cole's. A rush of energy spiralled up her body. The quartet stopped playing.

'It's not what you think!' she blurted.

'You're not trying to find me?' Cole asked, doubling over to catch his breath.

'Yes, yes I am! It *is* what you think.' Ana's body took over, legs running without instruction, until she was close enough to fling her arms around his neck. Sniffling and laughing, crying out in pain when he squeezed her ribs, she held on to him tightly.

'What's wrong?'

'I broke my rib. It's fine now, really, it's fine.'

Cole's firm hands combed through her hair.

'I thought I'd lost you,' he whispered, his breath still raspy and uneven.

'I don't love Jasper,' she said. She was sobbing and making an idiot of herself, but she didn't care.

'But why didn't you meet me? Why did you go back home?'

'Excuse me—' the girl with the cello said. 'We're trying to rehearse.'

Cole's fingers threaded through Ana's. 'We should get out of here.' She nodded. They left by the exit where he'd come in. Hand-in-hand, they wound through the York Gate basement, up a flight of stairs and on to a side street.

Fast-food huts and bric-a-brac stalls toppled off the pavement into the broad street. Six rows of rickshaws, bicycles and e-trikes travelled to and fro, many coming and going to the vast camp in Regent's Park.

Ana and Cole joined the bustle, keeping their heads down, squeezing each other's hands, Ana still half laughing, half crying.

'My dress,' she said.

Cole nodded, pulled her across the road to a rickshaw. He helped her up and got in behind her. They sank back beneath the curved roof, shoulders and legs and arms squeezed against each other.

'Where to?' the boy asked.

'The old tennis centre,' Cole said. 'A hundred metres beyond the bridge.'

'Minimum fare is three pounds.'

Cole nodded in agreement. The boy smiled, pleased he'd got a good deal, and began pedalling. Streaks of colour flickered through the plastic roof, like a kaleidoscope. They whizzed past a group of women lumbering with huge wash baskets on their backs, past a man talking to his shadow, a girl sitting on the roadside singing mournfully.

'Why did you hang up?' Ana asked.

'I thought the Wardens were probably listening to my calls,' Cole said. 'I didn't want them to know you were phoning me.'

'I thought after seeing me with Jasper . . . I thought you hated me.'

'Hardly. I almost got an aneurysm trying to get from St Johns Wood to the Academy so fast.' He winced, looked down, suddenly unsure of himself. 'When you didn't go back to the flat . . .' He swallowed. 'You have to be sure about your decision, Ana. You have to understand that if you come with me there might not be a way back if you change your mind. With me you're always going to be running from something. Even if your father stops looking for you, I can't give you any kind of security. I can't promise you'll be safe.'

382

Ana thought of her father's endless efforts to keep her safe and how miserable it had made her. She lifted his fingers to her lips and kissed them. He still didn't know why she hadn't made it to the flat. He thought she'd got scared at Three Mills and chosen to return home.

'They didn't give me the test,' she said. His eyes shifted. He looked at her oddly. 'I didn't come to the flat in Forest Hill the night I was supposed to because I didn't get out of Three Mills,' she explained.

'But the news . . .'

She shook her head. 'It wasn't me.'

'How long were you in there?' he asked, the happiness in his eyes shrinking.

'Four days.'

Cole's shoulders tightened. His hand grew icy. But surely it had to be her imagination. A silence fell over them. The rickshaw clattered across a bridge. Dense trees on either side stretched over them, leaves blocking the daylight.

'I can't let you come with me,' he said finally.

Confusion pooled in her heart. She dropped her hand from his frigid grip. Suppressing the desire to cry, she summoned up her self-control. Then she twisted her arm behind her back and unzipped her dress.

'What are you doing?' he asked.

She shimmied her arms from the dress sleeves.

He pulled the sleeves back up around her shoulders. 'What are you going to do, run away in your underwear?'

'If I have to.'

'Apart from freezing, you'll be attacked by every weirdo out here.'

383

'So give me your coat.'

'Ana, please.' Cole reached out to cup her cheek in his hand. She slapped him away. He tried a second time and as the tips of his fingers touched her skin, it was like he completed a circuit – the love and pain and confusion ripped through her again. She stared at him, unable to hide her roiling emotions.

'I thought you wanted us to be together,' she said.

'I do. But the thought of something happening to you again, because of me—'

'You tried to stop me from going to Three Mills, remember? Besides, I wouldn't change anything that's happened to me because of you.'

Hand still holding the back of her dress closed, he leant forward hesitantly and kissed the side of her mouth. She tilted her head so that their lips met. She kissed him gently, desire burning through her.

So this is what it feels like, she thought.

A cough sounded from somewhere beyond the cover of the rickshaw.

Ana whipped around, realising the vehicle had stopped.

'The old tennis courts,' the boy announced.

A head popped around the side of the curved roof. 'Haven't been wasting any time then,' Lila said.

The tips of Ana's ears burnt. Cole smiled, zipped up the back of her dress, then helped her down. He gave the boy three pounds and they followed Lila through a small gap in the bush, battering back branches until they came to a tumbledown hut.

'Here.' Lila chucked a drawstring bag in Ana's direction.

Disorientated, still warm from the feel of Cole's lips on hers, his hands wrapped in her hair, she picked up the bag. A bundle of clothes lay folded inside. A grey hooded sweater, a pair of jeans, socks and trainers.

'But, how did you know?'

'All part of the plan,' Lila said. 'It's why I've been waiting here getting cramp all afternoon. Though even I was a bit worried when I heard you'd joined with Jasper.'

Ana's eyes flashed guiltily towards Cole. She pulled the jeans up underneath her dress then stepped out of it and put Lila's grey sweater over her silk vest. Her fingers brushed the smooth wood of Jasper's star pendant. She pulled out the rusted chain and ran her forefinger across the engraving. She recalled the look in Jasper's eyes as he'd given it to her. His struggle to understand the truth that now lay buried beneath what they'd done to him. She thought of her best friend Tamsin and the girl, Helen, who'd been in the tanks with her. She thought of Cusher, Dannard and the orderly McCavern. She thought of all the girls and boys lost in the hell that was Three Mills. Their moans and sobs and crazy mutterings played in the corners of her mind.

'Ana,' Cole said. 'What's the matter?'

Her breath felt as though it was congealing in her throat. *It's not up to me to save anyone*, she thought. Jasper didn't even remember about the disc, so she hardly owed him to try and get it. No one expected her to risk going home. And yet she knew if there was a chance and she didn't take it, she would never be worthy of Cole. Or Tamsin.

Or Jasper. Each of her friends had risked their freedom to stand against the injustices of the Pure tests.

Her eyes stung. She tried to massage the ache in her throat.

'I—' All she'd wanted was for Cole to rescue her, to be with him again. She should leave with him now while she still had the chance. 'I . . . I can't go with you,' she said.

The light in Cole's eyes died. His shoulders sagged. He nodded once, gaze flitting away from the pendant, as though he knew who'd given it to her. He thought she was changing her mind.

'It's a lot to ask,' he said.

She circled her arms around his neck and stood on tip-toes. As she spoke her skin brushed his stubble.

'My father has the research disc. Jasper doesn't remember what it is, but he remembers giving it to him.'

Cole tried to pull away, but she held on, pressing their cheeks together. She couldn't look at him or the hurt in his eyes would dissuade her. The thought of leaving him again, of jeopardising the one thing she truly desired was already hard enough.

'My father must have taken it before admitting Jasper to Three Mills. He must still have it.'

She didn't mention the disc might be useless or empty, even if she did manage to find it.

Cole broke free. He shook his head.

Lila's eyes gleamed. 'You have to listen to her, Cole.'

'My father keeps his office at home locked,' Ana said. 'I'm going to break into it.'

'Half the Wardens in London are looking for you right

now,' Cole said, jaw clenched tight. 'Do you know how many were in the Academy? Within five minutes the place was totally swarming. And Wardens follow orders. If your father realises what you're up to and orders them to stop you, that's what they'll do. I saw a government minister get run over in the street near a security checkpoint and it was done without the slightest hesitation.'

Ana met his glower. Anger she could deal with.

'Cole,' Lila said. 'This is it. This is what you saw.'

'No.'

Ana's heart soared. This wasn't about some Glimpse for Cole. He wasn't here for information or because he needed her to do something. She approached him and cupped her hand around his cheek, mirroring the touch that had brought her around moments before. She had not been raised in a world where people spoke of their emotions. She didn't know how to lower the barriers, how to make him understand.

'A week ago,' she began, 'Nate came to my father's house in the Community.'

Cole's expression darkened.

'He told me you'd gone abroad. Lila too. That you were on a ship to America. He said there was no way I could get in touch with you. When I thought I wouldn't see you again, I couldn't make myself care any more. I wanted to be declared Active. But then I realised there was only one way to get revenge against the Board, to undermine them, to justify all the sacrifices you and Jasper and others had made. So I agreed to go through with the joining. To make the Board look stupid. And because if I couldn't be with you, it didn't seem to matter. But when I saw you at the ceremony—' Emotion stuck in her throat. She tried to swallow, but couldn't go on.

Cole gazed at her so long, she wondered if he understood what she was unable to say.

After a pause, he straightened her dishevelled sweater. His hand moved carefully up her shoulder to her chin. She trembled at his touch.

'On one condition,' he said. 'You let me take you.' He tilted her chin to his lips. She closed her eyes and met his kiss.

32

Destiny

Ana sheltered her body against Cole's as the Yamaha burred down the Archway Road heading for the Highgate Community's northerly checkpoint. Toyne Way had one security guard and a basic 2025 ID Scanner. Information had to be sent to the central checkpoint and manually processed before it entered the security system. If Ana's father still had her tagged it would mean an extra few minutes before the red flag alert arrived on his system. She had to hope he wouldn't be anticipating her return home. There was no reason for him to imagine she might go back for Jasper's pendant.

With any luck, he was still searching the Academy. It would take him at least half an hour to get to Highgate. And if he'd had the foresight to plant a tracer in her joining dress, he would be chasing a ghost right now because Ana had instructed Lila to give it away.

Cole drew up in a road adjacent to Toyne Way and cut the engine. Ana descended. He reached out and slid his fingers into the short hair at the base of her neck.

'This is hard for me,' he said. 'I feel like we're standing outside Three Mills again, and I've been given a second chance. I don't want to let you go, Ana.'

'I know.' She leaned in and pressed her lips against his, amazed once more at the warmth and tenderness of his kiss. It was like sunshine rousing every cell in her body. After a minute they broke away. He opened her palm and placed her old ID stick inside it.

'I've been looking after this for you. But you'll have to come back to me if you want your interface,' he said.

'I'll come back.'

'Promise?'

'I promise.' He stroked a hand over her hair, down to her cheek.

A pang of anxiety hit her. 'This isn't what you saw, is it? Us standing here now?'

'No.'

'Good.' She smiled, relieved. He unstrapped his wristwatch and set the countdown for twenty-five minutes.

'I have an interface,' she said. 'My dad lent me his spare one.'

'Don't switch it on. It might be tagged. Besides this isn't just a watch. This is your promise to me. You keep this until I get to kiss you again. And when the time is up, you run back to me. No matter what.'

'OK.' She kissed him quickly, afraid of changing her mind. As she broke away, he reached into her with his eyes and kissed her one last time. She savoured the moment. When he finally let her go, she turned and stepped around the wall into Toyne Way.

At the checkpoint, she handed over her ID to the security guard. The pulse in her neck popped in and out. The guard glanced at her. She braced herself for his questions.

His gaze wandered to his interface projection. Some TV series made twenty years ago. Then, as though reading her thoughts, he shook his head.

'I don't wanna know . . .' he said. He pressed her ID into the 2025 scanner and waved her through the foot passage at the side of the barrier.

Heart pounding, Ana strolled down the sycamore-lined street, veered into a narrow passage – a pedestrian short cut joining Toyne Way to Sheldon Avenue – and began to run.

The early evening filled with drizzle. Moisture collected on her cheeks, making them tingle. A scent of grass permeated the air. Holding her ribs, she jogged through pools of yellow streetlights that had just blinked on, past huge driveways and bay windows set back from the road.

After several minutes, she stopped at the gates to her home and typed in the code. The gates opened. She ran up the driveway, entered a second code for the front-door and sidled down the hall into the living room. The shutters had been drawn over the French windows. Diffuse light from the solar-charged panels framing her father's rock-star photographs made hazy outlines of the furniture. She wove around the coffee table up to the platform where her piano stood. She flicked the switch to raise the shutters, clicked open the French windows and stepped out into the waning daylight. On the patio, she seized a trowel from a terracotta pot and wiping the drizzle from her face, crept back inside.

Upstairs, near her bedroom, the photographs sensed her and lit up. She tried to ignore them as she padded to the end of the hall. She didn't want to see the tribute her father had raised to her perfect Pure-girl image. They couldn't tell her who she was any more. The girl in those photos no longer existed.

At her father's office door, she wedged the tapered blade of the trowel into the crack by the lock and yanked back with both hands. The wood splintered. She tried again. Part of the silver lock bent away from the frame. But it wasn't enough. She was a long way from breaking through. She jabbed at the lock with the point of the trowel, over and over. Shattered flakes piled up on the cream carpet. Her body began to shake with the thrill of destroying something of her father's. She kept hacking away, even as the lock broke off and dangled from its casing.

A beep broke through her frenzy. She stopped, recollecting herself. Cole's stopwatch signalled the halfway mark. Only twelve and a half minutes left to find Jasper's pendant and get back to the checkpoint. She pulled down the lopsided handle, thrust wide the door and froze. As she stood on the threshold of her father's office all her rage and hate evaporated.

Above her father's cherry-wood desk hung a giant black and white photograph taken the morning Ana'd returned to school after learning from the Board she was a Big3 Sleeper. Grey furious eyes stared out at her. Hurt and defiance poured through the silky paper. It was September; the first day of Year 11. Her father had been acquitted of the charges against him and the Board had announced her reprieve. She remembered how he'd escorted her to school. How he'd told her it would be the first of many things to test her mettle, one of many trials she would have to endure to earn her place among the Pures.

But he'd also made her face it alone. He had watched her enter the school gates, and as she'd tiptoed away from him she'd heard the smooth whirring of his chauffeur-driven saloon powering up. She'd turned and seen her father in the back seat reading something on his interface, his thoughts already far away, her plight already forgotten. She was sure that that was the exact moment the photo had been snapped.

But by whom?

The study's three other walls held the answer. An array of snapshots featured her in her mid-teens. In each she was unaware of the camera. The photos had obviously been shot by someone hired to discreetly trail and observe her. They were a record of her looking furious, defiant, proud, sad. All the emotions her father, once the Board knew of her mother's suicide, encouraged her to suppress. The wall was like a memorial to the vulnerable, tempestuous part of her he'd tried to extinguish.

Fumbling to his cherry-wood desk, she pulled open the twin drawers on either side and threw out paper receipts, small archaic notebooks, and strange paper diaries. Her fingers grasped around for Jasper's pendant. But the drawers came up empty. She flung open the mahogany humidor on top of the desk. A spicy aroma of cigars shot up her nose. Her father's presence solidified in her mind. Instinctively she turned to the door, checking he wasn't there. Light from the hallway shone against the battered, empty frame.

Resuming her mission, she tipped cigars across the desk, pulling the flap of the humidor's lift-out tray. Gold glinted as the tray came up. With trembling hands, she retrieved

Jasper's watch and signet ring. Her father must have taken them the night he admitted Jasper to Three Mills. But the pendant – the pendant wasn't there.

Panic shot through her. She ran to the bookcase, the only other furnishing in the room aside from the desk, desk chair, and a low leather sofa. She pulled haphazardly at the books, knowing it was hopeless. Because now she understood. Her father had been hiding something in his office, but it wasn't incriminating evidence to his fraudulent research. Ashby Barber had been hiding his volatile, imPure daughter.

Ana let out a sob of frustration. Through the blur of tears she strained to see the escaping seconds on Cole's watch. In nine minutes she was supposed to meet him. She couldn't have risked everything to turn up empty handed!

*

The order had been given. Ariana would not be permitted to leave through any of the Highgate checkpoints.

Ashby flexed his fingers. The bones in his knuckles ached. His shoulders were knotted with tension. Jack Dombrant sat up front, alert like a pointer, tail practically wagging. The girl they'd picked up sat beside Ashby, ghostly white. Ashby glanced at her and thought of her half-brother, Cole Winter. A jealous ache surfaced. Ariana had tried to leave Ashby for a bum she'd met a few weeks ago. His daughter had never understood, had never wanted to understand that someone had to teach her self-control, restraint, unrelenting advance towards a goal. It was the only way to ensure she would survive the world's brutality. His wife, Ariana's impetuous, unbalanced mother, had meant he'd had to work doubly hard to succeed.

He gazed out of the tinted window. There were two choices in life. Survive or succumb. And most people weren't even conscious of the path they chose. Because they chose for all the wrong reasons. Love, principles, dreams, desire. The world hadn't changed. It had always been survival of the fittest.

*

Ana could barely see through her tears as she tumbled down the wooden stairs, staggered through the living room and on towards the front door. Outside, it was spitting. The fresh evening rain hit her face as she began to run.

She ran past houses she'd seen every day for seven years. Houses with children she'd grown up beside. There were no cars and no people. She couldn't even hear the birds. Her sobbing began to subside. She didn't have the energy to run and cry.

As she reached the passage linking the avenue to Toyne Way, Cole's stopwatch beeped. The alarm sent a surge of energy through her. She tore through the shortcut and exited a hundred metres from the checkpoint. Slowing to a fast walk, she struggled to catch her breath. The security guard who'd previously paid her no attention, now watched her approaching. The cabin window slid open.

'ID,' he said. She passed him her stick. He ran it across his scanner, paused, studied the information. ''Fraid you'll have to wait here for a minute,' he said, 'while I fill out a couple of forms.'

Holding on to her ID, he entered information into his interface. She wiped the damp from her cheeks. If he was going to stop her from getting through, he'd have to do more than confiscate her ID.

She ducked down and crawled under the barrier. Dangling metal chains swung into her face. Her ribs bashed against each other.

'Oi!' The security guard shouted. 'Come back!'

She batted aside the chains and using her hands, pushed to her feet with a grunt.

There was a movement in the shadows. The tip of a mo-torbike edged forward, engine thrumming.

'Ana!' Cole shouted. Her heart leapt. She darted towards him. 'No, Ana, go back—' His voice cut off suddenly. She stopped, squinted around at the security booth. The guard stood in the half-open doorway, motionless. A sound of an engine grew closer. Except it was smoother and deeper than the throb of Cole's bike. And there was more than one.

A tingling sensation exploded inside Ana. She wobbled. Four men on motorbikes materialised from the misty drizzle. They fanned out around her, cutting their engines and descending, dark hooded tops drawn over their heads, faces in shadow. The thick silver rods they carried shone in the evening haze. The air around Ana vibrated like a mirage in a heatwave. She remembered the zombie attack outside the courthouse. Arashans. She thought of Lila and realised the rods these men carried had to be transmitting something.

Time to see if she could still move.

She sprung on her heel and channelling her own surprise

into motion, flew down Toyne Way. One of the men shouted. She didn't look back. In her mind's eye, she could see them shake off their cool advance and transform into lethal predators. She heard their light steps closing in.

The muscles in her thighs hardened with exertion. Wind ripped down the back of her grey sweater. She could make it to the alley. But then what? She couldn't outrun four athletic men.

She entered the passageway, weaving with it to the left, but as the road on the other side came into view she stopped dead. A car blocked her way. Headlights blinded her.

'Use the Stinger!' someone shouted. She spun around. A hooded man advanced with a thinner rod. He was so close she could hear the electricity buzzing.

'Wait,' a voice called. The headlights dimmed. Ana's father stepped into view, the Warden Dombrant flanking him. Both of them wore thin silver bands around the crowns of their heads.

The hooded men stopped advancing. As Ana watched her father approach, something behind him caught her eye. Nick the chauffeur sat immobile in the driver's seat of her father's saloon. Next to him, in Ana's bridal dress, was Lila. Ana's heart sank. Lila was supposed to have given it away, not played the decoy.

'Here,' her father said, offering her a metal band. She shook her head. 'That's a rare aptitude you have,' he said. 'I've only ever met one other person capable of resisting like that.' She scowled at him. 'Fine, we'll talk about it later.'

'I won't be around for later,' she said.

He fished something out of his suit pocket. Jasper's gold star pendant. Ana's senses prickled with the awareness of the wooden copy she wore beneath her blouse. It stuck to her perspiring skin. The pressure inside her head was growing. Soon the headache would be unbearable.

'Where have you been?' he asked.

'Home.'

'Looking for something?'

From the pouch in Lila's hooded top, she lifted out the tatty piece of photographic paper she'd snatched from her bedside drawer just before leaving. The picture showed Ana and her mother seated at an upright piano, playing a duet. Shorts and T-shirts, tanned skin, the same kink wrinkling both their foreheads where their eyebrows dipped in concentration. Ashby stared at it, then visibly relaxed.

'I'm not angry with you,' he said. 'I understand what you're going through. I admire your tenacity. I believe you can do whatever you set your mind to, Ariana.' His eyes coiled around her, refusing to let her go. She balled her hands into fists. It was too late for her father's admiration. She didn't need it any more. Didn't want it.

'But I won't let you throw your future away,' he went on. 'You have a crush on this boy . . .' Ana cringed. But of course he knew about her feelings for Cole. Everything she'd done since she got out of hospital had probably been photographed and psychologically analysed. 'How long do you honestly think it will last?' he asked. 'He's not like you. He's been in and out of trouble his whole life. He's always going to be struggling, fighting. It's his nature. It doesn't have to be that way for you.'

'You've made it that way for me.'

'All right, Ariana,' he said. 'We'll do this your way.'

Clipping open the hidden slot in the gold pendant, he took out a wafer thin disc and entered it into his interface. From his pocket he retrieved a magnetic grip. He placed the grip on the car bonnet, then ducked into the back of the saloon and picked up his portable pad. He secured the pad to the magnetic grip. His interface began transmitting information to the screen.

Scrawled handwriting appeared. Tight lines, crushed together, barely legible. Ana's heart thumped in time with the throbbing in her head. Her ability to focus was slipping. She reached towards the spare device around her father's wrist. He took it off and gave it to her. She secured it on her crown and felt an instant rush of released pressure.

I've found a way out, she read. *It's dangerous. But they know about the key. They want the key. I'm leaving it for Jasper. The only escape route still open is through a crack in the back of my skull. I will not be able to leave with my body. But I can't do any more here. Now it is up to Jasper. Everything rests on him. He knows about the key. He'll find the door, open it and release the world, before they find him.*

Ana breathed unevenly. 'No,' she said. 'No. I don't believe it. Tom wasn't crazy.' Her father reached out a hand to support her. She staggered away from him.

'After his death, the Wardens found this on his diary,' he said. 'His death wasn't an accident. Because of my background, I was asked to examine his case. To discover how a

Pure had become mentally unstable. To see if there wasn't some new genetic variant that hadn't yet been identified.'

Ana drifted for several moments, as though she'd been cut loose in the middle of the ocean. And then an idea seized her.

'Who's to say you haven't changed the disc? Made this up?'

'You have to believe me, Ariana,' he said. 'And I couldn't let Jasper abandon you for this! Throw everything away because of this rubbish. I knew what he was planning. I'd been keeping an eye on him and the Taurells for almost three years, ensuring none of them showed signs of a breakdown like Tom's. The day you two were bound he met with someone from the conspiracy-obsessed Enlightenment Project to pass on the information. His contact flipped out, went berserk in the street. Jasper panicked. He was afraid. He left the concert early because he was going to disappear too. He was leaving you. For what? For this!'

Ana hugged her arms around her shaking body.

'I thought putting him in an institution would keep him out of trouble until your joining,' her father continued. 'To say nothing of stopping him from attracting the Board's attention again. He was always going to be released after a couple of weeks. He needed time to appreciate everything he was about to throw away. I would have shown him the disc when he got out. When he'd calmed down and was ready to listen to reason.'

'Except you were saved the bother, weren't you?'

'I had nothing to do with his electric shock treatment.'

Ana clenched her jaw to stop her teeth from chattering.

Had her father really acted to save her Pure future or his own reputation? She regarded him, the man who'd always been so cold and calculating. His eyes were begging her to listen.

'Why was Warden Dombrant looking for *Enkidu*?' she asked.

Ashby ran a hand through his hair. His jaw flexed. She noticed the blood vessels on the side of his forehead pump in and out. She gasped. He'd almost fooled her. Almost convinced her.

'Because you were following up any loose ends,' she answered for him. 'At first, you hadn't discovered the disc in the pendant, so you weren't really sure whether there was something on it . . .' She stopped. The truth of her words sunk in. This might be Tom Taurell's 'proof' but her father hadn't known that at first. Which meant her father had been worried there was proof against the credibility of the Pure test. Which meant the man Cole had been meeting with, the Secretary of State for Trade and Industry, really had possessed a twenty-year-old recording of a meeting where people now in government and heading the Board came up with the idea of Pures. The minister had been killed because of it.

Her father wasn't a genius. He was nothing but a pawn.

It had stopped raining. The moisture on Ana's face began to dry in the evening breeze. The wooden star pendant lay flat against her chest.

'It's over,' she said. 'I don't want anything more to do with you. You only know how to crush people.'

'I preserve,' he said.

And at that moment, she knew he would not let her go. She was an object to him. A prize possession.

'Would you still want to leave,' he said, 'if you couldn't have the boy?'

She glanced back to the passage leading to Toyne Way. Only two of the hooded men remained in sight. The others must be with Cole.

'I want you to stay one year in the Community, as Jasper's wife,' he said. 'Tomorrow is your eighteenth birthday. The day you turn nineteen, if it's still what you want, I will not stop you from walking away. Though if you choose to leave, you leave everything you have here behind you.'

He still thought she could be bribed by luxury, forced by habit and fear. She thought of Cole somewhere in the shadows behind the checkpoint. Unable to run. Unable to fight. Frozen by the immobilising device. They could apprehend him right now. He would wait up to a year for his trial. He would face a possible lifetime prison sentence in the hands of the prison's Special Psychs.

Ana's legs gave way. She crumpled, smacking on to her knees.

Her father knelt down beside her. 'I'm doing this for you,' he said. 'One day you'll understand.' His words clawed at the numbness. His fingers pressed on the arch of her spine. In her imagination, she saw them reaching through, feeling, searching, trying to extract her very soul. A strange quiet fell over her, like thick, fluttering snow. She closed her eyes.

And suddenly she was surrounded by stars. Clusters of galaxies burnt in the dark sky. Dazzling. Infinite. The Milky

Way lay on the horizon, its spiral arms orbiting a golden centre. A sound reverberated towards her. Something close to music, yet it swept through her whole being as though she were a vibration, and it was tuning her to its strength, its power, its wholeness.

Her eyes flicked open. She regarded her father through tangles of hair. Two years eleven months and eight days ago, when the Board confirmed her mother's suicide and announced she was a Big3 Sleeper, she'd sworn never to let her father touch her again. Now she realised it didn't matter. He could no longer reach in and take her. He couldn't steal the beauty she saw, the compassion she felt for Jasper, the love she felt for Cole. She was beyond him.

She stood and crossed to the car, aware of her father's trained gaze. She opened the back door and scooted in beside Lila. As she placed the metal deflector on Lila's head, Lila came around drowsily. Her baffled expression grew fearful as she absorbed their surroundings.

'We haven't got long,' Ana said. 'My father will let you and Cole go if I stay. You have to make sure Cole doesn't try and come back for me. Whatever he hears about me and Jasper, don't let him doubt. I choose him. I'm staying with Jasper because I've chosen Cole. And I'll find a way for us to be together, as soon as I can.'

Lila's lips trembled. 'I won't let him doubt you,' she said.

Ana squeezed her hand.

'You got it, didn't you?' Lila asked.

Ana paused. It looked like Lila's faith in the Glimpse had been justified all along and strangely, that no longer scared her.

'I got it,' she whispered, touching the wooden star where she'd hidden the minister's disc.

'It was always about you,' Lila smiled, tears in her eyes. 'Not Cole. It was you who stood at the centre of it all.'

Ana embraced her friend, then took the deflector band from Lila's head and slid across the back seat to the door.

On the street, she strode past her father and the hooded men, heading up the alley that linked to the checkpoint. She felt them following, but as long as they didn't stop her from speaking to Cole, she didn't care.

Cole sat astride his motorbike, the engine still turning. Two hooded men stood beside him. They moved to halt her approach.

'It's all right,' her father called from behind.

The men withdrew. Ana put the band over Cole's head and waited as he blinked to life, eyes flexing in confusion. As his muscles relaxed, his motorbike almost slipped from his grip. He grabbed it and steadied it. His eyes darted from the hooded men to Ana's father.

'Get on! We've got to get out of here!'

'Cole—' She reached up to touch his cheek. She could see him trying to understand what was going on. She leaned in and kissed him. 'I won't forget you,' she said. She took off the wooden star pendant and placed the chain over his head. 'Now you have something belonging to me and I have something of yours.' She smiled weakly and turned, not sure she could really walk away from him. He grabbed her arm.

'Wait,' he said. 'What happened? Where are you going?'

Her legs wobbled. Her heart hurt so much she thought

it would implode. Leaning close to him, breathing in the scent of soap powder and summer, she said:

'It's in the pendant.'

'No.' He held on tight. 'This wasn't supposed to happen. I saw this, so that I could change it. I'm not letting you go this time.'

'This was the moment.' As Ana spoke, she knew the truth of her words. There was something about this precise point in time. Like a star exploding in the wide, dark universe. This place, this instant, stood out from all the others.

'Ana, please. You have to tell me how I can change this.'

'It's OK. He can't get to me any more. I understand now.'

'Ana, please . . .'

'You have to leave now, or my father will have you arrested. But I'll come to the Project. I'll come as soon as I can.'

'Please, I can't lose you again.'

She moved into him and opening up her heart, letting everything she felt flow through her, she kissed him a second time. Long, deep, unbound. When she broke away, she saw wonderment in his eyes, as though the touch of her lips had sent the vibration of strength and wholeness inside her, through him too.

'We're linked,' she said. 'We could lose each other a thousand times and the universe would still bring us back together. Will you wait for me?'

'Yes.'

She smiled. 'Don't forget the star.'

Understanding lit up his eyes. It hurt her how beaten he suddenly looked. Unwilling to accept how he knew this would end – for now – but knowing he had to. Realising there was something hidden in the pendant.

'My father's got Lila,' she told him. 'Go quickly. His car is on the other side of the passage.'

Cole revved the engine, but didn't advance.

'Go!' she shouted. 'Please.'

'Ana—'

'I know,' she said. 'I've known since the first time I saw you.'

He clicked the motorbike into gear. The engine thrummed against the silent evening. He looked at her one last time, as though trying to memorise everything about her, then sped off, disappearing down the alley.

Ana turned to her father. In the lamplight, his long shadow stretched towards her like the finger of a beckoning hand. Blood pulsed in her ears, her throat, her wrists. The electric energy was building up around her again, slowing her down. Her brain seemed to contract and expand, beating against her skull.

'You won't regret this, Ariana,' he said. 'I've given Warden Dombrant instructions to take the boy and his sister through the main checkpoint. As long as you keep your word, I guarantee their safety. And in one year, I will wipe the boy's arrest record and everything implicating him in Dr Peter Reed's death.'

For a split-second, Ana saw herself back in her father's office, tears streaming down her face. With a final cry of frustration she'd swept away the last books on the shelf, revealing a silver disc stuck to the wall. The numbers 12.04.2021 were engraved across it. Not numbers. A date!

She'd grabbed it, barely thinking. But the realisation had caught up with her slowly: she'd found a copy of the recording Peter Reed, ex-Secretary of State for Health, had been killed over. And now Cole had it, tucked away in Jasper's wooden star pendant.

'How can I trust you?' she said.

'You don't have a choice.'

'You want me to stay with Jasper among the Pures for a year. That's all you're asking?'

'And you will have no contact with the boy, his family or anyone that isn't Pure.'

'That's it?'

'That's all I'm asking. Only what you've wanted all along.'

Beyond the narrow passage, an engine strained as it accelerated away. If Cole was safe, Ana knew she could deal with anything. She listened as the motorbike hum faded. It sank out of range, but still she heard the gentle drone. It had melded with the vibration inside her as though they were part of a symphony that played on, even when no one was listening.

The evening bore down on her. She knew it would grow darker before she felt the light again. She followed her father through the alley to his car. She climbed in. Lila's lavender scent lingered on the leather seats. She closed her eyes and tilted back her head. In her mind, she felt Cole's lips, warm and soft, imprinted on her own.

33

The Wall

Three weeks later.

Ana lay on a chaise longue by the tennis courts while David Taurell and her father played an aggressive match of singles. It was a warm, Saturday afternoon in mid-May. Jasper was lying down inside the west wing with one of his headaches, his sister was staying at a friend's, and his mother was drinking cocktails and neurotically digging up the garden.

Putting down a book she was only pretending to read, Ana sat up and sipped her freshly squeezed lemonade. Her father caught her eye and winked. She looked away. She didn't want to make him suspicious by appearing to have forgiven him.

A twinge of pain shot through her temples. She set down her drink and pressed her fingers to the sides of her skull. Jasper wasn't the only one suffering from headaches and lack of sleep. In the last three weeks, Ana had woken often from nightmares. She'd been frozen and buried alive a hundred times. Night after night, she'd been drowned and drugged and torn apart by zombies. She would jolt awake to the sound of her own shouting or Jasper's howling from across the hall. While days drifted by in a surreal pretence of normality to fool the Board, reporters and their fathers, at night she and Jasper were prisoners of Three Mills.

Ana stared at her father considering why, if he'd kept his promise and allowed Cole and Lila to leave the Community, there had been no news of the minister's recording. It should have made the headlines. But she'd heard nothing, which meant one of three things: Cole was rotting in some prison or psych dump; the minister's disc was a sham like Tom Taurell's research; or Cole was holding on to it. Waiting for her. A silent message that he wouldn't trade her freedom for information that could hurt the Board. Because he understood that once Ashby Barber knew his daughter had not only ransacked his office and found the dead minister's recording, but that she'd also managed to filter it out of the Community, he'd tighten up his round-the-clock surveillance.

Ana stretched and stood up. Despite a general lack of sleep, she'd been exercising rigorously for the last ten days – swimming a hundred lengths morning and afternoon.

'They invited me next door,' she said. 'They said I could use their pool until ours is fixed.'

Her father leapt for a shot, grunted as he struck the ball. Jasper's father slammed the tennis ball back over the net. Her father skidded to reach it in time.

Ana stripped off her skirt and shorts down to her swimsuit. She slipped her arms through her fluffy dressing gown and languidly wedged her feet into the slip-ons she'd borrowed from Lucy.

'Bye then,' she said.

'See you tomorrow at lunch,' her father panted. David waved absently.

Ana trudged through the small copse beyond the tennis courts, towards the neighbours. Coiled up against an oak tree, exactly as she'd left it, she found the rope. Quickly, she checked the noose before hoisting the rope over her shoulder. She began to run. Tree roots, twigs and prickly undergrowth pressed through the soles of her pumps. But at least Lucy's shoes wouldn't have tracers in them. And she was fairly sure her father wouldn't have bothered hiding tracers in her dressing gown or swimsuit.

Sprinting across tended lawns, some in full view of porches, back doors, and verandas, Ana retraced the path she'd gone over a dozen times using an aerial map program on her interface. She'd already decided if she ran into anyone she'd simply keep going. But her luck held. By the time she reached the boys' school football field she hadn't seen a soul. To avoid the road, she scrambled up a high fence. After days of nothing but rest, swimming, and practising her breathing exercises, her fractured rib had healed, the bruises gone. She jumped down into the playing field and bolted across the football pitch, breathing deeply and steadily. A tingling sensation radiated out from her chest, down her arms, and into her fingers. Anticipation. Nerves. She was almost there. Almost at the wall.

Reaching the road, Ana huddled down beside a cluster of young trees demarcating the field. From where she crouched, she had a clear view of three hundred metres of road in each direction. She concentrated on her breathing. Imagined one heartbeat for every two, the way she used to when she would practise holding her breath underwater. She listened. Birdsong. A distant rumble of a lawnmower. But no electric buzzing of a hybrid engine. No patrol cars.

Now! she cried inwardly. She leapt up and bounded across the two-lane road. As she ran, she unhooked the rope from her arm and swung the knotted end towards the wall's ten-foot-high spikes. The noose snagged. She flicked the rope. The slipknot descended to the base of the metal pole. She yanked it tight then began pulling her hands one over the other, pressing her feet into the wall as she climbed.

Her dressing gown flew apart. Her hands burnt as they rubbed the rope. Her heart leapt wildly.

At the top of the wall she grabbed a pointed iron pole. Then she slid through the thin gap between spikes, gathered up the rope and dropped it over the other side. Beneath her, scattered between the thicket of horse chestnuts, oaks and sycamores were a thousand bluebells. Their deep violet-blue heads bobbed in the dappled sunshine. Ana smiled. With a last look back at the quiet Community road, she gripped the rope and abseiled down into the Project.

Acknowledgements

My deepest thanks to my editor, Susila Baybars, whose insight and intelligence guided me through revisions, asking all the right questions and generously allowing me to explore the answers in some unexpected ways.

I would like to thank everyone at Antony Harwood, especially Jo Williamson my agent extraordinaire, who was the first to love Ana and Cole the way I do, and whose constant support and enthusiasm is all a girl could want.

To the Faber team – Rebecca, Lizzie, Susan, Laura, Donna and everyone behind the scenes that I haven't yet met – thank you!

Thanks to Cassandra Griffin and Leandra Wallace, who read the earliest drafts of *The Glimpse*. Your advice and encouragement was invaluable. Likewise thanks to all my QT friends who helped out at various stages, particularly Julie Fedderson, Rachel Wickham, Ruth Kollman, B. L. Holliday, Cate Peace and Jennifer L. Armentrout. And 'aloha' to my new critique group, Mina, Tioka and Sandra. Looking forward to working with you guys on the next one!

Thanks to my Mum who always welcomed strange people into her house – rock bands and film crews – while I pursued my 'artistic ambitions'; and Dad who infiltrated this story on several levels and who was probably responsible for the 2018 Collapse.

Thanks to my sister Kate Lewis, and my dear friend Andrea Kapos. Your constant support, insight and encouragement over the years will always be deeply appreciated.

Finally my thanks and love to my three boys – my eldest son, Sean, who graciously accepted that when Mummy's writing she can no longer hear what he's saying; my youngest, West, whose afternoon naps and good nature allowed me to keep drafting and revising through those pre-nursery years; and my husband, Claude, whose belief in me has never waned despite the fact that he's had to rely on my garbled ramblings as to what this book is about, and won't read *The Glimpse* until it's released in French.